THE BODY IN THE THAMES

Also by Susanna Gregory

The Matthew Bartholomew Series

The Thomas Chaloner Series

THE BODY IN THE THAMES

Susanna
Gregory

SPHERE

First published in Great Britain in 2011 by Sphere

A CIP catalogue record for this book
is available from the British Library.

ISBN 978-1-84744-253-6

Typeset in Baskerville MT by Palimpsest Book Production Limited,
Falkirk, Stirlingshire

Printed and bound in Great Britain by
CPI Mackays, Chatham ME5 8TD

Papers used by Sphere are natural, renewable and recyclable
products sourced from well-managed forests and certified
in accordance with the rules of the Forest Stewardship Council.

Mixed Sources
Product group from well-managed
forests and other controlled sources
www.fsc.org Cert no. SGS-COC-004081
© 1996 Forest Stewardship Council

Sphere
An imprint of
Little, Brown Book Group
100 Victoria Embankment
London EC4Y 0DY

An Hachette UK Company
www.hachette.co.uk

www.littlebrown.co.uk

For Hendrick Berends
My Dutch consultant

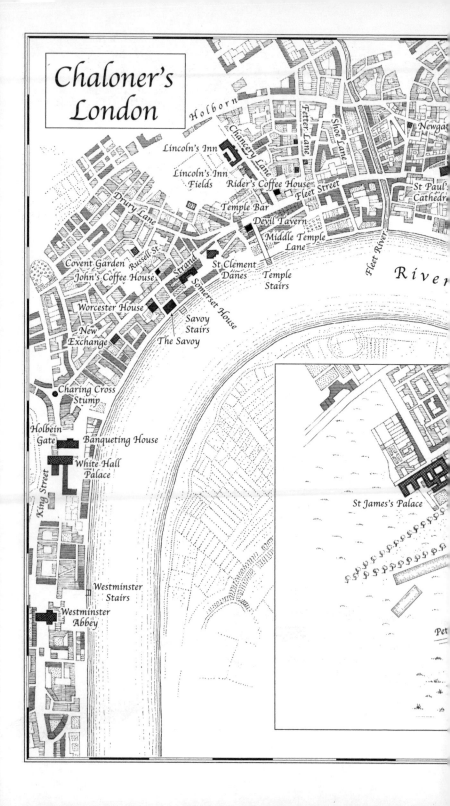

Prologue

Early June 1664

The marriage of Thomas Chaloner to Hannah Cotton in St Margaret's Church, Westminster transpired to be an occasion few of their guests would ever forget. It was not because the ceremony took place during one of the fiercest storms in living memory, raining so hard that the roof was unequal to it and began to leak. Nor was it because the ship bringing the bridegroom home from Holland was a week late, and he arrived at the church with only seconds to spare. Rather, it was because Philip Alden was murdered during it.

Alden was a man down on his luck. He had been a Royalist spy during the Commonwealth, and at the Restoration the King had rewarded him handsomely for his courage. Unfortunately, Alden loved to gamble, and the money had slipped through his fingers like quicksilver. Now, four years on, he could not remember when he had last eaten and he had no proper home. He was cold, hungry and feeling very sorry for himself as he slouched past St Margaret's. Then he happened

1

to overhear the name of the man who was to be married there that day.

He could scarcely believe his luck! Chaloner had also been an intelligencer, albeit one who had worked for the opposition, but even so, he would not see a brother officer starve. He would invite Alden to the wedding feast, and perhaps even slip him a few shilling afterwards, to see him back on his feet. Grinning in anticipation of his problems being solved, Alden brushed himself down, pulled back his shoulders and marched boldly into the church.

The wedding was a grand affair, far grander than Alden would have expected for a reticent, unassuming fellow like Chaloner, but eavesdropping soon explained why: Hannah was a lady-in-waiting to the Queen, and she had invited not only Her Majesty, but a number of high-ranking courtiers, too – such as the Duke of Buckingham, the Earl of Clarendon and members of the Privy Council. Alden's spirits rose further still: with such august guests, the feast was likely to be sumptuous.

Afraid his shabby clothes might see him expelled before he could corner the bridegroom, Alden selected a seat at the very back of the nave, and settled down to watch and to wait.

Sitting a few rows in front of him were a wealthy brothel-keeper named Temperance North, and Richard Wiseman, the Court surgeon. They were an unlikely pair, but Alden had seen them together on several occasions – although no longer active in espionage, old habits died hard, and he made it his business to know who was sleeping with whom. To pass the time, he listened to their conversation.

'There was no sign of Tom's ship again this morning,' Temperance was saying. 'Do you think it will arrive in time? Or do you think he has had second thoughts, and has paid the captain to be late deliberately?'

'No!' exclaimed Wiseman, clearly shocked by the notion. 'The ship is late because of these terrible storms. I cannot tell you how many patients I have tended because of them – broken limbs from being blown over, cuts and bruises from flying objects . . .'

'It *has* been windy,' agreed Temperance, and as if to give credence to her words, the bright sunlight that had been streaming through the windows was suddenly dimmed as black clouds scudded across the sky. The inside of the church grew dark.

And then it began to rain. At first, it was just a light patter, but it quickly became a roar, and water splattered furiously to the ground outside from overtaxed gutters. The racket it made drowned out the discussion between Wiseman and Temperance, but it did not matter, because a sudden flurry of activity at the door heralded the bride-groom's eleventh-hour arrival.

There was a collective sigh of relief from the congregation when he took his place at the altar rail, although Hannah only smiled serenely, as if she had known all along that raging seas and gale-force winds would not keep him from her that day.

As soon as Chaloner was in position, Rector White began the service, eyes fixed firmly heavenwards, although it had nothing to do with piety – he was concerned for his roof. His was not a wealthy parish, and could not afford costly repairs.

'—and keep her in sickness and in health,' he bellowed, struggling to make himself heard over the storm. 'And, forsaking all other, keep thee only unto her, so long as ye both shall live?'

Any response Chaloner might have made was lost amid a rippling roll of thunder.

'Did he say he would?' asked Temperance of Wiseman.

The surgeon shrugged. 'The vicar is asking him to repeat himself.'

Next, it was the roar of rain that drowned out Chaloner's reply. There was a sharp squeal as some hapless lady found herself standing directly under a leak, and Alden smirked. This was far better entertainment than the gaming houses! Rector White indicated Chaloner was to try again.

'I will,' shouted Chaloner for the third time.

Unfortunately, his yell coincided with a lull in the storm, and his words reverberated around the building like a challenge. Hannah beamed at him, then prodded White, who reluctantly dragged his attention away from his ceiling and back to the Book of Common Prayer. The respite did not last long, though, and the elements were soon battering the church with renewed ferocity.

A loud crack from above had the congregation gazing upwards in alarm, and almost immediately, water began to ooze through the ancient timbers. People edged towards the aisles, and the shuffle turned into a stampede when there was a second snap and the trickle became a deluge. The scene was illuminated by an eye-searing flicker of lightning, and Alden laughed openly at the sight of elegant courtiers making an undignified scramble for shelter.

Rector White continued valiantly, but the storm was directly overhead, and the thunder now sounded like

4

crashing booms from a whole field of cannons. Alden noticed that Chaloner's hand was on the hilt of his sword – an instinctive reaction from a man who had seen more than his share of fighting. The racket was so intense that Alden doubted the bridal couple could hear the vicar's words, while their guests were more interested in staying dry than in the ceremony.

Alden was so diverted by the spectacle that he did not sense the presence of the killer behind him until it was too late. There was a searing pain in his back, and he started to topple forward, but strong hands fastened around him, holding him upright. They continued to support him until his heart finally stopped beating, and then they arranged him so he was slumped in the pew with his hat over his eyes.

The storm abated the moment White hollered a final blessing. Immediately, sunlight shafted through the stained-glass windows, painting a mosaic of bright patterns on the wet floor. The rector gripped the newly-weds' hands in a sincere but brief gesture of congratulation, and then dashed away to inspect the damage to his tiles.

Dodging the ribbons of water that continued to flood through the roof, Hannah and Chaloner made their way up the aisle. When they passed Alden, Chaloner paused, frowning. The battered hat and grubby coat were in stark contrast to the finery worn by the rest of the guests.

'*I* did not invite him,' said Hannah, regarding the shabby figure in distaste. 'I was careful to keep the guest-list respectable, because the Queen is here. He must be a vagrant.'

5

One of the Queen's ladies-in-waiting, Judith Killigrew, had been leaning idly against the pew in which Alden was slumped, but when she straightened, there was a vivid blot of red against the pale yellow of her gown. She gazed at it in horror, then screamed. Her husband regarded the mess dispassionately: as Master of the Savoy Hospital, Dr Henry Killigrew was used to bloodstains. He touched Alden's neck, to feel for a life-beat, but shook his head.

'Dead,' he announced to the people who were hurrying to see what was happening. 'But there appears to be a letter pinned to his back by a knife. How very peculiar!'

There were exclamations of revulsion when he grabbed the dagger and tugged it out. Then he removed the paper from the sticky blade, and scanned it quickly before passing it to Chaloner.

'"Do not interfere",' Chaloner read, looking around to assess whether the message might mean something to one of the guests, but he was met by blank stares and puzzled frowns. And it could not be for *him*, because he had been in the country for less than an hour after an absence of four months – he had not had time to do anything to warrant grisly warnings.

'Interfere with what?' asked Hannah unsteadily. 'And who is he, anyway?'

'His name is Philip Alden,' supplied Killigrew. 'One-time Cavalier spy and inveterate gambler. He has been loitering around my hospital recently, begging for money. A bit of a scoundrel, but not one who should warrant execution.'

'He must have been killed during the ceremony,' declared Wiseman. 'I am a surgeon, and I am good at spotting corpses – he was certainly not dead when I saw him earlier.'

'Did anyone see or hear anything suspicious?' asked Chaloner, although without much hope: the storm had provided a perfect diversion for the crime.

There were shaken heads all around.

'This will be the work of fanatics,' said Killigrew with a grimace. 'Throw their damned note away, Chaloner, because I refuse to waste time considering it. Especially when we have a feast waiting for us at White Hall.'

But one man stared in open-mouthed horror at the corpse and its grim warning. Rector White knew exactly at whom the communication was aimed *and* what it meant. He staggered to a pew, feeling terror and nausea wash over him in alternate waves. Something dark and deadly was about to be unleashed, and he was not sure whether he – or anyone else – could stop it.

Ten days later

Willem Hanse carried a terrible secret, and had no idea what to do with it. He was a stranger in a foreign land, and did not know whom he could trust – not among his fellow Dutchmen, who had travelled to London with him in a final, desperate attempt to avert a war with Britain, and not among his English hosts. He was also unwell, suffering from an unsettling, gnawing ache in his innards. He pulled off his gloves – stupid things to wear when the city was in the grip of a heatwave, but they had been a gift from a friend and it comforted him to don them – and wiped sweat from his eyes.

He glanced behind him as he walked, pretending to gaze across the river at the twinkling lights of Southwark, but really looking for the malignant Oetje. His heart sank when he saw she was still there: he had not managed to lose her, despite his best efforts. She had followed him out of his lodgings at the Savoy Hospital – the rambling Tudor palace that had been lent to the Dutch Ambassador and his staff for the duration of their stay – and then she had lurked outside the Sun tavern while he had spent the evening with his friend, Tom Chaloner.

Poor Chaloner had been exhausted. He had spent the ten days since his wedding desperately trying to solve Alden's murder, while simultaneously struggling to pay court to a new wife and serve a demanding master. He had wanted to go home, but Hanse had detained him with idle chatter, hoping Oetje would tire of her vigil and leave. Unfortunately, her patience appeared to be infinite, because she had stood in a doorway all evening, silent and watchful.

Eventually, Chaloner had fallen asleep at the table, which had relieved Hanse of the burden of pretending all was well when it was not – the vicious murder in St Margaret's Church attested to that. Hanse had let him doze for a while, then had reluctantly shaken him awake when he knew he could dally no longer, and would have to leave the safety of the tavern – Oetje or no Oetje.

Chaloner had wanted to accompany him back to the Savoy – London was unsafe for Dutchmen, and one out alone at such an hour would be an attractive target for English 'patriots' – but Hanse, unwilling to embroil him in such a deadly matter, had refused. In the end, they had compromised: Hanse had taken a hackney carriage, instead of walking as he had planned. Chaloner had not been happy with the arrangement, but had been too tired to argue. He had seen Hanse into the coach, tried one last time to accompany him and, after being shoved away firmly, had turned towards home.

Once he had gone, Hanse had made a spirited effort to lose Oetje, directing his driver on a tortuous journey through a maze of narrow alleys. In a particularly dark spot, he had scrambled out and paid the man to keep going without him. Then he had visited several crowded taverns, entering through front doors and slipping out through the back ones, but all to no avail – Oetje had stuck to him like glue. Now he was all alone in a particularly dangerous, squalid part of the city.

Hanse believed, with all his heart, that the business he had undertaken was worth his life, and he was prepared to do anything to see it through. Of course, he thought grimly, as he broke into a trot, he could not complete what he had started if he was killed. Pushing such macabre thoughts from his mind, he blundered on.

A figure materialised ahead, so Hanse jigged down the alley to his left, but there were footsteps everywhere, echoing in his aching head. Clutching his stomach, he began to run, unease blossoming into full-blown fear as his pursuer gained on him. Then he tripped over a pile of rubbish in the darkness. He knew he was near the Thames, because he could hear its gentle lap on the muddy shore. He tried to climb to his feet, but his limbs were like lead. Someone came to stand over him.

'Please!' he whispered. 'Do not—'

His adversary issued a low, mirthless chuckle that turned Hanse's blood to ice, despite the heat of the summer evening. 'You should not have interfered.'

Chapter 1

Saturday 18 June 1664

St James's Park was a pleasant place to be on a hot day. It stood upwind of the steaming, stinking, crowded metropolis that was London, and smelled of scythed grass and summer flowers. High walls kept the general populace out, which allowed the King and his Court to lounge in indolent splendour, and to swim in the newly created stretch of water known as 'the Canal'. They were enjoying its cool waters that morning, laughing and shrieking as they frolicked.

A short distance away, in the shade of some elms, sat the Earl of Clarendon. He was England's Lord Chancellor, a short, fat, fussy man who favoured expensively frothy clothes and large wigs, neither of which were suitable for heatwaves – and London was currently enduring some of the driest, most sultry weather anyone could remember. His chubby face was shiny with sweat, and he was acutely uncomfortable. It was also clear, from his black scowl, that he was in a very bad mood.

He had accumulated many enemies during his four

years in office, so he and his staff – a secretary, four soldiers and a gentleman usher – had positioned themselves well away from the rest of the company. Not only did he feel safer when he was not among folk who itched to see him dead or disgraced, but the Court preferred it that way, too – the King's lively debauchees did not want their fun spoiled by his critical glares.

'The Lady emits some very uncivilised guffaws,' he remarked waspishly. So intense was his dislike of the King's mistress that he could never bring himself to say her name: the Countess of Castlemaine was always just 'the Lady'. 'I imagine they can hear her uncouth hooting in Chelsey.'

His staff exchanged wary glances behind his back, but held their silence. He had not wanted to join the royal party that day, and was itching to vent his spleen on someone for having been forced to do so. He had planned to spend the time writing letters to avert a war with the Dutch Republic. Unfortunately, most Englishmen thought that a fight with Holland was a very good idea, and his efforts to prevent one were regarded with irritation. The King, perhaps in a subversive attempt to keep him from such work, had informed him that a morning in the sunshine would do him good, and when the Earl had demurred, the invitation had become an order.

'It is too hot to loll about here,' Clarendon snapped, swabbing his forehead with a piece of lace. 'It is an omen, you know.'

'An omen, sir?' asked Secretary Bulteel nervously, when no one else spoke.

The Earl glowered at him. John Bulteel was a small, unattractive man with bad teeth and gauche manners. Clarendon treated him abominably, despite the fact that his loyalty, devotion and talent for administration made him almost indispensable.

'Yes!' the Earl snarled. 'The weather is an omen for evil to come – probably this damned war everyone seems so determined to have. Where is Chaloner? I have a question for him.'

Thomas Chaloner stepped forward. He had been a gentleman usher for exactly two weeks – the post had been the Earl's wedding gift to him. The promotion had not entailed a change in his duties, though. He was still an intelligencer, with a remit to protect his master from harmful plots and to investigate any matter Clarendon deemed worthy of attention.

He was in his thirties, of medium height and build, with brown hair and grey eyes. The sword at his side was more functional than ornamental, but there was nothing else remarkable about him. This was a deliberate ploy on his part – he had not survived more than twelve years in espionage by standing out from the crowd.

'Your question, sir?' he asked politely.

'Is it as hot as this in the States-General?' demanded Clarendon, using the popular name for the seven provinces that had united to form the Dutch Republic.

He scowled dangerously, suggesting there would be trouble no matter how the question was answered. Chaloner had been in his service for eighteen months, but was still not fully trusted. Perhaps it was because espionage was considered a distasteful occupation for gentlemen, or perhaps it was because Chaloner had been employed as a spy by the Parliamentarian government before he had come to the Earl. Regardless, his master always gave the impression that he did not like him, and employed him only because he needed to stay one step ahead of his enemies.

13

The antipathy was wholly reciprocated: Chaloner heartily wished he was hired by someone else. Unfortunately, opportunities for ex-Commonwealth intelligencers in Restoration London were few and far between, so he had no choice but to continue working for Clarendon.

'Well?' the Earl barked, when he thought Chaloner was taking too long to respond.

'It varies from year to year, sir,' replied Chaloner warily, not sure quite what his master was expecting to hear.

Clarendon sighed peevishly. 'I do not care about the time you spent there spying for Cromwell. I want to know what the weather was like when you visited the place for *me*. You have been skulking there since February, after all, and only deigned to return two weeks ago.'

Chaloner regarded him askance. The remark suggested that it had been *his* idea to linger in Amsterdam, when the reality was that he had written several times to say that Lord Bristol – the enemy he had been ordered to hunt down – was not there. It was only at the beginning of June that the Earl had finally accepted that his quarry must be elsewhere, and Chaloner had been given permission to come home.

'You told me it was much cooler, Tom,' said Bulteel helpfully, seeing his friend struggle for a polite response.

Clarendon nodded his satisfaction. 'I thought so! The omen is intended for England only. The Dutch will win if we go to war, and we shall look foolish for taking them on in the first place.'

Avoiding conflict with the United Provinces was one of few things upon which he and Chaloner agreed – both knew it was a fight Britain was unlikely to win.

'Is it true that the whole of the States-General is

ravaged by plague?' asked the Earl, kicking off his fashionably tight shoes and waggling his fat little toes in relief.

'No, sir,' replied Chaloner. 'Just Amsterdam.'

The Earl regarded him uneasily. '*You* were in Amsterdam. Did you see evidence of the disease?'

Chaloner nodded, but did not elaborate because the subject was a painful one for him. When he had first been sent to spy on Holland, some twelve years before, he had married a Dutch lady, but had lost her and their child to plague. It had not been easy to see the same sickness at work in the same place, and he had been unsettled by the intensity of the memories it had stirred.

'But you stayed away from sufferers?' Pointedly, Clarendon held the piece of lace over his nose.

'Of course.'

The Earl regarded him coolly. 'You are taciturn today, even by your standards. What is wrong? Are you concerned that you have made no headway on the cases I ordered you to investigate – these White Hall thefts and that missing Dutch diplomat? Or is married life not to your liking?'

'I have identified the thieves, sir, while married life is . . .' Chaloner trailed off. Two weeks was hardly long enough to tell, although it had occurred to him that he had made a mistake – spies made for poor spouses, and Hannah had already started two quarrels about the unsociable hours he kept.

'You have the culprits?' pounced the Earl eagerly. 'Why did you not say so? They stole my wig, you know. I set it down on a bench next to me, and when I turned around, it had gone.'

'Unfortunately, the evidence is circumstantial as yet,'

replied Chaloner. 'The only way to ensure a conviction will be to catch them in the act of stealing, and—'

'Then why are you not watching them?' the Earl demanded. 'Now? At this very minute?'

'Because you ordered him to accompany you here, sir,' explained Bulteel, when Chaloner hesitated, not sure how to respond without sounding insolent. 'You wanted him to brief you on his investigation into that vanished Dutchman – Willem Hanse.'

'Oh, yes.' The Earl mopped his face with the lace again. 'Well, he has finished telling me about his lack of progress there, so there is no need for him to linger. Go and catch the thieves, Chaloner. At once. How dare they lay sticky fingers on *my* property!'

Chaloner regarded him unhappily, sorry he should consider a wig more important than a man's safety, and sorrier still that tracking thieves would take time away from his search for Hanse. He had not told the Earl – or anyone else, for that matter – but his first marriage meant he and Hanse were kinsmen. And Chaloner was extremely worried about him.

He took his leave of Clarendon, but did not go far, because the two men he suspected of committing the White Hall thefts – a pair of courtier-stewards in the service of a diplomat named Sir George Downing – had just arrived and attached themselves to the royal party. He would far rather have resumed the hunt for Hanse, but he knew he would have no peace from the Earl until the thieves were under lock and key. With a sigh, he forced himself to concentrate on them.

The case had not been difficult to solve; interviews with victims and the application of basic logic had quickly pointed to them as the culprits. Moreover, discussions with their previous employers – Downing had only hired them recently – told him that they had not been honest in the past, either, and had probably forged the testimonials that claimed them to be men of good character. Unfortunately, he needed more than that to confront them. They were reputed to be cunning, and would wriggle out of any accusations made without hard evidence.

He crouched behind a bush, and watched. Abraham Kicke was a tall, handsome fellow with luxurious blue-black hair and a confident swagger. His accomplice, John Nisbett, was shorter and bulkier, with lank ginger locks and bulbous blue eyes. Both were said to be skilled swordsmen, although Chaloner had no intention of finding out whether that was true – while perfectly able to hold his own in a skirmish, he saw no point in taking unnecessary risks.

He winced when a particularly loud shriek rent the air. The Earl was right: Lady Castlemaine *did* have a piercing voice. He glanced towards her, and could not help but notice that she was by far the most scantily clad of the cavorting crowd – her dress was made of some thin, filmy stuff that turned transparent in water. She had borne three children, but her clothing showed she had retained her perfect figure. No one was quite sure how, and there were rumours that the Devil was involved.

Meanwhile, shy, lonely Queen Katherine watched her with haunted eyes. Two years of marriage had not provided *her* with a baby, despite fervent prayers and visits to spas. Her inability to conceive meant she was shunned by the Court, and Chaloner's heart went out to her when he saw her ladies-in-waiting had abandoned her and she

17

sat alone. Then one appeared, and distracted her with a barrage of merry chatter. He smiled when he saw the kindly Samaritan was Hannah.

Dragging his attention back to his duties, Chaloner watched Kicke and Nisbett pause by the edge of the Canal, ostensibly to marvel at His Majesty's new parterres. He braced himself, sure they were about to indulge their penchant for other people's property.

Suddenly, there was a roar of manly appreciation: the Lady had left the water to perform a series of exercises. They had the immediate effect of drawing every eye towards her, the men to ogle the display, and the women to regard it rather more critically. Chaloner glanced at the Earl, and saw that even he was transfixed, although he at least had the decency to pretend to be reading.

While people were distracted, Kicke and Nisbett aimed for the nearest bundle of clothes. A brief rummage saw them emerge with a copper-coloured wig that would have cost its owner a fortune. It was distinctive, and Chaloner recognised it as belonging to a courtier named Charles Bates. Kicke shoved it down the front of his shirt. In the next pile, Nisbett found a purse, which he slipped into his pocket. And so they continued.

'Hey!' Chaloner yelled, when he felt they had stolen enough to condemn themselves. 'Thieves!'

Kicke and Nisbett froze in horror, and in the Canal, heads whipped around towards them. Lady Castlemaine stopped her gyrations with a glare: she hated not being the centre of attention.

'Thieves!' Chaloner yelled again, pointing to Kicke and Nisbett.

Kicke held a necklace in his hand, and an expression of panicky guilt crossed his face as he dropped it. Nisbett spun around quickly, but thought better of making a bid for escape when he saw his way barred by the Earl's soldiers. Several younger, fitter members of Court, led by the Duke of Buckingham, splashed out of the water and trotted towards the commotion; some even had the sense to collect swords en route. But Kicke was jabbing his thumb at Chaloner.

'We are not the felons here,' he declared, injecting indignation in his every word. '*He* is.'

Accusations of criminal behaviour were not uncommon in White Hall, and most courtiers lost interest once they had assured themselves that their own belongings were safe. One by one, they drifted back to the water. Part of the reason for their departure was because the Earl was waddling towards them – they often expressed their dislike by refusing to be in his company – but also because the Lady had resumed her exercises. Buckingham was among the few who remained, and so was Bates, a sad-faced gentleman who was old and ugly without his auburn wig.

'Well, Chaloner?' demanded the Duke, a tall, elegant fellow whose good looks were being eroded by high living; his eyes were yellowish, and his skin was sallow. He was one of the Earl's most bitter enemies, and gleeful malice gleamed in his eyes when he heard the accusation levelled against a member of his rival's household. 'What do you say?'

'Thomas is not a thief.' Chaloner turned to see Hannah. For reasons beyond his ken, she and the Duke were friends, and Buckingham often listened to what she had to say. Unfortunately, she often listened to what Buckingham had to say in return, and what emerged

19

from the dissipated nobleman's mouth was not always sensible. 'I would not have married him if he were.'

'No, you would not,' agreed Buckingham. He sighed, sorry not to be able to strike a blow at the Earl through his most recently appointed gentleman usher.

'My wig is missing,' said Bates quietly. 'I left it here, and it has gone. It is quite distinctive, because no one else at Court has one that colour.'

'I lost one, too,' added Clarendon, fixing the thieves with a baleful eye. 'They must have a penchant for them. Or a penchant for the high prices such items fetch on the open market.'

'We have stolen nothing,' declared Kicke hotly. He pointed at Chaloner. 'But *he* has. He—'

'Search me,' suggested Chaloner. 'Then search them. That will tell you who is telling the truth.'

'If anyone comes near me, I will cut off his hands,' snarled Nisbett, drawing his sword when Buckingham nodded that it was a good idea, and took a step towards him. 'You insult us by giving credence to these slanderous lies.'

'Put up your weapon,' ordered Buckingham, his eyes pure ice. 'How dare you threaten me! And your actions do nothing to convince me of your innocence, sir. Quite the reverse, in fact. Now, I *am* going to search you, so I strongly recommend—'

'We refuse to submit to this outrage,' declared Kicke. He glowered haughtily at the Duke. 'And *you* cannot make us. We are in Downing's service, not yours, so you have no jurisdiction over us.'

'Actually, he does,' put in Clarendon. He was a lawyer by training, so this was the sort of thing he knew about. 'By virtue of his appointment as—'

Bored with the debate, Buckingham made a grab for Kicke. There was a tearing sound as stitches parted company, and Kicke bawled his indignation. Nisbett took a threatening step towards them, but a glimmer of common sense warned him that it would be unwise to skewer a peer of the realm. He faltered just long enough for the Earl's soldiers to disarm him.

'That is *my* wig,' Kicke shouted, as the Duke brandished what he found. 'I bought it last week.'

Bates took it from Buckingham's hand. 'No, it is mine. As you can see, it fits me perfectly.'

The Duke turned his attention to Nisbett, and it was not many moments before the purse was located, along with several items of jewellery. Nisbett's face flamed red with rage and humiliation.

'I think we have seen enough,' said the Earl, regarding both men contemptuously. 'They are caught red-handed.'

'They must be responsible for all the other thefts, too,' said Hannah. 'The method is the same: preying on the wealthy when they are otherwise engaged. I am glad my husband has solved the case, because ever since these crimes started back in April, White Hall has been full of suspicion and unpleasantness. Thank God it is over.'

'We are innocent of those,' began Kicke, alarmed. 'Chaloner must have—'

'Do not even *think* of accusing Tom,' declared Bulteel. The secretary's voice was unsteady: he hated pushing himself forward in such august company. But he took a deep breath and plunged on. Chaloner was touched by his support, knowing what it cost him to make bold with his opinions. 'He was not in the country when these crimes began. He was in Holland.'

Buckingham puffed out his cheeks in a sigh. 'I suppose

we had better search these villains' homes, to see whether they have hidden their ill-gotten gains there. Meanwhile, we shall keep them under lock and key until their fates are decided.'

'No!' screeched Kicke, as the soldiers laid hold of him. 'I will kill you for this, Chaloner! I have powerful friends, and you can expect retribution for—'

'Enough!' snapped Buckingham. 'He caught you fair and square. Besides, stealing in full view of half the Court was just plain stupid.'

Kicke's violent objections were loud enough to interrupt Lady Castlemaine's exhibition a second time. Petulantly, she flung away the branch she had been using, and stamped towards the water. The King was waiting for her, and Chaloner saw the Queen look away.

'I think your mistress needs you,' he whispered to Hannah.

At the Earl's insistence, Chaloner went with Buckingham to the chambers in White Hall where Kicke and Nisbett had their lodgings. He resented the wasted time, as he did not for a moment anticipate that they would be so foolish as to leave incriminating evidence in the place where they lived. He had been so certain of it, in fact, that he had not bothered to look himself. Thus he was amazed to discover that one of the rooms had been fitted with a false ceiling, and the space above it was crammed to the gills with jewellery, coins, clothes and costly trinkets.

The Duke's jaw dropped. 'Good God! I would never have thought of looking up there.'

To a professional spy, it stood out like a sore thumb, and Chaloner could not imagine *not* noticing it. He stood on a chair to retrieve the loot, passing it into the Duke's eagerly waiting hands.

'What made you suspect Kicke and Nisbett in the first place?' Buckingham asked as they worked. 'They do not strike me as especially villainous types.'

'No?' asked Chaloner, surprised.

'Well, I suppose there *is* something unpleasant about them,' conceded the Duke. 'They work for Downing for a start, which says nothing to commend them.'

Prudently, Chaloner did not mention that *he* had once worked for Downing, too. Downing was Envoy Extraordinary to The Hague, and had been for years, first under Cromwell, and then the King. He had dismissed his entire staff at the Restoration, and had appointed Royalists instead, to demonstrate his commitment to the new regime. Intelligence on the Dutch had suffered a serious setback, and was still well below par four years later, but Downing had 'proved' himself loyal.

Buckingham had been inspecting a beautiful necklace, but he looked up at Chaloner when a thought occurred to him. 'Do you think *he* put them up to this? He is certainly unscrupulous and greedy enough.'

'I doubt it,' replied Chaloner. Downing *was* unscrupulous and greedy, but he was not stupid, and would know better than to embroil himself in brazen thievery.

But Buckingham narrowed his eyes, unconvinced. 'The thefts started in April, which was when he was recalled to London to help us negotiate with the Dutch. The timing fits.'

'It fits because April was when he first hired Kicke and Nisbett,' explained Chaloner. 'He said he needed more stewards, so he could host receptions to further the cause of peace.'

Buckingham released a sharp, mirthless bark of laughter. 'Further the cause of peace? Downing? He is the greatest threat to it, with his nasty innuendos and bullying manner! But it suits me. Our country is not yet at ease with itself after the civil wars and the Commonwealth, and a foreign campaign is just what we need. It will unite us all in a common cause.'

'Only until the first battle, which we will lose. Then there will be more trouble than ever.'

Buckingham's expression hardened. 'Cromwell won when *he* tackled the Dutch. Are you saying the King is less of a warrior than the Great Usurper?'

Chaloner was saying nothing of the kind, although he suspected it was true: Cromwell had been a talented general. 'It boils down to resources and money. The States-General have more of both.'

'That is an unpatriotic attitude! Have you been listening to your traitorous master? Well, it does not matter, because the doves on the Privy Council will *not* prevail. We *shall* have our war.'

'Probably,' acknowledged Chaloner unhappily. 'But there is to be a convention in the Savoy Hospital next Sunday. Perhaps our politicians will see sense there, and agree that peace—'

'It will be a waste of time,' predicted Buckingham. 'Although the doves have high hopes for it. But I am not interested in debating politics with you. I would rather you told me how you came to suspect Nisbett and Kicke.'

Chaloner was more than happy to discuss something less contentious. 'I asked victims and witnesses to name everyone in the vicinity when the thefts were committed. Kicke and Nisbett appeared on more lists than was innocent.'

Buckingham frowned. 'Is that all? No wonder you held off tackling them until you caught them in the act. Hah! Here is Clarendon's hairpiece. Return it to him, and I shall see to the rest. Do not look dubious, man! Do you think I might help myself to the belongings of friends and colleagues?'

Chaloner did: few courtiers had much in the way of ready cash, and were quite happy to acquire more by any means arising. But he accepted the proffered wig and left, feeling that monitoring dishonest barons went well beyond his remit. Besides, he had more urgent matters to attend – namely finding Hanse. Stuffing the wig in his pocket, he determined to make the most of what remained of the day.

The following morning, heavy-eyed from lack of sleep – his enquiries had lasted well into the night, after which Hannah had been waiting to rail at him for the unsociable hours he kept – Chaloner walked to The Strand, a bustling thoroughfare where palaces rubbed shoulders with ramshackle shops and grimy public buildings. A number of nobles had homes there, their ownership reflected in the buildings' names – Essex House, Arundel House, York House, Somerset House, Bedford House. There was also Worcester House, an untidy Tudor monstrosity rented by the Earl of Clarendon while he built himself something better in the pretty fields around Piccadilly.

As it was Sunday, the Earl would be at home, rather than at his offices in White Hall, so Chaloner went directly there. Bulteel was hovering in the hallway when he arrived, waiting to be told whether their master needed him that day. The secretary looked tired, and Chaloner

25

was sorry Clarendon could not see the man's weariness, and let him have a few hours to himself.

'You did well yesterday,' Bulteel said, smiling shyly. 'People were beginning to think those thieves were uncatchable – that they would plague us until no one had any valuables left.'

'Success made them reckless,' replied Chaloner, feeling he had done nothing particularly remarkable. 'It was foolish to steal in plain sight of half the Court.'

'Yes, but they would have got away with it, if you had not been there. Do not denigrate what you did – *I* know it was cleverly done. I told the Earl so, too, but he did not listen. He never does.'

Chaloner did not reply, because Bulteel was right: the Earl rarely heeded his secretary's opinion. It was a pity, because Bulteel's views were usually far more sensible than those of his master.

At that moment, the door opened and a gentleman and his servant were shown in. The gentleman was exquisitely attired in pale blue satin, and, despite the steadily rising heat, looked cool and debonair. He held a piece of lace, which he flicked back and forth as if swiping dust out of the way. His cheeks were powdered, and he wore a 'face patch' cut in the shape of a crescent moon. Face patches were popular with ladies, but Chaloner had never seen one on a man before.

'There you are, John, dear!' the fellow exclaimed. He sank on to a chair, while his servant – a sober, silent fellow in brown – fetched him a footstool. 'I thought I would *never* find you. And the weather . . . well!'

Although Bulteel told everyone that he was happily married, Chaloner was party to a secret: the wife and child were an invention, designed to make his colleagues believe him capable of procuring them. But it had never occurred to Chaloner that his friend's tastes might run in other directions.

'No!' gulped Bulteel, seeing what he was thinking. 'This is my cousin. His name is Griffith.'

'*Colonel* Griffith,' corrected the man languidly. 'Introduce me to this fine fellow, John.'

'He is Tom,' obliged Bulteel. 'The Earl's spy.'

'No, no, no!' cried Griffith, putting a hand across his eyes in apparent despair. 'Have you listened to *none* of my lessons? Introduce him properly, as I have taught you.'

'Allow me to present Mr Thomas Chaloner, gentleman usher to the Lord Chancellor,' intoned Bulteel, blushing uncomfortably as he did so.

'Better,' acknowledged Griffith. 'Although he ranks more highly than I, so you should have presented me to him first, not the other way around.'

'My cousin is tutoring me in Court etiquette,' explained Bulteel to the bemused Chaloner. 'So I will not be so awkward when in the company of great people. I have always admired his elegant manners, and when he arrived in the city, I invited him to stay with me for a while to teach me his skills. By the time he has finished, wealthy patrons will be clamouring to hire my services, and I will be popular and loved by *everyone* I meet.'

'Oh,' said Chaloner, thinking Griffith should have refused the challenge, because it was not one that could be won. Bulteel had many admirable qualities, but his unprepossessing appearance and innate gaucheness meant he would never have the respect he craved. It was cruel and unfair, and Bulteel deserved better, but it was the way White Hall worked.

27

'What brings you to London, Colonel?' he asked, changing the subject before Bulteel could ask whether he had noticed any improvement. 'Military matters?'

'Lord, no!' exclaimed Griffith in distaste. 'I am a man of business now. I buy and sell fine cloth. My martial days are over. And I thank God for it, because I never did like the noise and dirt.'

'Which regiment?' asked Chaloner. An image of this foppish creature on a battlefield crept unbidden into his mind, and he fought down a smirk.

'Prince Rupert's,' replied Griffith proudly. 'I served with Clarendon once, too, at the Battle of Edgehill. He was minding the young princes, and I was minding Rupert's dog. Both were sacred trusts, but especially mine. Rupert was very fond of that beast.'

'The Earl was delighted to meet my cousin again,' said Bulteel, smiling fondly. Then the expression became pained. 'Griffith has settled nicely in my Westminster house. My wife and son are away, as you know, so there is plenty of room.'

Before he had left for Holland, Chaloner had advised Bulteel to send his 'family' on an extended visit to the country; the fiction was beginning to unravel, and he did not want his friend exposed as a liar. He was surprised Bulteel was willing to deceive a cousin, though – kinsmen were more difficult to mislead than colleagues, because they would want to know to whom they were related.

'I am pleased to have his company,' Bulteel went on, although he looked anything but pleased, and Chaloner wondered whether the strain of having a houseguest accounted for some of his weariness. 'He has been here since February.'

'I have,' agreed Griffith. 'And I am sure you have

28

noticed a great improvement in John's deportment and speech in that time. He is very nearly a gentleman.'

'He has never been anything else,' said Chaloner, using a compliment to avoid saying that Bulteel had not changed at all.

Bulteel blushed and hastily turned the conversation away from himself. 'Griffith lived in The Hague once.'

Griffith took the abrupt switch in his stride. 'But I did not like it. It smelled of cheese.'

Chaloner had never noticed a smell of cheese, and was beginning to suspect that a penchant for fabrication ran in the family.

'Did you know that one of the Dutch diplomats vanished on Friday?' Bulteel asked his cousin conversationally. 'Ambassador van Goch told me today that he fears for the fellow's safety.'

So did Chaloner, and heartily wished his enquiries into Hanse's disappearance had yielded clues. For all his efforts, he knew no more now than he had when it had first been reported.

'Then let us hope he is found safe and well,' said Griffith, not very interested. He brightened. 'Come with me to the New Exchange, John. One of its merchants has some *lovely* taffeta for sale.'

The Earl snatched the wig Chaloner handed him, and studied it minutely. 'There is a hole in it!' he cried in dismay. 'It will cost a fortune to repair.'

'It was shoved inside a false ceiling,' explained Chaloner.

'I never did like Kicke and Nisbett,' said Clarendon, placing the hair on a special stand. 'Unfortunately, Downing hired them when you were fooling around

29

overseas, or I would have ordered you to watch them from the start. Has there been any word on that Dutchman, by the way?'

'No, sir. Not yet.'

'He has been gone for almost two days now. And if he is as crucial to peace as Heer van Goch maintains, we must do all in our power to locate him. I thought I made that clear to you yesterday.'

'You did, sir,' said Chaloner, itching to remind the Earl that he had actually been more interested in catching the White Hall thieves. 'But all I can tell you about Hanse is that he was last seen at half-past eight on Friday evening, climbing into a hackney carriage outside the Sun tavern in Westminster. The driver was instructed to take him directly to the Savoy, but no one saw him arrive.'

'How do you know? Have you interviewed his fellow diplomats?'

Chaloner nodded. 'And their servants.'

'Perhaps he decided London is too dangerous, so elected to leave. I would not blame him. Hollanders are unpopular here – they cannot leave their lodgings without threats being hurled.'

'Never. He thinks war will be bad for both our countries, and is determined to avert one.'

The Earl regarded him soberly, and Chaloner tensed, waiting for the obvious question: how did *he* know what a foreign diplomat believed? He had not concealed his kinship with Hanse from any desire to be secretive, but because he had been trained never to share personal information, and found it a difficult habit to break. He had not even confided in Hannah.

'Do you think he is dead?' asked the Earl instead.

'I hope not,' replied Chaloner, although the possibility

had crossed his mind. 'It would deal the peace process a terrible blow. And his wife travelled from the States-General with him . . .'

Jacoba, he thought to himself, recalling the disconcerting experience of seeing Aletta's eyes smiling at him when they had met the previous week. They had been sisters.

'Then I shall pray for his safe return,' said the Earl, rather insincerely. 'But if he *is* dead – murdered – then who are your suspects?'

Chaloner tried not to let his master's callous attitude annoy him. 'Anyone who wants a war, I suppose. Including some of his colleagues.'

The Earl's eyebrows went up. 'But the Dutch came here specifically to argue for peace.'

'Heer van Goch did. But his retinue of diplomats, servants and soldiers comprises more than two hundred people. Among so many, differences of opinion will be inevitable.'

'Yes, I suppose the delegation *is* that large,' acknowledged Clarendon. 'Of course, you are in a unique position to know their real thoughts, given that you speak the language.'

'I do not spy on them,' said Chaloner immediately.

'You should,' countered the Earl. 'You might learn something useful.'

'And I might hear it in the wrong context, and tell you something inaccurate or misleading,' replied Chaloner. 'There is more to spying than just repeating what is overheard.'

'Yes, I have been told that the reports you composed when you were stationed overseas were good in that respect. But you *know* these people and their ways, so I do not see why you cannot manage a little eavesdropping to help your country.'

'I would need to be there on a full-time basis to be of any real value,' explained Chaloner, striving for patience. They had discussed this before. 'Besides, I am sure Spymaster Williamson has his own people in place. Too many intelligencers will cause confusion and be counter-productive.'

The Earl was thoughtful. 'The negotiations are proceeding far more slowly than they should, and mistrust and suspicion are rife. Perhaps you have just explained why – a surfeit of spies.'

'Perhaps. Of course, there is also the fact that the Dutch know that most of our country would much rather go to war. It is hardly an attitude that encourages them to make concessions.'

The Earl grimaced. 'I am aware of that, believe me! But there is another reason why you must find Hanse as quickly as possible. It pertains to the Privy Council papers that were stolen.'

'What Privy Council papers, sir?' asked Chaloner warily.

The Earl glared at him. 'I am sure I told you about them in the park yesterday. They went missing on Friday evening. From this very room! And I want them back.'

'I see,' said Chaloner, biting back his exasperation that the Earl had neglected to inform him of such an important matter immediately. It certainly had *not* been mentioned in the park, and the passage of time would make them that much harder to locate. 'But how do they relate to Hanse?'

'On Friday morning, just hours before they disappeared, I entertained two men here: van Goch and Hanse.

They must have seen these documents, and decided to steal them.'

Chaloner gazed at him, not sure whether he was more startled by the suggestion that two high-ranking diplomats would resort to theft, or that the Earl should have left such items lying around for foreign visitors to spot in the first place.

'Hanse and van Goch are not thieves, sir,' he began. 'They are—'

'Well, someone made off with them,' snapped the Earl. 'And they went on Friday evening, between six and eight o'clock, when I was dining with my wife and the papers were up here unattended. They could not have been taken before then, because I was reading them.'

'But van Goch and Hanse left you at noon,' said Chaloner, recalling the pair walking away to the accompaniment of bells striking twelve o'clock. 'They were not here between six and eight.'

'So? All that means is that they saw the papers, and elected to come and steal them later.'

'How? There are guards on all your doors *and* patrolling the garden. Or are you suggesting that Heer van Goch climbed up the side of the house and slipped in through a window?'

'Do not be impertinent!' barked the Earl. 'Hanse must have done it.'

'He has an alibi. He was in the Sun tavern from six o'clock until roughly half-past eight.' Chaloner did not mention that *he* was the alibi. 'He could not have stolen these papers.'

'I do not believe it,' snapped the Earl. 'He *did* steal them, and *that* is why he has disappeared. He is ferrying them back to the States-General as we speak.'

33

'I will interview your staff this afternoon,' said Chaloner, declining to argue.

'The thief is no one in my household!' shouted the Earl. 'They are all above reproach.'

They might have been once, thought Chaloner, but the Earl treated them badly, and one might well have made off with the papers to give him a good fright. He tried another avenue of questioning.

'What was in these documents, sir? Matters of interest to the States-General?'

'Maybe,' replied the Earl cagily. 'But do not ask me to elaborate, because I am bound by oaths of secrecy. Suffice to say they are highly sensitive.'

Chaloner smothered a sigh. How was he supposed to discover who had stolen the papers, when he did not know who might benefit from reading the things? And if they were so important, why had the Earl waited two days before ordering their disappearance investigated? He was about to press the matter further when there were footsteps outside, followed by a knock on the door. It was Bulteel.

'There is news, sir,' said the secretary. 'Nisbett and Kicke have just been released from custody.'

'What?' spluttered the Earl. 'But their guilt was beyond question!'

'Apparently, now most of what they stole is back with its rightful owners, people are inclined to see the matter as a bit of harmless fun. Anger has turned to admiration, especially as Kicke claims he did it to protect White Hall – to draw attention to its lax security, so something could be done to remedy the situation.'

'If that were true, then why did he not say so in the park?' pounced Chaloner.

34

.'Quite,' said Bulteel acidly. 'But it is all the Lady's doing. She is taken with their daring, and the story is that it was *she* who persuaded the King to let them go.'

'Then let us hope they learn from their narrow escape and leave the city,' said the Earl.

'They have not,' said Bulteel. 'Downing immediately dismissed them, lest people think *he* put them up to it. But the Lady has offered them posts instead. At a much higher salary.'

The Earl scowled. 'She is doing it to spite me, because it was my retainer who caught them.'

Petty though it sounded, Chaloner suspected he might well be right.

Despite the Earl's contention that he would be wasting his time, Chaloner spent the rest of the morning and much of the afternoon interviewing Worcester House's staff about the missing papers. Unfortunately, his master was right: no one had seen or heard anything out of the ordinary. Chaloner pursued the matter diligently until four o'clock, when most of them went home.

He had a talent for sketching and a good memory for faces, so he drafted a reasonable likeness of the hack-neyman who had taken Hanse to the Savoy, and showed it to every driver who would talk to him. It was almost three hours before he found one who nodded recognition. He was a Scot named Murdoch, who had helped him with information before.

'That is Saul Ibbot. He used to work over in Smithfield, and rarely came this way, but he was here on Friday. We shared a pipe together while we watered our horses.'

The use of the past tense did not escape Chaloner. 'Has something happened to him?'

'You have not heard? He was killed when his coach overturned in Long Lane yesterday.'

Such events were commonplace in a city where carriages were not very roadworthy, and although Chaloner had overheard people discussing the incident, he had not thought much about it.

'An accident?' he asked.

Murdoch shrugged. 'Probably, although his horse – he called it Cromwell – seemed a steady nag to me. Still, it happens.'

But not normally to drivers whose passengers had mysteriously gone missing, thought Chaloner worriedly. He walked to Smithfield in the bright, arid blaze of the setting sun, and set about finding someone who would direct him to Ibbot's house. It took a while, but eventually he was led to a dark, dirty alley near Aldgate Street. His knock was answered by a woman with a howling baby in her arms. She was jigging it up and down furiously, so its swollen red face was a blur of continuous movement. Chaloner felt sick just watching, and was not surprised it was making such a racket.

'They told me Cromwell bolted,' she shouted, snaking out a bony hand to snatch the coins he offered. 'But Cromwell is a quiet beast, and he never bolted before.'

'What do *you* think happened?' Chaloner asked.

'I think Saul took a job he shouldn't have done.' Mrs Ibbot's voice was bitter, and she rocked the baby more vigorously than ever. 'He told me he had given up that line of work, but the money was easy. And it was too much temptation for a weak man.'

'What line of work?' Chaloner grabbed the baby from her before she shook it senseless. It immediately

36

quietened, and contented itself with the occasional relieved sob.

She folded her arms. 'Work for the Hectors, mostly – one of the gangs what operates round here. I told him to have nothing to do with them, but he wouldn't listen. Now he's dead, and if it was an accident, then my name is Lady Castlemaine.'

'You think the Hectors killed him?' Chaloner's heart sank. If so, then it boded ill for Hanse.

'It wouldn't be the first time they hired a driver, then murdered him to make sure he kept his mouth shut. You got a nice way with babies, sir. This is the happiest she been all day.'

'Did Saul ever mention a particular Hector? A contact, perhaps?'

Mrs Ibbot nodded slowly. 'There was one he talked about – a woman called Mrs Riley. But I can't say no more, because I don't want word getting back that I been talking about her. I got the young one to think of, and Saul told me that Mrs Riley can be nasty.'

Chaloner nodded his thanks as he handed back the baby and took his leave, but the information was not very helpful. Every spy knew that 'Mrs Riley' was the codename used for the King during the Commonwealth – the Hectors had been having a joke at Ibbot's expense. Or perhaps Ibbot had just been cautious with a wife who had, after all, been willing to gossip to a stranger who had paid her. Either way, Chaloner knew this particular line of enquiry was at an end: the Hectors were not the kind of men to answer questions, and trying to locate 'Mrs Riley' would be futile.

So what had happened? Had someone hired the Hectors to snatch Hanse, perhaps in an effort to sabotage the

37

peace talks? Somehow, Chaloner did not believe it was coincidence that a driver with dubious connections – now mysteriously dead – should have been the one to drive Hanse home. Bowed down with anxiety for a man he liked, Chaloner turned homewards.

Hannah was asleep when he reached their cottage on Tothill Street, which was not surprising given that it was well past midnight. It was unbearably hot in the bedroom, because she believed that night air caused fevers, and never slept with the windows open. As she had lost her first husband to a sudden and inexplicable illness, Chaloner had been unable to dissuade her of the notion.

His concern for Hanse and the stifling heat meant he slept badly in the few hours before it became light, and he found himself reviewing again and again the last moments of the evening they had spent together. They had walked outside the Sun, and Hanse had raised his arm to flag down the hackney that had been trundling towards them. Ibbot had smiled in a friendly fashion, and there had been nothing about him – not even with hindsight – to suggest anything untoward. Chaloner had started to follow Hanse into the coach, but the Dutchman had pushed him back.

'You are tired,' he had said firmly. 'Go home to your new wife.'

'Not too tired to see an old friend home,' Chaloner had argued, trying to enter a second time.

The next shove had been rather more forceful. 'What can happen between King Street and the Savoy? It is a journey of a few minutes! But to take your mind off it, accept this gift – two pairs of fine Dutch stockings. The ones you wear are a little tatty.'

Hanse *should* have been safe, Chaloner thought bitterly, as he tossed and turned. So where was he? Dead? Or were the Hectors holding him somewhere until the peace talks foundered?

He rose as soon as it was light enough to see, donned clean clothes and left while Hannah was still asleep, unwilling to risk another row about the long hours he was working. He wandered through the wakening city, aiming for nowhere in particular, and had just reached King Street when he met Bulteel, who lived in nearby Old Palace Yard.

'I *know* I am up early, but my cousin snores,' explained Bulteel. 'And I cannot cook while he is there, either. He tells me that baking is an unsuitable pastime for gentlemen, and recommends dancing lessons instead. However, making cakes has a soothing effect on me: if I am tired, unhappy or worried, then producing a tray of biscuits makes me feel so much better.'

'Playing the viol does the same for me.' Chaloner spoke hesitantly, unused to sharing such intimate confidences. 'Unfortunately, Hannah does not like me making a noise at inconvenient hours, so . . .'

'So you cannot do it as often as you would like,' finished Bulteel sympathetically. 'There is a lot to be said for living alone. But you once told me that all intelligencers have accommodations away from their homes, lest they are working on a dangerous case, and do not want villains to know where they live. Why not take your viol there?'

Chaloner experienced a twinge of guilt. All spies *should* have boltholes, so as not to endanger their families, and he knew he was remiss in not finding a refuge to replace the one he had lost in February. The fact that he had not had a spare moment since his return from the United Provinces was a poor excuse.

'I have a second home in Chelsey,' said Bulteel. He smiled, revealing his brown teeth. It was a sinister expression, and went some way to explaining why he was not popular in White Hall. 'I use it rarely, so you may take your viol there, if you like.'

Chelsey was an attractively rural village two miles to the west. It was too far away to be practical as a regular sanctuary, although Chaloner appreciated the offer, and thought a distant safe haven might come in useful in the future. He nodded his thanks.

'You have bought a new house?' he asked, wondering how the secretary could afford it. Clarendon did not pay his people well, and Bulteel was known for declining to supplement his income with bribes.

'An uncle left it to me in his will. I wanted Griffith to live in it while he teaches me manners, but he insisted on staying with me in Westminster instead. When the weather cools, perhaps you will come to see it. It is a lovely place, near the church. You could bring Hannah, too. I suppose.'

To Chaloner's great sorrow, his wife and friend did not like each other, and the fact that Hannah had 'forgotten' to invite Bulteel to the wedding had not helped. Bulteel still had not forgiven her, while she treated him with a disdain that ran contrary to her usually easy-going nature. Bulteel was trying to build bridges by inviting her to Chelsey, but Chaloner suspected it would not be a good idea to accept on her behalf. There would almost certainly be trouble if he did.

'You have not mentioned the message I sent last night,' Bulteel said, as Chaloner struggled to think of a polite way to decline. 'About the missing Dutchman. Did anything come of the matter?'

Chaloner stared at him. 'What message?'

'Hannah probably recognised my writing and threw it away,' said Bulteel resentfully.

'She was asleep when I arrived home, and I left without waking her,' said Chaloner defensively, although Bulteel's claim was not entirely without foundation – she had 'mislaid' missives before, and had been defiantly unrepentant when Chaloner had tackled her about it. 'She did not have the chance to pass me anything.'

Bulteel sniffed disbelievingly. 'My note was about Hanse. Mr Kersey, down at the charnel house, has a body matching his description.'

Westminster's mortuary was a grim building, located between a granary and a coal yard. It comprised a long, low cellar for storing bodies, with two more pleasant rooms near the door. One of these chambers was the office in which the charnel-house keeper collected his takings. John Kersey charged an admission fee for spectators, and also ran a small museum containing some of the more unusual artefacts he had collected from his charges over the years. The other was a comfortable parlour in which he explained formalities to grieving friends and families.

Despite the early hour, Kersey was at his place of work. He was a neat, dapper little man whose fine clothes and expensive wig said he made a decent living from his grim trade. Chaloner might have suspected him of dressing himself with garments retrieved from his wealthier corpses, but they fitted him far too well, and were obviously the work of bespoke tailors.

41

Soberly confiding that the hot weather meant he was much busier than usual, Kersey conducted Chaloner to the main chamber, where the stench was enough to make a man light-headed. The place hummed with flies, and Chaloner's stomach began to churn. Although not a religious man, he found himself praying that the body he was about to be shown would not be Hanse's.

'Here,' said Kersey, stopping next to a table that was about halfway down the room and lifting the sheet that covered it. 'Is this him?'

Chaloner felt a great wave of sadness wash over him as he gazed at his brother-in-law, a man he had liked and respected, despite the fact that they had met rarely since his first wife's death twelve years before. Familial ties were important in both Dutch and English society, and were rarely severed because someone died or remarried, so Chaloner was still kin as far as Hanse was concerned, and vice versa.

Their paths had crossed by pure chance in White Hall the previous Wednesday, and Hanse had been so delighted that he had hauled Chaloner immediately to the Savoy to pay his respects to Jacoba – his own wife and Aletta's sister. Their next meeting had been in the Westminster tavern two days later, after which Hanse had disappeared.

'You look as though you could do with a drink,' said Kersey gently, after some time had passed, and Chaloner had done nothing but stare.

Wordlessly, Chaloner followed him through the mortuary to the parlour, flapping bluebottles from his face as he went. Once there, he sat on a chair and watched Kersey pour wine into a pair of handsome crystal goblets. He usually avoided drinking from Kersey's cups, on the grounds that the charnel-house keeper was

42

in the habit of letting them be used for unpleasant procedures in the mortuary, but such considerations were a
long way from his mind that day, and he accepted without
thinking. When he sipped the brew – dawn was a little
early in the day for wine, but Kersey was right in that
he needed something – he was surprised by its fine quality.
Clearly, Kersey was a man who knew how to cater to
his personal comforts.

Gradually, the wine settled Chaloner's roiling innards.
Seeing Hanse dead had upset him more than he would
have anticipated given the number of people he had lost
in his life – to the civil wars, to sickness, and because he
had chosen a dangerous occupation. He could only
suppose that meeting Hanse in London, combined with
his recent visit to the States-General, had resurrected
memories and feelings about his first family that he had
thought were well and truly buried.

'Can I assume it *is* the Dutchman?' asked Kersey, his
voice intruding on Chaloner's thoughts. 'I need a name,
you see. For my records.'

'It is Willem Hanse,' replied Chaloner, wishing with
all his heart that it was not.

Kersey went to a desk and began writing. 'We have
Surgeon Wiseman to thank for getting him identified.
He is the one who matched the description of the missing
diplomat to this corpse.'

'Was he able to deduce how Hanse died?'

'He said he drowned – could tell by the state of the
lungs, apparently.'

Silence reigned again, broken only by the buzz of flies
and the scratch of Kersey's pen. Chaloner berated himself
yet again for not overriding his kinsman's objections and
accompanying him back to his lodgings anyway. Then

he took a deep breath and pushed such thoughts from his mind: wallowing in guilt was helping no one, and he needed to concentrate on what *had* happened, not what might have been different. *How* had Hanse come to drown? Was it an accident? Chaloner could not see how, given that Ibbot should have taken Hanse nowhere near the river.

Had he tossed himself in the Thames deliberately, then? Chaloner thought that was unlikely, too. Hanse had mentioned pains in his stomach, but surely they would not have driven him to take his own life? And he had not seemed worried or in low sprits. As always, he had done the lion's share of the talking, chatting about good times spent in Amsterdam when Aletta had been alive, his hopes for successful peace talks, and a book he was writing on stockings. Chaloner had raised his eyebrows at this last subject, but Hanse had always been interested in decorative legwear.

Absently, he watched Kersey sprinkle sand on his wet ink. So if accident and suicide could be discounted, then all that was left was murder. The conclusion came as no surprise, given Ibbot's connection with the Hectors.

'I heard about the man who was killed at your wedding,' said Kersey conversationally as he wrote. His profession meant he tended to be interested in unusual deaths. 'Did you know him?'

'Yes, but not well. His name was Alden, and he was a one-time Royalist spy who had fallen on hard times. I suspect he was there to see whether he could inveigle a free meal.'

'So he was in the wrong place at the wrong time? Someone wanted a warning delivered to one of your guests, and pinned it on him because he happened to be sitting at the back?'

'It looks that way.'

Kersey shook his head in disgust. 'So who was the intended recipient of this vile communication? What did it say? "Do not interfere"?'

Chaloner only nodded, unwilling to admit that he had failed to unravel *that* mystery, too. Most of the guests had been strangers to him, because Hannah had invited a large number of courtiers, not to mention members of the Privy Council. Being politicians and aristocrats, many indulged in shady dealings, but – not surprisingly – no one had been inclined to discuss them with him.

'What about your colleagues?' asked Kersey. 'Fellow intelligencers? Could the message have been intended for one of them?'

Chaloner shook his head. Hannah had not invited any of those to her elegant celebrations. Besides, espionage was a dangerous way to earn a living, and most of them were dead.

'Are you looking into the matter?' persisted Kersey, trying a third time to solicit a verbal reply.

Chaloner made a noncommittal gesture. Hanse's death, along with the missing Privy Council papers, meant Alden would have to be shelved for a while. But only for a while, he determined, because no villain was going to commit murder during *his* wedding and get away with it.

'Well, at least there is no suggestion of foul play with Hanse,' said Kersey, setting the lid on his inkwell. 'He must have fallen in the Thames. It was an accident.'

'I disagree. He had no reason to be near the river. I think he was pushed.'

'It is possible, I suppose,' acknowledged Kersey, although he did not sound convinced. 'But I hear he was fond of his wine, and he would not be the first drunkard to topple into water.'

'He did drink a lot,' conceded Chaloner. 'But he was not drunk the night he disappeared.'

Kersey regarded him curiously. 'How do you know?'

'Was anything recovered with his body?' asked Chaloner, unwilling to tell him.

'You mean did I find the Privy Council papers he stole from Clarendon, so that when our two countries go to war, he will have given the States-General an advantage over us?' enquired Kersey archly.

Chaloner regarded him in horror, aghast that a charnel-house keeper should know about a matter that should have been contained within the Earl's household.

'It is common knowledge,' said Kersey defensively, when he saw Chaloner's shock. 'Everyone knows Worcester House was burgled the day that Hanse and Ambassador van Goch visited it.'

'Christ!' muttered Chaloner, more appalled than ever. 'Are you saying Hanse had the papers, then? Where are they?'

'I did not find them. The body was stripped by the time it came to me.'

Chaloner winced. 'By the people who found him?'

'No, they said he was naked when they stumbled across him. I believe them, because they often bring me bodies from the Thames, and they have never undressed one before.'

Chaloner stared at him. Was this evidence of murder? That Hanse's killer had removed his victim's clothing to hinder identification? Or perhaps to inflict some final humiliation on him?

'The only thing left was a stocking,' Kersey went on. 'And that was tied on so tightly that I needed a sharp knife to remove it.'

Chaloner's pulse quickened. Hanse had owned a peculiar habit of securing valuables in his hose, and kept them tight around his knees to prevent money and papers from spilling out. 'Do you still have it? May I see?'

Kersey's eyebrows went up. 'I threw it away. An odd stocking is of no use to me, and I cannot imagine his next-of-kin wanting it. It will be with the other rubbish outside. Why?'

Chaloner shrugged, feigning indifference. 'If it is all that is left, then I had better examine it.'

Chapter 2

Chaloner left the pungent building with relief, and went to rummage in the pile of refuse behind it. Most did not bear too close an inspection, and the feasting flies he disturbed buzzed in an angry cloud around his head. The stocking was near the bottom, recognisable by the high quality of its wool and an intricate design that rendered it unmistakably Dutch. It was unmistakably Hanse's, too, because he had always prided himself on his immaculate footwear. It had been slit near the top, presumably by Kersey to allow it to be pulled off, but was otherwise undamaged.

Chaloner glanced around carefully before picking it up, but the lane was deserted. The proximity of the Thames with its sun-baked cargo of sewage and rubbish, along with Kersey's odoriferous domain, meant the alley was not a pleasant place to be, and anyone who lived nearby had taken themselves off to more conducive surroundings. He was definitely alone.

He sat on a crate and turned the stocking over in his hands. Hanse had harboured an especially strong horror of robbers, and his family had always been amused by his habit of secreting valuables in his hose – he spurned pockets in coat or breeches, on the grounds that thieves knew how to find those. To ensure the stockings did not slide down, he took needle and thread each morning, and sewed them tight. The fact that the sock had resisted attempts to remove it – by whoever had stripped his body and later by Kersey – suggested it had been anchored very firmly. And that meant there was something within that Hanse had deemed worthy of protection.

But Chaloner's hopes were soon dashed – it contained nothing. Disgusted, he flung it away, but as it landed, it caught the sun, and he saw silver thread had been used to sew a pattern near the top. If the design had been on the outside, he would have thought nothing of it, but it was on the inside, where it would never be seen. Puzzled, he bent down and picked it up again. Two letters, an S and an N, had been embroidered, but the material was too filthy to allow any more to be made out.

He went to a water butt – almost empty because of the recent drought, but containing enough for a rinse – and inspected it again. He was able to make out a word: *Sinon*.

He frowned. Sinon was the original spy who had persuaded the Trojans to take a wooden horse into their city, so that the Greek soldiers hiding inside could emerge after darkness and destroy it. His name was synonymous with deceit, and was often used to describe plots involving traitors. It was hardly original, and Chaloner had lost count of the times he had taken part in 'Operation Sinon' through the years. But what did it mean now? Was Hanse suggesting there was a traitor in the Dutch delegation?

He examined the hose again, and found more words embroidered opposite the first. They were difficult to read, as if Hanse had been hurrying, and indeed, the last letter was incomplete: *Bezoek Nieuwe Poort.*

Chaloner translated it in his head. *Visit new gate.* But knowing its meaning did little to illuminate matters. What new gate? Or did it refer to Newgate, one of the gate-houses that had been built to protect the medieval city from attack? Chaloner hoped not. Newgate was also a prison, and harrowing experiences in such places, especially one in France had taught him to hate them intensely.

Eventually, realising that staring at the stocking was not going to provide him with answers, he left that grim little pocket of Westminster, aiming for the open squares and wider streets that would take him to White Hall. He needed to tell Clarendon that Hanse was found, so the Dutch ambassador could be officially informed. And then there was Hanse's wife. Chaloner stopped walking abruptly. Clearly, it was his duty to tell her first. The Earl would have to wait.

When Ambassador Michiel van Goch had arrived in London for the talks he hoped would avert a war, he had requested lodgings that would allow all his retinue to be together under one roof. It was a tall order, given that he had brought with him some two hundred diplomats, clerks, lawyers, servants and guards, plus several ship-loads of luggage, and the government had been obliged to commandeer the Savoy Hospital to accommodate them all.

The Savoy had once been a palace, but currently served as a charitable foundation for the poor. It comprised not only a hall, chapel, kitchens, stables and dormitories, but a number of fine mansions that were usually leased to nobles and high-ranking clergy. The precinct was self-contained, with secure courtyards in which vulnerable foreigners could take the air without fear of being attacked by those Londoners who thought the delegation should never have come in the first place.

Its master, Dr Henry Killigrew, had not been pleased when he had been told what was going to happen – the Dutch were to pay no rent, which meant he would lose revenue for as long as they remained – but the Court was happy. The Savoy was near enough to be convenient for negotiations, but not so close that the visitors would impinge on the revelries for which White Hall was famous. As he walked there, Chaloner recalled that Killigrew had been at his wedding – it had been the master's wife whose dress had been stained by Alden's blood.

He dragged his feet as he made his way up King Street, not relishing the prospect of informing his first wife's sister that she was now a widow. He traversed Charing Cross slowly, and turned into The Strand, which was carpeted in a thick layer of manure impregnated with discarded scraps of food, rotting vegetables, urine and copies of the many broadsheets – usually rabid and ill-informed rants on politics and religion – that kept London's printers busy. The blazing sun baked all, and the resulting stench was enough to make his eyes smart.

The Savoy was located about a third of the way along, protected from the outside world by a fortified gatehouse. It was guarded by soldiers, English ones in buff jerkins with stripy sleeves, and Dutch ones in sleek uniforms of black. Anyone wanting to enter the hospital

51

complex was obliged to explain himself twice, once to each nationality.

Chaloner was disinclined to tell anyone his business, so, as Worcester House, where Clarendon lived, was next door, he entered that, then climbed over the wall that divided them. The Dutch had pickets prowling the grounds, but they represented no challenge to a man of his experience, and it was not many moments before he reached the hospital's main door.

The man in charge of the delegation's security was a burly, humourless officer named Captain van Ruyven, whom Chaloner had met before, some twelve years earlier, when he had been on his first assignment in the United Provinces. They had fallen in love with the same woman, and Chaloner had been somewhat surprised to learn that Ruyven had still not forgiven him for winning Aletta. When Hanse had dragged Chaloner to the Savoy the previous week, Ruyven had glowered and sulked through the entire encounter.

'How did you get in?' Ruyven demanded coldly.

Chaloner realised he should have braved the guards, because it would not do to admit that he was skilled at breaking into houses. No one in the Dutch delegation had the slightest inkling that he had spent years spying on them. As far as they were concerned, he had been a minor diplomat in the service of the British ambassador.

'I have come to see Jacoba,' Chaloner replied in Dutch – Ruyven's English was poor – deftly avoiding the question.

'The sister-in-law you have neglected for so long?' asked Ruyven nastily. 'When Aletta died, you disappeared within a week of burying her, and seldom bothered to visit afterwards.'

It had not been Chaloner's idea to leave Amsterdam so abruptly, but his Spymaster had decided that a grieving man was too great a liability, and had ordered him to France instead. Five years later, Chaloner had been posted back to the United Provinces, but to The Hague, where Aletta's family rarely ventured. He had always felt guilty about abandoning Jacoba at such a time.

'Jacoba will not want to see you,' Ruyven went on. 'She told me only last night that you remind her too painfully of Aletta.'

Chaloner felt the same way about Jacoba, especially after his recent visit to Amsterdam. He saw Ruyven was expecting some sort of response, but did not know what to say, and the Dutchman turned to other matters when the resulting pause had extended long enough to be uncomfortable for both of them.

'Envoy Downing came this morning. Apparently, some documents have been stolen from Worcester House, and he told us the general belief is that Hanse is responsible – that he took the papers and has disappeared with them. Do you know anything about this horrible tale?'

'Only that it is circulating.'

At that moment, the door opened and someone else stepped out, taking deep breaths and rolling his shoulders, as if he had spent too long at work. It was Peter van der Kun, an elderly, mild-mannered gentleman with a friendly face and a scholar's stoop. He was van Goch's secretary, and Chaloner was glad the cause of peace had a gentle, careful man like Kun fighting its corner.

'Thomas Chaloner,' he smiled. 'The man who shares his name with the regicide who fled to our country and died there two years ago. You translated some documents for us the other day.'

'It was unnecessary, though,' replied Chaloner, declining to address the issue of his relationship to one of the men who had signed the old king's death warrant. His flamboyant uncle was not someone to boast about in Restoration London. 'Your English is perfect.'

'You are too kind.' Kun's expression turned eager. 'Do you bring a message from your Earl? He was going to address the Privy Council today, urging them to look favourably on the convention to be held here next Sunday evening.'

'I doubt he will succeed,' said Ruyven bitterly. 'Our two countries do not trust each other enough to agree on anything, and these peace talks are a waste of time.'

'You are wrong: we *will* have a truce,' countered Kun stoutly. Then he grimaced. 'But you are right about the mutual distrust. As soon as I disprove one set of lies about us, another appears. Maligning us is some villain's way of hindering progress.'

'The English do not have the wit for such tactics,' said Ruyven, shooting Chaloner a challenging glare. 'Their idea of damaging the talks is far less subtle. Such as refusing to bow to Heer van Goch at banquets, and calling the rest of us names.'

Kun's pained expression said he was sorry for Ruyven's hostility. 'What is your master's message?' he asked keenly. 'Is it good news?'

'Actually, I have come to visit Jacoba,' replied Chaloner.

'Oh,' said Kun, disappointed. 'Well, perhaps your company will take her mind off—'

'No,' interrupted Ruyven. '*I* control who enters the Savoy, and I do not trust this man. He called himself

Tom Heyden in Amsterdam, but now we learn his real name is something else entirely.'

Most intelligencers used aliases when working overseas, and the practice did sometimes backfire. But Chaloner was ready with an explanation, just as he had been when Hanse had been startled to learn from an inconveniently garrulous Clarendon that his brother-in-law did not hail from a Bristol mercantile family, but was the youngest son of a country squire in Buckinghamshire.

'I had debts in Holland. I had no choice but to use a different name there.'

'So you say,' snarled Ruyven. 'But spies—'

'Chaloner is not a spy,' said Kun firmly, while Chaloner thought it ironic that Ruyven should think so now, when he was *not* gathering intelligence, but had never raised an eyebrow when he had been doing little else. 'Let him pass. Jacoba will be pleased to see him.'

In resentful silence, Ruyven conducted Chaloner to the quarters that had been allocated to Hanse and his wife for the duration of their stay in London. They comprised a pair of comfortably furnished rooms near the chapel, both pleasantly cool after the burning sunlight outside. Their size and location underlined the high esteem in which Hanse had been held by his ambassador – space was in short supply at the Savoy, and most envoys only had one.

Jacoba was sitting at a harpsichord when Chaloner arrived, although her playing was lacklustre, and he could tell her heart was not in it. She was a small, dark haired woman with a neat figure and a regal bearing. For a moment, with the sun in his eyes, Chaloner mistook her for Aletta, and his stomach lurched. But Aletta had been twenty-two when she had died, and Jacoba was approaching forty: he forced himself to acknowledge that they were nothing alike.

'Tom!' she exclaimed, abandoning the instrument and coming to take his hand. 'Is there any word of Willem?'

Chaloner nodded, and then spoke quickly, unwilling to prolong the agony for her. 'He is dead, Jacoba. I am so sorry.'

'Why did you not tell me this immediately?' cried Ruyven, shocked. 'And why break the news in so brutal a fashion? What is wrong with you? It is—'

Jacoba's wail of grief cut through his tirade, and was loud enough to bring Kun and several others running to see what was happening. A maid rushed to comfort her, while Ruyven glowered at Chaloner, fists clenched. The knife Chaloner always carried in his sleeve slipped into his hand.

'Easy, Ruyven,' said Kun, coming to lay a hastily soothing hand on the captain's shoulder. 'We cannot afford to be seen as ruffians, no matter what the provocation.'

'I would not be itching to punch him if he had spoken more gently,' said Ruyven between clenched teeth.

'Unfortunately, there *is* no gentle way to impart such terrible tidings,' said Kun quietly. 'And I am sure he did not mean to be unkind.' He turned to Chaloner. 'Where is he?'

'In the Westminster charnel house. I will arrange for him to be brought here later.'

'How did he die?' demanded Ruyven, white-faced. 'He was fit and healthy, so his death cannot have been natural.'

'He drowned,' replied Chaloner. 'In the river, apparently.'

'You mean he fell in?' asked a man with a sharp, pointed face, small teeth and russet hair. The combination made him look like a fox, and Chaloner recalled Hanse saying his name was Gerbrand Zas, one of the ambassador's most talented lawyers. 'How in God's name did that happen?'

'He would not have *fallen in*,' spat Ruyven scathingly. 'He was not stupid! Someone must have pushed him. He was *murdered*!'

Chaloner kept his voice and expression neutral, knowing the peace talks would be doomed for certain if the Dutch delegation accused England of assassinating one of its number. And that was the last thing Hanse would have wanted.

'It is unclear what happened,' he replied truthfully.

'It is not unclear to me,' snarled Ruyven. Chaloner was surprised to see tears glinting in his eyes – he did not remember the captain as a sentimental man. 'It is obvious! He was pushed in the Thames in the expectation that his body would be washed away and never seen again. And why? Because of this rumour that says he stole Clarendon's papers! Someone wants *him* blamed for the theft, even though we all know the tale is nothing but a slanderous lie!'

Kun raised his hand to prevent him from saying more. 'Before jumping to wild conclusions, let us review what we know of his movements that last day,' he said with quiet reason. 'He went with Heer van Goch to Worcester House on Friday morning. He worked here all afternoon, and left a few minutes before six o'clock for his rendezvous in the Westminster tavern with Chaloner.'

57

'It is a pity you enticed him there,' said Ruyven accusingly.

'It was his idea,' countered Chaloner, recalling how he had tried to postpone the occasion to a time when he might not have been so tired. Hanse had chosen the Sun, too, whereas *he* would have picked somewhere quieter. 'He mentioned stomach ache, but was not otherwise anxious or uneasy.'

'In other words, he did not look like a man who had made off with a great stack of sensitive papers,' concluded Zas.

'He did not,' agreed Chaloner. 'We arrived at the Sun at about six o'clock, and stayed until half past eight, during which time he did not stop talking. I am afraid I fell asleep.'

'He did enjoy holding forth,' acknowledged Kun with a fond smile. 'And a weary companion would have been an irresistible temptation: tired men are less likely to interrupt with their own opinions. His behaviour with you sounds reassuringly familiar.'

'He woke me as the daylight began to fade,' Chaloner continued. 'He said Jacoba would be worried about him, so we left the tavern—'

'And you abandoned him, despite the fact that London is full of men who would relish the opportunity to shove a Dutchman in the river,' concluded Ruyven coldly.

'He would not let me in the carriage,' said Chaloner, trying to keep the guilt from his voice. He did not need Ruyven to tell him he should have insisted.

'You should be ashamed of yourself,' declared Ruyven. 'It was unthinkable to let an unarmed diplomat travel alone. Especially with darkness approaching.'

'Yes,' acknowledged Chaloner bleakly. 'And I shall regret it for the rest of my life.'

The maid was still struggling to quieten Jacoba, and Chaloner was not sure what to do. There were no words he knew to comfort her, and it was possible that his presence might exacerbate her distress – he had, after all, gone home to sleep, rather than ensuring that her husband arrived safely at the Savoy. But he was loath to slink away until he was certain there was nothing she wanted from him.

But Jacoba was a strong-minded woman, like her sister had been, and once the initial shock had worn off, she dismissed the maid and indicated that she wanted to speak to him alone. Ruyven was reluctant to leave her, and Kun and Zas were obliged to pull him away. None went far, though, and Chaloner knew they were hovering just out of earshot, lest they were needed again.

'I knew Willem was dead the moment I realised he was missing,' Jacoba said, when the door had closed. 'We were married for fifteen years, and wives just *feel* these things. But it was still a terrible thing to hear even so. Do you know how it happened?'

'He drowned. Ruyven and the others think it was murder.'

'Do you?'

'I will look into it, and if they are right, I will find his killer. I promise.'

She shot him a wan smile. 'Thank you. I suspect you are his sole hope of justice. Ruyven is brave and determined, but he is a stranger here – he will fail if *he* tries to investigate.'

'He is brave and determined,' agreed Chaloner, recalling that these were the qualities Aletta had admired. Of course, Ruyven was also surly, feisty and bore grudges.

'He is not the hot-tempered youth you knew,' Jacoba went on. 'He has learned how to be gentle, although Willem says . . . Willem *said* he is dangerous, and would not like him as an enemy.'

'Did he?' asked Chaloner. Ruyven was one of those Dutchmen who thought a pact with Britain was a mistake. Could *he* have drowned a man whose death would deal peace a heavy blow?

'Ruyven did not hurt Willem,' said Jacoba quickly, seeing what he was thinking. 'He liked Willem and considered him a friend.'

'Did Willem make any enemies while he was here?' Chaloner asked, thinking he would make up his own mind about what Ruyven might or might not do.

'Well, there are three hundred thousand Londoners who do not want a truce. Your countrymen itch for war, although it will cost them dear – in money and well as lives.'

'Not all of us are spoiling for a fight,' objected Chaloner. 'Clarendon wants peace, and so do—'

'Clarendon is a bumbling old man whom everyone ignores,' Jacoba interrupted bitterly. 'Heer van Goch is wasting his time here. And my poor Willem has wasted his life.'

'Does "Sinon" mean anything to you?' asked Chaloner, after a short and uncomfortable silence.

Jacoba frowned. 'No, why?'

'Willem had the word sewn into his stocking, along with "Visit new gate".'

60

Jacoba's eyes filled with tears. 'That would have been a message for you. You are the only one who knows about his habit of hiding valuables in his hose.'

Chaloner did not believe that. 'There must be others who were aware of—'

'No,' interrupted Jacoba. 'It was a family secret. And they are all dead now, except you and me. If he sewed words in his stockings, then *you* were the one he wanted to communicate with.'

'Or you,' Chaloner pointed out.

Jacoba smiled rather sadly. 'He did not trust women with business matters. But he trusted you. He told me so the night before he went missing.'

Chaloner regarded her unhappily. Did this mean Hanse had anticipated that he would die, and had worn those particular hose in readiness? And if so, had there been more messages in the other stocking? But then he thought about Hanse's last evening: he had not behaved like a man on the brink of death.

'May I see his other hose?' he asked eventually.

Jacoba stared at him. 'You think he might have embroidered more words into them?'

'It is possible. I recall he had a strange habit of changing them every day, and—'

'And he would not have worn that particular set unless he knew he was going to die,' finished Jacoba. 'They *were* clean on that morning. I remember him stitching them up.'

She left the room, and returned a few moments later with her arms full. They inspected the hose together, but there were no other messages. Hanse had, however, given Chaloner two pairs when they had been arguing about who should ride in the hackney coach. It had been done casually, and Chaloner had not looked at them closely. Clearly, he would have to do so when he went home.

'Did he mention anything that was worrying him?' he asked.

'No. He was uneasy in the few days before he went missing, but he was a foreigner in a hostile city, so that is not surprising. Besides, if he had been really concerned, he would have told you.'

'Jacoba, we were not close,' said Chaloner gently. 'We met too infrequently to stay firm friends.'

Jacoba sniffed in a way that said she did not believe him. 'You know he did not steal those papers, do you not? That horrible Downing accused him . . . but Willem was *not* a thief.'

'I know. He was with me when these documents were said to have disappeared.'

'It is a tale put about to discredit our delegation,' declared Jacoba tearfully. 'And Downing picked on Willem, because he is not here to defend himself.'

'Very possibly,' acknowledged Chaloner. 'But to return to Sinon—'

'I never heard Willem or anyone else mention it,' said Jacoba firmly. 'What does it mean?'

'Then do you know of any new gate in the Savoy?'

'There is nothing "new" about this place. It is falling to pieces!'

She could add nothing more to help him, so Chaloner took his leave, promising to keep her appraised of his progress.

As he left the hospital complex, Ruyven at his heels to make sure he really went, Chaloner met Henry Killigrew.

He had been cornered by the Master of the Savoy at his wedding, just after the speeches, and had been compelled to spend a long time listening to the man's complaints about the cost of maintaining a lot of elderly buildings. Killigrew, it seemed, was more interested in profit than in the wellbeing of his residents.

'And housing these damned Dutchmen is not helping,' he grumbled when their paths converged, as if the conversation had not suffered a two-week break. Uninvited, he fell into step at Chaloner's side and began to walk with him towards the gate. 'They are costing me a fortune. Not only do they live here rent-free, but they are very demanding. One even asked me to empty the latrines, which had overflowed into the room where he was sleeping.'

'How very unreasonable,' murmured Chaloner.

Ruyven strained forward. 'What is he saying about us?' he demanded in Dutch. 'All he ever does is make disparaging remarks. Personally, I think *he* might be a spy, too.'

'And he is the worst,' spat Killigrew, jerking a thumb towards Ruyven. 'Always criticising my security arrangements and carping on about hygiene. He does not even speak English, the ignorant pig! If he cannot converse in our language, then he should not have come here.'

'I suspect him of being Catholic,' said Ruyven, not understanding Killigrew's words, but guessing they were offensive. 'He has that look about him – devious, scheming and greedy.'

'Is there a new gate in your hospital?' asked Chaloner of Killigrew.

'No, why?' said Killigrew suspiciously. 'Did that butter-

63

eating lout just tell you that I am going to install one? Well, I am not! He claims the back door is flimsy, but I am not made of money, and if he is so worried, then why does he not go out and buy one himself? With his *own* silver!'

'I did *not* break the brazier in the State Room,' snapped Ruyven, scowling as he tried to follow Killigrew's rapid sentences. 'And you can tell him so, because I know that is what he is carping about. I was nowhere near it when it fell. Go on, tell him.'

'Ruyven did not break the brazier,' obliged Chaloner in English.

Killigrew narrowed his eyes. 'I never thought he did, but now he denies it, I begin to wonder. Could it be his conscience speaking? Between you and me, I suspect him of being Catholic, and you know what *they* are like with guilt.'

'Christ!' muttered Chaloner, reaching the gate with relief.

Ruyven caught his arm before he could step through it. 'It is best if you do not come here again. Your presence will only distress Jacoba.'

'But she has asked me to look into what happened to Willem,' said Chaloner. 'And she wants reports on my progress.'

Ruyven stared at him. 'Then you can give them to me. I shall also be investigating.'

'I would not recommend it. You are right in that London is hostile to Hollanders, especially ones who cannot speak English. You are likely to land yourself in trouble.'

'Is that a threat?' demanded Ruyven.

'It is friendly advice. You are unlikely to succeed, and

a second suspicious death in the ambassador's retinue would ruin the negotiations for certain. Hanse would not want that.'

'No,' conceded Ruyven reluctantly. 'Very well. I shall not interfere. But I want you to keep me abreast of your findings. I am in charge of security here, so I am within my rights to ask.'

Chaloner inclined his head, although he had no intention of obliging. Not until he was sure Hanse's killer was not a Dutchman, at least.

'I had no idea Hannah was marrying a fellow who spoke Hollandish,' said Killigrew, watching Ruyven stride away, and then turning to glare accusingly at Chaloner. 'It is not seemly, man. Not in this day and age.'

'Where is the nearest new gate that you know of?' asked Chaloner. He suspected Killigrew was not alone in his convictions, and wondered what chance there was for a treaty when there was so much dislike between the two countries. And it was not even a dislike he understood. Both were Protestant nations, and they had been allies in the past.

Killigrew regarded him askance. 'What is this obsession with new gates? Are you sun-touched?'

'I am thinking of replacing the one at home,' lied Chaloner, supposing he had better furnish an explanation. Killigrew was inclined to gossip, and he did not want it put about that he was short of wits. Or that his familiarity with Dutch was leading him into suspicious activities regarding doors.

'And you want to inspect a few before you make a final decision? Well, why did you not say so?' Killigrew frowned in thought. 'No one around here has brought one recently. In fact, the only "new gate" I can think of is Newgate itself, and you will not want one of those in your garden!'

He roared with laughter as he stepped out of the hospital precinct and turned right along The Strand, leaving Chaloner staring after him thoughtfully. *Did* Hanse's message refer to the prison? But Hanse had known nothing about Chaloner's career as a spy, so had no reason to expect him to unravel cryptic clues. So why had he left one for him? Or was Jacoba wrong, and the words sewn in the hose were intended for someone else?

Before he went to White Hall, he stopped at his house in Tothill Street to inspect the stockings Hanse had given him. They were lying on a bench in the parlour, where he had tossed them when he had arrived home on Friday night, too tired to think of putting them away.

They were thin summer ones, obviously intended to be worn while the weather was warm. Was that significant? It did not take him many moments to see that it was. There were words sewn into the finer of the two pairs – the ones he was most likely to have used first. They were: *Sinon* and *Bezoek Nieuwe Poort* again. So Jacoba had been right: Hanse's message *had* been intended for him.

Hanse had often praised his brother-in-law's sharp mind, and Chaloner could only assume that Hanse had left him the riddle because he believed him to be capable of solving it. Uncomfortably, he suspected Hanse had overrated his abilities, because he had no idea how even to start unravelling what it meant. He stared at the stockings for a long time before standing reluctantly and going to tell the Earl of Clarendon that the missing diplomat was dead.

*　　*　　*

The Palace of White Hall was a sprawling, chaotic affair, said to contain more than two thousand rooms. It boasted elegant halls that rubbed shoulders with laundries and coal sheds, and was a maze of twisting lanes, cobbled yards and covered walkways. Because it was the King's main London residence, it was always busy, and that Monday morning it thronged with servants, courtiers, nobles and clerks. Many had ridden there, or travelled in carriages, so there was a lot of traffic, too.

White Hall was not just home to the King, his Queen, his mistress and the immediate members of his family. It was also a seat of administrative power, and some of His Majesty's most important ministers had offices there. These included the Lord Chancellor, who had been provided with a suite of rooms overlooking the manicured elegance of the Privy Garden.

Bulteel occupied a small, windowless room at the top of the great marble staircase. Its stone walls meant it was frigid in winter, and cool in summer. Chaloner stepped inside gratefully, relishing the sudden drop in temperature after the blistering heat of outside.

'Have you found the Earl's papers yet?' the secretary asked. He wore a coat, and blew on his fingers to warm them as he sat back to smile a greeting at Chaloner.

'Not yet. It would help – a lot, I imagine – if I knew what was in them. For example, there is a rumour that Hanse stole them, but if they pertain to agricultural policy in Wales, then I doubt he would have been very interested.'

'Apparently, the rumour that Hanse is to blame was started by Sir George Downing. And I wish I *could* tell you what is in them, but I cannot, because Clarendon says they are sensitive.'

'Does that mean you think they are not?'

'Stop!' ordered Bulteel nervously. 'There is nothing I would like more than to answer your questions, but he has forbidden me, so my hands are tied. I cannot disobey him.'

'No,' said Chaloner, disappointed. Bulteel was nothing if not obedient.

'I was going to make knot biscuits this morning,' said Bulteel unhappily, in the silence that followed. 'My cousin tends to rise late, so I thought I could bake a batch before he was awake. But he must have heard the pantry door open, because he came down while I was measuring out the flour, and I had to concoct a tale about lending it to a neighbour.'

Chaloner was sorry. Bulteel's cakes were often the only pleasant thing about visiting White Hall. 'How much longer will Griffith be staying with you?' he asked, mostly out of self-interest.

Bulteel looked pained. 'My lessons are taking rather longer than we expected, and he says it will be at least another month before I am converted into a proper courtier. I want my kitchen back, but I want to be respected and admired more. It will be worth the inconvenience in the end.'

'He cannot think badly of you for cooking,' said Chaloner, resisting the urge to flinch at the desperate hope in Bulteel's eyes. If he had known how to say it without causing hurt, he would have advised his friend to stop wasting his time.

'He says I should expend all my spare energy in learning to dance, and he is right, of course. I dislike dancing, but it is an art I *shall* master.' Bulteel's small face was full of grim determination.

'Are you sure this is a path you want to follow?' asked Chaloner gently. 'It is not—'

'I have no choice,' said Bulteel shortly. 'I do not want to be a secretary for the rest of my life, because I am capable of much greater things. But never mind me. Griffith is with the Earl at the moment. He spied for him during the Commonwealth, you see, and they often reminisce together. You should be glad, because Clarendon is usually in a good mood when they have finished.'

'Is it true?' asked Chaloner. He could not imagine Griffith being subtle enough for espionage. 'He really was an intelligencer?'

'Oh, yes. He and Clarendon have dozens of stories to tell about their exploits. I think I have heard them all now, thank God, but for a while, they insisted that I sat and listened. My cousin is a lovely man, but he can be very long-winded. I pity his valet, having to wait hours while he gabbles.'

Bulteel lowered his voice as he pointed to the antechamber at the far end of the hall, where the soberly clad manservant sat. The man was so still that Chaloner wondered if he was asleep, but he saw them looking, and raised a hand in greeting. He did not smile, though, and Chaloner did not think he had ever seen a more impassive visage.

'Roger Lane,' said Bulteel in a whisper. 'I cannot say I like him. In fact, he makes me uneasy.'

'Why?'

'I cannot explain – it is just a feeling. Perhaps it is because he so rarely speaks.'

'Your cousin makes up for his taciturnity.'

Bulteel grinned, revealing his sadly decayed teeth. 'Yes, he does.'

Both turned when a door opened, and Griffith stepped out. He was followed by a roar of laughter and some jovial farewells, and was beaming as he minced towards them, lace kerchief flapping back and forth. Immediately, Lane came to his feet and followed, treading as silently as a cat.

Griffith turned to him. 'Summon a carriage, if you please. It is too dusty for walking, and I have been invited to watch His Majesty and the Duke of Buckingham play tennis at noon.'

'Surely, it is too hot for that sort of thing?' remarked Bulteel, watching as Lane slunk away to do as he was told. 'Tennis, I mean.'

Griffith fanned himself theatrically. 'Gentleman do not allow a mere inconvenience like the climate to prevent them from doing what they like. Besides, the King has invited the Dutch ambassador to watch, and he will not want *him* disappointed.'

Chaloner doubted van Goch would mind a cancellation, and he would certainly have more profitable things to do than sit in a stuffy room and watch two sweaty Englishmen run about.

'But first, I shall visit the Spares Gallery,' Griffith declared. The Spares Gallery, so named because it was a repository for duplicate or unwanted pieces of art, was a long hall used by courtiers and minor nobles as a common room. Chaloner often eavesdropped in it, because it was a great place for gossip. 'Where I shall enjoy a refreshing glass of ale.'

'I will join you,' said Bulteel, removing his coat in anticipation of a walk outside. 'And while we drink, I shall recite the romantic poem you suggested I write. It is called "Reflections on a Stale Biscuit". Keep looking for those papers, Tom. Do your best to find them.'

Chaloner was astonished when he opened the Earl's door to find fires lit within. His master suffered from gout and hated the cold, but he should not have been chilly when all London wilted, and plants had turned brown and crunchy under an unrelenting sun. He felt himself break into a sweat as he went from the hall to the oven-like atmosphere of the main office.

The Earl had endured great privation during the Commonwealth, when he had gone into exile with the King, and was busily making up for lost time. His offices were crammed to the gills with fine works of art and exquisite pieces of furniture, while the rugs on the floor were the best money could buy. Personally, Chaloner found the chambers vulgar, and thought they would have been more pleasant with less ostentatious wealth.

'There you are,' said Clarendon. He scowled, suggesting the good temper arising from Griffith's visit had already evaporated. 'Where have *you* been? The Dutch ambassador met the Privy Council this morning, and I wanted you there, to ensure there was no trouble.'

'You were afraid the Privy Council might assault him?' asked Chaloner. He had not imagined the King's inner circle of ministers would stoop to those sorts of depths, but at Court, nothing could be taken for granted.

The Earl's scowl deepened. 'Do not be ridiculous! I wanted you there to prevent fighting among the minions. Some of the soldiers in his retinue are very feisty, and our own guards love nothing more than a skirmish.'

'I am sorry, sir. I have been—'

'Have you retrieved my stolen papers yet?' demanded the Earl. 'Is that why you came? To tell me you have them?'

'It is difficult to know who might have taken them, sir, when I do not know what they contain.'

'Why should that make any difference?'

Chaloner strove for patience. 'Because it will allow me to identify potential suspects.'

'But I *cannot* tell you what is in them. They pertain to matters of national security.'

'National security?' pounced Chaloner. 'Do you mean statistics for naval—'

'I said I cannot tell you,' snapped the Earl. 'So do not try to trick me with guesses. All you need to know is that I want them back.'

'But they have been missing for three days now,' said Chaloner unhappily. 'Even if I do recover them, their contents will be compromised. They will have been read by—'

'That is for *me* to worry about,' interrupted Clarendon. 'Not you. I discussed the matter with Sir George Downing last night, and he told me I am right to suspect Hanse. He says he has met the man on several occasions, and considers him sly, because he is always smiling.'

Chaloner was disgusted. 'Unfortunately, Downing then went to the Savoy and said the same thing there. He has dealt the peace talks a serious blow, because no diplomatic mission likes to be accused of theft. Moreover, the rumour seems to be circulating in White Hall, too.'

The Earl regarded him in horror. 'Downing shared our conversation with others? But he is Envoy

Extraordinary to the States-General – an expert on Dutch affairs, and a man who should be working for peace between our two nations! It is why he was recalled from The Hague, after all. What was he thinking? I spoke in confidence!'

Suspecting Clarendon would not take kindly to being called a fool for airing such a sensitive matter with the duplicitous Downing, Chaloner made no comment.

'Hanse went missing the same night that the crime was committed,' the Earl said after a moment. 'So of course he is the guilty party, although I wish the Dutch delegation did not know I think so.'

'There is no evidence to link the loss of your papers with his disappearance. And he has been murdered, anyway. His body was found in the Thames last night.'

Clarendon gazed at him. 'Really? Did you visit the corpse and retrieve the papers?'

'There were no papers, sir.' Chaloner wondered whether the Earl was being irritating on purpose.

'Then you must scour the river bank and locate them, even if they are waterlogged and illegible. They are far too important to be left for just anyone to peruse.'

'Most of Hanse's clothes were missing, and I suspect his killer removed them. *Ergo*, if there had been documents on his person, they would have been taken, too. But Hanse did not—'

'So Hanse was drowned by someone who wanted my papers?' asked Clarendon, bemused.

Chaloner struggled to suppress his exasperation. 'I have no idea why he was killed, but he did *not* steal your documents.'

The Earl's eyes narrowed. 'You seem very sure of this. Why?'

Chaloner decided it was time to be open: Downing knew about Aletta, so it was only a matter of time before he told the Earl that his gentleman usher was related to Hanse by marriage.

'Because I was with him when your documents went missing. We met at six o'clock, and we were together in the Sun tavern until dusk. He had no papers with him – I would have noticed – and he could not have taken them *after* we parted company, because you had noticed them missing by eight o'clock, and he was with me for at least half an hour beyond that.'

'Then he *hired* someone else to burgle my house,' persisted Clarendon. 'It *must* have been him, Chaloner. He and van Goch were the only ones who visited me that day.'

'No,' insisted Chaloner doggedly. 'He was not a thief. And nor was he a spy. I know, because we were kin. He was my brother-in-law. Married to my wife's sister.'

Clarendon frowned. 'Hannah has no siblings – she is an only child. What nonsense is this?'

'My first wife. Aletta. She died of the plague twelve years ago.'

The Earl's jaw dropped. 'Aletta? But that is a Dutch name! Are you saying you wed a *Hollander*? Why in God's name did you do that? To allow you to blend into their society, so you could be a better intelligencer?'

'No,' replied Chaloner stiffly. 'I married her because . . . well, she was dear to me, and . . .'

Clarendon softened at the confidence, such as it was. 'Then I am sorry for your loss. But I had no idea you are kin to a Dutch spy! This could be awkward for me, if the tale gets out.'

'There is no reason for anyone to accuse me – or you – of anything untoward. There are plenty of Anglo-Dutch marriages. And mine did end twelve years ago.'

'Even so, I wish you had told me sooner. Sometimes, I wonder whether I know you at all. You are full of peculiar surprises.'

'It is not . . .' began Chaloner, stung into attempting an explanation. 'Aletta is not a subject . . .'

'You find it too painful to discuss,' surmised Clarendon, when he faltered into silence. 'That is understandable. I did not enjoy losing *my* first wife, either. Very well, then: we shall say no more about it. We shall talk about Hanse's death instead. You will have to find out who killed him. You understand that, do you not? No matter where it leads.'

Chaloner regarded him uneasily. 'What are you saying, sir?'

'I am saying that your confidence in this Dutch kinsman may be misplaced – he may have changed since you first met him. And I am also saying that you will have to ask questions in the Savoy. Not all Hollanders want peace, just as not all Englishmen want war. You may uncover all manner of treachery and betrayal.'

Chaloner nodded. It had already occurred to him that Hanse may have been dispatched by one of his own countrymen. And there was the message in the stocking to consider, too: Sinon, the traitor.

'Do the words "new gate" mean anything to you?' he asked. 'Or does Sinon?'

'Newgate is a prison, Chaloner,' replied Clarendon contemptuously. 'Surely you know that?'

'And Sinon?' asked Chaloner. His master had avoided addressing that part of the question.

The Earl looked decidedly shifty. 'Nothing. Why would it?'

'It relates to Hanse's death,' said Chaloner quietly. 'I will have to find out what it means if I am to solve the case, and it will be quicker and easier if you just tell me.'

Clarendon stared at him for a moment, then indicated he was to shut the door.

With a sense of misgiving, Chaloner did as he was told. It never boded well when the Earl insisted on speaking behind closed doors.

'How did you hear about Sinon?' whispered Clarendon. 'It is a secret and only the Privy Council and Spymaster Williamson are party to it. Them and Sir William Compton. Do you know him?'

'I met him last week, when I was investigating the White Hall thefts.'

Clarendon was shocked. '*He* was one of your suspects?'

'No, of course not. Everyone agrees that he is a man of integrity. But Kicke was one of his stewards – before he was dismissed and hired by Downing, that is.'

The Earl regarded him critically. 'I sense from your tone that you disapprove of anyone hired by Downing. Yet you were in his employ yourself. Of course, that was when you were in the service of that villain Cromwell. At least Kicke can claim he worked for Downing *after* Downing shifted his loyalties to the King. You cannot.'

'I visited Compton to ask why Kicke had been dismissed,' said Chaloner, declining to acknowledge the remark, partly because he did not know what to say to it, but mostly because he did not want to talk about the difficult days when he had been obliged to report to a man he neither trusted or liked. In fact, he thought wryly, looking at Clarendon, it had not been so very different from now.

'And why had he?' asked the Earl.

'For theft. Compton also told me he had not written the glowing testimonial that Kicke used to secure himself the post with Downing. Kicke penned that himself.'

'Downing has certainly been telling everyone at White Hall as much.' Clarendon smirked. He, like most people who had met the envoy, considered him a rogue. 'He wants to distance himself from what Kicke and Nisbett did. And who can blame him?'

Chaloner knew the conversation was being manoeuvred away from where he wanted it to be. He brought it back on track. 'What does Compton have to do with Sinon, sir? What is it, exactly?'

The Earl sighed, and for a moment Chaloner thought he was going to change the subject again, but he began to reply. 'It is something Compton uncovered. He came immediately to tell me, and we went together to inform Spymaster Williamson. And the Privy Council had to know, of course. It was a very dark business.'

'Involving what, exactly?'

'Riches beyond your wildest dreams,' replied Clarendon shortly and not very helpfully. 'But why do you want to know? What does Sinon have to do with the dead Dutchman and my papers?'

Chaloner hesitated, loath to reveal too much, given his master's reckless habit of confiding in men like Downing. 'There is evidence that it may be connected to Hanse's death.'

77

Clarendon frowned. 'What evidence?'

'It might be safer for you if you did not know,' hedged Chaloner.

The Earl regarded him in alarm. 'Very well, if you think that is best. But are you *sure* you need to know about Sinon? We all swore an oath, you see, to say nothing to anyone.'

'Who swore? You and Compton?'

'Yes, along with Spymaster Williamson and the whole Privy Council. Sinon is a codeword for a particular plot. We arrested the perpetrators, and they are all incarcerated in Newgate. We did not dare put them in the Tower, because it is too public.'

Newgate, thought Chaloner. At least that explained part of Hanse's message: he had wanted Chaloner to go to the prison and question the Sinon Plot conspirators. If the Earl ever got around to telling him what they had done, of course.

'Does it involve treason?' he asked. It was the obvious conclusion to draw from the name the plot had been given, and there was always some rebellion brewing in a country that was still reeling from two decades of war and regime change.

'No, not treason,' said the Earl. 'It was something else.'

'What?' pressed Chaloner, beginning to be annoyed with him.

The Earl sighed. 'They were going to commit a robbery. Three weeks ago. They were going to make off with the crown jewels.'

Chaloner left the Earl with a sick feeling in the pit of his stomach. The last thing he wanted to do was visit Newgate, and he detested cases that involved treasure.

78

Large sums of money invariably brought out the worst in people, and anyone audacious enough to steal the crown jewels was unlikely to be someone whose company he would enjoy.

'Sir William Compton,' Clarendon called after him. 'He is the best man to approach for information about the Sinon Plot, because he is the one who brought the matter to our attention in the first place. Speak to him about it. He lives on Drury Lane.'

Chaloner winced. The Earl's voice had been strident, and if the Sinon Plot really was a closely guarded secret, then bawling was unlikely to keep it that way. He walked down the marble staircase and stepped outside, where the afternoon heat hit him like a physical blow. Sweating uncomfortably, he crossed the Pebble Court, supposing he should visit Compton immediately.

He had liked the man when he had interviewed him about Kicke, and hoped he would be helpful and co-operative a second time – it would certainly be a relief if Compton provided enough information to obviate an excursion to Newgate. Unsettling images of the place filled Chaloner's mind as he passed through the passage that linked Pebble Court to the Great Court, and he shuddered. They distracted him, along with the sudden blindness caused by going from bright sunlight to the comparative gloom of the tunnel, and he collided heavily with someone.

'Come now, sir!' came Colonel Griffith's indignant squawk. 'Watch where you are going, or I shall be obliged to call you out. And neither one of us will enjoy that, because I am never at my best at dawn, and I shall look an absolute fright. I will win the duel by *terrifying* you to death.'

Chaloner laughed as the effete colonel flapped his lace.

'The Spares Gallery was deserted,' said Bulteel. His dull brown clothes were a striking contrast to his cousin's bright silks, and the comparison did him no favours. 'Which is unusual.'

'People must be lying down,' said Griffith, fanning himself with his hand, and looking for all the world like a finicky old dowager. 'And in a few moments, I shall be doing the same.'

'I thought you were going to watch the King play tennis,' said Chaloner.

'I have changed my mind,' declared Griffith. '*He* may be able to prance around in this heat, but *I* am delicate. I have tendered my apologies, but tempered the disappointment he will surely feel at my absence by agreeing to attend a performance of the King's Private Musick tonight.'

'Tom is going to that,' said Bulteel. Then an expression of malicious glee stole across his face. 'Oh, I am sorry! Hannah arranged it as a surprise, and now I have ruined it for her. What a pity. I imagine she will be terribly disappointed.'

'Really?' Chaloner was delighted by the news. He loved music. Bulteel pulled a face when he saw his friend's pleasure.

'All that scraping and screeching. It is a waste of time, and I would far rather be bak—' He stopped abruptly, shooting a guilty glance at Griffith.

'Baking,' finished Griffith in distaste. 'A pastime for peasants. How am I expected to turn you into a gentleman if you persist in enjoying such demeaning activities?'

'I do it in private,' Bulteel flashed back. 'So I do not

see how it will interfere with my desire to join the sophisticated elite. But never mind this. At the moment, I am more concerned about Kicke and Nisbett. I was incensed when I heard they had been set free.'

'They are the kind of men who give White Hall a bad name,' agreed Griffith. 'The common people believe Court is full of villains, and this will make them even more convinced of it.'

'Well, it is true!' declared Bulteel. 'Here are two thieves, caught in the act. And do they face the rigours of the law, to show what befalls men who steal from their colleagues? No! They are hailed as loveable rogues and rewarded with promotions.'

'Did they steal from you, then?' asked Chaloner. 'And your property has not been returned?'

Bulteel looked hurt. 'That is a wretched thing to say, Tom! It implies my indignation stems from self-interest. Well, it does not. I am just furious that these felons are not only getting away with their crimes, but are being feted for them.'

'Not by everyone,' said Griffith soothingly. 'Apparently, not as much stolen property was recovered as first thought. A lot is still missing.'

'But the Lady does not care,' snapped Bulteel, while Chaloner supposed that Buckingham had helped himself to rather more than was reasonable. 'She does not care about anyone except herself. Horrible woman!'

'Not so loud,' warned Chaloner, looking around uncomfortably.

'Chaloner is right, cousin,' said Griffith, amused. 'I have no wish to be arrested for maligning the King's mistress, and I would rather you were not, either.'

'I am sorry,' said Bulteel, blushing as he lowered his

voice. 'But it seems to me that the best way to succeed at White Hall is to break the law. I have always followed my principles, and lived an ethical life, but no one else does. And who is rewarded? Not me!'

'But people know Kicke and Nisbett have light fingers now,' said Chaloner. 'So accusing eyes will look to them every time something goes missing, regardless of whether or not they are guilty.'

'True,' acknowledged Bulteel, brightening.

'Do not even think of making off with something to see them blamed,' said Chaloner, reading the secretary's mind. Bulteel was a novice at such games, and would end up in trouble.

'Damn!' muttered Griffith, pointing. 'There they are, coming towards us. I do not want to exchange words with them. They are unmannerly louts, and no company for gentlemen.'

Chaloner turned to see Kicke and Nisbett strutting confidently across the Great Court. They wore Lady Castlemaine's livery, flaunting it with pride. Kicke looked handsome and prosperous, his dark locks tumbling around his shoulders in a glossy mass. Nisbett fared poorly by comparison: his lank ginger hair and bulbous eyes were not attractive features, and the uniform did not suit his bulk. Chaloner's inclination was to slip out of sight. He was not afraid of them, but he had no wish for a confrontation. Unfortunately, Griffith's voice had carried, and they had spotted him.

'We will not forget what you did to us on Saturday, Chaloner,' hissed Kicke in a low, threatening voice as he approached. 'And you will pay for it.'

'He helped you get promoted,' countered Bulteel. 'You owe him your gratitude and—'

Kicke turned suddenly, and Bulteel's eyes widened in alarm at the fury in his face.

'Leave him,' ordered Chaloner, stepping between them. 'He has no quarrel with you.'

His back was towards Nisbett, but he ducked when he heard the man lurch forward, and the punch went wide. Then he whipped around and shoved him while he was still off-balance. Nisbett went sprawling.

Kicke drew his knife, but the one from Chaloner's sleeve was already in the palm of his hand, and he moved fast. It thudded into the wall near Kicke's head, and by the time Kicke had recovered from his shock, Chaloner had grabbed the one from his boot and held it ready.

'I will not miss next time,' he said softly. 'But the King does not approve of brawling, so I suggest you help your friend to his feet, and we go our separate ways before we are all arrested.'

Nisbett was clearly ready to risk a spell in White Hall's cells to exact revenge on the man who had dared to assault him, because he surged to his feet with murder in his eyes, but Kicke was no fool. He jerked his companion away.

'No,' he said shortly. 'We will deal with him another day. We have plenty of time.'

'I will set Spymaster Williamson on them,' vowed Bulteel shakily, when the pair had gone. 'He and I are not friends, exactly, but he might be prepared to do me this one favour.'

'Do not try it,' advised Chaloner. 'It is better just to stay away from them.'

'He is right,' said Griffith, holding his lace to his nose, as if Kicke and Griffith had left a disagreeable smell

83

behind. 'They will soon slip up, and then the Court will not be so accommodating.'

Bulteel sniffed. 'It would not surprise me to learn that Hanse is innocent of stealing the Earl's documents, and that the real culprits are *them*. They are thieves, after all.'

Chapter 3

Chaloner left White Hall, but had not taken many steps towards Drury Lane when he saw two familiar figures. He glanced around, but there was nowhere to hide, and he was reluctant to go back the way he had come, lest it was seen as a retreat – and he did not want the men who were striding towards him to think he was frightened of them. Or worse, that he had something to hide.

Spymaster Williamson, tall, aloof and haughty, was clad in well-tailored clothes that boasted an inordinate amount of ribbon. He blamed Chaloner for the death of a friend, and had proved himself to be a dangerous enemy. He was with Sir George Downing, a large, florid man in a coat that was too tight for his paunch. Downing was a decade older than Chaloner, and his eyebrows had turned grey. Perhaps his hair had, too, but it was concealed under a sumptuous black wig. Uncharitably, Chaloner wondered whether the two men were together because no one else wanted their company.

'I thought *you* would be dead by now,' said Downing, regarding Chaloner in distaste as their paths converged.

'You led a very precarious life when you worked for me.'

Downing was a deeply repellent individual. He had changed sides with greasy aplomb when the Commonwealth fell, and in order to prove himself to his new masters, had kidnapped three of his own friends – regicides, who had signed the old king's death warrant – and smuggled them back to England to face the horrors of a traitors' death. His self-serving actions had shocked even Royalists, although Downing had genuinely failed to understand why.

Williamson gave one of his ambiguous smiles. 'He leads a precarious life here, too. Why, only two days ago, he solved the White Hall thefts. My people have been investigating those since April, but with no success. Yet Chaloner comes to London and has the culprits exposed within a fortnight.'

Chaloner could tell, from the malignant gleam in Williamson's eye, that he was seething. It was not the first time he had exposed the ineptitude of the intelligence services, and Williamson would certainly resent it. But, he thought, if Williamson did not want his people revealed as deficient, then he either needed to invest more money in their training, or hire more capable ones.

'I had nothing to do with that,' said Downing, very quickly. 'It was not my fault they forged the testimonials that convinced me to hire them as stewards. Indeed, I am as much a victim as anyone.'

'Of course,' Williamson went on, ignoring him, 'it is a pity Chaloner trapped them in a way that earned them instant popularity. My intelligencers would not have made that mistake.'

'No,' acknowledged Chaloner, suspecting that Kicke

and Nisbett would have been quietly dispatched, to save the country the expense of a trial.

Williamson looked down his long nose at him. 'So what task has your Earl assigned to you now the thieves are caught? This business of blackmail?'

'Blackmail?' asked Chaloner, not understanding.

'You do not know?' Williamson's expression was smug. 'I thought you were a decent spy – that nothing happened in White Hall without your knowledge.'

'Much as it pains me to admit it, he was the best intelligencer I ever had,' said Downing before Chaloner could reply. 'He is cunning, resourceful, brave and daring, and nothing was beyond him.'

'Why did you dismiss him, then?' asked Williamson. 'And do not say it was because he was committed to serving the Commonwealth, because my researches suggest he was nothing of the sort. Like many men, he owns a loyalty to his country, not to any particular faction.'

Chaloner did not know he had been the subject of 'researches', and was astonished that the Spymaster should deem him sufficiently important for what was probably a costly exercise.

'If you say so,' said Downing. He chuckled suddenly. 'Did I tell you about the time he burgled Grand Pensionary de Witt's bedchamber? The place was heavily guarded, because de Witt was asleep in it at the time. Well, he is the Dutch head of state, so of course they are protective of him.'

Chaloner could scarcely believe his ears. Downing knew it was bad form to chat about the past exploits of intelligencers – treaties between countries had been torn up for less. Then there was the danger to the spy himself, although Downing would not care about that.

'This is not a story for—' he began, trying to mask his horror.

'He evaded all the guards, and crept past the slumbering de Witt,' Downing went on, smirking. 'Then he stole the key to the strongbox where de Witt kept his most secret papers. He opened that box, emptied its contents into a sack, and brought them to me. I had an hour to read them, after which he put all back as he had found it. The Dutch never knew he had been.'

Williamson raised his eyebrows. 'You had better hope this tale does not find its way to the Savoy, Chaloner, because I doubt the Dutch delegation will find it very amusing.'

'No,' agreed Downing slyly. 'They might have him assassinated. And good riddance! It will teach him to embarrass me by arresting two of my stewards. Why could he not have dealt with the matter discreetly? He did not have to do it in front of the whole Court.'

Chaloner had not really considered the implications for Downing when he had tackled Nisbett and Kicke, not that he would have acted any differently if he had. As far as he was concerned, it was Downing's own fault for hiring villains.

'I do not care if he is executed by the Dutch,' said Williamson. 'But I *do* care about the peace talks. Please do not share this tale of de Witt's bedchamber with anyone else.'

'Peace!' sneered Downing. 'There is no hope of that.'

Williamson regarded him in surprise. 'I thought you were summoned back from The Hague to assist with the negotiations – to help avert needless hostilities.'

Downing winked at him. 'I was summoned back. Let us leave it at that.'

Williamson's expression was dark. 'War with the States-General is not a good idea. It will cost a lot of money, for a start – money we do not have. I am hoping for an amicable solution.'

'Well, I am not,' declared Downing baldly. 'As Envoy Extraordinary, I will be able to claim a much higher income if I am stationed in hostile territory.'

Williamson's jaw dropped. 'You would put personal gain above duty to country?'

Downing raised his eyebrows. 'Oh, come, Williamson! You are as unscrupulous a rogue as I have ever met, so do not pretend you are full of lofty principles.'

'You mentioned blackmail,' said Chaloner, when Williamson did not seem to have an answer. And while Chaloner was amused by his discomfiture, it seemed prudent to steer the discussion to other matters.

'Several high-ranking courtiers have received letters,' explained Williamson, although he continued to stare at Downing. 'They demand large sums of money in exchange for silence about delicate secrets. Obviously, I cannot disclose names, but the victims are extremely distressed.'

Downing sniggered. 'I imagine so! I have heard that one is being threatened with the exposure of an unmarried sister's pregnancy, while another had a duel in which he killed an opponent. These are not tales "high-ranking courtiers" will want bandied about.'

'How do *you* know?' demanded Williamson, rounding on him. 'These gentlemen came to me in confidence, and no one else is supposed to be party to the details of their transgressions.'

'I have my spies, just as you have yours,' replied Downing, tapping the side of his nose in a way that was calculated to irritate. 'But do not worry: these courtiers' misdeeds are safe with me. *I* shall not reveal your department as the source of scurrilous gossip.'

Chaloner could tell by the fury in Williamson's eyes that Downing had just earned himself an enemy. Downing was a fool, he thought – the Spymaster had all manner of ruthless villains at his disposal, and was not above making nuisances disappear.

Downing doffed his hat, grinning malevolently. 'I must bid you good day, gentlemen. I am expected at the Savoy, so I had better make an appearance. We cannot offend the Dutch, eh?'

He swaggered away. Chaloner was tempted to broach the subject of the Sinon Plot – Williamson was, after all, one of those who knew about it – but the Spymaster's dark, angry expression suggested it would not be a good time.

'I am beginning to understand why so many people hate him,' Williamson said between gritted teeth. 'No wonder he was posted to the States-General. It was to keep him out of London!'

Relieved to be away from two of the most odious men in the city, Chaloner strode towards Drury Lane. The afternoon was so hot that even the pigeons were wilting, and the air was thick with dust. By the time he arrived, he felt sweaty and soiled, and sooty smudges covered his clothes. He wiped his face on his sleeve, brushed himself down as well as he could, and knocked on Compton's door.

A maid conducted him to a large, pleasant parlour overlooking the street. All the windows had been flung open in an attempt to catch a breeze, but the room was stifling even so.

Sir William Compton, Master of Ordnance and Member of Parliament for Cambridge, was a devoted Royalist, but was honourable enough to be popular with Parliamentarians, too. That afternoon, he was slumped in a cushion-filled chair, a damp cloth on his forehead and his eyes closed. Chaloner glanced uncomfortably at the maid, sure she should not have admitted him while her master was so clearly indisposed.

'It is all right,' said Compton, looking up tiredly. 'I am not dying.'

Chaloner was not so sure, because Compton looked terrible. He was an unhealthy greenish colour, and his eyes were sunken. Sweat dampened his hair, and a bowl had been placed near his head.

'If you are unwell, I can come back another time.' Chaloner was eager for information, but was not so ruthless as to pester a sick man for it. Spy he might be, but he had his scruples.

'It is just the heat,' said Compton. 'And you are doubtless here on the Lord Chancellor's behalf. As I said the last time you visited, I applaud his efforts to broker peace with the Dutch, and if I can do anything to assist him, I am at your service.'

'Thank you.'

'I confronted Kicke,' Compton went on. 'About his forging a testimonial from me in order to acquire himself a post with Downing. I had dismissed him for theft, if you recall.'

'What did he say?'

'He denied writing the report himself. I pressed him, and eventually he claimed that if there *was* a character reference from me, then it was penned by someone who wished him ill.'

'Someone who wished him ill would not have produced such a fulsome recommendation.'

'I know he was lying,' said Compton wryly. 'Just as he was lying when he professed to have the good of White Hall at heart when he stole. Lady Castlemaine is a fool to hire him, because he will cheat her. But he is no longer our concern, thank God. How may I help you this time?'

'Clarendon sent me to ask questions about the Sinon Plot.'

Compton regarded him in horror. 'I cannot talk about that! I swore a sacred vow never to break my silence, and I take such matters seriously.'

Chaloner hesitated, but then forged on, wanting Compton to know why it was important. 'A Dutch diplomat was murdered on Friday.'

Compton struggled upright in his chair. 'What Dutch diplomat?'

'Willem Hanse. He left a message mentioning Sinon, along with an instruction telling the recipient to visit Newgate.'

'Did he?' Compton was aghast. 'But the only people who are supposed to know about Sinon are the perpetrators, the Privy Council, Spymaster Williamson, and me.'

'And the gaolers at Newgate,' added Chaloner, thinking it a substantial list. The Privy Council comprised a dozen men, few of whom were noted for their discretion.

Compton gave a humourless bark of laughter. 'Hardly! Williamson has an arrangement with Newgate's Keeper. One wing, deep underground, is for his exclusive use, and his wardens never go anywhere near it. That is where the would-be perpetrators of the Sinon Plot are being held.'

'Did they have a trial?' said Chaloner uneasily. 'In a court of law?'

'The Privy Council did not want the affair made public. The culprits were quietly incarcerated, and there they will remain until they die.'

Chaloner could not help but shudder. The notion that such a place existed was bad enough, but the admission that its inhabitants comprised people who had been denied an opportunity to prove their innocence was appalling.

'I really cannot talk about this,' warned Compton. 'I took a vow.'

'I appreciate that, but Hanse is dead, and it seems he thought the Sinon Plot was important – he left several messages about it. He was a good man, and I would like to bring his killer to justice. But I cannot, unless I know more about this business.'

Compton looked troubled. 'Then ask your questions. Perhaps I shall be able to answer without breaking my oath.'

'Why does the Privy Council want the matter kept quiet? It is only the theft of a few jewels.'

'A few jewels?' echoed Compton, shocked. 'These are the *crown* jewels, man! They cost more than twelve thousand pounds. Cromwell sold off the old ones, if you recall, so we had to commission a new set. Have you ever seen them?'

'No. I was out of the country when the King was invested.'

Compton smiled. 'Actually, I was asking whether you had visited them in the Tower. You can buy a viewing for a few pennies, and it is well worth the expense. *I* think they are magnificent.'

'How far had the plot gone before you discovered it?' asked Chaloner, hoping he could avoid the experience. The Tower was a prison, as well as a repository for the King's baubles.

'The culprits had befriended the Assistant Keeper of the Jewels, drawn up plans of the Tower, and hired a carriage in which to escape. Unfortunately for them, I overheard their discussion in the Feathers tavern on Cheapside. I reported it to your Earl, and we went together to the Spymaster. Williamson spent several days investigating, then gave the order for the culprits' arrest.'

'Did he investigate thoroughly?' asked Chaloner, thinking it would not be the first time a busy spymaster had ordered the detention of suspects based on poor, erroneous or partial evidence.

'I believe so – I accompanied him on some of his fact-finding missions. Then, when we were both satisfied that these plotters posed a genuine threat, I took four of my men and arrested them.'

'*You* did? Why? It should have been Williamson's doing, not the Master of Ordnance's.'

'That is what I said. But Williamson and his creatures are unpopular in London, and the last time they tried to arrest a party of villains, they were attacked by a mob – and their suspects got away. The Sinon plotters could not be allowed to escape, so I agreed to apprehend them for him.'

'What are their names?' asked Chaloner. Compton was right: Williamson and his henchmen *were* unpopular among the people.

'Swan, Swallow and Falcon.'

Chaloner raised his eyebrows in disbelief. 'And they met in the Feathers?'

'Yes,' replied Compton. 'I know it does not sound very likely, but those *are* their real names.'

Chaloner did not believe it, and sighed unhappily when he saw he was going to have to visit Newgate, and speak to the trio himself. Compton seemed to guess what he was planning.

'Do not even *think* of trying to interview them, Chaloner. It will be more than the Keeper's life is worth to let you in. Williamson has some sort of hold over the fellow, and I have been told that not even promises of fabulous wealth can weaken his resolve.'

Chaloner nodded, but did not say that the Keeper's character and wishes were irrelevant to him – he had made a career out of entering places that wanted to keep him out, and he would visit the felons if he felt it necessary. The difficulty, of course, would be in leaving again.

'Hanse seemed to think an interview with them would be a good idea,' he said. 'Do you know why?'

Compton shook his head. 'Perhaps he heard Sinon mentioned by one of the Privy Council – they are apt to assume foreigners speak no English, and are always babbling incautiously in front of them – and was afraid it might adversely affect the peace process.'

Suddenly, there was a commotion in the hall outside, as someone thrust his way past the indignant servants and made his way towards Compton's parlour. Chaloner winced, recognising the strident tones of Surgeon Wiseman, the most arrogant, opinionated and conceited man in London.

Richard Wiseman had been appointed Surgeon to the Person at the Restoration, and loved the adulation the post had brought him. He was huge man, and never wore any colour except red. His detractors – and his acerbic tongue meant he had a lot of them – said it was to conceal the spilled blood of his victims, but Chaloner suspected the flamboyant *medicus* just liked to be noticed.

That day, he wore a scarlet long-coat, breeches of a paler crimson, and his boots were maroon. His thick hair fell in vibrant auburn curls down his back. He followed a curious regime of lifting heavy stones each morning, which gave him the muscles and physique of a wrestler. He was a very powerful man, and Chaloner pitied anyone unfortunate enough to be treated by him.

'Chaloner!' Wiseman exclaimed in genuine pleasure, thrusting aside a maid, when she tried to prevent him from bursting in on what was a private meeting. 'What are you doing here?'

'He was talking to me,' said Compton coolly. 'Would you mind waiting outside until we have finished? We will not be long, and you can tend me afterwards.'

'Absolutely not,' declared Wiseman, striding towards him. 'I am a busy man, and you are clearly in need of my services. Besides, Chaloner and I are old friends. He will not mind me being here.'

Chaloner minded very much, and he minded people being told he was Wiseman's friend, too. He owned a grudging respect for the surgeon, but Wiseman's universal unpopularity meant it was not sensible for a man who liked to stay in the shadows to admit friendship with such a man. Moreover, Wiseman's abrasive manner meant it was difficult to like him much of the time.

'Surely *I* have some say in the matter?' said Compton. 'And I would like you to wait outside.'

Wiseman crouched next to him and peered into his

eyes. 'That would be unwise. You are gravely ill, and need my expertise immediately.'

'I have a mild fever brought on by riding without a hat. All I want is a draught to relieve the pain in my temples. My brother said you gave him one that set him to rights within moments.'

'True,' said Wiseman, preening. 'But *his* sore head resulted from too much wine. Yours requires surgery, to relieve pressure on the brain. I have invented a new implement to remove small parts of the skull, and you shall be the first to have it tested . . . to *benefit* from it.'

Compton was aghast. 'You will not touch me! Chaloner, remove this madman from my house!'

'You are a fool,' declared Wiseman, flouncing out before Chaloner could oblige. 'But I shall wait in the street for a few moments to give you time to reconsider. If you come to your senses, I *may* deign to save your life.'

'Lord Christ!' breathed Compton, when the surgeon had gone. 'Is he always like that?'

Chaloner nodded.

'Is he good at his trade?' asked the Master of Ordnance worriedly. 'Should I be concerned, do you think?'

Chaloner would not have let Wiseman near *him* with a surgical implement, because the man was known to experiment. However, despite his natural antipathy towards the medical profession in general, he was forced to concede that Wiseman did know his business. 'A second opinion might be a good idea,' he hedged.

Compton lay back. 'Then I shall send to Chyrurgeons' Hall for another butcher. If he concurs with Wiseman, I shall consent to be examined. But I am not letting either saw my head off!'

*   *   *

97

Chaloner left with his thoughts full of how Hanse could have become aware of a plot to steal the British crown jewels. Was Compton right, and he had overheard an indiscreet remark made by a Privy Council member? Or had he, like Compton, overheard Swan, Swallow and Falcon plotting? Hanse had liked taverns, so it was not inconceivable that he had visited the Feathers. Then, being a foreigner, he would not have known to whom to report the information. Of course, it did not explain why he had sewn messages in his hose. Or why he had not mentioned the matter during the evening he had spent with Chaloner in the Sun.

Chaloner had not gone far when he felt his shoulder grabbed. He was about to knock the hand away when he saw it belonged to Wiseman. And he rarely manhandled the surgeon lest the surgeon did some manhandling back.

'You should have supported me in there,' Wiseman said accusingly. 'You know I am right.'

'Perhaps you are. But you cannot go around sawing people's heads off. It is unethical.'

'So is letting them die. But no matter. It was his choice to reject me, and on his head be it.'

'At least he still has one,' muttered Chaloner. 'Which he would not, if you had had your way.'

Wiseman stared blankly at him for a moment, then released a bellow of laughter that brought Drury Lane to a standstill. He clapped Chaloner on the back in what was probably intended to be a friendly gesture, but that almost knocked the spy from his feet.

'Where are you going now?' he asked, once he had controlled his mirth. 'To see Temperance?'

Temperance North was Chaloner's friend and

Wiseman's mistress. She ran a high-class bordello in Hercules' Pillars Alley, just off Fleet Street.

'Not today. Hannah is expecting me home.' Chaloner brightened when he recalled that she had arranged for him to hear the King's Private Musick that evening.

'Rent yourself some separate lodgings,' advised Wiseman. 'Then you will have more freedom.'

'I would, but I have not had time to—'

'There is a spare garret in my house in Fleet Street. You may lease that, if you like.'

'You live in Fleet Street? I thought you had rooms in Chyrurgeons' Hall.'

'The Master of the Company of Barber-Surgeons suggested I move out, because my experiments were upsetting the other residents. But I do not mind: Fleet Street is closer to Temperance. As my friend, you may have the attic for a very reasonable price.'

Chaloner would rather sleep in an alley than lodge with the surgeon. For a start, Wiseman might conduct unpleasant procedures there, and the screams of his victims would be unsettling.

'Well, I must be off,' said Wiseman cheerfully, when Chaloner did no more than nod cautious thanks. 'There is an increase of gaol-fever in Newgate, and I have been asked to look into it.'

'May I come with you?' Chaloner heard himself say. He rubbed his eyes. The last thing he felt like doing was visiting a prison – and he might be late for the concert. He had had scant opportunity for music since returning from Holland, and its absence from his life was beginning to depress him. He *needed* to hear the performance that night.

Wiseman stared at him. 'Why? I thought you hated gaols.'

'I have to do something there for the Earl,' replied Chaloner vaguely.

'You cannot come today, because the Keeper will not admit you without prior warning,' replied Wiseman. 'But I can arrange for you to accompany me on my next visit, which is on Thursday. I shall tell everyone that you are my assistant. Just remember to wear old clothes.'

Chaloner was tired and dispirited as he walked down Drury Lane. Despite all he had learned, he still did not know why Hanse had been murdered. *Was* it connected to the Sinon Plot? Or because a lot of people wanted Ambassador van Goch to go home without negotiating a treaty? In which case, had Hanse been killed by an Englishman or a Dutchman? And was it wise to delay interviewing the Sinon Plot conspirators until Wiseman could sneak him inside Newgate? Perhaps he should go sooner. He shuddered at the thought, and told himself that he could gather a lot of intelligence in three days, and with luck, he might not have to go at all.

Still deep in reverie, he joined the stream of carts and pedestrians lining up to pass through Temple Bar, an inconvenient gate that divided Fleet Street from The Strand. It restricted the flow of traffic, and he narrowly missed being kicked when a horse, alarmed by the press, began to buck. It was such a common occurrence that no one paid it any heed, and the conversations around him continued as though nothing had happened.

'Our fleet can be ready in eight days,' a merchant was saying to his companion. 'I say we declare war on the cheese-eaters and be done with it. There is no question that we will win.'

'The newsbooks agree with you,' the friend replied

worriedly. 'But Samuel Pepys of the Navy Board – who knows what he is talking about – told me they are wrong.'

'Pepys is an old woman,' sneered the merchant. 'He is no better than Clarendon with his wailings for peace. Peace be damned! Let us show these devils who is master of the oceans.'

Chaloner walked on, his spirits sinking further still. Why were people so keen to inflict damage on a country that had done them no harm? Had the King forgotten the kindness showed to him by the Dutch when he was in exile? Moreover, the United Provinces were Protestant, which alone should have ensured some sort of bond between the two nations.

Without conscious thought, he turned up Chancery Lane and headed towards Rider's Coffee House, a dimly lit, smoky little establishment sandwiched between two much larger buildings. Coffee houses were springing up all over London, and were popular with men – women were not allowed – who gathered to enjoy a dish of the beverage and to discuss politics, religion and current affairs in an atmosphere of amiable gentility. It was not uncommon for nobles to rub shoulders with apprentices, and anyone had the right to express an opinion.

He pushed open the door and walked inside, peering through the oily brown smog created by roasting coffee beans, his eyes smarting. He smiled when he spotted the man he wanted to see.

John Thurloe was sitting in the shadows near the back, reading a newsbook. Newsbooks were twice-weekly papers – *The Intelligencer* on Mondays, and *The Newes* on Thursdays – that were supposed to keep the public abreast of domestic and foreign affairs. The reality was that their editor believed it was undesirable for the general populace to know what its government was up to, so news of any description was in frustratingly short supply.

Thurloe had been the Commonwealth's Secretary of State and Spymaster General, and there were those who said Cromwell would not have clung to power for as long as he had, were it not for his quietly efficient and loyal first minister. Thurloe had been dismissed at the Restoration, and now lived in peaceful retirement, dividing his time between Lincoln's Inn and his home in Oxfordshire. He was slightly built with brown hair and blue eyes, and his mild manners had led more than one would-be traitor to underestimate him and live to regret it. He was the most ethical man Chaloner had ever met, but there was a core of steel in him that explained why he had risen to such power.

'I heard you caught the White Hall thieves, Tom,' he said, looking up. 'And the culprits have been punished by being given lucrative posts in Lady Castlemaine's retinue.'

Chaloner was not surprised to learn that Thurloe knew what was happening in White Hall. His old spies still supplied him with gossip, and although he had taken a definite and final step away from politics, he was still one of the best informed men in London. Of course, given that there were a lot of people who thought his severed head should be on a pole outside Westminster Hall next to Cromwell's, he was wise to keep himself abreast of current affairs.

'I cannot imagine what she thinks she is doing,' said Chaloner. 'They might steal from her.'

'Or steal *for* her,' Thurloe pointed out. 'They are said to be good at it, and she has a penchant for other people's property. I suspect there is a lot she could do with such men.'

'Christ!' muttered Chaloner, supposing it was true. 'I hope I will not be ordered to investigate burglaries that show *her* to be the instigator. She is far too deadly an opponent for me.'

'For anyone,' agreed Thurloe. 'But she is not such a fool as to use them straight away, so you need not concern yourself just yet.'

'They are angry with me for catching them,' said Chaloner, sitting on the bench opposite. 'And so is Downing, who had employed them as stewards.'

'Downing,' said Thurloe in distaste, folding the news-book and pushing it to one side to give Chaloner his full attention. 'But do not worry about him. Heer van Goch will go home when war is declared, and Downing will accompany him back to The Hague. All you have to do is stay out of his way until he has gone, which should not be too difficult in a city this size.'

Chaloner gazed at him. 'You seem very certain that the peace talks will fail.'

Thurloe sighed. 'Fighting the States-General would be disastrous for our country, so of course that is what the Privy Council will decide to do. I would not say this to anyone else, but those ridiculous hedonists deserve to be shot. They will lead us all into chaos and disorder.'

'It is a sorry state of affairs.'

'Very sorry. I wish Downing was not here, though. He knows it was your hard work and diligence that kept him in office during the Commonwealth, and he resents being in debt to you.'

'Hardly!' exclaimed Chaloner, startled. 'We both supplied you with—'

'Your intelligence was accurate and useful, whereas

103

his was street gossip. Doubt me if you will, but do not underestimate the malice he bears you. He is an unsavoury villain.'

'Yes,' acknowledged Chaloner, not wanting to dwell on it.

Tactfully, Thurloe changed the subject. 'It has been another glorious day, although I imagine it will be unpleasantly sultry again tonight. I wish the weather would break. Such oppressive heat is not good for a man with a delicate constitution.'

Thurloe was always worried about his health, and swallowed many tonics, pills and purges in his quest for an efficacious cure-all. Chaloner often wondered if he might be healthier if he threw them all away and concentrated on devising himself a healthy diet instead.

'You seem distracted,' said Thurloe, after a moment during which a coffee-boy came and poured a dense black sludge into two dishes. 'What is the matter?'

Chaloner took a sip of the drink and winced. Rider's brew was better than most, because he knew how to cook most of his beans without burning them, but the beverage was not pleasant, even so. It was not as bad as tea, which tasted of rotting vegetation, and it was a considerable improvement on chocolate, which was bitter and greasy, but they were all unpleasant, and Chaloner doubted any would remain popular for long.

'It is much nicer with sugar,' said Thurloe, watching him.

Chaloner nodded, but did not take any. A year ago, he had vowed not to touch it, as a silent protest against the plantations, although he knew his stance would make no difference to the people forced to labour in appalling conditions just so Britain could enjoy sweetened drinks.

'Willem Hanse is dead,' he said, placing the dish back on the table. 'I identified his body this morning, and then went to tell his wife.'

'I am sorry, Tom,' said Thurloe sympathetically. 'It must have been dreadful. How did he die?'

'Drowned. Murdered, probably. He spent his last evening with me, at the Sun tavern in Westminster, and I should have seen him back to the Savoy. But I was tired, and I let him go home alone. The hackneyman was in the pay of the Hectors, and now he is dead, too.'

'Blaming yourself will do no good,' said Thurloe kindly. 'It is better to invest your energies in bringing his killer to justice. What have you learned about his death so far?'

'Almost nothing.'

Thurloe was thoughtful. 'If I were in your position, I would return to the Sun, and question the landlord again. People are apt to remember more once they have had a chance to reflect.'

Chaloner doubted it would help, but was willing to try. 'I will do it tomorrow. But this evening, I am going to listen to some music.'

Virtually every courtier at White Hall had been invited to hear the King's Private Musick, because the players were to perform in the vast expanse of St James's Park, which meant the audience could be as large as His Majesty chose to make it. The players occupied a barge in the middle of the Canal, which was to be punted back and forth by four men with poles, while the guests had ranged themselves along both banks – the lesser ones on blankets, and the more important ones on chairs.

The King, his Queen, his mistress and his favourite

105

companions were housed in a purpose-built gazebo. Among them were Buckingham and the dissipated Alan Brodrick, cousin to Clarendon. The Earl himself was some distance away, talking animatedly to the Bishop of Hereford. Hereford was something of a fanatic, and, Chaloner thought acidly as he watched them, was probably picking the Earl's brains for new ways to suppress anyone who was not an Anglican.

Sitting on the fringes of the royal party were several members of the Dutch delegation, stiff and tense in company they knew wished them ill. Their attention was fixed on the spectacle of Colonel Griffith, who had donned a startling orange suit for the occasion, and was holding forth in his high-pitched, effeminate way to members of the Privy Council. There was no sign of Bulteel, although that was not surprising: the secretary disliked music, but would never have been asked to attend such an august occasion, anyway. And, despite Griffith's grooming, probably never would.

Chaloner was pleased to note that Kicke, Nisbett and Williamson were not there: it would be difficult to give his full attention to the music if he was surrounded by men who meant him harm. Unfortunately, Downing *had* been invited. The envoy was clad in a green long-coat that was too tight for his lard, and was busily ogling any ladies who came within leering distance.

'I have heard that Downing will not pay for clothes that fit, because he is too mean,' whispered Hannah in Chaloner's ear, following the direction of his gaze. The spy had managed an admirable job of pretending to be astonished when she had announced she was taking him to hear the music that evening, so Bulteel's hope to cause a spat had been thwarted. 'He hates parting with cash.'

Chaloner knew it, because although Thurloe had paid his spies regularly and well, the money had gone through Downing, and Downing had not always been willing to pass it on. He tried to steer Hannah away when he saw their path was going to cross the envoy's, but she did not understand what he was trying to do, and resisted. And then it was too late. Downing eyed her salaciously.

'Is this your new wife, Chaloner? Perhaps you would introduce me. I am always eager to meet pretty ladies, even ones married to reprobates.'

The open lust on his face made Chaloner want to punch him, and a curt rejoinder was on the tip of his tongue, but Hannah was there first.

'My husband is *not* a reprobate, sir,' she said icily. 'Moreover, I do not consort with low-mannered men, so please remove yourself from my presence. The Queen is watching, and I will not have her thinking badly of me.'

Downing's jaw dropped. 'I assure you, madam, she holds me in the highest esteem, and—'

'The Queen is a *lady*!' interrupted Hannah haughtily. 'And her esteem is reserved for those who deserve it. She does not deign to pass judgement on the loathsome.'

Chaloner regarded her uneasily, wondering whether she had gone too far, but Downing merely bowed and moved away. Hannah watched him go.

'What a *revolting* creature!' she declared. 'He has no place in a genteel gathering like this.'

'The King likes him, and it is unwise to make an enemy of such a man. You should not have—'

'He was my enemy long before I put him in his place. First, because he was nasty to you. And second, because he is a lecher. No decent woman should give him the time of day, and I am not having *my* reputation sullied by simpering at him.'

Chaloner experienced a surge of affection as he looked down at her determinedly jutting chin and flashing eyes. Her fierce opinions were one of the reasons why he had married her.

Hannah had agreed to meet some friends in the park, and among her little party were Killigrew, his wife Judith and Charles Bates, the sad-faced man with the copper wig. While Killigrew and Judith chatted to Hannah in French – a Court affectation to let everyone know they were civilised – Bates started to thank Chaloner for saving his hairpiece, but then stopped abruptly, and backed away.

Chaloner turned to see the Earl approaching, Griffith mincing at his side. Clarendon beamed at Hannah, for whom he felt a fatherly affection, although the fondness was not reciprocated. Hannah disliked him on two counts: the irritating delight he took in being a killjoy, and the shabby way he treated her husband. As she seemed to be in a feisty mood, Chaloner braced himself for trouble.

'You look well, my dear child,' said the Earl, taking her hand and patting it paternally.

She smiled pleasantly enough as she pulled it away. 'Thank you, My Lord. You look terrible.'

'Your wife has a discerning eye,' said the Earl to Chaloner, who was holding his breath for fireworks. 'I *do* feel terrible. But my spirits have been lifted by my old friend Colonel Griffith. He always did know how to make me forget my troubles with laughter.'

Griffith effected an elegant bow, all waving lace and

bobbing wig. 'The pleasure of diverting you is all mine, sir.'

'Such fine manners,' said the Earl admiringly, watching him flounce away. 'Do you know why Bulteel took him into his home, by the way? So that Griffith can transform him into a such a *beau ideal* that we will all fall helplessly at his feet.' He sniggered at the notion.

'Not even Griffith is equal to *that* task,' said Hannah. 'Of course, Bulteel has never had anyone decent to emulate, given where he works.'

The Earl regarded her uncertainly, then smiled. 'You refer to White Hall as a whole, and you are quite right, my dear. The rakes of Court do *not* set a good example.'

'I meant—' began Hannah, although she faltered when Chaloner shot her an agonised glance. While he admired her independence of thought, it would be unfortunate if it saw him dismissed.

'Of course, Griffith has changed since the wars,' the Earl went on, blithely unaware of the attempt to insult him.

'You mean he is older?' asked Chaloner, relieved when Hannah returned to the Killigrews, openly disgusted that her barbs had failed to hit their target.

'Well, *obviously* he is older.' The Earl shot him an irritable glance. 'The wars started more than twenty years ago. But I do not recall him prancing so. And his face was thinner in those days.'

Chaloner imagined the Earl's had been thinner, too, because he was gaining weight at a rate of knots. And his gout was not helping: it meant he was often immobile, but still ate a lot.

'Yet he still has the ability to make me laugh,' said the Earl fondly. 'I had forgotten how amusing he can be.

109

Escort me back to the Bishop, Chaloner. The Lady keeps looking my way, and I do not like it. However, she will not do anything untoward if I am with him.'

By the time Chaloner had obliged, the musicians had tuned their instruments, and were ready to start. Immediately, a hush fell over the assembled guests.

The first strains of an air by Matthew Locke drifted towards them. One bass viol was joined by another, the melodies intertwining, delicate and light on the still evening air. Then the treble came in, soaring above them. In the distance, a blackbird sang, as if in answer. The four watermen poled the barge slowly up and down the Canal, and its changing position, along with the hint of a breeze, played with the notes, so they were sometimes loud and sometimes soft, but always exquisite.

Eventually, the sun began to dip, turning the trees in the distance into dark silhouettes against a blaze of orange-gold. Bats flitted, feasting on the insects that proliferated in the hot weather. The air was full of the scent of scythed grass and scorched earth, overlain lightly with the odour of still water. Then, as the light faded further, lanterns were lit on the barge, which created shimmering paths of silver on the darkening Canal.

The last piece had been written specially for the occasion by the French composer Louis Grabu. It began with a lively dance, with all the musicians playing together, but gradually evolved into a haunting fugue. This time, when the barge was punted into the gloom, it did not return, and the music grew ever softer, until just a single bass viol was left. Its notes hung in the air, sad and sweet. Then, one by one, the lamps were doused. The last flickered, matching the viol's fading melody. And finally, the music diminished into nothing and the

110

light winked out. There was a brief pause, then rapturous applause.

Chaloner did not join in. He had been moved by the performance, and the sudden clamour of hands and voices seemed somehow sacrilegious. He sat with his head bowed, trying not to lose the magic of the last moments. No one else seemed to share his sensibilities. The King shot out of his chair and aimed for his carriage, the Lady hot on his heels; doubtless, they had more lively entertainment planned for the rest of the night. The Queen lingered to exchange pleasantries with Ambassador van Goch, Secretary Kun and the fox-faced Zas, then she left, too.

Once the royals had gone, there was a concerted move towards the gates. People clambered inelegantly to their feet, and servants hurried to gather up the blankets on which they had been sitting. Bates claimed that night-dew had seeped into his joints, and he had to be hauled to his feet. Nearby, Griffith was declaring to his companions that the performance had moved him to tears.

'Damned milksop,' muttered Killigrew. 'He was made a colonel during the wars, just because he minded Prince Rupert's dog. But he never saw any *real* action. I, of course, saw several battles.'

'Did you?' asked Chaloner, feigning polite interest.

'Mostly from a distance, I admit,' Killigrew elaborated. 'But I saw them even so. They looked very nasty. How about you? No, you would have been much too young.'

Chaloner was spared from having to reply, because Hannah interrupted: not everyone at Court would be impressed to learn that his regicide uncle had enrolled him in Cromwell's New Model Army when he was just fifteen. He had taken part in several major battles, the

111

last of which was Naseby, when he had been injured by an exploding cannon. His leg had never fully mended, and he still walked with a limp when he over-exerted it.

'Judith has offered to take Tom and me home in your carriage,' said Hannah, smiling at Killigrew. 'It is kind, because I do not feel like walking. It is too hot.'

But Chaloner *did* feel like walking, and was more than happy to give up his place to Bates, who was claiming that sitting on the ground for so long had done him irreparable damage.

'Do not be long,' warned Hannah. 'Or I shall be asleep when you come in, and there are things we need to discuss.'

Chaloner was not sure he liked the sound of that, but promised he would hurry. He said his farewells, and slipped away from the crowds, wanting time alone to reflect on the music, and to replay some of the more inspired sections in his mind. He aimed for the gate near Charing Cross, relishing the growing silence as he left the Court behind.

But it was a short-lived peace, because the moment he left the park, he found himself in an area that was thick with taverns. The patrons that spilled out of them were rowdy, and heat and large quantities of ale made them feisty, too. One apprentice collided with him as he passed, clearly in the hope of starting a fight, but Chaloner jigged away, ignoring the challenging jeers that followed.

There was a lot of traffic, too, much of it from St James's Park, as courtiers travelled home in private coaches or hackney carriages. One had had a mishap. It stood at a precarious angle, a wheel missing, and it was obvious that its driver had failed to negotiate one of the drainage channels that ran along the side of the road. A crowd had gathered, and there was a lot of shouting and shoving. Chaloner began to skirt around the mêlée, but stopped when he heard a familiar voice.

'Please!' It was Secretary Kun, and he sounded frightened. 'We do not want trouble.'

'Do you not?' sneered one onlooker. 'Well, I am afraid you have found it.'

With a sigh, Chaloner saw that whatever Hannah had wanted to discuss would have to wait.

The man taunting Kun had disguised himself by donning the kind of face-scarf intended to shield the wearer from London's foul air, but his voice and posture revealed him as Kicke. Chaloner looked around quickly, and saw a second figure that was the right size and shape to be Nisbett.

'We do not want trouble,' Kun said again, pleadingly. He had dressed for an evening with royalty, and although Dutch fashions were not as flamboyant as those of the English Court, his clothes were still fine. To the mob that was gathering, which comprised mainly the poorer kind of tradesmen, apprentices and the unemployed, they were like a red rag to a bull.

'We want only to go home.' It was Zas, similarly attired – and similarly alarmed by the situation.

'Home?' echoed Kicke. 'Do you mean the Savoy? Why should sly Dutchmen live in a grand palace, while honest Englishmen are forced into mean tenements, like animals?'

There was a rumble of approval from the crowd. Chaloner edged forward, careful not to jostle anyone who might use it as an excuse to fight him.

'You are probably spies, too,' Kicke went on. 'Stealing secrets, so you can cheat when hostilities break out. The tale is all over London that you stole documents from the Lord Chancellor.'

There was another growl from the onlookers, and this time there was anger in it. Chaloner wondered what Kicke thought he was doing: if van Goch's secretary was killed by a mob, the peace talks would stall for certain. Or was he acting under orders from the Lady, because she was one of those who itched for war?

'You look as though you are planning to intervene,' came a low voice at Chaloner's shoulder. He turned quickly, and saw Griffith, his elegant clothes hidden by a plain dark coat. His silent servant was at his side. 'Do not try it. Nisbett is an excellent swordsman, and will cut you to pieces.'

'What are you doing here?' asked Chaloner, glancing around hopefully. Perhaps other courtiers were to hand, and would help him extricate the diplomats from their predicament.

Griffith made a moue of distaste. 'There was no room for me in my friends' coach, so I was obliged to walk. *And* I was forced to borrow Lane's coat, to conceal my finery.' He lowered his voice. 'He was not very nice about it, either. I cannot abide the fellow, and will dismiss him as soon as I can find a replacement. How dare he—'

'How many English babies have you roasted on a spit?' Nisbett's voice was loud as he taunted his victims, and drew Chaloner's attention away from Griffith's tirade. 'And how many honest English merchants have you cheated, you piece of Dutch—'

The rest of his sentence was lost as the mob surged

forward with a furious roar. Kun screamed, and Chaloner whipped his sword from its scabbard.

'No!' cried Griffith, grabbing his arm. 'You cannot win against so many. Not alone.'

'He is not alone,' said Lane, the first words Chaloner had heard him speak. There was a grim smile on his face as he drew his weapon. It was an expression Chaloner had seen before, and told him Lane was a warrior, probably one who had cut his teeth during the civil wars.

Another howl from Kun, audible even over the vengeful yells of the mob, made Chaloner turn quickly and begin beating a path towards him, careful to use the flat of his blade. He had no wish to kill, not even men who were behaving like animals. It was not easy, though. People were pressed tightly together, and there was not enough room to wield any weapon effectively. He was aware of Lane at his back, similarly handicapped.

When he finally managed to reach Kun, the elderly secretary was on his knees, clothes torn and bloody. He was praying, and Nisbett was holding a dagger against his neck.

'Cut his throat!' yelled a butcher. 'Do it now!'

Chaloner stepped forward and knocked the dagger from Nisbett's hand. Furious that they were to be deprived of a show of blood, the onlookers began a chorus of boos and hisses.

'You!' exclaimed Nisbett, recognising him. Then his expression turned vengeful, and he raised his voice. 'Here is a traitor who wants to protect cheese-eaters! Will you let him do it? Tear him limb from limb, in the name of England and St George!'

Cheering patriotically, several apprentices leapt

forward to oblige, but fell back when Chaloner proved he could defend himself. Meanwhile, Lane had reached Zas, and was standing over him protectively. Griffith hovered nearby. He had drawn his sword, but made no attempt to use it.

'Kill the traitors!' screamed Kicke, launching himself at Lane. There was an ear-shattering clash as steel met steel, followed by an appreciative bellow from the crowd.

'Run him through!' shrieked the butcher, almost beside himself with delight at the spectacle. He was, however, careful to stand well back as the weapons began to flash.

Watching them almost cost Chaloner his life, because Nisbett attacked him while his attention wavered, and it did not take many moments for the spy to see he was in the presence of a master. Chaloner was accomplished, but Nisbett was better, and Chaloner was forced to give ground again and again.

Grinning malevolently, Nisbett began to toy with him. In a display that had the mob baying its approval, he performed a fancy manoeuvre that scored a gash down Chaloner's forearm. While the spy staggered, Nisbett strutted at the edge of the crowd, doffing his hat to their compliments.

Then there was a collective groan of disappointment. Lane had managed to disarm Kicke, who was cowering on the ground. At that point, Griffith minced forward, all effete flourishes and elegant footwork. Some of the onlookers started to laugh, causing the colonel to glare at them.

Piqued by the loss of attention, Nisbett attacked his opponent anew. This time, he came in earnest, and it was not long before Chaloner's sword was wrenched from his hand. The dagger in his sleeve fell to the ground at the same time. He managed to twist away from one blow, but he knew it was only a matter of time before he was skewered. The crowd began to chant for Nisbett to finish him, and with glittering eyes, the thief stepped forward to oblige.

Suddenly, there was an urgent clatter of hoofs, and horsemen bore down on the crowd, swords flailing. Chaloner recognised Buckingham and Sir Alan Brodrick among the riders, and understood at once what was happening: a gaggle of courtiers, at a loose end after the music in St James's Park, was looking for entertainment. And tackling a mob fitted the bill perfectly. Clearly afraid of being unmasked, Kicke and Nisbett joined the frantic horde that scattered in all directions.

Chaloner leaned against the broken carriage and watched. Whooping and shrieking, the horsemen pursued the panicking throng, jabbing wildly with their blades. Zas knelt next to Kun, a comforting hand on his shoulder, while the secretary wept his relief.

'Did you recognise the two men who started all this?' Chaloner asked, when Lane and Griffith came to join him.

Griffith regarded him askance. 'How could we? Their faces were covered by scarves. Damned villains! Parrying with them has put dust all over my best stockings.'

Chaloner's heart sank. He could not accuse Kicke and Nisbett without another witness – it would look like sour grapes on his part, and would probably make them more popular than ever.

'I think they were courtiers,' said Lane helpfully. 'They fought too well to be common men.'

'You do say some curious things,' said Griffith, gazing at his servant with wide eyes. 'And you cannot be right,

117

because Buckingham would not have attacked them if they had been from White Hall.'

'He might, if he did not know who they were,' Lane pointed out.

Chaloner watched Buckingham and his cronies drive away the last of the spectators, and it was not long before Charing Cross was empty. When it was, the Duke came to accept the gratitude of those he had saved. Zas made a pretty speech of thanks, but Kun was still too shaken for talking.

Buckingham peered at the Dutchmen in the dim light cast by a nearby tavern. 'Good God! It is van Goch's secretary and the lawyer from the Savoy!'

'Yes,' replied Zas. 'Our driver swerved to avoid a dog, but the manoeuvre broke a wheel. People immediately swarmed towards us, presumably to steal. But when they saw who we were, they dragged us out, and . . .'

'I see,' said Buckingham. He sounded disgusted, and Chaloner wondered whether he would have dashed to their rescue with such élan had he understood what was happening. He was, after all, one of those clamouring for war. 'Then I suppose we had better see you safely home. You can ride Brodrick's horse. He will not mind.'

The following day was hotter than ever, and Chaloner woke breathless and sweating from a nightmare in which he was locked in one of Williamson's Newgate cells with Aletta. He rarely dreamt about his first wife, but when he did, it invariably left him unsettled. A wave of guilt washed over him when he opened his eyes and saw Hannah lying next to him. Discomfited, he slid out of the bed, moving carefully so as not to wake her.

Unfortunately, he stumbled over a discarded blanket en route to the door, and she sat up.

'Where are you going?' she demanded. 'It is still dark, so it is far too early to be up. Come back to bed, or you will be tired in the morning.'

He smothered a smile – she was a true courtier in her horror of early starts. 'It *is* morning.'

'I doubt it is four o'clock yet, and *that* is the middle of the night. Do you have a fever? We should have summoned Surgeon Wiseman to tend your arm last night.'

'Christ, no! There is nothing wrong. Go back to sleep.'

'You still have not told me what happened. I am not sure how, but we ended up discussing my worries until we fell asleep, and I neglected to ask about yours.'

Which was exactly how Chaloner had engineered it, for her protection, as well as his own. He wondered how long it would be before she realised that he always sidetracked her when she asked about his day. And how long it would be before their marriage suffered because of it.

'You were telling me about Charles Bates,' he said, hoping the subject that had put her in such a lather the previous night would distract her again that morning. 'And his wife Ann.'

Hannah grimaced. 'Yes. After the music, when we were travelling home in Killigrew's carriage, Charles told us how Kicke is intent on seducing her. He had confided in the Duke, too, who said Charles should call him out. But Charles is no fighter, and Kicke is likely to kill him.'

'Duelling is illegal, anyway,' said Chaloner, supposing he should not be surprised to hear that Buckingham dispensed such impractical advice.

'Yes, but it does not stop anyone from doing it.' Hannah regarded Chaloner in sudden alarm. 'Is *that* how you came by the cut on your arm?'

'No, of course not.'

'But there is worse,' Hannah went on. 'Some villain is blackmailing Charles – demanding money in return for not braying that Ann is as besotted with Kicke as Kicke is with her.'

'Bates should not pay. If you and the Duke know about the situation, it cannot be a very closely guarded secret. People will start talking about it soon anyway.'

Hannah scowled. 'It *is* a closely guarded secret. And I think Charles *will* pay, because he does not want Ann's reputation sullied with gossip.'

Then the man was a fool, thought Chaloner. 'Thank you for arranging the invitation to the park last night. It was . . .' He faltered, unable to find the words to describe such hauntingly beautiful music.

'Yes, I was bored, too.' Hannah narrowed her eyes. 'You are not thinking of getting your viol out now, are you, Thomas? It will disturb the neighbours.'

Chaloner shook his head, although it had been exactly what he had intended. Sourly, he wondered when he *would* be permitted to play, since she complained if he did it during the day, too.

'Then come back to bed,' she ordered. 'Or are you hoping I will make you some breakfast?'

Chaloner shook his head again, trying not to do so too fervently. Hannah had many talents, but cooking was not one of them. And when she had turned her hand to brewing ale, it had put Buckingham in bed for the best part of a week.

'Incidentally, the Queen talked about you yesterday,'

Hannah went on. 'She enjoyed our wedding – except for the murder – and told me that I am a lucky woman. She also said that if ever Clarendon dispenses with your services, she will find you a post in her household.'

'Really?' Chaloner doubted the Queen would have much use for a spy. Or perhaps it was just that he knew Portuguese, and she preferred speaking her native tongue to struggling with English.

'Personally, I think you should abandon your Earl before he sends you on any more dangerous missions. I have been widowed once, and I do not want it to happen again.'

'The United Provinces were not dangerous.' Except for the plague and the uncomfortable memories of his first wife, Chaloner had enjoyed himself there, and had seriously considered not coming back. Not least among his concerns was the prospect of marrying Hannah, a woman he thought he loved, but who was as different from him as it was possible to be. Failed relationships in the recent past had made him acutely aware of his own shortcomings in selecting suitable partners, and the last thing he wanted was to trap her in a problematic marriage – he certainly loved her enough to want to avoid inflicting that on her. 'Of course, that might change if we go to war, although even then, I cannot see Dutchmen attacking our diplomats on the streets.'

'Has Ambassador van Goch been assaulted, then? I am sorry, but not surprised, given that the Dutch are so unpopular in London at the moment. If they had any sense, they would stay inside the Savoy, where they are safe. Of course, Hanse – the man who was fished from the Thames – was always out on his own, so no eyebrows were raised when *he* met an untimely end.'

Chaloner stared at her. 'Who told you Hanse was always out alone?'

Hannah shrugged. 'Everyone – Charles Bates, the Duke, Brodrick, Henry and Judith Killigrew. And the last two live in the Savoy, so *they* know what they are talking about. Apparently, Hanse liked visiting taverns, so someone must have recognised him as a Hollander and killed him. I am not saying such behaviour is right, but it is certainly predictable.'

'Which taverns?' demanded Chaloner.

Hannah started, unnerved by the sudden harshness in his voice. 'I am not sure anyone knows – just that he liked to frequent such places. What is wrong? Why are you glaring at me?'

'Sorry. I am supposed to be investigating his death, but I have not heard these tales.'

'Then speak to Killigrew. He will confirm them.'

Chaloner nodded his thanks, and it occurred to him that this would be a good opportunity to tell her that Hanse was related to him through Aletta. They were alone, with plenty of time for her to air any grievances she might feel, and it was not the sort of thing one should keep from a spouse. As he flailed about for the right words, he became aware that she was smiling at him in a way that drove all thoughts of Aletta from his mind. One hand beckoned a sultry invitation, while the other patted the empty bed at her side.

Afterwards, as Chaloner retrieved the clothes that had been tossed carelessly around the room, it seemed inappropriate to broach the subject of his first wife. He smiled fondly as Hannah yawned and began to burrow back under the bedcovers.

'If you plan on visiting Mr Thurloe today, take the

biscuits I made for him,' she murmured. 'You keep forgetting, and they will be stale soon.'

He nodded, manfully resisting the urge to remark
that the biscuits would never go stale, because that
assumed they were edible, and few of Hannah's culi-
nary creations could claim that distinction. The warmth
of his feelings for her suffered a jolt at her next remark,
however.

'I am going back to sleep, so no scraping on that
wretched viol, if you please.'

Chaloner left her to her slumbers with a vague sense
of unease. How could they be happy together if she kept
him from his music? Or was she worth the sacrifice?

Chapter 4

It was still not fully light when Chaloner opened his front door and stepped outside, savouring the freshness of the air after the stuffiness of the house. Tothill Street was semi-rural; St James's Park lay in one direction, and the wilder area known as Tothill Fields in another. It was rich with the scent of bramble blossom, new leaves and scythed grass. Sheep bleated in the distance, and two blackbirds were engaged in a battle of song, shrill and bright.

As he walked, Thurloe's biscuits tucked under his arm, he thought about Hannah's aversion to his viol. It was the third time she had asked him not to practise since he had returned from Holland, and while he could have overridden her and done it anyway, the resulting quarrel would have spoiled the experience. He decided that as soon as he had solved Hanse's murder and retrieved the Earl's papers, he would find lodgings of his own, a bolt-hole to which he could escape when he and Hannah did not see eye to eye. The more he thought about it, the more it seemed like a good idea – a solution that would benefit both of them.

To take his mind off his marital hiccups, he reviewed

yet again the evening he and Hanse had spent in the tavern on King Street, trying to recall whether there had been remarks that should have alerted him to the fact that Hanse knew about a plot to deprive the King of his jewels. Or that Hanse thought he might be in danger, for that matter. For the life of him, Chaloner could not recall any.

Deciding to follow Thurloe's advice, he went to the Sun, where its owner, Edmond Waters, was closing for the night – it might be early morning for most of London, but there were plenty for whom the night's revels were only just drawing to a close.

Waters was an elderly man with grey hair. He yawned hugely as Chaloner approached to ask his questions, and wiped grimy hands on what had, at the beginning of the evening, been a clean white apron. Now it was stained not only with wine, but with what looked ominously like blood, too.

'The Duke of Buckingham was in here last night,' was all he said in explanation.

'I see.' Chaloner moved to the business in hand. 'You were more than patient with my questions on Saturday morning, but would you mind going over your answers again?'

'Of course not. Mr Hanse is a lovely man, and I will do anything to help you find him. I do not make a habit of letting Hollanders drink here, though. I do not want *my* tavern set alight because I open my doors to men who will soon be our enemies. But Mr Hanse is special.'

'How so?'

'He lets me keep the change when he pays his bill. Unlike that miserly Buckingham, I might add. If all Hollanders were like Mr Hanse, we would not need to go to war. Have you news of him?'

'He died,' replied Chaloner baldly. 'Probably late on Friday, after he left your tavern.'

Waters' eyes opened wide. 'Dead? I hope you are not here to suggest my wine was responsible. I know he had more than his share that night, but . . .'

'He drank a lot?' Chaloner was disgusted that he had not noticed.

'Perhaps not a *lot*,' backtracked Waters. 'But he had far more than you. He said he was not feeling well, and that wine would settle his stomach.'

'I know I have asked you this before, but do you remember anything odd about that night? Anything that might have a bearing on his death?'

'I am afraid not,' said Waters. 'And I *have* been thinking about it. As I said, I liked Mr Hanse.'

Chaloner was thoughtful. 'Did he drink here regularly? You speak of him as though he did.'

Waters nodded. 'He met four other men here, although I cannot tell you their names. One was a vicar, though. I know, because he always wore clerical garb.'

'Was there anything distinctive about him?'

There were hundreds of clergymen in London – parish priests, clerks and chaplains to various bishops and nobles, not to mention those who had been extruded from their churches for nonconformism, and were in London because they had nowhere else to go. Tracing one would be next to impossible without a good description.

'Not really,' came the disappointing reply. 'Although *he* was generous with tips, too.'

'What can you tell me about the other three?'

'One was a handsome fellow with long, dark hair and a regal bearing. He and Mr Hanse were of an age – late thirties. He was kind to the serving wench when she acci-

126

dentally spilled wine in his lap. And not everyone would have been so gracious, because she made a terrible mess.'

'A clergyman and someone who sounds like a gentleman,' mused Chaloner. No one came to mind, and he wondered what Hanse had been doing. 'And the other two?'

'The third was the antithesis of the gentleman – fat, sweaty and ordinary. The last was a medical man, who always carried a bag of surgical weapons. He was elderly with a birth-stain on his neck.'

Chaloner supposed he would have to return one evening and ask the same questions of Waters' customers. Perhaps one might have overheard what was discussed, or would have a name to put to the descriptions. He nodded his thanks and started to walk away, but Waters caught his arm.

'You seem a decent sort, so let me give you some advice. Do not consort too openly with Hollanders, not even nice ones like Mr Hanse. There *will* be a war, and then anyone with Dutch friends will become suspect. I heard that some of Heer van Goch's retinue were attacked last night, and there is bitter rumbling against three villains who stepped in to rescue them.'

'A lot of courtiers rode in to rescue them,' countered Chaloner.

'That was later. Two patriots were about to slit the diplomats' throats, but these rogues stopped them. People did not like it. So, if you must consort with Hollanders, do it discreetly.'

Mulling over the warning, Chaloner walked towards Lincoln's Inn, one of London's four great legal foundations, moving carefully to avoid being doused in the night-soil that was being hurled from the windows of the houses he passed.

Hanse had been a stranger in London, so his mysterious meetings were unlikely to have been social. The obvious conclusion was that he was embroiled in something untoward, although Chaloner refused to believe that it might have been a plot to steal the crown jewels. However, the fact that one of his associates was a vicar did not bode well. England was undergoing a period of religious turmoil, and the city was full of dangerous clerics. Yet Hanse had not been particularly devout, and Chaloner could not see him involving himself in another country's spiritual problems.

So what else could he have been doing? Something in the name of peace? He had certainly been passionate about that, and would have done almost anything to secure a non-violent solution to the discord. Chaloner supposed he would have to ask Hanse's colleagues about it.

The Strand was already busy as he strode along it, mostly with carts bringing produce from the country – vegetables, fruit, eggs and grain to feed London's vast rumbling belly. Livestock was being driven to the markets, too – ducks, geese and chickens to Covent Garden, and cattle to Smithfield. And there were other goods – baskets, pots, linen, books, maps and charts, soap, ornaments, scientific instruments, perfume, clothes, tools, furniture and building materials. It was not said for nothing that anything under the sun could be bought in the city.

Street shows were setting up, too, ready to draw the custom of the idle. The Bearded Lady of Holborn had relocated in an effort to attract new admirers; she could be viewed for a penny. Meanwhile, a glimpse of a calf with six legs would cost two pennies, and the two-headed

Barbary Ape three. Uncomfortable amid such noisy, colourful bustle, Chaloner left the main road, and weaved through a maze of quiet lanes until he reached the open area known as Lincoln's Inn Fields.

The Fields had once been much larger, but land near the city's centre was worth a fortune, and bits had been sold off to developers. There was, however, a core of ground that had retained its ancient trees and heath-like vegetation. It was popular in the summer as a place to relax, giving the illusion that London was rural. But after dark and at dawn, it became a different place altogether.

That morning, a duel was in progress, one of the several that were alleged to occur there each week. Both combatants and their seconds were drunk, and Chaloner thought that if any of them did score a hit, it would be more by luck than design. There was a sharp crack, and he turned just in time to see a bundle of feathers drop from a tree. He winced at the ensuing guffaws: he liked birds.

Lincoln's Inn's gate was opened by a sleepy porter, who knew Chaloner well enough to wave him inside without asking the nature of his business. Chaloner aimed for the garden, where Thurloe liked to stroll each morning. A veritable army was required to maintain its neat little hedges, gravelled paths and themed flower beds, but the benchers – the Inn's governing body – did not mind. Theirs was a wealthy institution, and could well afford it. And they all loved the garden.

Chaloner found Thurloe admiring the roses. The air was rich with their scent, although even they could not mask the stench of sun-baked sewage, manure and rotting rubbish that hung in a pall over the city – and would do so until rain sluiced it away.

'I was hoping you would come today, Tom,' said Thurloe. 'I heard a tale last night about "evil-minded traitors" preventing some of the Dutch delegation from being lynched. The description of one of these villains sounded uncannily like you. I trust it was not.'

'Why? You did not train me to stand by and watch the murder of innocents.'

'I did not train you to leap wildly into dangerous situations, either.'

Chaloner grimaced. 'Then I wish I had listened. Nisbett is a much better swordsman than me.'

'It was Nisbett doing the lynching?' asked Thurloe uneasily. 'Was Kicke with him?'

'Yes. They were taunting Kun and Zas, fuelling a mob with inflammatory remarks.'

'Will you tell Clarendon, so they can be arrested? Such antics cannot be tolerated.'

'Unfortunately, they took care to conceal their faces, and someone is sure to give them an alibi if I accuse them. Lady Castlemaine, probably. Moreover, I imagine they would receive even more adulation for attacking Hollanders than they did for thieving. London hates the Dutch.'

'But we are a civilised nation! We do not assault visiting diplomats!'

'No? That was not how it appeared last night.'

Thurloe shook his head in disgust. 'Is our country mad? We cannot win a war, and anyone who thinks otherwise is a fool. I am told the Privy Council is divided, with some crying for peace, but most baying for a fight. This would never have happened in Cromwell's time. There is no unseemly squabbling among government ministers when you have a military dictatorship.'

Chaloner did not share his friend's views on the joys of repressive regimes, so he handed over the package as a way of moving to less contentious matters. 'Hannah made you some biscuits. However, I should warn you that she gave one to Buckingham, and he claims it broke two of his teeth.'

Thurloe weighed the parcel in his hand. 'The porter's dog would not touch the last batch she baked me – and that ravenous beast eats anything – so I put them on the fire. She should patent the recipe, because they made for a lovely blaze.'

'I have to go to Newgate,' said Chaloner gloomily, falling in beside Thurloe as the ex-Spymaster resumed his stroll. 'And as if that is not bad enough, I must do it with Wiseman.'

'Wiseman has his faults, but he is a good man. Do not reject his overtures of friendship. But my breakfast will be waiting, and you look hungry. Come to my rooms and partake of a little pottage. And then you can tell me why you must visit Newgate.'

Chaloner followed Thurloe out of the garden, to the building that housed Chamber XIII. Thurloe's home comprised a pleasant suite of rooms overlooking Chancery Lane. They smelled of beeswax, books and wood-smoke, and were the one place in London where Chaloner felt truly safe.

A servant brought some thin, unappetising gruel, then left. Thurloe drank his with obvious relish, then washed it down with an alarming array of medicines bearing names like Stinking Pills, Lazarus Lozenges and Aqua Digitalis. When he had finished, he regaled Chaloner with the latest city gossip: the shipyards had

131

not stockpiled enough victuals to send the navy to sea, Sir Edward Montagu was dismissed from Court for squeezing the Queen's hand, and the learned men of the Royal Society had sent a dog to sleep by injecting something into its hind leg.

'There is a rumour about Cromwell, too,' Thurloe went on unhappily. 'It says he broke into the royal tombs in Westminster Abbey, and swapped all the bones about.'

Chaloner regarded him askance. 'Why did he do that?'

'He did *not* do that,' snapped Thurloe. Cromwell had been a much-loved friend. 'It is a lie put about by his enemies. He is dead, and his poor rotted body torn from its grave to be hanged and beheaded, so why can they not leave him in peace now? Why invent monstrous tales?'

Chaloner had no answer, but Thurloe had not expected one. He went on bitterly.

'All I can think is that the King and his licentious Cavaliers hope to improve their own ghastly reputations by "reminding" London that Parliamentarians were worse. It is transparent and sly, but people are too gullible to see through these tricks. They love nasty stories about Cromwell.'

'But people will ask *why* he despoiled these graves,' Chaloner pointed out soothingly. 'Then they will recall that he was a religious man, and excavating tombs was not something he—'

'They remember him giving orders to smash churches,' interrupted Thurloe. 'And it is a small step from iconoclasm to desecrating tombs. Moreover, it is said that he emptied these grand mausoleums to make room for his own body when the time came – that it was not *his* corpse the Royalists dragged out to be mutilated, but some long-dead monarch's, which was ousted from its own resting place and shoved in his more modest sarcophagus.'

'I half wish that were true. It would have a certain irony.'

Thurloe smiled at last. 'It would, although you had better not say so to anyone else. But we have discussed my worries long enough. Do you want to tell me why you must visit Newgate? I know how you feel about prisons, so I imagine it is not something you undertake lightly.'

'Sinon,' replied Chaloner, to see whether the word meant anything to his friend.

'The conspiracy to steal the crown jewels,' replied Thurloe promptly, thus proving that the affair was not as confidential as the Earl and Sir William Compton believed. 'But it has been foiled, and the would-be villains are incarcerated in the Tower.'

'In Newgate,' corrected Chaloner. 'It is common knowledge then? I was told it was a secret.'

'There is no such thing, not when the Privy Council leaks its business like an old boot. France, Denmark, Sweden *and* Russia have all hired spies to monitor our dealings with the Dutch, but they could have saved their money. All they need do is listen to street gossip. Of course, it explains why no headway has been made on the peace talks.'

'It does?' asked Chaloner, bemused.

Thurloe nodded. 'It is obvious that a foreign intelligencer is at work, listening to these rumours, and using them to sabotage progress. We would have reached *some* agreement by now, otherwise.'

'There are high hopes that advances will be made on Sunday, at the convention in the Savoy.'

'High hopes from the doves,' corrected Thurloe. 'The hawks want it to flounder.'

Chaloner was sure he was right, but discussing politics was not helping his enquiries. 'What else have you heard about Sinon?' he asked.

'Just that three men plotted to steal the crown jewels, but were thwarted. Efforts were made to keep the matter quiet, because there was fear of a public outcry. But such concerns are ridiculous.'

'Why?'

'Because it assumes people care. They might have done four years ago, when the King first returned to London, but his debauched, corrupt Court has turned them against him. Are you going to Newgate to speak to these would-be thieves? Why? Presumably, they confessed to their crime?'

'I am not sure whether they confessed or not. Williamson did most of the investigating . . .'

'I share your distrust of my successor's abilities, but I imagine he would have been thorough in a case like this. He will want to know whether it might have succeeded, for a start – his would be the first head to roll, if the plot *had* been successful.'

'Hanse sewed two messages in his stockings. They were "Sinon" and "Visit Newgate". There is nothing to say they are connected to his death, but . . .'

'I imagine they are. Even I, with all my informants, did not know the Sinon plotters are in Newgate. Yet Hanse did. You are right to secure an interview with them.'

'He met four men in the Sun tavern,' Chaloner went on. 'They included a cleric, a gentleman, someone fat and sweaty, and a medical man with a birth-stain on his neck.'

'Wiseman might be able to advise you about the medical man.'

Chaloner smiled. It was a good suggestion, and a good way forward.

Chaloner's restless night had left him drained and woolly-headed, so he went to the Rainbow Coffee House on Fleet Street, hoping a dish of the toxic beverage would serve to sharpen his wits.

Already, the streets were swelteringly airless and tempers were frayed. A horse had dropped dead in its traces outside St Dunstan-in-the-West, blocking the passage of traffic. No one was inclined to help the bereft carter haul the carcass out of the way, but no one wanted to stand around while he fetched his family to do it, either. Furious yells were traded, then punches started to swing. Chaloner dodged around the mêlée, scrambled over the hapless nag and continued on his way.

He reached the Rainbow with relief. It was owned and run by a man named Thomas Farr, an opinionated individual with views on everything, from fashion and current affairs, to music and science. That morning, he was telling his patrons about a series of terrible infernos in Amsterdam, which had coincided with a 'blazing star' that had passed over the city like a pillar of fire.

'God created all these portents, as a sign that they will lose the war we are going to have with them,' he concluded, as Chaloner sank on to a bench, grateful to be out of the sun.

'How do *you* know what God was saying?' asked Joseph Thompson, rector of St Dunstan-in-the-West. He was sitting next to a fellow cleric – Edward White, the amiable vicar who had married Hannah and

Chaloner in St Margaret's Church. 'It might be a sign that they are going to win.'

There was a shocked intake of breath, and Chaloner reached for the most recent newsbook. He usually ignored such discussions, on the grounds that the participants rarely knew what they were talking about. That day was a good example. He had been in Amsterdam when the conflagrations had started, but they had been caused by careless servants. And the blazing star had been a meteorite shower, like many others he had seen on clear nights.

'The Dutch will *never* win,' declared Farr. 'Incidentally, did you hear what happened at Charing Cross last night? Two patriots cornered a couple of cheese-eaters, but three traitors rescued them.'

'But the patriots fought very bravely,' said Fabian Stedman, a young printer, who always seemed to be in the Rainbow; Chaloner wondered whether he ever went to work. 'And one villain was stabbed so badly that his arm was virtually severed. He slunk away with his tail between his legs.'

Casually, Chaloner tugged his sleeve down over the bandage, marvelling at the way facts could become so distorted within such a short space of time.

'You cannot *slink* anywhere if your arm is hanging off,' argued Rector Thompson pedantically. 'So I am inclined to doubt the veracity of this tale.'

Stedman ignored him. 'London's surgeons have been ordered to report any such injuries to Spymaster Williamson, so I am sure the villain will be caught.'

'And when he is, I shall pay him a visit,' said Farr darkly. 'With a cudgel and several like-minded friends. I am not alone in thinking we do not need Judases in our midst.'

'No!' cried White, appalled. 'You cannot go around

136

attacking people! We have courts of law to deal with these matters.'

'Traitors do not deserve courts of law,' Farr flashed back. 'And there *is* treason afoot, because Clarendon's papers were stolen by a Dutchman. That is an act of war, as far as I am concerned.'

'The thief's name was William Hands,' supplied Stedman confidently. 'But he is murdered, by all accounts. Some say Ambassador von Gauche killed him, for not being sly enough.'

'*Van Goch*,' corrected White quietly. 'And the poor man who died was named *Willem Hanse*. He was said to have been an honourable, decent fellow, wholly dedicated to peace.'

'Then he *is* a villain!' declared Farr. 'Because peace will damage England. I want war, and I am looking forward to slitting a few Dutch throats. Especially men like this Hands.'

Chaloner could bear it no more. 'There is a report in the newsbooks that the hot weather will cause a shortage of peas later in the year,' he blurted. Then he winced. It was hardly a subtle way of changing the subject, and a startled silence followed his announcement.

'Peas?' asked Thompson eventually, regarding Chaloner as though he had just sprouted horns. 'Why should we care about peas? I do not even like them.'

'I do,' said Stedman, somewhat provocatively. 'And a shortage of them will be terrible. I imagine the Dutch brought some sort of pea-plague with them, and—'

'No,' said White, shocked. 'You cannot blame diseased peas on the Dutch. They are—'

'We are *not* discussing peas,' interrupted Farr firmly. 'Not in my coffee house. I forbid it.'

'Well, *I* do not want to talk about lynching Dutchmen,' countered White. 'It is unchristian.'

'Let us chat about blackmail instead, then,' said Farr, after a moment of consideration. 'I heard several courtiers have been victims – money demanded in exchange for silence about unsavoury doings. What do you say, Bates? You are a Court man. What can you tell us about it?'

Chaloner had not noticed Hannah's sad-eyed friend sitting at the far end of the room. Bates did not often grace the Rainbow with his presence, and Chaloner suspected that when he did, it reminded him how acrimonious the company could be, driving him away again.

'Nothing,' squeaked Bates, when all eyes turned towards him.

'You must know something,' pressed Farr, impatiently. 'You are at White Hall all day, and we all know it is a great place for gossip. Come on, man. Tell us! We can keep a secret.'

'No,' said Bates. He stood hastily, upsetting his coffee dish. The spilled liquid slid across the table in a malignant black streak. 'I know nothing.'

He aimed for the door, jostling people in his haste. Farr watched him go in astonishment, although Stedman, White and Thompson were already on another debate, and did not notice.

'The King is *not* corrupt,' Stedman was saying fiercely. 'Some of his courtiers could benefit from acquiring a few morals, but White Hall is far more ethical than it was in Cromwell's time.'

'I beg to differ,' said Thompson stiffly. 'At least Cromwell and his ministers went to church. This Privy Council does not bother.'

'Perhaps they are bored with long-winded sermons,' Stedman shot back.

Chaloner stopped listening. He opened the newsbook, and settled down to read an account of the Spanish ambassador's recent holiday in Rome, which was the government's idea of keeping its people abreast of international affairs.

It was not long before the coffee began to have an effect. Chaloner's weariness diminished, and his heart began to beat faster. He folded the newsbook, paid for the coffee and left Farr, Stedman, White and Thompson debating whether going hatless in the sun was dangerous. He was surprised when Bates emerged from an alley as he stepped outside, and indicated that he wanted to talk.

'Hannah told me you frequent the Rainbow,' he said softly. 'Of a morning.'

'Did she?' asked Chaloner, wishing she had not. It was dangerous for a spy's haunts to be known, and he disliked the fact that she talked about him to men he barely knew.

Bates nodded. 'So I have been waiting for you. I need to talk to you about something, but I could not go to your house, because I do not want our meeting witnessed.'

Chaloner gestured around him. 'Then why accost me here, on a busy public thoroughfare?'

Bates looked stricken, so Chaloner beckoned him down Hercules' Pillars Alley, a lane named for the tavern that stood on the corner. About halfway down was a large house with a paved courtyard, separated from the road by railings. The shutters were closed, and there was no sign of life. It was Temperance North's gentleman's club, and at that hour in the morning, its owner and her ladies were in bed, sleeping off the excesses of the previous night. Chaloner stepped into the shadows created by a little willow tree, and pulled Bates after him.

'How can I help you?' he asked.

Bates swallowed hard, and would not meet Chaloner's eyes. 'I hate Kicke,' he whispered. 'He has set lustful eyes on my wife, and woos her with silvery words. Ann is weakening fast.'

'I am sorry to hear it,' said Chaloner, although it went through his mind that most women would probably prefer the handsome, confident Kicke to poor Bates.

'It is wicked that he was allowed to wriggle free of the charges brought against him,' Bates went on bitterly. 'And I wanted you to know that I wholeheartedly support what you did in the park.'

'Thank you,' said Chaloner, wondering where the discussion was going.

'I spend a lot of time in the Spares Gallery,' Bates blundered on. 'The place where courtiers go to relax, or for refreshments.'

'Yes, I have seen you.'

Bates gave his sad smile. 'No one else has. They forget I am there, and I hear things. So if you decide to tackle Kicke again, come to me first. I know a lot about what goes on in White Hall. But more importantly, I know how and where to get written evidence for some of it.'

Chaloner regarded him warily. 'I have no idea what you are trying to tell me.'

'I am volunteering my help, should you decide to bring him down a second time,' hissed Bates, a little desperately. 'I am not bold enough to stand shoulder to shoulder with you wielding a sword, but I know where to find documents.'

Chaloner was still none the wiser. 'Are you saying that

you know something detrimental about Kicke and Nisbett? And that there is a written record of it?'

Bates winced. 'No. If there were, I would have made sure copies were left lying around for the right people to "discover". But I know how to locate deeds of owner-ship, and I know who goes where and when. I may be able to unearth witnesses if you catch Kicke stealing again.'

'I see,' said Chaloner, sorry for him. He knew what it was like to feel powerless in the face of overwhelming odds. But he doubted Bates's 'help' would be much use. It sounded precarious at best, and smacked of contrivance at worst.

The sun was blazing as Chaloner trudged towards the Savoy to ask what Killigrew knew of Hanse's drinking habits. He was not the only one to be travelling at half his normal speed. Horses plodded with drooping heads, and street vendors could barely summon the energy to push their carts. Everywhere, people had shed clothes in an effort to stay cool, and burned skin was in abundance, from the blistered pate of a hatless merchant to the scarlet shoulders of a baker's lad.

Chaloner wandered to the river in search of a cooling breeze, but the air around the Thames was as still and sultry as the rest of the city. Moreover, the rubbish that had been dumped in the water when the tide was coming in was now oozing back downstream. Some of it would reach the sea, but the lack of rain had rendered the great stream sluggish, and most of it was likely to revisit the city yet again later.

Despite the squalor, children shrieked and whooped in the shallows, splashing each other and taking turns to

141

clamber aboard a makeshift raft. It threatened to capsize at every jump, eliciting excited laughter. Chaloner was tempted to cool his feet at the water's edge, but came to his senses when several lumps of sewage and a dead cat drifted past. When the clocks struck nine, he sighed, and made his way back towards The Strand.

A rabid Puritan minister named Preacher Hill was bawling doom-laden prophecies in the street. 'God will not let it rain again until we have declared war on the Dutch,' he hollered.

Hill earned his daily bread by working in Temperance's brothel as a doorman, and Chaloner had never liked him. Several people nodded agreement with his declaration, although most were so used to being regaled with diatribes as they went about their business that his words did not register.

'War is His will,' Hill raved on. 'He will strengthen our arms and sharpen our swords. We must drive the cheese-eaters off the oceans, and wrest their trade routes away from them. And then we shall all be rich, which will be God's reward for doing what He wants.'

Chaloner doubted the likes of Hill would grow fat from ousting the Dutch from the high seas, because any profit would go directly into the pockets of a few powerful merchants. He skirted around him, wondering what hope van Goch had, when even the lowliest citizen howled for war.

He smiled when he saw three familiar figures walking towards him.

'What a *dreadful* man!' exclaimed Griffith, regarding Hill in distaste. Bulteel was next to him, and Lane was a few diffident paces behind. 'His strident voice pains the ears.'

142

'You were not at the church this morning, Tom,' said Bulteel. 'You said you would be there for the singing, and I was worried when you did not appear.'

'I forgot,' replied Chaloner, and wished he had not. Listening to the Chapel Royal Choir might have made up for him not playing his viol. 'Did you go? I thought you did not like music.'

'I detest it,' said Bulteel. 'But Griffith says I should acquire an appreciation, and if learning to like a largo is the cost of my admission to high society, then I shall persevere. And I *will* succeed. How can I not, when my future success and happiness depend on it?'

Chaloner regarded him worriedly, hoping he would not be too disappointed when his labours did not bring him the adulation he anticipated. Mentally, he cursed the Earl, whose callous indifference was likely to have been the catalyst for Bulteel's sudden display of determined ambition.

Griffith smiled fondly. 'Good. Because you cannot charm White Hall into submission until you are conversant with *all* the finer things in life. I hope you will remember my lessons after I leave, cousin, because I would not like all this hard work to be wasted.'

Chaloner looked at Griffith. 'Are you leaving?'

'I think I must. London is so *dirty*. Lane is for ever wiping soot from my clothes.'

'I told you to stay in my Chelsey house,' said Bulteel, a little vindictively. 'I said Westminster would prove too grubby for your elevated tastes.'

Griffith flapped the lace. 'Yes, but you did not warn me that London's summers are so wretchedly *hot*, and I yearn for the cool, green hills of home.'

'Where is your home?' asked Chaloner politely.

'Buckinghamshire. A lovely place called Great Hampden. And you?'

Chaloner smiled. 'Steeple Claydon. You must know it, because it is not far from Great Hamp—'

'You have never told *me* where you were born,' interrupted Bulteel, stung. 'And *we* are supposed to be friends. Yet you confide in my cousin within a few days of meeting him.'

Chaloner regarded him in surprise. 'You have never asked me where—'

'Yes, I *have*,' declared Bulteel. 'But as I have been under the impression that you hail from Guiseborough, you must have lied to me!'

Chaloner rarely fabricated that sort of detail, because there was too great a danger that the truth would out in an embarrassingly awkward manner, such as had happened when Clarendon had cheerfully informed Hanse that his brother-in-law's real name was something else entirely.

'My uncle came from Guiseborough,' he said. 'You must be thinking of him.'

'I most certainly am not,' declared Bulteel coolly. 'He was a regicide, and not fit to bear the same name as you. But let us talk of happier things. Have you caught Hanse's killer yet?'

'I heard he liked to drink in taverns,' said Griffith, while Chaloner wondered why Bulteel should consider murder a 'happier' subject. 'With friends.'

'Really?' asked Bulteel. 'I have not been told that particular tale.'

'Because you do not move in the right circles, cousin,' explained Griffith loftily. 'Not yet, at least. I heard it from members of the Privy Council, when I happened to be in the Spares Gallery. I usually visit the place when I know it is graced by persons of quality.'

'Why were they talking about Hanse?' asked Chaloner.

'Because they had just learned of his death, and were telling each other what they knew of him. They did not know the names of these friends, though. And I *did* ask, knowing you are looking into the matter. All they could tell me was that they were local men, not Dutch.'

'How did they know that?' asked Chaloner doubtfully.

'Their clothes. Dutch fashions are plainer and duller than our own. In fact, you could be a Hollander, given your preference for muted colours and a sorry lack of lace. No insult intended.'

Chaloner supposed he would have to let Hannah loose on his wardrobe, because it was not a good idea to be thought of as a foreigner.

'Lane, fetch me a cup of wine from that tavern, will you?' said Griffith, holding his hand to his head dramatically. 'My throat is so clogged with dust, I can scarcely breathe.'

'I want one, too,' said Bulteel, then sighed irritably when it became obvious that Lane was not going to oblige. A sulky expression suffused his face as he followed the servant to the alehouse. When they were alone, Griffith turned to Chaloner and spoke softly.

'If it is all the same to you, I would sooner keep my role in last night's skirmish quiet. *I* do not want to be lynched because I went to those Hollanders' rescue.'

'You did not go to their rescue,' Chaloner pointed out. 'Lane did.'

'Yes, and I have berated him soundly for it,' said Griffith disagreeably. 'He had no business rushing into such a situation without my consent, and I would dismiss him

145

if I had a suitable replacement. And I *did* do my part last night, by the way – I am *not* a coward. I drew my sword.'

'Yes, you did,' acknowledged Chaloner, seeing he had hurt the man's feelings. 'I understand your reluctance to be associated with the matter. So am I. But we were recognised. Buckingham—'

'I have asked for his discretion,' interrupted Griffith, flailing furiously at a fly that had developed an interest in the pastes that gave his face its fashionable pallor.

'And you trust him to give it?' asked Chaloner doubtfully.

'Yes. I promised him a length of fine silk for a new waistcoat if he forgot about the matter, and I believe he is sufficiently bribed.'

'But he was in company with several members of the Privy Council, while Brodrick is—'

'They were more interested in chasing commoners. Besides, I met them in Temperance North's bordello later, and it was clear they did not connect me with the "villains" who defended the Dutch. And you were deeper in the shadows than I.'

'Then what about the masked men?' persisted Chaloner. 'They saw us very clearly.'

'They were masked,' said Griffith acidly. 'That means they do not want to be identified, so they are hardly likely to break cover by pointing fingers at us, are they!'

Chaloner was tempted to tell him who they were, but held his tongue. It was better to leave matters as they were. Kicke and Nisbett would soon do something else to disgrace themselves, and thus bring about their own downfall. He turned as Bulteel came back.

'We are going to Rotherhithe, to pick cherries,' the

secretary said, wiping his lips on his sleeve as he watched Lane present the wine to Griffith. 'Clarendon is lending us his second-best carriage.'

Chaloner was astonished. The Earl was not noted for his generosity, and he could not imagine why his largesse should so suddenly be extended to Bulteel. The secretary saw his reaction.

'All right – he is not lending it to *me*,' he said bitterly, as Griffith took a sip of the claret, then went through an elaborate series of gags to demonstrate it was anathema to his refined palate. 'He is lending it to my cousin, whom he says is a *real* gentleman. When I become one, too, do you think he will be sorry for treating me so shabbily all these years?'

'He might,' said Chaloner, although without conviction.

When they had gone, Chaloner walked the short distance to the Savoy. He was just girding himself up to talk his way through the gamut of guards on the gates, when Killigrew emerged.

'Lord!' the Master of the Hospital exclaimed. 'What a night! After that *tedious* music in the park, I felt the need for something more stimulating, so I dropped off the wife, and went to Temperance's club. I was only there an hour, but when I came back, everyone acted as though I had been gone for a week! How was I to know I would be needed?'

'Why?' asked Chaloner uneasily. 'What had happened?'

'Kun and Zas were attacked by a mob. Well, it was their own fault. They should have stayed in the Savoy, not gone gallivanting around after dark.'

'I imagine they had no choice. They were invited by the King, and refusing would not have furthered the cause of peace.'

Killigrew glared. 'You argue their case? What are you, some kind of rebel?'

'No! But it is not—'

'Word is that Lady Castlemaine was behind the attack,' interrupted Killigrew, waving a hand that said Chaloner's explanation was of no interest to him. 'She denies it, of course. But it was *her* driver who took their carriage into a ditch, then ran off when a rabble converged.'

'Why would she do something like that?'

'Because the King is a member of the Company of Royal Adventurers Trading to Africa,' explained Killigrew. 'And the Adventurers stand to profit enormously if certain shipping routes can be wrested from the Dutch. Obviously, it is in her interests to provoke a war.'

'I see.' Chaloner was disgusted, but not surprised. He caught Killigrew's arm as the Master of the Savoy turned to leave. 'The Lord Chancellor has charged me to look into Hanse's death, and I have been told that you noticed he went out alone a lot.'

'Every two or three days. He said he liked to browse the markets for stockings, but I suspect it was an excuse to get into a tavern. Old Hanse liked a drink, and I saw him in the Sun at least twice.'

'On his own?'

'No, but I cannot tell you who was with him – I did not really look at them, although they all left very quickly after I wished him good evening. Almost as if they were sorry I had spotted them.'

'You think they were doing something untoward?'

148

'With Hanse? I doubt it! He was a nice fellow. For a Dutchman.'

'Are you sure you cannot recall who was with him? Not even a vague description?'

'No. It is dark in that tavern.'

'Is there anything else you can tell me? *Anything*, no matter how insignificant it may seem?'

'You sound desperate,' said Killigrew with a smirk. 'Of course, I know why. A lot of people want to know who murdered Hanse, so the pressure on you to solve the crime must be immense. Moreover, you could destroy the peace talks if you produce a culprit who proves to be controversial – whether he is a Hollander *or* an Englishman. I would not be in your shoes for a kingdom.'

'Is that so,' said Chaloner shortly. He was beginning to dislike Killigrew.

'And whatever you discover is unlikely to satisfy Ruyven,' Killigrew prattled on. 'He would like to investigate himself, but he has no English. And if he tried to interrogate *me*, I would give him short shrift – I cannot abide the fellow. But there is one snippet you may find interesting. My wife Judith mentioned something . . .'

'Yes?' asked Chaloner impatiently, when Killigrew hesitated.

'She said a woman was following Hanse. I thought she was imagining it, but I saw the lass myself once. Judith was right.'

'Do you know this woman's name?'

'No, it was too dark to see. She might have been anyone.'

The day was passing quickly, and Chaloner had made scant headway with Hanse's death, while he had not spared the Earl's missing papers a single thought, other than to dismiss out of hand any notion that Hanse had had anything to do with their disappearance. So, as he was there, he decided to question the Dutch delegation about both crimes. He was admitted to the hospital by a sturdy Dutch sergeant called Taacken, a pleasant, round-faced fellow with yellow hair.

'I shall take you to the Brown Room,' Taacken said, as they crossed the expanse of withered grass and plants that had once been a verdant courtyard. 'It is reserved for high-ranking members of our delegation, and is usually off-limits to foreigners, but they will not mind you.'

Chaloner stopped abruptly. The Savoy was busy, not only with Dutchmen, but with English clerks, lawyers and envoys, who had been sent to grease the wheels of diplomacy. He did not want them to see him escorted into some sensitive inner sanctum. They might assume he was a spy.

'The Brown Room is best,' said Taacken, when Chaloner voiced his reservations. 'All our senior officials are there at the moment, because the ambassador is hosting a dinner in the State Room.'

'And these senior officials are not invited?' asked Chaloner, bemused by the information.

'Not *needed*,' corrected Taacken. 'And none of them are eager to volunteer, because the guests are Lord Buckingham, Lady Castlemaine and Sir George Downing. Need I say more?'

Poor van Goch, thought Chaloner. Still, it was part of an ambassador's duty to meet disagreeable people, and he was probably being well paid for it.

The Brown Room was aptly named. Its walls had been painted a dirty tan, and there were thin, coffee-coloured rugs on the floor. Pictures had been hung, but they were black with age, so it was impossible to make out what they depicted. The result was dismally drab, and Chaloner wondered whether the government's aim was to depress the Dutch into going home early.

Kun and Zas were sitting near the door, working on a pile of documents. The elderly secretary wore a handsome suit of green silk, and his white hair was neatly trimmed. His face was pale, though, and there was a bruise under one eye. Zas wore a russet coat, and bared his foxy teeth in a welcoming smile as Chaloner approached. He had not escaped unscathed, either, and there was a graze on his chin and dried blood in his ear.

'You saved our lives, Chaloner,' said Kun, coming to seize his hand in tearful gratitude. 'There was murder in the eyes of our attackers, and if you had not been there . . .'

'We did not have so much as a dagger to defend ourselves,' Zas elaborated. 'The ambassador does not want his diplomats armed, lest it is interpreted as a hostile act.'

'Personally, I suspect the driver broke the wheel deliberately,' said Kun. 'He ran away very quickly, leaving us to fend for ourselves.' He shuddered: the incident had shaken him badly.

'Perhaps you should not venture out again,' suggested Chaloner. 'London's mood is volatile, and crowds turn quickly into mobs.'

'Unfortunately, that is not possible, because we are expected to attend meetings and functions,' replied Kun. 'And to refuse might damage the negotiations. Still, we have learned our lesson. We will not be going anywhere without a proper escort again.'

'Buckingham, Lady Castlemaine and Downing have been sent here to make amends,' said Zas wryly. 'Unfortunately, none have offered anything remotely approaching an apology. They did bring a bribe, though, to encourage us to pretend the incident did not happen.'

'Do you know what it was?' asked Kun. He shook his head, torn between indignation and amusement. 'A lot of cheese and butter! Downing even had the temerity to inform me that it is common knowledge that my countrymen will forgive anything in exchange for dairy produce.'

'What is going on?' came an angry voice from behind them. Chaloner had been watching Ruyven's approach through a reflection in the window, so did not jump as the others did. The burly captain's face was angry. 'The Brown Room is closed to foreigners.'

'Taacken brought him,' explained Kun. 'And I am glad he did, because I was in no state to thank him for helping us last night. But why *did* you come, Chaloner? Have you news of Hanse's killer?'

'Not yet. But I am trying to learn more about his life here. Will you answer some questions?'

'We will try,' agreed Kun. 'But I doubt we will be of much help.'

'Why would you think that?' asked Chaloner.

'Because we are always so busy. The root of the dispute between our nations lies in trade – the complex net of arrangements and treaties that have been agreed over the past few decades—'

'And that the English have consistently broken,' interjected Ruyven.

'There have been infractions on both sides,' said Kun, shooting him a warning glance. 'And we are not here to dwell on them, but to find ways to heal the rifts.'

'We are obliged to comb through these treaties,' added Zas. 'So we work from dawn to dusk, with barely a moment to spare. I know I *never* notice what my colleagues are doing, because I am too intent on my own work. The others are the same.'

'You will appreciate that we are talking about hundreds of documents here,' elaborated Kun. 'And we did not bring copies of all of them with us. Hanse was obliged to visit Westminster several times, to inspect the ones stored there.'

'How many times?' asked Chaloner.

Kun shook his head helplessly. 'I really could not say. A dozen, perhaps. He was braver than the rest of us – he did not mind leaving the safety of the Savoy.'

'And look where it took him: to an early grave,' muttered Ruyven. He spun around suddenly as someone else approached. 'Jacoba! What are you doing here? I thought you were lying down.'

Chaloner was sorry to see his sister-in-law looking so low. There were rings under her eyes, and her face was reddened and puffy from weeping. She came to take Chaloner's hands.

'Do you know yet what happened to Willem?'

'No,' said Ruyven, before Chaloner could reply. 'Or he would not be asking *us* for clues.'

'Then we must help him,' said Jacoba with quiet dignity. 'We shall sit down together – all of us – and tell him everything we know.'

It did not take Kun long to clear a table and summon everyone who had worked with Hanse. A number of people arrived to take part in the proceedings, and Ruyven's expression was resentful as he watched them take their places.

'Hanse was one of us,' he said bitterly. '*I* should be the one investigating his murder.'

'How?' asked Kun gently. 'You speak no English. Besides, Heer van Goch wants Chaloner to do it. He is afraid people will take umbrage if *we* ask questions that look as though we are accusing them of a crime. And that will do nothing for peace.'

'Peace!' spat Ruyven. 'London does not want peace! We are wasting our time here.'

'I disagree,' said Kun. 'With patience and determination, we *can* succeed.'

'But we *have* been patient and determined,' argued Ruyven. He sounded tired and frustrated in equal measure. 'Yet for every step forward, we take two back. We should have the basis of a treaty by now, but we have nothing. Indeed, the two sides regard each other with even greater suspicion and mistrust than ever.'

'All that is true,' said Kun quietly. 'But we cannot give up while there is still hope – and there *is* hope. Sunday evening's convention will see progress made.'

'And butter grows on trees,' muttered Ruyven. 'We should just declare war and be done with it.'

'He was fond of Willem,' Jacoba whispered in Chaloner's ear, as Ruyven slouched away to take a seat as far from Chaloner as possible. 'And it is grief that makes him angry. Take no notice of his sour remarks. He does not mean to offend.'

Ruyven had never been good at controlling his temper, Chaloner thought, recalling their old rivalry over Aletta. He started to make a noncommittal reply, but the light caught Jacoba's face in such a way that the resemblance to her sister was uncanny, and the words died in his throat. He was startled, confused and unsettled.

Desperate to escape emotions he could not begin to understand, he dragged his attention back to Kun's little assembly.

The men who sat around the table were all sober, serious fellows from good families, who had been hand-picked to accompany van Goch on his frantic mission for peace. Some were lawyers or clerks, and others were experts in English affairs or talented negotiators. All were said to be committed to negotiating a truce.

But were they? Ruyven made no secret of *his* preference for war, and there were bound to be others who felt the same. Had one of them killed Hanse for his fervent commitment to peace? The Savoy was on the banks of the Thames, so it would be easy to deliver a well-timed elbow when the tide was running fast and deep.

'Could Hanse swim?' Chaloner winced, realising he should have phrased the question more subtly. Fortunately, no one seemed to guess why he had asked it.

'I think so,' said Kun, frowning. 'It was not something we ever discussed.'

'He could not,' replied Ruyven. He shrugged when everyone looked at him. 'Amsterdam is full of canals, and I once asked what he would do if he fell in one. He did like a drink on occasion.'

'What did he say?' asked Zas, while Chaloner wondered whether it was significant that Ruyven should know Hanse would be unable to save himself once in water.

'That he only ever imbibed when the tide was out.' Ruyven looked sheepish. 'I was not sure if he was joking. It was often difficult to tell with him.'

'Did he have friends in London?' asked Chaloner. *He*

had never had any problems understanding Hanse's dry wit: his brother-in-law had been amusing himself at Ruyven's expense. 'Other than the people here at the Savoy?'

'Well, there was you,' muttered Ruyven.

'He knew no one,' replied Kun, ignoring him. 'Like all of us, he was a stranger here. And he did not try to make new acquaintances, because it is not safe to go out socialising. As last night showed.'

'He did not even know *you* were in London until you met in White Hall,' added Zas.

'But he was delighted,' said Jacoba softly. 'He always was fond of you.'

Chaloner returned to Hanse's excursions. 'You said he was obliged to visit Westminster several times. How did he travel there? By coach?'

'Yes, always,' replied Zas. 'But in the evenings, when his work was done, he liked to walk around the city.'

'He enjoyed shopping for stockings,' explained Kun. An expression of great sadness suffused his face. 'He was generous with them, too. He often gave them as gifts to his friends.'

'He did,' agreed Zas. 'Although, I looked in the ones he gave me, but there was no secret message sewn in them, as Jacoba said there was in yours, Chaloner.'

'Nor in mine,' added Kun, while all around the table there were similar denials.

'He bought a lot of stockings,' said Jacoba in a choked voice. 'He was writing a book about them, you know. They were his passion.'

For several moments, the only sounds in the Brown Room were her broken sobs. Ruyven shot Chaloner a furious glare, making it clear he blamed him for her distress. Chaloner supposed he was, and resumed his questions quickly, eager to bring her ordeal to an end.

'How late did Hanse return from these evening jaunts?'

'Usually before sunset,' replied Zas. 'But not always. I noticed him returning quite late once or twice, and I told him it was not a good idea.'

'So did I,' added another man. 'God only knows where he went.'

'He loved long summer evenings,' explained Kun, while Chaloner wondered why this had not been mentioned when Hanse had first gone missing. 'You said it was half-past eight when you left him, so there would have been daylight left. He hated retiring early, so perhaps he *did* go for a walk after you parted ways.'

Chaloner stared at him. If Hanse had been in the habit of wandering around after dark, then his murder took on a whole new dimension. Perhaps his being a foreigner, with secret messages about the Sinon Plot sewn in his hose, was irrelevant, and he was just the victim of a common robbery. Or the victim of someone who did not like Hollanders.

'Did any of you accompany him on these evening rambles?' he asked. 'Or follow him, to see where he went?'

'No, of course not!' said Ruyven indignantly. 'We do not spy on each other.'

'He valued his privacy,' added Zas. 'We all have our own way of relaxing, and solitary evening rambles were his. Obviously, with hindsight, we should have stopped him. But what is the rationale behind this particular line of questioning?'

Chaloner saw no reason not to enlighten them. 'He was seen meeting four men on a regular basis in a tavern

157

– a cleric, a surgeon, a gentleman and a fat, sweaty fellow. They are—'

'So this quartet killed him?' pounced Ruyven eagerly. 'Why did you not tell us you had solved the case? Who are they? Give me their names.'

'I do not know them yet. But there is nothing to say *they* harmed him. On the contrary, the meetings sounded amiable. They were friends.'

'But he *had* no friends besides us,' objected Ruyven, while all around the table, his countrymen concurred. So did Jacoba. 'We would have known.'

'But he *did* meet these men, and you did *not* know,' Chaloner pointed out. 'So you are not as familiar with his habits as you seem to think.' He turned to another matter. 'Did he ever mention the word Sinon? Or have any of you heard it spoken?'

'No,' said Kun, accompanied by a chorus of denials from everyone else. 'But Sinon was the original traitor, of Trojan horse fame. What does he have to do with Hanse?'

'I am not sure,' said Chaloner, loath to furnish explanations. 'It is just an avenue of—'

'I hope you are not suggesting Hanse was a traitor,' said Ruyven, rather dangerously. 'Because if you are, I shall defend his honour with my sword.'

'No!' cried Jacoba, dismayed. 'Stop it! Willem is gone. Is that not enough? Why do men always insist on resolving everything with blood? Well, I will *not* have it!'

Kun rested a fatherly hand on her shoulder. 'There will be no fighting, Jacoba. Moreover, if these witnesses are telling the truth, then Chaloner is right to question our understanding of the man we thought we knew. So, I suggest we all go away and review our exchanges with

Hanse. Perhaps, with hindsight, something will come to mind that will answer these questions.'

It was a good idea, and the meeting broke up with everyone – even Ruyven – agreeing to do as Kun suggested.

Chapter 5

As Chaloner emerged from the Brown Room with Jacoba clinging tearfully to his arm, he found Sergeant Taacken waiting for him.

'The ambassador wants to see you,' he said. 'Would you mind sparing him a few moments? His other visitors are on the verge of leaving.'

Chaloner did mind, because he had a lot to do. He scrabbled around for an excuse. 'I have—'

'Do not slight him, Tom,' begged Jacoba. 'There are only so many insults from your countrymen he can be expected to endure. Besides, he will *need* to meet someone decent after two hours with Buckingham, Downing and Lady Castlemaine.'

Reluctantly, Chaloner followed her to the chamber that Killigrew had decked out as a State Room for his Dutch guests. He had not done a very good job. A few paintings had been mounted on the plain white walls, but they were so variable in size, theme and quality that it looked as though he had just had a quick scout around his domain and grabbed whatever was to hand. Meanwhile, the rugs were such a wild assortment of shapes and colours that they made the place look untidy, and the banners hanging from the rafters were mostly Swedish.

When Jacoba and Chaloner arrived, the State Room was busy. There were pages to conduct van Goch's guests out, valets to carry their hats, and an army of minions to open doors and form a guard of honour. Chaloner hung back, having no wish to exchange words with the haughty trio, especially Downing. He pretended to inspect the pictures as they approached, so as to keep them from seeing his face, although he could not help but hear what they were saying to each other.

'This looming conflict is of your own making,' Downing admonished the ambassador. 'Your sailors started it, by being offended when our ships do not salute them at sea.'

'The terms of our previous treaty stipulate that we dip our flags to English vessels,' said van Goch tiredly. 'And we do. Would it cost so much to return the courtesy? To acknowledge us by dropping your own pennants in return? It seems a small price to pay for peace between our nations.'

'But do we *want* peace?' asked Buckingham provocatively. 'Our countries have been at loggerheads for years now. Perhaps we should just battle it out, and let the best side win.'

'Perhaps you and I could make a little peace, Heer van Goch,' suggested Lady Castlemaine with a sultry smile. She was walking at his side, rather closer than was socially acceptable.

'I want peace with *all* your countrymen, madam,' replied van Goch, edging away. 'Not just you.'

She ran her fingers down his sleeve. 'Yes, but none of them desire it as much as I do. Perhaps we should go somewhere private, and discuss terms. With wine. I hear you keep a fine cellar.'

Van Goch tried to distance himself a second time, but she caught his arm in a way that meant he could not do so without using force – which would be unwise with Buckingham and Downing watching. Defeated, he submitted to her mauling, although it was clear he was uncomfortable.

'She is trying to seduce him, in the hope that it will make him concede detrimental terms,' whispered Jacoba to Chaloner. 'She does it every time she comes, although I imagine it is Buckingham's idea.'

Not necessarily, thought Chaloner: the Lady had an eye for attractive men, and van Goch was unquestionably handsome. Rich, too, which was always a consideration where she was concerned.

'We are wasting our time here,' said Downing, regarding the ambassador with undisguised disdain. 'You have no intention of listening to our demands.'

'I will listen to reasonable suggestions,' countered van Goch, taking the opportunity to dislodge the Lady when both Buckingham and Downing turned their backs on him. 'But demands have no place in any negotiations. We are none of us barbarians, gentlemen.'

'I am not so sure about that,' Jacoba whispered. 'Downing is crude and brutal. Willem told me you were in his service for five years in The Hague. I cannot imagine how you bore it.'

Nor could Chaloner. He pretended to inspect the paintings again as the entourage moved closer. Lady Castlemaine and Buckingham sailed past him without a second glance, but Downing's roving eye was drawn by Jacoba's pale loveliness. And then he saw who was next to her.

162

'What are you doing here?' he hissed. 'Consorting with the friends you cultivated in The Hague, so you can pass them information detrimental to your own country?'

Jacoba spoke poor English, but she had understood the first question. She replied in Dutch, of which Downing owned a smattering, drawing herself up to her full height to address him icily.

'He is here to see me, sir. My husband died on Friday, and Thomas has been very kind.'

Desire flashed in Downing's eyes as he looked her up and down. 'My condolences, madam,' he said in English, all oily charm. 'But I doubt there is much *he* can do to alleviate your suffering. I, however, have considerable experience in such matters, and I have taken a house overlooking St James's Park. If you visit me there, I am sure a little frolic will take your mind off—'

'You low dog,' interrupted Chaloner, unable to help himself. 'Stay away from her.'

'Or what?' sneered Downing. 'I will have to account to you? I could crush you like a worm.'

'Come, Tom,' said Jacoba, regarding the envoy with loathing. She had understood little of what had been said, but Downing's open lust had told her all she needed to know. 'Heer van Goch will see you now.'

Unwilling to draw attention to himself with a scene, Chaloner started to do as she asked, but Downing had other ideas. Offended by Jacoba's disdain, he lashed out at an easier victim.

'I enjoyed your tale about spying on Grand Pensionary de Witt, Chaloner,' he said loudly. Several people turned to listen. 'You broke into his bedchamber, stole his secret papers, and had them all back again before he woke.'

Chaloner's stomach lurched, although he was careful

163

to keep the alarm from his face. It was bad enough that Downing had shared the story with Williamson, but to bray it in a Dutch embassy was madness itself. Did he want them both arrested? Because if Chaloner was taken, Downing's own role in the affair would quickly be exposed, regardless of what his old spy might or might not reveal under questioning.

'You are mistaken.' Chaloner spoke with a lightness he did not feel. 'I was in Middleburg when all that happened. You sent me there to deliver letters, and I still have the receipts to prove it.'

Or rather, Thurloe did. The ex-Spymaster had taken to organising alibis for his intelligencers when dispatched on especially dangerous missions. It was partly for their protection, but also for England's, so she could be ready with a denial if things went wrong.

Downing glowered, his temper up. 'I am not mistaken. It *was* you that I . . .'

'Me that you ordered to invade de Witt's privacy?' Chaloner smiled. 'You should watch what you say, Sir George. I doubt many people here think that incident was amusing, and may not know that you are in jest when you claim you were behind it.'

Downing leaned towards him, eyes glittering with thwarted fury. 'You think you can best me with your lies and twisted words,' he hissed. 'But you cannot. I *will* have my revenge.'

Jacoba watched him stalk away. 'Did he just accuse you of raiding Grand Pensionary de Witt's documents, and passing his secrets to Cromwell?'

Chaloner nodded, aware that a servant was translating the altercation for Ruyven. De Witt had vowed to execute

164

the culprit, should he ever be caught, and Ruyven would no doubt be delighted to see his old rival shot. Downing's attempt to see Chaloner in trouble might succeed yet.

Jacoba scowled at the envoy's retreating back. 'He is a revolting man, and it is not the first time he has made nasty accusations against the innocent. I cannot imagine why your King chose him to be a diplomat, because tact and charm are anathema to him.'

Chaloner had often wondered the same thing, and could only suppose that Downing had managed to black-mail His Majesty in some way. And blackmailed Cromwell before him, too.

Van Goch had slumped wearily on a large leather chair at the end of the State Room, looking drained and discon-solate. A man dressed in black stood behind him, and was whispering in his ear. There was something odd about the fellow – about the intensity of his gaze – but he had a pleasant enough face. He stepped back when Jacoba approached, Chaloner in tow.

'De Buat reads lips,' said van Goch, acknowledging Chaloner's bow, then indicating the man behind him with a wave of his hand. 'And he just told me what Downing said to you. We searched a long time for the fellow who burgled de Witt, but eventually decided one of his staff was responsible – had sold our secrets for money. Downing chose a very sensitive matter about which to joke.'

'He has a habit of doing that,' said Chaloner. His heart was pounding. Could he fight his way out of the Savoy if van Goch ordered him detained? Or should he stand fast, and insist that the tale had been Downing's idea of humour?

'I know your King is a comparative novice at running

165

a country,' van Goch went on irritably. 'But surely there is *someone* at Court who can help him appoint suitable officials?'

Chaloner was not sure how to reply, loath to denigrate his country by acknowledging that His Majesty was not always a good judge of character, but equally unwilling to defend Downing. Yet van Goch's remarks were hardly discreet, and should have been beneath a skilled diplomat. Then Chaloner looked at the ambassador's pale face, and supposed it was exhaustion speaking. He said nothing, and van Goch took a shuddering sigh and pinched the bridge of his nose.

'Forgive me,' he said in English, his voice low and hoarse. 'We have been here since April, and should have made *some* progress, but we are no further forward now than when we arrived. I have no idea why, because we have all worked extremely hard.'

'Downing is a brute,' declared Jacoba in Dutch; she had not understood the ambassador's words, and thought he was still talking about the envoy. 'He propositioned me the moment he heard I was a widow. Tom defended me, and Downing responded by making those stupid allegations.'

'Ignore him,' advised van Goch. 'I do, or our countries would have been at war months ago.'

'Perhaps the crime against de Witt should be re-examined, sir,' said Ruyven, stepping forward keenly. 'There was no evidence that a member of his staff was responsible, and Downing was—'

'Downing probably did it himself,' interrupted Jacoba, still angry. 'He is unscrupulous enough.'

'He is,' agreed van Goch with a faint smile. 'But if he had, he would not be so foolish as to make jokes about it. He is just trying to cause trouble, and I refuse to let his spiteful tongue plunge us even deeper into distrust and suspicion.'

'I agree that Downing is unlikely to have been involved,' said Ruyven tightly. 'But his claim was that *Chaloner* is the culprit, and—'

'A malicious riposte, because Chaloner defended a lady's honour,' van Goch cut in. 'So we shall dismiss his sly remarks for what they are – hateful mischief.'

Ruyven opened his mouth to argue, but van Goch raised an imperious hand and he shut it again. 'I will take Jacoba to lie down,' he said stiffly. 'Chaloner's visit has been one ghastly experience after another for her, and she looks tired.'

'I am tired,' admitted Jacoba, sagging at the realisation. 'But not through any doing of Tom's.'

Chaloner watched Ruyven escort her away with self-conscious gentleness, and the servants went back to work. It was not long before he was alone with the ambassador and the black-garbed de Buat. He wondered who the man was – he did not look big enough to be a body-guard.

'Do you have questions for me, sir?' asked Chaloner, when the ambassador did nothing but massage his temples with his forefingers.

'No,' said van Goch, pulling himself together. 'I would like you to take a message to Clarendon. Tell him we did not take those papers from his house.'

'I know it was not Hanse,' said Chaloner carefully.

'It was not any of us! These negotiations are far too important to risk by dabbling in espionage.'

'But if they fail, such intelligence may help you win whatever conflict follows,' Chaloner pointed out, thinking that if the situation had been reversed, *he* would have been gathering all the information he could lay his hands on.

'Is that the nature of these lost documents?' pounced van Goch. 'Military facts and figures? We have been accused of stealing them, but we have not been told what they contain.'

Neither have I, thought Chaloner ruefully. 'I have been ordered to retrieve them.'

'Why? They have been missing for days now, so the information in them is tainted. You would do better to work out who took them, and take steps to prevent it from happening again.'

Chaloner made no reply, recalling his unsuccessful efforts to tell the Earl the very same thing.

'I understand it was you who found Hanse,' said van Goch, abruptly moving to another matter. 'Thank God you thought to look in that charnel house, or he would have been buried anonymously, and we would never have known what happened to him. He was murdered, you know.'

Chaloner nodded cautiously. 'Pushed in the river. He could not swim.'

'Oh, he did not drown, although that is what we are supposed to believe. He was poisoned.'

Chaloner stared at him. 'Poisoned? How do you know?'

Van Goch indicated the man in black. 'De Buat is my personal physician – the man who ensures Downing and Buckingham do not give me a seizure with their insolent manners. When Hanse's body arrived from the charnel house, he examined it. You tell him, de Buat.'

'The signs are there, clear to anyone who knows where

168

to look,' obliged the physician. 'There are blisters in his mouth and bleeding in his eyes.'

Chaloner was appalled. Had his kinsman been dying in front of him all evening, and he had not noticed? Hanse *had* complained of stomach ache. Yet Wiseman had not mentioned poison . . .

'I can show you, if you like,' offered de Buat, misreading Chaloner's dismay for scepticism. 'Then, when he was dead or dying, his killer stripped off his clothes and tossed him in the river.'

'Why do that?' asked van Goch in distaste. 'It seems unnecessarily brutal.'

'Because removing anything of value would make us think he was attacked by common robbers,' explained de Buat. 'It was all part of a plan to conceal what really happened.'

'He is not the only member of my retinue to die, either,' said van Goch, when, still horror-struck, Chaloner remained silent. 'I have not made it public, because I suspect it is just another way to disrupt the negotiations, but I lost a maidservant, too. Oetje was also poisoned.'

Chaloner found his voice. 'By the same substance?'

'It is impossible to say for certain,' replied the physician. 'But yes, I think so.'

'What kind? If it is an unusual one, I might be able to trace who bought it.'

'There are many such compounds, and London is a big city,' replied de Buat. 'I doubt that avenue of enquiry will bring you answers. You will be wasting your time.'

'Oetje was . . .' The ambassador sighed. 'There is no point in eulogising. She was a bitter, sharp spinster, whom I wished I could have left behind. But my wife argued

169

that she possessed a unique talent with wigs, so, suffice to say, she joined my retinue.'

'Once here, she began to behave oddly,' de Buat went on. 'She kept strange hours, and went out alone. I believe she was a spy.'

Chaloner regarded him uneasily. 'What made you reach that conclusion?'

'Hanse liked to walk of an evening,' said de Buat. 'And I saw Oetje follow him several times.'

So Killigrew and Judith had been right, thought Chaloner. They *had* seen a woman pursuing Hanse. 'Why would she do that?'

De Buat shrugged. 'Heer van Goch and I questioned her at length, but she had answers for everything. She said it was coincidence that she had left at the same times as Hanse. So unfortunately, we have no idea what she was doing.'

'Could *she* have taken Clarendon's papers?' asked Chaloner.

Van Goch shook his head. 'I doubt she could have infiltrated his household – she spoke poor English. Besides, as I have already said, none of my people took those documents.'

'Why are you telling me all this – about Oetje and your suspicions?'

'Because it is probably pertinent to Hanse's death,' replied van Goch. 'And it may help you to identify his killer. He and I were friends for years, and I want his murderer brought to justice. Clarendon tells me you have a talent for solving complex cases, so solve this one.'

'You are our only hope,' added de Buat. 'None of *us* can go out and ask questions. We are foreigners, unfamiliar with your ways, and it would be dangerous – not just for us, but for peace.'

'Besides, Jacoba informs me that you married her sister,' said van Goch. 'That makes you kin, so I know you will do your best to find the culprit. For her, if not for Hanse.'

The bodies of Hanse and Oetje were being stored in the Savoy chapel until they could be buried, and de Buat insisted on showing Chaloner why he thought they had been poisoned. Chaloner would have been content to take his word for it, but the physician was adamant. He begged a few moments to prepare a tonic for van Goch's headache first, so Chaloner went to wait for him in the dusty courtyard, thinking of all he had learned.

What manner of spy had Oetje been? One who had grown suspicious of Hanse's curious meetings with foreigners in taverns? But then why not tell van Goch so when he had asked? Or had her intentions been more sinister, and she had followed Hanse with the intention of harming him? Van Goch and de Buat certainly seemed to think so, while Killigrew and his wife had both noticed the peculiar behaviour of the woman who had dogged Hanse's footsteps.

Chaloner stood in the shade of a porch, gazing absently across the scorched yard. Downing had not yet left the precinct, and was making a nuisance of himself with two pretty serving maids. They giggled nervously at his attentions, not sure what to make of him. Then Ruyven approached, and said something curt that made them scamper away. He and Downing began to talk, although it was clear they were having trouble understanding each

171

other – neither spoke the other's language well enough for an easy conversation.

Chaloner watched them. What were they discussing? The raid on de Witt's bedchamber? Surely, even Downing would have the sense to understand that was not a wise subject to pursue when he was likely to implicate himself? But the envoy was complex and unfathomable, and Chaloner had no idea what games he might play. All he hoped was that Thurloe had kept the evidence that would 'prove' his spy had been in Middelburg when de Witt had been burgled.

There was a sudden flurry of activity near the gates, which were flung open to admit Clarendon's private carriage. The driver drew up outside the State Room, and Chaloner went to help when he saw his master was having trouble climbing out – the steps were narrow, and the Earl could not see them over the bulk of his stomach.

Bulteel was there, too, his face hot and red beneath his hat. He was staggering under the weight of a portable writing desk, pens and ink, and several boxes of documents. When Chaloner started to take some from him, the Earl scowled and held out his arm, indicating that his gentleman usher was to escort him inside the building and let the secretary fend for himself. Bulteel tried not to look resentful at the brazen disregard for his welfare, but did not succeed. Chaloner did not blame him.

'I assume you are here looking for my missing papers,' the Earl said, as Chaloner assisted him up the steps. 'Have you found them?'

'Not yet.'

The Earl sighed irritably. 'How much longer will you take? I told you it was urgent.'

'I am working as fast as I can, sir.'

172

'Are you, indeed! Because it looked to me as though you were lounging in the shade when I arrived, and that is *not* working fast. Do not lie to me.'

Chaloner started to protest his innocence, but the Earl waved him to silence. Once inside the hall, a number of Dutch retainers hurried forward to greet the new guest. They were all smiles and polite concern, offering wine to wash away the dust of his journey – although as the Earl lived next door, the distance was hardly significant – and a cool cloth to mop his face.

'They always fuss over him,' remarked Bulteel to Chaloner. 'They do not fawn over Downing, Buckingham or the Lady, though. *They* are taken straight in, with no genial welcome.'

'They know he is committed to peace, I suppose,' said Chaloner.

'I hate it here,' said Bulteel, looking around with a shudder. 'I feel unsafe, as if I am entering the lair of a lion. I much prefer it when van Goch comes to White Hall.'

'I imagine you are safer here. White Hall is full of people who dislike Clarendon.'

'It is full of people who dislike *me*, too. No, do not deny it, Tom. I know the truth. But at least there I know my enemies. Here, I cannot tell friend from foe. I do not like that Ruyven, for a start. What do you think he is saying to Downing?'

'God knows,' muttered Chaloner.

'Well, *you* may feel at ease here, but I am terrified. Someone may decide to murder an Englishman in revenge for Hanse. Clarendon is too important, so they will pick on me.'

'I doubt it,' said Chaloner. 'You just said they fuss over

173

him, so they will not risk his goodwill by depriving him of his secretary. You are perfectly safe.'

'Only as long as he remains their friend. But the moment he declares for war, I am a dead man.'

Chaloner laughed. 'Then you will live a very long time, because he is deeply opposed to any form of conflict with the States-General.'

Bulteel sniffed. 'I hope you are right, Tom. I really do.'

There was a flurry of trumpets as the Earl began to walk towards the ambassador, head held high. Bulteel stepped behind him, and Chaloner's jaw dropped when the secretary effected an elaborate mince. It was grotesque, and he could only assume that Griffith had given him a lesson in courtly walks – one that had badly misfired. He could not bear to watch, afraid that at any moment Clarendon would turn around and see what was happening. And then there would be trouble, because he would assume that Bulteel was mimicking his stately waddle. He followed de Buat out of the hall and towards the chapel with considerable relief.

The chapel was spacious and light. It was also hot, and Chaloner immediately became aware that it was home to two corpses. According to de Buat, Oetje had died the day after Hanse, which meant three or four days in searing heat. The stench permeated the whole building, which was a pity, because it was rather lovely with its spectacular ceiling and carved pews.

It did not take Chaloner long to see that de Buat was right about the poison. The marks were obvious on Oetje, but they were clear on Hanse, too, when he knew what he was looking for. He wondered how Wiseman could have missed them.

'Where was Oetje found?' he asked.

De Buat was leaning over the bodies, inspecting their eyes. When the physician did not answer, Chaloner touched his hand, and repeated the question when de Buat looked at him.

'On the Savoy's private wharf. Well, I say *private* wharf, but anyone can moor a boat there. It is thus a place that can be reached from both the hospital complex and the river.'

'In other words, Oetje may have been murdered by someone in the Savoy, or by an outsider who came by water,' surmised Chaloner. 'Were you able to glean any other clues from her body?'

'No, but I found this on the pier.'

De Buat reached into the bag that was hanging over his shoulder, and produced the smallest firearm Chaloner had ever seen. It was no longer than the length of his hand, and so tiny that he wondered whether it would be effective. He was sure of one thing though: it would have been extremely expensive, and a maidservant's salary would not have covered the cost.

'Is it hers?' he asked. 'Or do you think her killer dropped it by mistake?'

The physician shrugged. 'There is no way to know. But keep it – it may help you unravel what is going on, and it is no use to me. I do not have any ammunition, for a start, and I can hardly go out and buy some. It would finish the negotiations for certain!'

When de Buat looked back to the corpses, Chaloner touched his arm a second time, to regain his attention. 'How long have you been deaf?' he asked, once the physician's eyes were on his face.

De Buat gave a crooked grin. 'It takes most people

175

rather longer to guess, by which point they have either yelled at me for ignoring them, or accused me of being impolite. It happened during your civil wars, as a matter of fact. I served under General Fairfax, fighting for Cromwell.'

'You did? Why embroil yourself in another country's troubles?'

'Because I was young, idealistic and stupid, and fighting for a republic seemed a good idea at the time. But a cannon exploded near me, and I have been deaf ever since.'

Chaloner nodded his sympathy. He knew all about exploding cannons. 'But you read lips.'

'I do now.'

Chaloner turned the subject back to the victims. 'Do you know anyone who wanted Hanse or Oetje dead?'

De Buat smiled ruefully. 'Well, Hanse disliked his every move being dogged by Oetje, but he died first, so he cannot be responsible for what happened to her. And he was not a man who would have resorted to violence anyway. Not even when he drank too much.'

'He drank too much?'

'I thought his consumption had increased over the last few weeks, and drunkenness can turn gentle men into demons. But Hanse was not one of them. Rather, he became introspective and sad.'

'Then do you think Oetje brought about Hanse's death somehow, and was killed in revenge?'

De Buat considered. 'No. Both died from poison, which suggests a single culprit.'

'Then we are left with a puzzle. Hanse enjoyed solitary walks, and he often met four men in a tavern. Oetje spied on him, which suggests she was reporting his activ-

176

ities to someone else. Hanse may have been killed to bring an end to these clandestine meetings, but then why murder Oetje?'

'Perhaps it was to ensure she would never reveal what she had been doing to anyone else. Or for whom she had been doing it.'

'Who in the Savoy was uneasy enough about Hanse's wanderings to recruit Oetje?'

De Buat shook his head slowly. 'I really cannot say. Perhaps someone who does not think peace between our nations is a good thing.'

Ruyven did not want peace, Chaloner thought as he took his leave. Could *he* have set Oetje to follow Hanse, then poisoned them both? He sighed, feeling his time in the Savoy had raised more questions than answers. One thing was clear, though: Hanse had been involved in something that had cost him his life and Oetje hers. So now what? He rubbed his head tiredly when he saw what he had to do next: take the bull by the horns and visit Spymaster Williamson, to find out exactly what *he* knew about the Sinon Plot.

Because Williamson's dislike of Chaloner ran deep, it would be suicide to walk into his lair without taking precautions, so he went to St Martin's Lane first, where a gun shop was operated by three brothers named Edmund, George and William Trulocke. As his previous dealings with them had not been congenial, he bought an old hat and coat from a rag-seller, and trusted the inside of the shop would be shadowy enough to prevent the trio from seeing his face. He also purchased a bone.

The Trulockes' domain was seedy. The sign above their door was so faded as to be unreadable, and the

177

whole place was ill-kept and dirty. Its window shutters were closed, and a snarling dog was tethered outside, to ensure pedestrians kept their distance. Chaloner tossed it the bone, and walked past unchallenged when the animal put stomach before duty. As the door opened, a bell clanged, and three hulking men immediately materialised from the workshop at the back. The place was very dark, and all Chaloner could see was a trio of bald-headed silhouettes.

'We are closed,' said the largest.

'I want ammunition for this,' said Chaloner, setting Oetje's little dag on the counter.

The eldest Trulocke gestured to tell his siblings that he would deal with the matter; they nodded back and returned to their workshop. Within moments a metallic clattering began, along with a lot of hissing. The place reeked of smoke and oil: gun manufacture was a noisy, smelly process.

'Three shillings,' said Trulocke, beginning to count paper-wrapped metal balls into a little tin. 'Expensive, you may say, but the bore is unusual, and that costs.'

'Does it work?'

Trulocke picked up the dag and began to prime it. Immediately, the dagger in Chaloner's sleeve dropped into the palm of his hand.

'You think it is too small to be effective,' surmised the gunsmith, handing it over with a grin. 'Well, I understand your reservations, but they are groundless. Shoot at that matting on the far wall. Do not worry about the noise. Our neighbours are used to it.'

The matting had patterns painted on it, so Chaloner selected a red circle, took aim and fired. There was a sharp report, and the ball thudded neatly into the centre of the blob. He was impressed. Its accuracy was excellent, and it was more than powerful enough to stop a man in his tracks.

'Who bought it from you?' he asked.

Trulocke placed the tin and a packet of gunpowder on the counter. 'Never seen it before.'

'Your name is engraved on the barrel, and you carry its ammunition,' said Chaloner mildly. 'So who bought it from you?'

'I ask no questions and get told no lies,' said Trulocke. 'Do you want the shot or not?'

Chaloner put the money on the counter, then moved fast when the gunsmith started to take it. Before Trulocke realised what was happening, he was pressed against the wall with a knife at his throat. He opened his mouth to yell to his brothers, but Chaloner applied pressure to the blade, and the mouth snapped closed again.

'I will ask you one last time,' he said softly. 'Who bought it?'

'I cannot say!' gasped Trulocke. 'I *will* not say! I am more frightened of him than of you.'

Chaloner pushed harder, and a dribble of blood began to ooze down Trulocke's neck. 'Who are you more frightened of now?'

'But he will kill me if I talk! Me *and* my brothers. And he can do it, too. He has more villains at his disposal than any man in London, although you would not know it to look at him, fine gentleman that he seems.'

'Williamson,' said Chaloner heavily, a sinking feeling in his stomach. If the Spymaster had commissioned Oetje to watch Hanse – or had dropped the weapon when he had killed her himself – then the investigation had just taken a decidedly sinister turn. 'This is his gun?'

'No! I never said that!' Trulocke was appalled at himself. 'You misunderstood.'

Chaloner sighed. 'It seems a pity to kill you, but if you will not cooperate, then . . .'

'Wait!' cried Trulocke. 'Please! Williamson buys a number of these small pieces, because his spies often need dags that are easy to conceal. Sometimes, when they have done their work, it is necessary to dump the things. Then they find their way into circulation among a certain kind of . . . That is why I did not ask how *you* came by it.'

Chaloner put the gun and ammunition in his pocket, still keeping the blade at Trulocke's throat. 'Will you tell him I was here?'

'Christ, no! He does not take kindly to men who reveal his secrets. And if *you* tell him, I shall deny it. He and I have done business for months now, and he will believe me over some villain who bursts into an honest man's property and starts brandishing daggers.'

Chaloner gave him a shove that saw him trip over a stack of muskets. Trulocke immediately started to bawl for help, but long before his brothers came racing to his aid, Chaloner had disappeared into the crowds outside.

Discarding the coat and hat in the nearest available alley, Chaloner left St Martin's Lane in a thoughtful frame of mind. Had Williamson hired Oetje because Hanse had found out about the Sinon Plot? And then killed both to be sure of no loose ends? Chaloner supposed he now had even more reason to interview the Spymaster.

After a short walk in the blazing late-afternoon sun, he reached Charing Cross, which was full of lethargically moving people. Near the stump of the medieval monument – a cross raised by Edward I in memory of a beloved queen – a man keeled over suddenly, stone dead. The interest from passers-by was short-lived: the heat was causing the old and weak to drop like flies, and sudden deaths were becoming increasingly commonplace as the heatwave dragged on.

Two men lingered though, prodding the corpse with their feet, and exchanging remarks that said they found the victim's demise entertaining. Chaloner was not surprised to recognise Kicke and Nisbett, both resplendent in the new livery Lady Castlemaine had provided.

'This could be you,' said Kicke with a nasty grin, stepping in front of Chaloner to prevent him from passing. 'People die inexplicably all the time these days.'

'They do,' agreed Nisbett, coming to stand behind Chaloner, thus trapping him between them. 'Especially ones that bleat about what they think they have seen. How is your arm, by the way?'

'Was it your idea to kill defenceless Dutchmen?' asked Chaloner archly, safe in the knowledge that they could hardly commit murder in such a public place. 'Or did someone hire you to do it?'

'If you had run him through last night, instead of flaunting your skill with the sword, we would not be having this stupid conversation,' Kicke snapped at his accomplice.

'So you have said,' retorted Nisbett with affected weariness. '*Ad nauseam*. But he will not escape me next time.'

Chaloner supposed he would just have to stay out of their way, because he had no intention of fighting them again. He eased to one side, then jigged quickly the other way when they both moved to block him. The manoeuvre saw him free.

181

'You are living on borrowed time, Chaloner,' hissed Kicke. 'Or you could save yourself by leaving the city tonight. It is your choice. However, bear in mind that we do not appreciate men who accuse us of theft and murder, so consider the offer carefully if you want to live.'

He started to walk away, but Nisbett was less inclined to leave the encounter unresolved. He drew his dagger, and Kicke exclaimed his alarm when he saw his friend prepare to lunge.

'Not here!' he grated, knocking the weapon down and then looking around quickly to see if anyone had noticed. 'If we are caught killing him, people will say we lied over the White Hall thefts – that we silenced him because we have something to hide.'

Chaloner raised his hands in the air. 'The Court chose to believe you over me, but that is its prerogative. The matter is over, as far as I am concerned.'

'Well, it is not over for me,' declared Nisbett. 'You have caused us too much trouble. Kicke may be willing to let you escape, but I plan to slit you open like a pig and dance in your blood.'

Kicke hauled him away before he could add anything else, glancing uneasily over his shoulder as he did so. Chaloner turned to see why, and saw Wiseman approaching. In deference to the heat, the surgeon had dispensed with his normal clothes and wore a bizarre gown of flowing red silk. It accentuated the solid muscles of his chest and arms, and gave him the appearance of an extremely powerful prostitute.

'Charming,' Wiseman said, having heard Nisbett's parting remark. 'I assume they are still vexed because you showed them to be villains?'

'It would seem so.' Chaloner supposed he should ask Wiseman why he had failed to notice that Hanse had been poisoned, but he was tired, hot and did not feel equal to another confrontation.

'You have accrued a lot of enemies of late,' Wiseman went on. 'That pair issue wild threats, while George Downing is not enamoured of you, and neither is Spymaster Williamson.'

'How do you know?'

'I am always listening for rumours that affect my friends, and I eavesdropped on a discussion between Downing and Williamson only this morning. The bit of their discourse regarding you was none too flattering. These are dangerous men, Chaloner. You should take care.'

Wiseman was hardly someone to be dispensing such advice, given that he had accumulated a list of detractors that comprised virtually everyone at Court. Chaloner nodded acknowledgement of the warning, and started to walk away. The surgeon followed, falling into step at his side.

'But there is a reason for Downing's hostility,' he chattered on. 'He is being blackmailed. And blackmail is especially dreadful for him, because he is so indescribably miserly, and does not want to pay what the extortionist is demanding.'

That secured Chaloner's attention. 'Blackmailed about what?'

Wiseman shrugged. 'I overheard him tell Williamson that he had received a letter demanding payment in return for silence over some past misdeed. Williamson tried his best to find out what, but Downing was not saying. Personally, I suspect it is some dalliance with another man's wife – the fellow is a shameless and unrelenting lecher.'

'He is, but he does not care who knows it.' Chaloner recalled the envoy's improper advances to Jacoba and Hannah. 'I cannot see him paying to keep his indiscretions quiet.'

'He might, if the husband is in a position to do him harm,' countered Wiseman. 'He is ambitious, and will not want a casual affair to spoil his chances of advancement. Anyway, whatever he has done, a blackmailer is demanding fifty pounds to keep it secret. And Downing is deeply concerned – it is what has turned him so petulant and spiteful.'

Chaloner raised his eyebrows. Downing was always petulant and spiteful, although he supposed it was possible that worry had made him worse. 'Does Williamson know the identity of this blackmailer? Other nobles are being held to ransom, too, so he will want him caught quickly.'

'He does not. And he is mightily embarrassed about it.'

'How did you come to overhear this discussion?'

Wiseman grinned sheepishly. 'I was asleep in a yew thicket, and they started talking right next to me. I suppose decency should have compelled me to cough and advise them of my presence, but I do not like them, and what they were saying intrigued me. Besides, you do it all the time.'

'Yes, but I know what I am doing, whereas such behaviour by you is asking for a dagger between the ribs. But your explanation begs another question: why were you asleep in a yew thicket?'

'I rarely drink to excess, but Temperance and I have quarrelled.' An expression of abject sorrow filled

Wiseman's face. 'So I let myself become intoxicated and I collapsed there. The spat was about my wife, who is incarcerated in Bedlam, as you know. She is quite out of her wits.'

'Who? Temperance or your wife?'

Wiseman glared at him. 'My wife. But then Temperance said *she* was mad, too, to have accepted me as her lover. Do you think she meant it? I could not bear it if she did.'

Chaloner had never understood what had possessed Temperance to take up with Wiseman, and was inclined to believe it *had* been during a moment of insanity. But he could see her remark had hurt the surgeon, and had no wish to make matters worse.

'She can be unkind,' he said, thinking of all the cruel remarks she had made to him since she had abandoned her Puritan lifestyle and turned to brothel-keeping. 'But she is often sorry afterwards.'

'Will you talk to her?' Wiseman looked uncharacteristically pitiful. 'It will not take long, and I would be very grateful. In fact, if you oblige, I will break one of the cardinal rules of being a *medicus* and let you into a secret about one of my patients – one that may save your life.'

Chaloner supposed his confrontation with Williamson could wait until the following day, and it would be good to have information that might allow him to steal a march on one of the many people who meant him harm. He nodded agreement. Relieved, Wiseman squeezed his shoulder in a gruff gesture of appreciation, and began to talk.

'Nisbett is a superb swordsman, but he has a major weakness: his left knee is very easily dislocated, leaving him in agony and all but defenceless. If you do fight him, make him stumble. It might even the odds a little.'

It might, and Chaloner was grateful for the information.

It was early for the gentleman's club in Hercules' Pillars Alley, and although its doors were open, most patrons would come later, after carousing in White Hall or the Fleet Street taverns. Only a handful of men were present so far, listening to a consort of players from the King's Private Musick, or conversing quietly with the *filles de joie* who had draped themselves around the room.

In the centre of the main parlour sat Temperance North, a large woman recently turned twenty-one. Her exquisitely elegant clothes were a statement of how wealthy the establishment had made her. Unfortunately, they could not disguise the fact that the fine fare available to her on a nightly basis was going directly to her middle, and her friends should have told her that the delicate bodices designed for slender souls like Lady Castlemaine did not suit those with fuller figures.

She had recently acquired the habit of smoking a pipe, too, which had darkened her teeth and roughened her complexion. To disguise this, she had smeared her cheeks with white paste, aiming for a fashionable pallor, and her black face-patches were stark against it – three of them, all star-shaped. She also wore a wig of yellow curls, although her own chestnut locks were far prettier.

'Thomas,' she said with a marked lack of enthusiasm. 'What brings you here? Some investigation, and you want to know what gossip we have heard about it? I cannot imagine why else you have deigned to grace us with your presence.'

The brusque remark reminded Chaloner that although they had been close once, they had grown apart. She considered him too staid, while he did not like what she had become. 'I wanted to see you,' he replied coolly. 'Although I can leave if it would make you happy.'

'Come now, children,' chided Maude, the matronly woman who was Temperance's helpmeet. 'There is no need to be nasty to each other.'

'I was not being nasty,' retorted Temperance sullenly. 'I was being honest. And he is the one always rattling on about the importance of telling the truth.'

Chaloner raised his eyebrows in surprise, sure he had never done anything of the kind. Spies lied as a matter of course, and he was not such a hypocrite as to demand from others what he failed to do himself.

'Wiseman asked me to visit,' he said, deciding to state his business and leave before they quarrelled. 'You have upset him, and he wants to know how badly he is out of favour.'

'Actually, he upset *me*,' said Temperance sulkily. 'I want to visit his wife in Bedlam, but he will not let me. All I want is to *see* her, to know what manner of lady captured his heart.'

'I doubt that is the woman you will find there,' predicted Chaloner. 'Illness will have changed her. And such an encounter is likely to distress everyone involved, but especially her.'

Temperance stared at him. 'She is insane. You cannot distress the insane.'

'I imagine you can. How would *you* feel, if you were locked away, your mind tormented, and your husband brought people to gawp at you? Wiseman is right to refuse.'

Temperance sniffed. 'You think he is acting out of compassion? Not because she might be prettier than me, and he does not want me to know it?'

'He once told me that you were the loveliest woman alive.' Chaloner did not add that he had thought the surgeon was joking, because even to his brotherly eyes, Temperance was plain.

Slowly, she began to smile. 'He said that? You are not making it up?'

'No,' he replied truthfully. 'He really did.'

'Thank you, Tom,' she said, the smile turning to a beam. 'You have brought me great peace of mind. I should have known never to doubt him, wonderful man that he is.'

She reached up to scratch her head – wigs were hot, rough and attractive to lice, so itching was an occupational hazard. Chaloner felt his jaw drop when her fingers dislodged the hairpiece, and it fell to the floor, revealing the bald pate underneath.

'What have you done?' he gasped, unable to help himself. 'Your hair . . .'

Temperance bent to retrieve the curls. 'Everyone shaves their heads these days.'

'Some men do,' he acknowledged, unable to take his eyes off the spectacle. 'Women do not.'

'Perhaps not yet, but they will. It is what fashion dictates.'

'Christ!' Chaloner sincerely hoped she was wrong. He was relieved when she replaced the wig, and wondered whether he had been right to repeat Wiseman's remark about her beauty. Perhaps the surgeon had revised his opinion when he went to bed and found bristle on the pillow beside him.

188

'Are you investigating the murder of that Dutch diplomat?' asked Maude, before they could debate the matter further. 'Willem Hanse? There is a rumour about him.'

'Is there?' asked Chaloner, forcing himself to sound disinterested. He did not want Temperance to accuse him of visiting purely for the purpose of eliciting information again.

'It is said that Hanse was different from the other Hollanders,' Maude went on. 'He went out alone, and he visited taverns. Kicke and that foppish Griffith had an argument about it here the other night. Kicke said Hanse was murdered by another Dutchman, but Griffith disagreed.'

'I like Kicke,' said Temperance warmly. 'He is a handsome, charming man. But I cannot take to Colonel Griffith. I do not know why he bothers coming here, because he is not interested in girls.'

'What reason did Griffith give for disagreeing with Kicke?' Chaloner asked of Maude.

She frowned. 'I think it was something to do with Hanse meeting Englishmen in taverns, and plotting with them. Griffith said that he was murdered for it.'

Chaloner went home after he had taken his leave of Temperance. He was tired after sleeping badly the night before, and his arm hurt. He declined to play his viol when Hannah informed him that he might do so for half an hour while she was in the kitchen, and he could not bring himself to eat the stew she had prepared. It comprised lumps of undercooked meat in a grey, watery gravy, and he felt sick just looking at it. After forcing down two mouthfuls at considerable risk to his health, he retired to bed while it was still light.

189

Hannah was solicitous of him the following morning, and sent out to a cookshop for a pie when he said he was hungry. He was grateful, because the stew had developed a hard plate of grease across the top, and smelled rancid.

'You are unwell,' said Hannah kindly. 'You have not said a word since you woke.'

'Willem Hanse's funeral is today,' said Chaloner, saying what had been on his mind since he had first opened his eyes. 'I liked him.'

She laid a sympathetic hand on his shoulder. 'Then I shall come with you.'

'No!' He had not meant to sound sharp, but it would not be a good idea to bring Hannah into contact with the Dutch delegation when so many Londoners meant them harm. Moreover, he was not sure how he felt about her meeting Jacoba, either. It would be too much like introducing her to Aletta, and he was eager to keep those two parts of his life separate, although he could not have said why.

Hannah drew back, hurt. 'I thought you would appreciate my support.'

'I do,' he said quickly. 'Very much. But . . .'

He knew he should tell her that his first wife's sister was in the city, and he also knew that there was no time like the present. He took a breath, but then was not sure what to say. Why did he find such matters so difficult? Surely, it could not be entirely attributable to his life as a spy? He was angry with himself, because Hannah deserved better. Moreover, he would have liked to regale her with affectionate remarks – the kind he imagined most men murmured to their wives on a regular basis. So far, he had not managed one, and his inadequacy both annoyed and exasperated him.

'Well,' said Hannah, when the silence had extended for some time, 'I think I *had* better come. It is what spouses are expected to do, and I do not want to be seen as uncaring. You can collect me from White Hall half an hour before it starts. Now eat the pie while it is warm.'

The pie was past its best, too, because hot weather spoiled food fast. He ate a little, and tried again to tell her about Jacoba, but she interrupted with a tale about Kicke's improper fascination with Charles Bates's wife. He let her talk, feeling cowardly for ducking the issue.

'The Duke has invited us to a soiree,' said Hannah brightly, once she had exhausted the topic of the Bates's marital hiccups. 'A week on Monday.'

'Oh,' said Chaloner without enthusiasm. The Duke's parties tended to involve a lot of drinking and lewd behaviour, and he was always surprised when Hannah enjoyed them. Moreover, there was rarely any decent music. 'You go. I may be working.'

'Working!' spat Hannah in disgust. 'That wretched Earl demands far too much of you. In fact, he sees you more than I do, and it is hardly fair. We are newly wed!'

'Yes,' said Chaloner. Was he being unreasonable by declining to accompany her? He decided he was, and that he should make an effort, regardless of what he thought about the Duke and his hedonistic companions. 'But I am sure I can arrange to—'

'Do not bother,' said Hannah huffily. 'I will have more fun without you.'

Chaloner had no wish to quarrel. He smiled, and tried to make amends. 'Perhaps we could go to the theatre today. I understand *Worse and Worse* is playing at the Duke's House.'

Hannah glared at him. 'It is, and I asked you to see it with me last week. But you were too busy trying to learn who killed that dirty old spy during our wedding, so I went with Charles Bates and the Killigrews instead. I told you it was boring, but apparently, you did not listen.'

Chaloner could not recall her saying a thing about it, and supposed he had neglected to pay attention, as often happened when he was preoccupied with murder and she was prattling on about something he did not find very interesting.

'My friends warned me that I had nothing in common with you,' said Hannah, when there was no reply. 'But I thought it would not matter, because we love each other. Do you think the storm at our wedding was an omen? That God was trying to tell us we were making a mistake?'

She was not the first person to suggest a supernatural significance for the events of that day: Bulteel had, too, although mostly because he had been hurt by not receiving an invitation. Chaloner had spotted him lurking by the church door, but had not understood why he had failed to join the celebrations until the situation had been explained to him the following day. He wished he had known sooner, because Hannah had invited a lot of people *he* did not like, and he did not see why she should have had everything her own way.

'No, of course not,' he said, when he saw it was one of the rare occasions when Hannah *did* expect an answer, and was prepared to wait until she had one. 'It meant nothing more than that you chose a month notorious for its turbulent weather.'

'I will be late if I stay chatting here,' said Hannah, standing abruptly and reaching for her hat. 'And the

192

Queen will be wondering where I am. I will see you later. For Hanse's funeral.'

Chaloner left Tothill Street feeling unsettled and confused, and was relieved to push Hannah to the back of his mind and consider the day ahead instead. His first task was to tackle Williamson, so he set off towards Westminster, where the Spymaster had been allocated a suite of rooms from which to conduct the sordid business of espionage. He had Oetje's gun with him, and made sure there was a dagger in his sleeve, in his boot and in his belt. And he stopped at White Hall to collect Bulteel, too.

'Why do you want me with you?' asked the secretary, trotting along at his side. 'I know nothing about murdered Dutchmen. Or about the Earl's lost papers, although I wish I did. I worry about those.'

'Williamson likes you,' explained Chaloner. 'He will be nicer to me if you are there.'

Bulteel smiled. 'He and I do spend the odd evening together. We share a number of interests, you see, such as a dislike of music and exclusive soirees. Not that we are ever invited to any, of course. However, that will change when I complete my training with Griffith.'

'About that,' began Chaloner, feeling it incumbent on him as a friend to warn Bulteel that the outcome he was anticipating might not come to pass. Then he hesitated, not sure how to put it.

'He has been working on my gait this week,' Bulteel went on happily. 'He says I have not *quite* mastered a courtly bearing yet, but urges me to practise as often as possible.'

'Not here,' said Chaloner hastily, as Bulteel began the

bizarre mince he had affected in the Savoy the previous day. It attracted the attention of passers-by, who gazed at him warily. 'It is better done in the privacy of your own home.'

'Griffith said the same,' confided Bulteel, reverting to his normal walk. 'Although I cannot imagine why. Surely, all practise is good?'

Chaloner was spared from answering when something struck him on the shoulder. Immediately, he dropped into a defensive stance, ready to repel an attack. But it was only hail. Pieces of ice the size of musket balls began to fall, and Bulteel yelped when one bounced off his head. Chaloner pulled him into the shelter of a doorway.

The hailstones grew harder and larger, causing pedestrians to scatter in alarm. A hackney driver abandoned his carriage and dived for cover in St Margaret's Church. His passengers peered out of the windows in alarm when they heard the staccato rattle of ice-balls on the roof, and Chaloner saw they were van Goch and Kun. Ruyven was accompanying them on horseback, with several well-armed soldiers at his heels. Van Goch called an order, but it was only reluctantly that they left him and went to wait out the barrage with the driver.

'Look!' exclaimed Bulteel, reaching out to retrieve one of the missiles. 'It is *huge*! What a pity it will melt. No one will believe us when we say it was the size of a hen's egg.'

The flurry stopped as quickly as it had started. There was one grey cloud in an otherwise azure sky, and Chaloner wondered what had caused it to release its burden so abruptly. Doubtless the street-prophets would have answers. They always did.

194

'No rain, though,' said Bulteel. 'And we could do with some. Are you ready to go?'

Chaloner watched Ruyven gather his troops and surround the ambassador's coach again. The captain railed at the driver for abandoning his duties, but the man only pretended not to understand. Eventually, the cavalcade clattered away.

'Tom,' prompted Bulteel. 'I cannot be gone too long, or the Earl will complain. If you want me to accompany you to Williamson's office, then we must go now.'

Chaloner nodded assent, but they had not gone far before they were intercepted by White, the friendly, smiling vicar of St Margaret's Church. He was not smiling that morning, however.

'My ceiling does not cope well with this kind of weather,' he remarked unhappily. 'As you no doubt remember from your wedding.'

'*I* do not,' said Bulteel bitterly. '*I* was not on the guest list. Incidentally, I heard those tales about Cromwell – how he excavated the bodies of Westminster Abbey's dead kings, and swapped them all about. You were his chaplain at the time, so you must have seen him doing it.'

Chaloner winced. Clearly, Griffith's lessons in gentility and tact had some way to go.

'I assure you, there is no truth in those accusations,' said White stiffly. 'Cromwell was a religious man, not in the habit of despoiling graves. Good day to you both.'

Bulteel watched him stalk away. 'Do you think I offended him?'

Chaloner regarded him askance. 'You suggested that he stood by and watched while the King's ancestors were desecrated, so yes, I would say he considers himself insulted.'

195

Bulteel looked crestfallen. 'I did not mean . . . Oh, damn it all! Perhaps I should not have spoken.'

'Perhaps not,' agreed Chaloner, beginning to walk again.

Westminster was the older of the two royal palaces that stood next to each other on the west bank of the Thames. It was dominated by medieval buildings, including the abbey and the Great Hall, and was full of gothic pinnacles, spires and gracefully arched windows. Parts looked like the religious precinct it had once been, and it was populated by clerks in sober robes.

Williamson had been provided with a modest building in the cobbled expanse of New Palace Yard. As usual, uniformed guards stood outside it, wearing buff jerkins with stripy sleeves. These represented the respectable face of his operation. The less salubrious one comprised criminals from London's gangs, who were employed when solutions were needed that broke the law.

Hoping he was not making a mistake by entering the place, Chaloner stepped past the guards, and found himself in an airy hall, where a dozen clerks laboured feverishly. The cells where Williamson conducted his interrogations were below it, reached by an ominously dark stairway. Chaloner tried not to think about them as he and Bulteel were conducted to the upper floor, where Williamson occupied a tastefully furnished office.

'Well,' drawled the Spymaster, leaning back in his chair as his guests were shown in. 'To what do I owe this pleasure? I thought you went to some trouble to avoid my company.'

'Hello, Joseph,' said Bulteel, peering out from behind Chaloner with a mischievous grin. He looked around.

'So this is where you work. It is lovely! Far nicer than my vile little office.'

Williamson understood immediately why Bulteel had been brought. He nodded an affable greeting to the secretary, but the moment Bulteel went to admire the view from the window and could not see him, his expression turned hard and dangerous.

'There is no need for insurances when you deal with me, Chaloner,' he said, making it perfectly clear that there was. 'You need not be afraid.'

'There,' said Bulteel, turning to smile. 'You see? I told you there was nothing to fear.'

A shadow glided soundlessly through the door and came to stand protectively at Williamson's side. It was John Swaddell, technically a clerk, although everyone knew he was really an assassin. He was clad in black from head to toe, with the exception of a spotlessly white 'falling band' – a decorative bib that lay across his chest. He had small, dark eyes that were never still, and was one of the most sinister men Chaloner had ever encountered.

'The Earl suggested I talk to you,' lied Chaloner, knowing Williamson was unlikely to learn that his master had done nothing of the kind. 'About the Sinon Plot.'

Williamson's eyes widened fractionally, but otherwise he betrayed no emotion. He indicated with an elegant gesture of his hand that Swaddell was to lock the door.

'Why is that necessary?' asked Bulteel, most of his attention on the window. It afforded an excellent view of the severed heads displayed on poles outside Westminster Hall, and explained why so many people who had tried to rescue Cromwell's skull had been apprehended.

'It is just a precaution to ensure your friend does not leave before we have enjoyed a full and frank exchange of information,' replied Williamson. 'If I am to provide him with intelligence, then he must reciprocate in kind, and I do not want him wandering off before we have finished.'

'That will not happen,' said Swaddell, moving his hand to reveal that he held a dagger. Chaloner did likewise, and alarm flashed in Williamson's eyes, no doubt predicting that it would not be his assassin who would be skewered first if the situation turned hostile. By the window, Bulteel gazed happily into New Palace Yard, oblivious to the deadly undercurrents that surged behind him.

'Make a start, Tom,' he said over his shoulder. 'I cannot stay much longer.'

Chaloner obliged. 'The Sinon Plot is not as secret as you believe,' he told Williamson. 'It is common knowledge.'

Williamson paled. 'You must have read Clarendon's private papers, and learned about Sinon that way. It is *not* common knowledge.'

'There is nothing about any Sinon in the Earl's correspondence,' said Bulteel, turning to face them and frowning his puzzlement. 'I would have seen it. What is this plot?'

'The tale *is* out,' Swaddell told his master. 'Although I would hardly call it "common knowledge". One of the Privy Council must have blabbed.'

Williamson sighed heavily. 'Damn them! It is not a good idea for London to know that three men came close to making off with the crown jewels.'

'What?' cried Bulteel. 'Are you serious?'

'Yes, and it is a secret.' Williamson winced. 'Or it should be. I am appalled to learn otherwise.'

'Why have you gone to such lengths to suppress it?' asked Chaloner. 'People do not care enough about the jewels to be angry about their disappearance. There will be no public outcry.'

'There will if London is taxed to replace the things,' retorted Williamson, truthfully enough. 'And, if we may be blunt, the King's popularity is at a low ebb at the moment, and we cannot afford the bad publicity. It is one reason why most of the Privy Council is keen for a war with the Dutch – a military campaign will settle people's eyes on problems outside our domestic hiccups.'

'That is hardly a good reason to plunge two countries into bloody conflict,' objected Chaloner.

'Nations have clashed for a lot less,' said Williamson soberly. 'I am not saying it is right – indeed, I am person-ally convinced that antagonising the Dutch is a very bad idea – but history tells us that our leaders do not always make sensible decisions. Still, perhaps progress will be made towards peace on Sunday night, at the convention in the Savoy.'

'What is the *real* reason for wanting the Sinon Plot kept quiet?' asked Chaloner, aware that the Spymaster had managed to change the subject. 'It is nothing to do with the King's popularity – if the plot had succeeded, people would have felt sorry for him, and perhaps liked him better.'

Williamson smiled coldly. 'You are too astute for your own good. But I suppose I can tell you, given that Clarendon seems to have taken you into his confidence. The three villains are named Swan, Swallow and Falcon. I know it does not sound very likely, but those *are* their

199

real names. Sir William Compton overheard them plotting together in a tavern on Cheapside.'

'Who are they, exactly?' asked Chaloner.

'Swan and Swallow are booksellers; Falcon is a cleric. And *that* is the reason why we have tried to keep the matter quiet.'

Chaloner frowned. 'Are you saying you acted to spare the Church embarrassment, by keeping from the public that one of their ministers was on the verge of stealing from the King?'

Williamson inclined his head. 'It is beset with problems at the moment, what with Quakers and Catholics refusing to obey its edicts. It does not need tales of criminal members, too.'

Chaloner supposed it might be true: the Church *would* be grateful for such help. And spymasters were always happy to have powerful organisations in their debt. 'I need to speak to these plotters.'

'No,' said Williamson immediately. 'I have given orders that no one will ever speak to them again. The affair is over, so let it alone.'

'Were Swan, Swallow and Falcon the only ones involved? Or did they have accomplices?'

'They said not, and I believe them,' replied Williamson curtly.

'Then what about witnesses? Did anyone other than Compton overhear what they were plotting?'

Williamson scowled. 'No, because they would have come forward to tell me.'

'Unfortunately, not everyone sees you as a benevolent soul,' said Swaddell, when Chaloner did not grace that claim with a response. 'Having Londoners afraid of you is good in some ways, but it does make them reluctant to confide. Chaloner may be right: a witness may well have blathered, and we might be wrong to blame the Privy Council for gossiping.'

'Then find him,' said Williamson to Swaddell. 'Thank you for bringing the matter to my attention, Chaloner. You may go now. But before you do, let me issue a warning: do not dabble in this matter any further. You will not look for this witness, and you will stay away from Newgate. Is that clear?'

'Clear enough,' said Chaloner, although he had no intention of complying.

'Disobey me, and you will be sorry.' Williamson's eyes bored into Chaloner's. 'I mean it.'

'There is no need for threats,' said Bulteel reproachfully. 'Thomas will do as you say.'

Chapter 6

Far from discouraging Chaloner, Williamson's threat had convinced him that a quiet word with Falcon, Swan and Swallow might be extremely useful, and he decided he would use Surgeon Wiseman to gain access to Newgate the following day. It would be risky – and certainly unpleasant – but he had faced far greater dangers in the past.

He returned to White Hall with Bulteel, and was just crossing the Great Court to report to the Earl, when Hannah waylaid them. A man was with her, arm extended to escort her over the cobbles. He appeared to be in his mid fifties, with a face that was lined and worn from a life outdoors. He was surprisingly clean shaven, though, and his uniform was smart. Bulteel made Hannah a graceless obeisance that caused him to stumble, and scurried away when she started to smirk.

'Are you feeling better now, Tom?' she asked sweetly, thus indicating that she considered their earlier spat his fault, not hers. 'You were sadly out of sorts this morning.'

'Probably the heat,' said her companion sympathetically. 'It is affecting us all.'

'This is Daniel Cotton,' said Hannah, in response to Chaloner's questioning look. 'My first husband's brother – or one of them. There are also Josias and William, and all three hold Court appointments. Daniel is a Yeoman Cartaker, which means he looks after the King's carriages.'

Chaloner bowed, thinking Daniel held the same relationship to him that Hannah held to Jacoba. Did it make them kin, or was the tie too tenuous?

'I have a bit of a problem,' said Daniel, bowing in return. He had a curious, gravelly voice. 'But Hannah says you have a way with problems, and may be able to help.'

Chaloner suppressed a sigh. There were not enough hours in the day for yet another enquiry. 'It is not a good time . . .'

'Because we are about to go to Hanse's funeral?' asked Hannah. 'I have not forgotten. I assume you are here to collect me?'

'It will not take a moment to tell you,' said Daniel. 'And then you can be on your way.'

'Daniel has the same difficulty as another of my friends,' explained Hannah. She grabbed Chaloner's hand and jerked him towards her, so she could whisper in his ear. 'Charles Bates is being blackmailed, and now Daniel is similarly menaced. You explore nasty happenings in White Hall, so . . .'

'Not this nasty happening,' Chaloner whispered back. 'I have other cases to solve.'

'Please, Tom,' said Hannah quietly. 'This is important to me.'

'We shall talk here,' determined Daniel, when Chaloner could think of no excuse, and Hannah indicated that the

Yeoman Cartaker should begin his tale. 'It is in the blazing sun, but we will see anyone coming, and I cannot afford to be overheard. You may wait in the shade, Hannah. What I am about to say is too delicate for the ears of ladies.'

Chaloner's heart sank, and he hoped he was not about to be regaled with anything too risqué.

'I shall leave you to it, then,' said Hannah, rather resentfully. 'Afterwards, we shall attend this funeral, and then Tom can take me to the Banqueting House, where the King is putting on a play.'

'I am not sure where to begin,' said Daniel, when she was out of earshot. Then he took a deep breath, closed his eyes, and spoke in a blurt. 'I am pregnant. There! It is out.'

Chaloner regarded him warily. 'Are you?' Daniel's only response was a curt nod, and the spy was clearly expected to say something else, so he added, 'Does your wife know?'

'I am not married,' snapped Daniel. 'Obviously.'

'It was an immaculate conception, then, was it?' asked Chaloner unable to help himself.

Daniel glared at him. 'Of course not. A man is involved – a fellow named John Nisbett. I know I should not have bedded him, but these things happen, and we were both drunk at the time. He has since confessed that he does not recall what happened. Thank God!'

Chaloner tried to understand why anyone – of either sex – should want to bed Nisbett. 'So you are a woman, then?'

'Of course I am a woman! I would not be pregnant if I were a man, would I?'

Chaloner felt it was unreasonable of her to bark at

him. 'You must forgive me, madam, but it is not every day that a Yeoman Cartaker confesses to being a lady.'

'Well, perhaps not, but this is White Hall, so you should be used to the unexpected. Of course, Hannah does not know I am a sister-in-law, and I would be grateful if you did not enlighten her.'

'Her first husband, Nathan, was he a woman, too?'

'Do not be ridiculous! It is only me, William and Josias who are of the fairer sex. Well, we had to do something to earn a crust, given that none of us are pretty enough to be ladies-in-waiting. And I am an excellent manager of His Majesty's carriages. Far better than any man.'

'I am sure you are,' asked Chaloner weakly.

'We have all done extremely well at White Hall, and we have made the name of Cotton highly respected. However, that will change should my secret emerge. It would hurt Hannah, too.'

Chaloner supposed it would. 'So, can I assume that someone found out about your . . . your *condition*, and is threatening to expose you?'

'Precisely! I shall disappear to the country to "visit kin" when my time comes, as I have done in the past, so no one should know anything about it. But some wretched villain found out, although I cannot imagine how. All I can think is that someone must have overheard me talking to my sisters.'

'Do you have any idea who?'

'If I did, I would call the villain out. I may be a woman, Mr Chaloner, but I am more than a match for most of these fops who strut about Court.'

Chaloner was sure she was. 'How does the blackmailer communicate?'

Daniel handed him a sheet of paper, on which the

writer informed the reader in a bold roundhand that the cost of concealing the pregnancy would be fifty pounds. It was to be paid by the end of the month, which was about two weeks hence.

'I do not have fifty pounds,' she said. 'It is more than I earn in a year. Yet I cannot have my family exposed to ridicule. People will say Nathan was a woman, too, and it explains why his marriage was childless. But he was a perfectly normal man, and it was just unfortunate that he and Hannah were never blessed with brats.'

'Not nearly as unfortunate as the fact that you are,' muttered Chaloner. 'All I can promise is to listen for rumours regarding his identity. And I will look into the matter when my current cases are closed, and I have more free time.'

Daniel sighed her relief. 'Thank you. Is there anything I can do for you in return?'

'Yes. You can take Hannah to this play in the Banqueting House.'

'So you can pursue your other work?' asked Daniel.

So I do not have to take her to Hanse's funeral, thought Chaloner. He nodded.

'Very well,' said Daniel. 'I will do a great deal to secure your help, even sit through a play.'

For convenience, Hanse was going to be laid to rest in St Martin-in-the-Fields, no longer rural, but still possessed of a decent sward of grass for burials. Aware that a large gathering of Dutchmen was likely to attract unwanted attention, Ambassador van Goch had permitted only a few of his staff to attend. All had been instructed to don clothes that would not reveal them to be foreigners.

There was a smattering of English mourners besides

Chaloner. Bulteel was there as the Earl's representative, and he had asked Griffith to join him. Bulteel had not bothered to change, and his pale-green coat was inappropriate. By contrast, Griffith had taken considerable care with *his* appearance, and every item of clothing was black. Chaloner could see him berating his cousin for his insensitivity, although Bulteel appeared bemused, not understanding what he had done wrong.

Chaloner wore a black coat for the occasion, and felt the sun burning through it as he stood at the graveside, listening to the priest drone the all-too-familiar words. Inevitably, he thought of his first wife and child, especially when Jacoba came to cling to his arm, as she had done at Aletta's funeral. It was a dismal occasion, and upset him more than he liked to admit.

Afterwards, everyone was invited to the Savoy for wine, biscuits and the distribution of mourning rings. Being sociable was the last thing Chaloner felt like doing, but Jacoba said she wanted him there, and it would have been churlish to refuse. Reluctantly, he climbed into one of the waiting carriages, and found it already occupied by Bulteel, Griffith and the Killigrews.

'Thank God that is over,' said Griffith, flapping his piece of lace and leaning back against the upholstery with a gusty sigh. 'I *detest* funerals. All that weeping and wailing . . .'

'I do not mind,' said Bulteel blithely. 'I am not asked to many, so it makes for a pleasant change. But I do not want to go to this post-burial reception. I hate the Savoy.'

'Do you?' asked Killigrew coldly. 'And why is that, pray?'

'It is not the place itself,' gabbled Bulteel, seeing he had offended. 'It is its current residents. I do not like being among Dutchmen when they are so unpopular. It makes me fearful for my life.'

'I can agree with you there,' said Judith. 'I cannot wait to see the back of them.'

'You amaze me,' said Griffith. 'I have always found the delegates extremely mannerly.'

'Oh, they are mannerly,' acknowledged Killigrew. 'But that does not mean we must like them. Besides, they are not *all* well behaved. That Ruyven is downright uncouth.'

'Hanse was the best of them,' said Judith sadly. 'And I am sorry he is the one who died. He was nothing but smiles and cheerful conversation.'

'I do not believe he stole those papers from Clarendon,' said Killigrew. 'Not him. Well, not any of them, if you want the truth. They are not thieves. Not even Ruyven.'

'Yet someone made off with them,' said Bulteel unhappily. 'And I hope to God they turn up soon. I shall not rest easy until I know what has happened, because the notion of someone breaking into Worcester House and helping himself to important documents does not bear thinking about.'

Chaloner felt guilty when it occurred to him that he had done virtually nothing about retrieving them, but then told himself that the Earl had only himself to blame. How could the theft be investigated when Chaloner had no notion as to what kind of person the papers might appeal?

When the coach drew to a standstill outside the Savoy, Griffith's servant, Lane, was waiting to help the occupants out. As usual, he was dour and silent, although the briefest of smiles cracked when he contrived to make Bulteel stumble. Griffith berated him soundly for his lack of care, although Lane did not seem to take the reprimand to heart. Or perhaps he did – it was difficult to tell with such a taciturn character.

'How is your arm?' he asked Chaloner, the last to alight. 'Nisbett fought like a scoundrel the other night. True gentlemen do not taunt their opponents.'

'I never thanked you for standing with me,' said Chaloner. 'I hope it did not see you in trouble.'

'It did, but there we are. I am glad *you* picked Nisbett, because I would not have lasted two minutes with him. Kicke, on the other hand, is all bluster. I wish I had slit his throat.'

And with that venomous remark, he bowed, and turned away to help the driver with the horses.

'I swear he just said more to you than he has uttered in three months to me,' said Griffith, who had been watching from the shade of the porch. 'He is a desperately uncommunicative rogue.'

'Is he given to fighting?'

Griffith raised his eyebrows. 'No, or I would not have hired him! But there is something odd about him. Something sly. I shall dismiss him the moment I find a suitable replacement.'

Chaloner recalled what Temperance had said about Griffith. 'I understand you have been listening to rumours about Hanse, and have learned that he drank in taverns with strangers.'

Griffith nodded. 'It is amazing what one overhears in the Spares Gallery. And my cousin ordered me to keep my ears open, in the hope that I might learn something to help you locate the villain who made off with Clarendon's papers. Unfortunately, I heard nothing useful about those, but I did catch a few whispers about Hanse.'

'What, exactly?'

209

'Just that he visited the Sun tavern and sat with four men, although no one seems to know their names. As far as I am concerned, that is peculiar behaviour for a foreign diplomat, so perhaps there *is* truth in the rumour that he stole the Earl's documents.'

The reception for Hanse was being held in the State Room, where were gathered many people who had wanted to attend the funeral, but who had been forbidden to do so by van Goch. They comprised not only every member of the ambassadorial delegation, but a large number of London-based Dutch merchants, too. The ten or so British guests formed a distinct minority, and stood together looking acutely uncomfortable. All except one.

'*He* was not invited,' Bulteel whispered in Chaloner's ear, pointing to where Downing was making a nuisance of himself with the women. Most fled before he could corner them, but Kun and Zas were obliged to rescue others who were less fleet of foot.

'Then why did he come?' asked Chaloner. A funeral was the last occasion *he* would gatecrash.

'For the funeral gifts,' explained Bulteel. 'And the free food.'

Chaloner regarded him in amused surprise. 'I hardly think—'

'I am right,' asserted Bulteel. 'His meanness is legendary, and he will do anything to avoid spending money. The food and wine served here will save him the cost of his dinner.'

Chaloner was about to argue when he saw Downing grab a handful of biscuits, eat half as quickly as he could, and slip the rest in his pocket for later. Bulteel nodded his satisfaction at this proof that he was right, then wandered away to admire the paintings, evidently trying to put Griffith's art lessons to good use. Chaloner went to pay his respects to Jacoba.

'You should not have come,' said Ruyven, standing protectively at her side. 'Your time would have been better spent hunting for the killer.'

'*I* wanted him here,' said Jacoba. Her face was pale: the occasion was a strain. 'It made me feel as though Aletta was with me. Have one of these biscuits, Tom. Ruyven has just told me that they are very good. And here is the funeral ring I would like you to have, to remember Willem by.'

Clearly disgusted that such honour should be bestowed on his old rival, Ruyven left abruptly, shouldering his way through the mourners so bullishly that they staggered and spilled their wine. Chaloner gazed at the biscuit in his hand. It was embossed with Hanse's family arms, as was the custom on such occasions, and he could not bring himself to eat it. He pushed it in his pocket, along with the ring, hoping no one would see and assume he was like Downing, storing treats for later.

'Ignore Ruyven,' said Jacoba, misunderstanding the reason for his lack of appetite. 'He is distressed, and does not mean to be rude.'

'It does not matter.' Chaloner looked up as someone approached. It was Bulteel.

'Are you the widow?' asked Bulteel baldly. 'Then I have a message for you: Clarendon sends his congratulations ... I mean his *condolences* on your tragic loss, and says that he hopes you will not blame England for the fact that Hanse was drowned and left naked on the banks of the Thames.'

While Chaloner gaped at the tactless choice of words, Bulteel took Jacoba's hand and started to bow, but someone jostled him, and he only retained his balance by hauling on her arm. She staggered, and Chaloner was obliged to catch her before she fell. She started to acknowledge the Earl's message – although, mercifully, her poor English meant she had not understood most of it – but Bulteel turned and fled with obvious relief. Jacoba stared after him in astonishment.

'What a curious little man!'

'This is a sad day,' said Kun, arriving at Jacoba's side with Zas at his heels, and saving Chaloner from the need to reply. 'I already miss Hanse. I found myself thinking to ask his opinion about a treaty I read this morning, and it will be a long time before I am used to his absence.'

'Have you found his killer yet?' asked Zas. His bright little eyes were everywhere as he spoke, and Chaloner had the sense that he was a man who missed nothing – that he was quite capable of holding a conversation with one set of people, while watching the interactions between others. He was paying especially close attention to Killigrew and Judith. Chaloner wondered why.

'Not yet.'

'You will,' said Kun, patting Chaloner's shoulder encouragingly, although it was clear from his eyes that he was disappointed. 'And if there is anything we can do to help, then do not hesitate to ask. We are all eager for this villain to be brought to justice.'

Jacoba began to talk about the book her husband had been writing on stockings, asking Kun and Zas whether they might be prepared to finish it. Leaving them fabricating diplomatically worded excuses, Chaloner made for the door, feeling he had already done more than his duty.

De Buat was standing outside, smoking his pipe away from the bustle.

'Oetje will be buried later today,' he said. 'Although I will be the only mourner. Incidentally, I re-examined her *and* Hanse, and I believe that the poison that killed them was not administered in food or drink. It may have been on a sharp point that was jabbed into their skin.'

'But there were blisters in their mouths. Surely, that means they swallowed something?'

'Not necessarily. I found blisters in their eyes, too, and when I opened Oetje up, her liver was—'

'Stop,' said Chaloner uneasily. 'I am not sure it is legal for foreign *medici* to conduct anatomies in London. I do not want to hear any more.'

'Her liver showed a lot of damage,' de Buat pressed on. 'And, had Heer van Goch given me permission, I am sure I would have found the same in Hanse. It was a particularly nasty substance, and would not have given them easy deaths. Whoever did this is more than a killer. He is a brute who cares nothing for the sufferings of his victims.'

Chaloner returned to White Hall, where he spent the rest of the day and all evening listening for rumours about the Sinon Plot, Hanse's murder, the Earl's missing papers and the blackmailer. He was a silent shadow in doorways and corridors that no one noticed, but although he lingered in the palace until well past midnight, his efforts went largely unrewarded.

He learned that Cromwell was indeed suspected of opening the royal tombs in Westminster Abbey, and there was a plan afoot to remove his rotting head from outside Westminster Hall, lest it actually belonged to someone else. Chaloner smiled, thinking Thurloe would be pleased: it was not easy for him, seeing the remains of his old friend treated in so barbaric a fashion.

He also learned that Downing had been making a nuisance of himself among the royal seamstresses, and that most people thought Hanse was guilty of making off with the Earl's papers. But it was all based on gossip, not fact, and he decided to give up his eavesdropping when the servants went home and White Hall was left to courtiers, who were even less well informed than their minions.

As he walked towards the gate, he saw that a private party was beginning in Lady Castlemaine's apartments. Her windows were open, and a lot of manly laughter was wafting out. White Hall's pitch torches illuminated a number of familiar faces making their way towards it – Buckingham and his cronies, who attended any event likely to turn debauched, and the foolish Lady Muskerry, whose services in the bedchamber were likely to be in demand later. Nisbett was there in an official capacity, welcoming guests and repelling anyone he deemed unsuitable.

Chaloner happened to glance to his left as he passed, and saw someone else he recognised, too, although it was the last person he would have expected to see there. Hannah was slinking towards the entrance, Bates at her side. Curious to know what they were doing, Chaloner stepped out of the shadows to intercept them. Hannah did not look pleased to see him and, sensing her irritation, Bates went to hover in a nearby doorway, tactfully out of earshot.

'You went to Hanse's funeral without me,' she said accusingly. 'After you promised to let me go.'

214

'I did not promise,' he said tiredly. 'It was a dismal affair, anyway – a dozen mourners, and a lot of soldiers nearby, ready to repel attacks by hostile Londoners.'

'You mean it was dangerous?' she demanded.

'It did not feel entirely safe. And it was certainly no place for you.'

'Did you attend the ceremonies in the Savoy afterwards? And think very carefully before you answer, Thomas, because Judith Killigrew was there, and I have been talking to her.'

Chaloner felt overwhelmed by the interrogation. Was this how people felt when *he* was asking them questions? 'Briefly, yes.'

Hannah's lips compressed into an angry line. 'Were there cakes and gifts?'

Chaloner handed her the biscuit and the ring, then wished he had not. The value of jewellery distributed at funerals expressed two things: the state of the deceased's wealth, and how close he had been to the recipient – the more expensive the item, the more intimate the association. The ring Jacoba had pressed on Chaloner was a costly thing of gold, and Hannah's eyes narrowed.

'This is an oddly generous gift for a passing acquaintance. Why is—'

'What are you doing here?' he interrupted, cutting off her offensive with one of his own. 'Do not tell me you plan on joining Lady Castlemaine's games?'

'I am, actually,' replied Hannah coolly. 'But since you are here, perhaps you will give me some advice. You are better at this kind of thing than I.'

'What kind of thing?' he asked suspiciously.

Hannah beckoned to Bates, who approached unhappily, shuffling his feet and looking for all the world as if he wished he were somewhere else. Chaloner knew exactly how he felt. 'Explain it to him, Charles,' she ordered.

'As you know, Kicke has taken a liking to my wife,' obliged Bates miserably. 'Well, more than a liking, if you want the truth . . .'

'And we suspect his wooing campaign has finally won Ann over,' elaborated Hannah. 'So we are going to slip into the Lady's soiree, to see if it is true.'

'Ann is already there, you see,' blurted Bates, close to tears. 'One of the Lady's grooms came to fetch her, saying the order to attend came from the hostess herself. But I believe it was all arranged by Kicke, and that the Countess of Castlemaine has nothing to do with it.'

'How do you plan on getting in?' asked Chaloner. 'Nisbett is guarding the door.'

'Charles will distract him while I slip past,' explained Hannah. She swallowed hard. These were desperate measures, and ones with which she was not entirely comfortable, although Chaloner admired both her determination and her loyalty towards an old friend. 'But now you are here, perhaps you can think of a better idea.'

'Go home,' said Chaloner, not liking the notion of her coming into contact with Nisbett – which she would, because the chances of her sidling past him undetected were negligible. 'I will do it.'

It was a measure of Hannah's relief that she did not argue. 'Thank you. Ann is wearing pale yellow skirts and a blue bodice. But all we want to know is whether our concerns are justified. Do not tackle Kicke, especially if Nisbett is with him. I do not want you hurt.'

'No,' agreed Bates miserably. 'Money is not worth a life.'

'He is being blackmailed,' explained Hannah, although she had already told Chaloner the tale. 'Some greedy villain wants fifty pounds from him.'

'In return, he will keep his silence over the fact that I am a cuckold and my wife is a whore.' Bates whispered the last word; it was painful to him. 'But Ann is *not* wanton. Just weak.'

'But if she cavorts with Kicke at this soiree, there will be no need to pay the extortionist,' Chaloner pointed out. 'Everyone will know what is happening anyway.'

Bates winced. 'Kicke genuinely admires her, and will not want her reputation sullied. In other words, he will not seduce her in front of witnesses. But I need to know how far they . . . whether the blackmailer is telling the truth about . . .'

It was all very sordid, and Chaloner wished Hannah had not let herself become involved. 'Take my wife home,' he said to Bates. 'I will contact you in the morning.'

When they had gone, Chaloner turned his attention to the sumptuous suite occupied by the King's mistress. Entering via the main door was out of the question, because Nisbett was taking his duties seriously. But it did not take him long to locate a loose window shutter, and then it was only a matter of moments before he was inside the building, where the boisterous laughter, loud music and womanly shrieks were all but deafening.

The Lady's home comprised six or seven large chambers on the upper floor. Every one was full of revellers, although the corridor that connected them was relatively empty. It contained several life-sized statues of Greek gods on heavy marble plinths, so Chaloner stepped behind Zeus, and settled down to wait.

217

Eventually, a woman in blue and yellow appeared, and tiptoed towards a window that was hung with long, thick curtains. She pretended to be gazing into the courtyard below when Buckingham tottered past, a giggling courtesan on each arm. When he had gone, she scanned the hallway carefully, then ducked quickly behind the draperies.

A quarter of an hour passed before Kicke arrived. He loitered in the hallway for several minutes, ostensibly admiring the artwork, then slunk towards the woman's hiding place. There was a soft squeal of delight when he disappeared behind the material, followed by low voices as the couple conversed. Then there was silence, although the bottom of the curtain began to swing in a suspiciously regular motion. It stopped eventually, and there was more muttering. After a while, Kicke poked out his head, peered around cautiously, and ushered her out.

Chaloner was not surprised to find Bates waiting anxiously for him when he finally made his escape.

'I took Hannah home,' he said. There was an agonised expression on his face, and when he removed his copper wig, he looked tired, old and ugly, a marked contrast to his vibrantly handsome rival. 'What did you learn?'

'Do not pay the money,' advised Chaloner kindly. 'Kicke and Ann were careful, but that sort of thing cannot be kept quiet for long. You will impoverish yourself for nothing.'

'I have made arrangements for us to leave London next week, so I *will* give him what he wants. He will keep his silence, and people will remember us as a happy couple, not as a cuckold and a . . .'

'Does Ann know of these plans?' asked Chaloner, suspecting she might decline to go.

'I will tell her tonight,' said Bates unsteadily. 'When I also tell her that she has been seen frolicking with Kicke, and will lose her reputation unless immediate steps are taken to repair the damage. Thank you for your help, Chaloner. And my offer of documents to incriminate Kicke still stands, but do not leave it too long to ask.'

Chaloner had had enough of White Hall and its sordid goings-on. He started to walk home, but met Wiseman by the Court Gate, a vast, unsettling figure in his flowing crimson robe.

'The King has wind again,' he confided in a booming voice. 'He should have laid off the onions, as I advised. And his summons is a damned nuisance, because there are parlour games at the club tonight, and I was enjoying myself.'

'You and Temperance are friends again, then?'

Wiseman grinned. 'Thanks to you. She sent me a note, inviting me to visit, and we made up for our quarrel in ways that only an experienced surgeon and a brothel-keeper could devise.'

Chaloner managed to stop himself asking for details. 'You should not bray remarks about the King's digestion. It is asking to be dismissed.'

Wiseman snorted his disdain for the advice. 'His Majesty would not deprive himself of the best surgeon in London – nay, in England and perhaps the world. He knows quality when he sees it. He is an observant man.'

'Unlike you,' retorted Chaloner, deciding to tackle the subject he had postponed the day before. 'You told me Hanse had drowned, but the cause of his death was poisoning.'

'I suppose you refer to the blisters in his eyes and

mouth. Yes, he certainly came into contact with a toxic substance before he died. But the actual cause of death *was* drowning. There was froth in his lungs, and you do not get that when a corpse goes in a river – the water needs to be inhaled, you see. *Ergo*, although Hanse *was* poisoned, it is not what killed him.'

Chaloner sighed in exasperation. 'And it did not occur to you to tell me all this?'

'I did not want to upset you. Kersey told me that Hanse was your friend.'

Chaloner was appalled. 'You withheld vital information in an effort to be kind?'

'I did,' replied Wiseman, unrepentant. 'It is one thing to probe the grisly deaths of strangers, but another altogether to do it with folk you know. For example, I did not like anatomising my brother-in-law. It made me feel quite disconcerted.'

Chaloner took an involuntary step away. Conversations with Wiseman were often unsettling. 'You sliced out the entrails of a kinsman?'

'My wife's sibling,' nodded Wiseman. 'He was a lunatic, too, and also a resident of Bedlam. It was decided to dissect him, to see whether we could learn anything about the nature of insanity.'

'And did you?'

'Not really. His brain looked the same as every other one I have excised. I keep it in a bottle on the shelf in my study, and I shall show it to you when you are my lodger.'

'No!' exclaimed Chaloner in revulsion, backing away farther. 'I will find other accommodation, thank you. I do not want to share a house with your relatives' body parts.'

'Only his brain. And it is an item of scientific interest. But I cannot stand here chatting with you when the King needs relief. Are you still coming to Newgate with me tomorrow?'

Chaloner nodded. 'And if you need to introduce me, say I am called John Crane.' Then if word did get back to Williamson that someone had interviewed the men he had incarcerated for life, the bird name might throw him off the scent.

'Until the morning, then,' said Wiseman. 'Eight o'clock sharp.'

When Wiseman had gone, Chaloner realised he had forgotten to ask about the surgeon with the birth-marked neck who had met Hanse in the Sun. What was wrong with him, that he could not remember to put his questions? Was he losing his touch? He started to run after Wiseman, but the man had already entered the royal apartments. Chaloner waited a while, but soon saw he was wasting his time: Wiseman might be with the King for hours, and there was nothing he could do about the matter that night anyway. He decided to leave it until the following day.

He was tired when he reached Tothill Street, but not so weary that he did not notice someone moving in the shadows opposite his house. He froze, and slipped into an alley to watch. It did not take him long to see that his home was under surveillance. But by whom, and why?

He eased forward, aiming to lay hold of the fellow and demand some answers, but the ground was crisp with withered leaves, and a stealthy approach was impossible, even for him. The shadow heard him coming and fled. Chaloner followed, but the night was dark and his quarry had too great a start. Moreover, there was a veritable labyrinth of places to hide. He prowled the streets for some time afterwards, but was too tired to be effective, and eventually gave up. He entered his house, and lay fully clothed on the bed, his senses on high alert even as he slept.

A curious sound snapped him awake the following day, and he was off the bed with a dagger in his hand before he was fully cognisant. It was just past dawn, and the streets were full of grey shadows. The roaring grew louder.

'It is a hailstorm, Thomas,' said Hannah crossly, jostled awake by his sudden movement.

Muttering an apology, he went to check that the strands of thread he had left on the stairs were still in place. They were, telling him that no one had passed. As he stared at them, he knew it was time to find a bolthole, because if he felt unsafe enough to set traps for intruders, then he had no business staying with Hannah. He would never forgive himself if anything were to happen to her.

'What are you doing?' she demanded.

'Looking for leaks,' lied Chaloner, as the thunder of hail on the roof intensified.

'Our roof does not leak, as you would know if you ever spent any time here.'

'I would have been home sooner, but you sent me on an errand,' he said defensively.

'You volunteered to help,' she shot back. She was rarely amiable first thing in the morning, something he had learned only after they were married. 'And you took a lot longer than I expected.'

'Did I wake you when I returned?' he asked, trying to sound conciliatory.

'I felt you flop beside me, all clammy and hot.' She

glanced upwards, as the hail came down harder than ever. 'Did you hear that yesterday's storm was so violent it broke the cupola in the King's Theatre? It caused a terrible panic as glass showered down on the audience below. It is a good thing I did not allow you to take me *there* when you suggested it.'

'The street-preachers claim it was a sign that God does not approve of the stage,' said Chaloner, recalling what had been whispered in White Hall the night before. 'But the Court maintains that God just does not like Ben Jonson, and wants the actors to perform something else.'

This coaxed a reluctant smile. 'Buckingham put that tale about. He is a great one for fun. And it was good to have something to laugh about, because I had a terrible day yesterday. There were Charles and Daniel upset, you being awkward about Hanse's funeral, and on top of all that, someone sent the Queen some baby clothes. She was distraught, and I spent hours calming her.'

Chaloner was puzzled. 'Is she with child at last, then?'

'It was a prank – if such an act of malice can be called such. Do you know there are tales that she made herself barren deliberately, as part of a Catholic plot to deprive England of its heir?'

Chaloner nodded. It was common street gossip.

Hannah bit her lip and stared at the bedcovers. 'I am assuming, from your ominous silence on the matter, that Kicke *did* seduce Ann last night. That vile scoundrel! If I were a man, I would call him out and put a musket ball through his black heart.'

'Most people duel with swords or handguns,' Chaloner said absently. 'Not muskets.'

Hannah regarded him oddly. 'I shall not ask how you come to be party to such information. Sometimes, you are a stranger to me, Thomas, and I wonder whether I know you at all.'

While she continued in this vein, Chaloner donned a thin vest – a collarless tunic with skirts to the knees, gathered at the waist by a belt – and an old pair of breeches. Both had seen better days, but were suitable apparel for what he planned to do that day. Hannah stopped berating him to stare.

'You cannot go out dressed like that! You will never get past the Court Gate.'

'I am not going to White Hall today.' He saw her eyebrows draw together in annoyance at the enigmatic answer, and hastened to elaborate. 'I am meeting Wiseman.'

The scowl lifted. For reasons Chaloner failed to understand, she liked the bombastic surgeon. Then the dark expression returned. 'I hope you are not leading him into anything dangerous.'

'He will be doing the leading,' Chaloner assured her. 'But the current case *is* transpiring to be troubling, and it might be better if I do not come home until it is resolved. It will be safer for you, because I could not bear it if . . .'

'If what?' asked Hannah, when he trailed off. 'It is perfectly all right to tell your wife that you harbour protective feelings towards her, you know. I appreciate the fact that you deplore admitting to anything that vaguely resembles a human emotion, but we *are* married.'

'I harbour protective feelings towards you,' mumbled Chaloner uncomfortably.

Hannah started to laugh. 'Very romantic! But it is a start, and who knows? Maybe one day, you might even manage to say you love me. I assume you do, but I have never had it confirmed.'

224

'Oh,' said Chaloner. He took a deep breath to oblige. And when he had made his long-overdue declaration of affection, he would tell her about Jacoba. 'I—'

But a sudden increase in volume from the hail made further conversation impossible. Then there was a crack as a windowpane broke. By the time he had replaced it with a panel of wood, all talk of love and other unsettling subjects had been forgotten. By him, at least.

'When will I see you again?' asked Hannah, as he made for the door. 'I know we are hardly star-struck youngsters in the throes of first love, but we are still newly-weds, and I am not happy to hear that you intend to disappear for an undisclosed period of time. I shall miss you.'

'Is there a friend you can stay with for a while?' He saw her horrified expression. 'I am probably worrying over nothing, but I do not like the notion of you being here alone.'

'I have been here alone for two years,' Hannah pointed out. 'While you have lived here on a permanent basis for less than three weeks. And who am I supposed to ask for refuge? Buckingham? I can imagine what the Court gossips would make of that!'

The sun was bathing London in a pale gold light when Chaloner began the long trudge from Tothill Street to the complex of streets near Pye Corner, where Newgate Gaol was located. But it was not yet six o'clock, and far too early to meet Wiseman, so he stopped at the Rainbow Coffee House.

'What news?' called James Farr. He had just burned his beans, and the place was thick with brown smoke. It covered everything in an oily pall, and Chaloner started to cough.

'The cupola in the King's Theatre cracked during a hailstorm,' he said, when he had caught his breath. No one looked impressed.

'We already knew that,' said Farr disdainfully. 'But here comes Rector Thompson. Perhaps he can do better. What news, Thompson?'

'The Dutch have just put sixty ships to sea,' replied Thompson, going to sit next to Chaloner. 'What are they thinking? We shall have no peace if they make that sort of gesture.'

'We can beat them,' declared Stedman dismissively. 'One of our ships is worth ten of theirs, and one of our sailors is worth fifty Dutchmen.'

There was a patriotic cheer from the dozen or so men who had gathered for an early-morning dose of coffee and conversation.

'Actually,' said Chaloner, recalling what he had heard at White Hall the previous night, and hoping to alleviate Thompson's concerns, 'they put *forty* vessels to sea, and of those, only fifteen are warships, which are needed to protect the rest of the fleet from . . . from pirates.'

He stopped himself from saying 'English ships', on the grounds that it was likely to lead to accusations of disloyalty. But he wished he had not spoken when Stedman regarded him warily.

'You are always defending the cheese-eaters. Why? Are you secretly on their side?'

'Do not speak nonsense, man!' chided Thompson. 'He is reporting a fact, as Farr asked him to do when he requested news.'

'Well, some facts are more acceptable than others,' sniffed Stedman. 'Or are you suggesting we greet all intelligence with equal enthusiasm? That smacks of despotism, such as we had when the tyrant Cromwell was in power.'

'Facts are facts,' argued Thompson. 'Regardless of what *you* think of them. The disciples did not appreciate some of the Lord Jesus's teachings concerning the Holy Spirit, but that did not give them the right to tell him to talk about something else.'

Stedman was silent, as were most sane men once the Holy Trinity had entered the equation. Chaloner took a copy of *The Intelligencer*, and pretended to be engrossed in an advertisement for a paste that could repair brown and broken teeth, to deter the printer from attempting to resume the discussion concerning his views on the Dutch. Then he read about the plague that still raged in Amsterdam, which made him think of Aletta. To take his mind off her, he asked Thompson whether he knew of any rooms for rent in the area.

'I thought you were just married,' said Stedman nosily. 'Is your union in difficulties already?'

'Hailstones damaged our roof,' lied Chaloner.

'There is nothing available that I know of,' said Thompson apologetically. 'The weather is causing crops to fail in the country, you see, so people are flocking to London for work, and living quarters are in short supply. But if you are desperate, you may lodge with me for a few days.'

Chaloner took him to one side. 'Will you take my wife instead? I am . . . in a little trouble, and I do not want her to stay at home.'

Thompson regarded him in alarm. 'You have not done anything illegal—'

'No!' Chaloner thought fast. 'I helped expose two

thieves at White Hall, and they are angry with me. I am worried that they may strike at me through Hannah.'

'Kicke and Nisbett?' asked Thompson. 'Their arrest was your doing? In that case, of course you may bring her. I detest that pair almost as much as I detest their erstwhile master, Sir George Downing. And my wife will enjoy Hannah's company. But that does not really help *you*, does it?'

'Actually, it does,' said Chaloner relieved and grateful. 'It helps enormously.'

When Chaloner left the Rainbow, it was late enough that the first rush of traffic had eased. The street vendors were already at their pitches, and he stopped to buy some early strawberries that had been picked from the fields near Islington. They were still slightly yellow, and could have been left to ripen a little longer, but they were the first he had eaten that year, and he supposed the unseasonably hot weather was good for something at least.

He was just crossing the filthy smear of the River Fleet, so deprived of water that it was little more than a grey trickle between two slopes of festering mud, when he saw someone he recognised. It was Sir William Compton, riding down Ludgate Hill with several soldiers in his wake. He was clad in a fine but plain uniform, which included a pair of very white gloves. He reined in when he spotted Chaloner.

'I am glad I did not heed Wiseman's advice,' he said grimly. 'He would have sawn off my head, when all I needed was a tonic and a good night's sleep. As you see, I am quite recovered.'

'I will tell him he made a mistake when I next see him,' offered Chaloner.

'Please do not!' exclaimed Compton, shuddering. 'He is the kind of fellow who would wreak revenge in ways only he knows how, and Clarendon tells me that you are indispensable.'

'He does?' asked Chaloner doubtfully. The Earl never gave *him* that impression. Indeed, most of the time he felt like an interloper, tolerated only because there was unpleasant work to be done.

'All the time,' averred Compton. 'Indeed, I am thinking of poaching you because, as Master of Ordnance, I can always use a good man. You will not be surprised to learn that large caches of weapons attract the attentions of some very dubious characters, and there are always plots to steal from me. If he ever dismisses you, come to me first.'

Chaloner smiled. 'Thank you.'

Compton took a deep breath of air, then gagged. 'Lord, this city reeks when the sun is on it. It is almost certainly an omen of evil to come. I know people are always saying that – about inclement weather, strange clouds, odd tides and collapsing buildings – but this is different.'

'Is it?' asked Chaloner, failing to see how.

'I cannot shake this peculiar sense of impending doom. I am not normally assailed by such wild notions, but this feeling is very strong. How much longer will the heat-wave last, do you think?'

Chaloner shrugged. 'Who knows? But we will all complain when it turns cold and wet again.'

'Not me,' vowed Compton fervently. 'I have never liked high temperatures.'

Chaloner nodded at the gloves. 'You might feel more comfortable without those.'

Compton flexed his hands. 'These were a gift from the Dutchman who died – Hanse – and I am wearing them for him. It sounds ridiculous, but there you are.'

'You knew Hanse?' asked Chaloner, surprised. 'How?'

'Through the peace negotiations – I am often called upon to give my opinion on the various treaties and pacts that have been signed in the past. But to return to this torrid weather, you should see what excessive heat can do to the barrel of a cannon. Moreover, I am always afraid that it will make my stocks of gunpowder ignite.'

Chaloner was doubtful. 'It would need a flame. Powder does not explode of its own volition.'

'The sun is a flame,' argued Compton. 'A great, big powerful one that only God can control. I tell you, Chaloner, if this weather does not ameliorate, we shall all be in trouble.'

But Chaloner suspected Compton had not stopped to chat about the elements. 'Have you remembered any more about the business we discussed on Monday? Something that perhaps slipped your mind when you were unwell and Wiseman was hovering?'

Compton leaned down from his horse, glancing around furtively as he did so. 'No, but something has happened since then. Another one of my men is dead.'

Chaloner frowned. 'What do you mean by "another"?'

Compton looked around again, and lowered his voice to the point where he was difficult to hear. 'I took four good lads with me when I arrested the Sinon plotters – fine warriors, whom I trust with my life. I had word last night that Upton is dead. He fell in the river and drowned.'

Chaloner was not sure what he was being told. 'Are you saying someone pushed him?'

'I do not know what happened. But when I took the plotters into custody, one of them – Falcon – started to curse. I am not an impressionable man, and neither are my soldiers, but there was something about this fellow's words that frightened all of us. We discussed it afterwards.'

'What did he say?'

'That we would all die before the next full moon. I put it from my mind, and when Osborn and Oates were killed by a speeding carriage last week, I told myself it was just an accident. But now Upton is drowned . . . Well, there were five of us, and now there are two. Only Fairfax and I are left.'

'Fairfax?'

'No relation to the Parliamentarian general, I hasten to add. My Fairfax brought me the news about Upton last night. And I am not ashamed to say that it unnerved me.'

'Where is Fairfax now?' asked Chaloner, glancing at Compton's men, who were waiting patiently for their master to finish talking.

'I told him to stay with his sister in the Fleet Rookery. It is the haunt of killers, robbers and the resentful poor, but they look after their own. He will be safer there than with me.'

'You said the first two were killed by a speeding cart—'

'Yes – one that that did not stop, and that witnesses have failed to identify.'

'It may be coincidence.'

'May it? The Sinon Plot was thwarted at the eleventh hour, and its leader cursed me and my soldiers as he was committed to Newgate. And now, just three weeks later,

Osborn, Oates and Upton are dead. Even if Falcon's vile threats are not the cause, there is still something amiss.'

And there was Hanse, Chaloner thought but did not say. He had some connection to the Sinon Plot, and he was dead, too, as was the sinister Oetje. *And* Ibbot the hackney driver, who should have taken Hanse home.

'I know I have asked you this before,' began Chaloner, 'but did you ever discuss Sinon with anyone other than the Privy Council and Williamson? With Hanse, for example?'

Compton stared at him. 'Why would I share that sort of thing with a foreigner? A plan to make off with our crown jewels hardly shows my country in a favourable light!'

And with that, he nodded a farewell, and rode off, his men streaming behind him.

Chapter 7

Wiseman was waiting when Chaloner arrived at Newgate. He, too, was wearing old clothes, although they were still scarlet, even down to his shoes. He had also donned a leather apron, like the kind worn by fishmongers.

'You are late,' he growled. 'I said eight o'clock.'

The words were no more out of his mouth before the bells of nearby Christ Church began to chime, to announce the start of its eight o'clock service.

'They are late, too,' declared Wiseman belligerently. Then St Martin's and St Sepulchre's added their clangs to the clamour, and his glower deepened. 'In fact, the entire city is late. What is wrong with people? Can they not read a clock?'

Chaloner did not waste his breath arguing. He was looking at Newgate, trying to control a sudden queasiness. The gate itself was ancient, a great, crumbling monstrosity that crouched over the road like a carrion bird. It was five storeys tall, and was where the Keeper and his more wealthy prisoners were accommodated. Attached to it were a number of grim extensions, where the remainder of the inmates were housed. Bars filled every small, mean window, and white, desperate faces could be seen behind them. Chaloner shuddered, and it took every ounce of his self control not to turn around and run away.

'I brought you this,' said Wiseman, shoving an apron at him. 'And you had better carry my instruments, too, if I am to pass you off as my assistant. I have no idea why you are set on coming here – and nor do I want to know, should you think to furnish me with an explanation – but we had better at least *try* to look convincing. I do not want to be accused of anything untoward.'

'You mean something untoward like offering to saw the head from a man you said was dying, but who was hale and hearty this morning?' asked Chaloner.

Wiseman raised his eyebrows. 'Compton survived? Well, there is a surprise! I was certain he was a dead man. Did you see him yourself? In person?'

'Just a few moments ago, and we held a perfectly rational discussion.'

Wiseman blew out his cheeks. 'Well, well! Wonders never cease.'

Chaloner remembered that he was supposed to ask Wiseman about the surgeon who had met Hanse, and in an effort to delay entering Newgate, he repeated the description of the elderly man with the birth-stain on his neck.

'Ned Molins,' replied Wiseman promptly. 'He was once called to tend Cromwell. As a medical man, he had no choice but to oblige. But as a Royalist, he made his objections known by refusing to take payment. Other than a drink.'

'So he cured Parliamentarians for nothing, but charged Cavaliers?' asked Chaloner, amused. 'Is that how he showed his allegiance to the Crown? I think there was something awry with his reasoning!'

Wiseman waved a dismissive hand. 'I applauded his courage in making a stand. And Cromwell was lucky his servants did not summon *me*, because *I* would have given the old scoundrel something to remember. And it would not have been a pleasant memory, either.'

'Which memories of you are?' muttered Chaloner, tying the apron around his middle. It was stiff with something he assumed was dried blood, and had a rank, rotten smell.

'Molins had the last word, though,' Wiseman went on, grinning nastily. 'He insisted that Cromwell be turned upside-down three times, to ensure the medicine was working. But afterwards, he told me that he had done to Cromwell what Cromwell was doing to our country.'

'He sounds quite a character,' said Chaloner flatly.

'Oh, yes! A man of strong opinions and rigid principles. What prompts your interest in him?'

'Clarendon's business,' replied Chaloner vaguely.

'Well, in that case, I shall take you to meet him myself. It will give me something to look forward to, because I doubt I shall enjoy what we are going to do *here* for the next couple of hours.'

'No?' asked Chaloner nervously. If it was something to disconcert the surgeon, then he was sure he would not fare any better. 'Why? What do you intend, exactly?'

'There has been a lot of gaol-fever recently, and while I am always pleased with new corpses to anatomise, there is a limit to the number I can accommodate. I mentioned the matter to the King, and he ordered me to look into it. So, after several preliminary discussions with Keeper

Sligo, I begin my inspection proper today. And I anticipate some very distressing sights.'

'Oh,' said Chaloner, swallowing hard.

'Will you stay with me, or am I to invent an excuse that will let you wander off alone? I would not recommend the latter – you may not find your way out again.' Wiseman roared with laughter, although Chaloner did not find the notion amusing.

'I need to find a cell in which three men have been incarcerated,' he said, when the surgeon had his mirth under control. 'Their names are Swan, Swallow and Falcon.'

Wiseman raised his eyebrows. 'Aliases?'

'Apparently not. They are said to be in a part of the prison that is closed to visitors.'

'That will be the ward they call Calais, where there are two layers of dungeons, one under the other. Prisoners only ever leave there in a coffin, so I have decided to exclude it from my reforms – there is no point in making improvements for people who are doomed anyway. It would be unethical to prolong *their* misery.'

Chaloner felt his resolve begin to crumble. 'I have to visit it,' he heard himself say.

Wiseman shrugged. 'Then I shall order you there to make an inspection on my behalf. Keeper Sligo will make a fuss, but I have the ear of the King, so I can force him to comply.'

Without another word, he led the way to Newgate's great iron-studded door and hammered on it. His fist caused hollow booms to echo in a way that was decidedly sinister, and it was all Chaloner could do to prevent himself from bolting. Then the gate opened, and a warden indicated that the surgeon and his assistant were to enter. It closed behind them with a resounding clang.

The warden who answered the gate was an obese, grim-faced man with rotten teeth that might have been responsible for his surly temper. He spat on the floor as Wiseman marched past him, and made an obscene gesture at his back. Chaloner followed more slowly, feeling his heart begin to pound and sweat break out all over his body. How much longer would his experiences in the French prison torment him? Or was he destined to be haunted by them for the rest of his life?

'We got better things to do than fuss over inmates,' the warden muttered, securing the door with one of the biggest keys Chaloner had ever seen. 'Keeper Sligo had us scrubbing all day yesterday. You could eat your dinner in here now.'

'I am glad to hear it,' retorted Wiseman, 'given that the prisoners are obliged to do just that.'

The entrance hall stank, although it was clear that an effort had been made to tidy up – rotten straw, rags and discarded food had been swept into a corner, where they festered gently. Parts of the pile undulated, and Chaloner looked away when he realised it was full of rats.

Sligo was waiting for them. He was a thin, cadaverous man, whose fiery red nose stood out like a beacon against his white face. The stench of wine on his breath made Chaloner recoil.

'I have been looking forward to your visit, Surgeon Wiseman,' the Keeper gushed. 'Perhaps you will join me for a glass of claret before you—'

'No,' interrupted Wiseman. 'There is too much to do. So, let us begin. My assistant, John Crane, will inspect

Calais, while I concentrate on the parts you call Tangier and the Press Yard.'

'Calais?' echoed Sligo, horrified. 'He cannot go down there! No one can. It is off-limits to everyone except Mr Williamson. And I dare not disobey *his* orders, because . . . well, I cannot.'

'In other words, he has a hold over you,' said Wiseman with exaggerated weariness.

'It is not a *hold*,' objected Sligo. 'It is an arrangement. I set aside a part of the prison for his exclusive use, and he does not meddle in the way I run the rest of it.'

'He overlooks your corruption,' surmised Wiseman. 'Of which he doubtless has a good deal of evidence. No, do not deny it. I am not a fool. What I *am*, however, is a close friend of the King. You may find yourself incarcerated in Calais yourself, if you do not cooperate with me.'

'I object most strenuously,' bleated Sligo. 'I have given you permission to pry everywhere else, so why can you not be content with that? Calais is closed.'

'Not to me. The King said I was to have unlimited access.' Wiseman turned to Chaloner. 'Calais is in that direction, and the sooner you start, the sooner we can finish.'

'I had better go with him,' said Sligo sullenly, seeing he was defeated. 'To unlock the doors and let him in. And out again, I suppose.'

Wiseman strode away, indicating with a snap of imperious fingers that the fat warden was to follow. When the man demurred, Wiseman hauled him along as if he were no more substantial than feathers, and Chaloner was reminded yet again that the surgeon was a very powerful man.

'Perhaps you and I can come to an arrangement, Mr

Crane,' said Sligo, smiling slyly once the surgeon had gone. 'Would five shillings suffice to see you write your report in my office?'

'Five shillings will see you charged with bribery,' retorted Chaloner tartly. 'I have my orders.'

Sligo glared at him. 'Very well, but do not blame me if the experience plagues your dreams. And you cannot talk to any of the inmates, either. I must have your word.'

'What would I have to say to such people?' asked Chaloner, deftly avoiding the condition.

With a final glower, Sligo led the way through a series of corridors, each marked by a set of double-locked doors. As they went deeper into the prison, Chaloner's heart pounded harder, and he could not take breaths deep enough to fill his lungs.

He was not unduly affected by the stench of brimming sewage buckets, the putrid straw that carpeted the floor, or even the unwashed, parasite-ridden prisoners, because he had been ready for those. What disturbed him was the crushing sense of helplessness and despair that seemed to ooze from the very walls of such places. It sapped his courage and filled him with a fear so dark that it threatened to overwhelm him. He struggled to fight it off, steadying himself with one hand on the wall when his legs threatened to fail him.

After what felt like an age, Sligo opened a door to reveal a flight of steps. There was a lamp at the bottom, and the fetid atmosphere that wafted upwards made even the Keeper gag.

'Calais,' he said, sleeve over his mouth and nose. 'Are you ready?'

When a prisoner in a nearby cell released a scream of mad laughter, Chaloner almost leapt out of his skin. Why was he putting himself through this ordeal? Was it really so important to learn what Hanse had known about the Sinon Plot? Why not leave it at the fact that Hanse, like Compton, had probably overheard the culprits planning their crime in a tavern? But Chaloner knew he would have no peace if he did not follow through with it – not from the Earl, not from Jacoba or van Goch, and not from himself, either. He took one step downwards, and then another, and eventually he reached the bottom, where Sligo was waiting impatiently.

'Here it is,' the Keeper said, still holding his sleeve over his nose. 'Satisfied?'

Chaloner looked around to see he was in a long hallway with a dozen doors off it, each with a board on which had been chalked a name. The floor was soft with filth, and his feet squelched as he forced himself to walk along it. The only ventilation – and light – came from a tiny window that was thick with cobwebs.

'Can we go now?' asked Sligo peevishly, when Chaloner had read all the names and determined that the Sinon Plot conspirators were not among them. He shivered. 'It is cold down here.'

'No,' said Chaloner, ignoring the instincts that clamoured at him to race back up the steps as fast as his legs would carry him. 'There is another level below this one, and I need to see that, too.'

Sligo regarded him silently, then without a word led the way to a second set of steps. The stairway was icy and damp, and the air felt as though it had not been changed since the place was built. Somewhere, a man was crying, babbling in a way that said his wits had gone.

'Rebel,' said Sligo, as if by explanation. 'Take the lamp. I will wait here.'

240

'You are not coming?' asked Chaloner uneasily.

Sligo shook his head. 'Not down there. A warden delivers food once a day – he opens a flap at the bottom of their doors and shoves it through – but other than that, we leave the place alone.'

Chaloner was horrified. 'But what if one of them is ill? Or dies?'

'There is nothing we can do about sickness. And when they die, we know, because they do not eat their food. We open the doors then, and remove the corpses.'

Chaloner took the lamp with a hand that shook, and began his descent. Twice he stopped, and it was only Sligo's irritable sighs that started him moving again. The stench of decay grew stronger with each step, and led him to wonder whether someone *had* died. Or perhaps it was the fact that Sligo had mentioned no facility for emptying slop buckets, and they were left to overflow until the prisoner perished from whatever foul diseases were carried within them.

He reached the bottom, and was faced with a low tunnel that ran in both directions. Doors were embedded in the walls, each with a sliding grille at its base. As on the level above, names had been chalked on a slate, and it did not take Chaloner long to find the one that said Swallow, Swan and Falcon. It was at the end farthest from the steps, and he knew Sligo would not be able to hear what he was doing. He knocked softly. Immediately, there was a scuffling sound.

'Swan?' he called. 'Swallow?'

There was an eerie laugh. 'They are gone. And Falcon flew away, like a bird. He escaped.'

'Then who are you?'

'I am Yarrow, from the room next door. But this one

241

is bigger, so I made a hole and helped myself. They will not be needing it. Falcon flew through the wall, and the other two are in Heaven.'

Chaloner returned to the stairs and called to Sligo. 'Your guests appear to be moving cells. You had better come down and check them.'

There was no reply, and for a moment, he thought he had been abandoned. He raced up the steps in a panic, only to find Sligo drinking from a bottle he had concealed inside his coat.

'I told you I was cold,' the Keeper said defensively. 'Have you finished? Can we go now?'

Chaloner repeated what he had said, watching as Sligo snatched some keys from a hook on a wall, and tore down the stairs in alarm. He followed, drawing his dagger as the Keeper unlocked the cell door. It swung open to reveal three people. One was sitting on his haunches, chewing a bone.

'Yarrow!' exclaimed Sligo, shocked. 'You should not be in here.'

A small hole in the wall explained how that had happened. The other two figures were huddled together on the floor, and for a moment, Chaloner did not understand what he was seeing. But then he turned away in revulsion. The heads of both had been burned away.

There was a room in Newgate that Wiseman had used to examine dead prisoners before. It was disconcertingly near the area where food was prepared, and Chaloner did not know which smell was worse – the corpses, or whatever rancid stew was being prepared for the prisoners' dinner.

'They died from inhaling smoke,' Wiseman said, after

doing something grisly with a knife that had Chaloner and Sligo looking studiously in the opposite direction. 'You can see soot here, if you care to look. It can only have entered their airways by them breathing it in.'

'We will take your word for it,' said Sligo shakily.

'There are no other injuries,' Wiseman went on. 'And no obvious incidence of disease. But where is Falcon? Unlike Yarrow, *I* do not believe he made his escape by flying through the wall.'

'I have no idea,' gulped Sligo. 'And I do not know how Swan and Swallow caught themselves alight, either, because we do not allow candles or lamps in Calais.'

Wiseman grimaced. 'Well, these two have been dead for some time – probably since soon after their arrival – which will certainly be in my report to His Majesty. It is not healthy to leave corpses lying around for weeks on end. You are lucky that my assistant struck up a discussion with Yarrow, or they might have lain undiscovered for years.'

'No!' objected Sligo. 'It would have been noticed!'

'Not if Yarrow was eating their food,' Chaloner pointed out.

'How can this have happened?' breathed Sligo, raising a bottle to his lips with a hand that shook. 'What will Williamson say? He will accuse me of ineptitude, but I run a tight ship. *And* I shall have to confess that I let you down there – a place where visitors are forbidden.'

'We will not tell him if you do not,' said Chaloner hopefully.

But Sligo shook his head. 'He will find out, so it is best to be honest.'

'You say visitors are barred from Calais,' said Wiseman. 'But one must have gone down there, because

243

how else would Falcon have escaped? Or is a gaoler responsible?'

'My men swear they know nothing about it,' said Sligo miserably.

'But?' asked Chaloner, sensing a caveat.

'But they do not get paid much, so few of them stay long. And no one questions a strange face.'

'I see,' said Wiseman. 'In other words, anyone can dress up as a guard and get inside?'

'Well, not *anyone*,' hedged Sligo. 'We challenge those who are flagrantly out of place.'

Wiseman regarded him very coldly. 'Some prisoners are here because they represent a serious threat to the public – killers, rapists and fanatical dissidents. But now we learn you do not have a secure hold on them. You should be ashamed of yourself!'

'We *do* have a secure hold on them!' cried Sligo, horrified by the accusation. '*They* do not have cunning associates who know how to break through our defences.'

'Why did Swan and Swallow allow themselves to be set alight?' mused Chaloner, more interested in what had happened than in berating Sligo. 'There is no evidence that they were restrained.'

Wiseman tapped his chin thoughtfully. 'You make a valid point. However, I detect the smell of oil on them.'

'They were doused in fuel to make them burn?' Chaloner felt slightly sick.

'I cannot imagine they went quietly,' said Wiseman.

'But why do it?' asked Chaloner, frustrated that what had looked to be a promising line of inquiry should be cut so brutally short. 'Why not rescue them with Falcon?'

'I know the answer to that,' said Sligo. 'One "guard" and one prisoner could deceive us, but not one "guard" and three prisoners. In other words, Swan and Swallow were sacrificed to allow Falcon – their leader – to go free.'

'Falcon must be very ruthless,' said Wiseman, 'to subject his friends to such a terrible fate.'

'Oh, he is horrible,' agreed Sligo. 'He cursed us when he was first brought here, and frightened some of my guards so much that they refused to go down there to feed him. And they are not easily intimidated.'

Chaloner recalled what Compton had said about Falcon's curses, and the odd deaths of his men. He began to wonder whether he had been told the entire truth about the Sinon Plot, and it occurred to him that it might involve something a lot more sinister than the theft of a few jewels.

'So now you have two more murders to investigate,' said Wiseman, as he and Chaloner left Newgate some time later. 'Along with the escape of a dangerous prisoner. And Falcon *is* dangerous, or he would not have been put in Calais.'

'Two more deaths associated with Sinon,' said Chaloner, more to himself than the surgeon. 'There are eight now: Hanse and possibly Oetje and Ibbot, Compton's three soldiers, and Swan and Swallow. Assuming the dead men in Calais *are* Swan and Swallow, of course. With their faces burned away, Sligo could not be sure.'

'No, but I can,' said Wiseman. He grinned at Chaloner's surprise. 'There was a detailed physical description of them in the pile of papers he left unattended when he went to refill his bottle. You were interviewing the guards, so I took the opportunity to flick through them.'

245

Chaloner smiled. 'Perhaps you should be the Lord Chancellor's spy.'

'I prefer surgery, thank you – it is not quite so sordid. But Swan had a mole on his knee, and Swallow had a scar on his forearm. I checked: they are the same men.'

'What about Falcon?' asked Chaloner. 'What description was given of him?'

Wiseman frowned. 'Now there is a curious thing: one was not included. Apparently, he possesses the ability to change his appearance, so the papers said there was no point.'

'Did these documents tell you anything else?'

'Just that these three prisoners had been planning to steal the crown jewels. I did hear a rumour that someone intended to try, but I did not believe it. It seems such an unpatriotic thing to do.'

'I spoke to the other Calais prisoners while you and Sligo retrieved the bodies,' said Chaloner. 'Swan and Swallow were killed the day after they were brought to Newgate – their screams were heard. The inmates tried to tell the warden who brought their food, but he would not listen.'

'The decomposition of the bodies confirms their claim,' said Wiseman pompously. 'Swan and Swallow have been mouldering for at least two weeks. And that means Falcon spent no more than a day in Calais before he was rescued.'

Chaloner nodded. Did it mean Compton was right to think the deaths of his men could be laid at Falcon's door? If the felon had been at liberty for so long, then it was not inconceivable that he had plotted his revenge on the soldiers who had arrested him. Chaloner rubbed his chin. So, if Falcon had killed Compton's men, then was he responsible for the other deaths connected to the Sinon Plot, too – Hanse, Oetje and Ibbot? And if so, how was Chaloner to find him, when he was such a master of disguise that no description of him was possible?

'You are very white,' said Wiseman, after a while during which they walked in silence. 'However, I did warn you that a visit to Calais would be distressing, and so did Sligo. You have only yourself to blame if the jaunt upset you.'

Chaloner looked away. 'I have experienced worse,' he said quietly. 'Far worse.'

Wiseman regarded him thoughtfully for a moment, then released a gusty sigh. 'I said earlier that I did not want to know the nature of your business in Newgate, but I spoke over-hastily. I suspect you need my formidable wits to solve this case. So you may confide in me, if you like.'

Chaloner saw no problem in doing so, given that much of what he had learned was in the public domain anyway. 'Falcon, Swan and Swallow plotted an audacious robbery, but Compton overheard them. Williamson investigated, and when he had convinced himself that the threat was genuine, he ordered them arrested. Compton obliged, because Williamson's own men are unpopular.'

'I suppose they were incarcerated in Calais to keep the affair quiet,' surmised Wiseman. 'Although these stories have a way of seeping out, and this one was bandied around in White Hall.'

Chaloner nodded. 'But Williamson was wrong when he claimed Falcon had only two helpmeets. He must have had more, and one disguised himself as a warden and came to let him out.'

'I would not like to meet this Falcon,' said Wiseman soberly. 'The manner in which he chose to murder Swallow and Swan indicates a malice and depravity that is terrifying.'

'I still do not understand how he did it. They would have fought with all their might to avoid being doused in oil and set alight. How did Falcon and one "warden" subdue them?'

'Perhaps they agreed to the dousing because they were told it was part of a ruse that would let them escape. And then Falcon applied a flame before they could guess that he had no intention of taking them with him.'

Chaloner found his hands were unsteady, and felt the stink of the gaol had seeped into every pore in his body. He could even smell it over the stench of the Fleet River as they crossed the bridge at Ludgate, and he could taste it in his mouth.

'Will you take me to meet Molins now?' he asked, eager to forge on with the investigation so he could make an end of it.

But Wiseman shook his head. 'He broke his leg a week ago, but it festered and I was obliged to amputate. It was a lovely piece of work on my part, and I am confident of a complete recovery. But I stipulated no visitors until tomorrow, and I cannot break my own rules, not even for you.'

'How did he break his leg? Did he fall?'

'He says he was pushed, but I think he was probably drunk. Old Molins likes his wine, and the combination of claret and age must have rendered him unsteady on his feet.'

Hanse liked a drink, too. Could that be the answer? That Hanse had sought the company of men who did not chide him for overindulgence? Chaloner supposed he would find out the following day.

It had been some time since Chaloner had reported to the Earl – he had tried the previous day, but had been prevented by Daniel Cotton's confession and Hanse's funeral – so he decided he had better visit White Hall without delay. He went to Tothill Street to change his clothes first. Two men loitered at the end of the road, leaning against a wall as they smoked their pipes. Had they been detailed to put his house under surveillance, or were they just enjoying a bowl of tobacco? Chaloner ducked into the shadows cast by the Westminster Gatehouse and settled down to watch.

It was not long before they were joined by two others. They chatted briefly, then the first couple wandered off, leaving the second pair behind in a classic case of changing the guard. Chaloner was about to question them – he could tell they were just common hirelings, so would be no match for him – when he saw three more men at the far end of the street. He grimaced. They had been placed to catch him coming *or* going, and while he could manage two, five would be a challenge.

Who had ordered them there, and why? Williamson, because he was afraid Chaloner would ignore his orders and investigate the Sinon Plot anyway? Downing, Nisbett and Kicke because they bore him a grudge? Ruyven, because he wanted to know how Hanse's murder was being investigated? Or even Falcon, at large and probably loath for anyone to interfere in his business?

Chaloner cut down the lane that ran parallel to Tothill Street, and entered his house via the back door. Inside, the hairs he had draped across door handles had disappeared, and there were marks in the powder he had scattered below shelves and chimneys. He was relieved that Hannah would be staying with Rector Thompson from now on: the house was no longer safe for her.

There was a bucket of water in the scullery, and he felt considerably better once he had scoured the reek of Newgate from his skin and hair. He donned clean clothes, then gathered a few of Hannah's possessions – items he thought she might need, and some of sentimental value. After a moment's hesitation, he included a book of poetry that had belonged to Aletta. Apart from his viol – not something that could be slipped into a pocket – it was the only thing he owned that he would not like to lose. He left the way he had come, noting that guards still stood at the ends of the road.

Hannah was busy with the Queen when he arrived at White Hall. Van Goch had been invited to another official reception, this one at the Banqueting House, and she was helping Her Majesty to dress for it, so he went to Clarendon's offices instead. For the first time in an age, there were no fires burning in the hearth, and all the windows had been thrown open.

'He is complaining about the heat,' whispered Bulteel, emerging from his cupboard-like office to intercept Chaloner. 'Of course, he would be a lot more comfortable if he removed that thick coat. I did suggest it, but he told me I was a savage to tell a gentleman to go about undressed.' He looked away. The remark had hit him where he was most vulnerable.

Chaloner patted his shoulder consolingly. 'You should hear some of the things he says to me.'

Bulteel gave a wan smile. 'Do you have any good news to report? About the stolen papers?'

'Not really.'

Bulteel sighed. 'It cannot be easy, conducting an investigation when there is a wife to keep happy. I know what it is like to live with another person. I love my cousin dearly – he makes me laugh and it is good to have someone who cares about me – but I do long for solitude.'

'He told me he planned to stay with you for one more month. It will soon pass.'

Bulteel nodded. 'It will, and I shall certainly miss him when he goes, but it will be good to be able to bake again. Incidentally, *you* are still kind to me, but others have cooled now I have no cakes with which to buy their friendship. So when Griffith leaves, you will be the sole recipient of my wares.'

He went back into his office abruptly, so Chaloner would not see the pain in his eyes.

'It is too hot,' the Earl grumbled, when Chaloner entered his office. 'And I cannot get comfortable. Moreover, the negotiations with the Dutch are floundering *again*. They promised to accept certain conditions pertaining to trade in New England, and we have spent weeks drafting the details. But now there is a rumour that they will refuse to sign what has already been agreed.'

'Is is true?' asked Chaloner. 'Or another tale put about to cause trouble?'

'It is impossible to say, but it is all very disheartening. What is in that bag? Have your investigations uncovered treasure that you are bringing to me for safekeeping? That would certainly cheer my flagging spirits.' The Earl's eyes gleamed; he liked money.

'Hannah's things, sir,' replied Chaloner. His master was terrible at keeping secrets, but a loose tongue had its uses, and this time he planned to use it for his own ends. He wanted the fact that they were no longer living together spread around White Hall, so that whoever had ordered his house watched would leave Hannah alone. 'She is moving out of Tothill Street.'

'Your marriage is in difficulties already?' asked the Earl, with rather salacious interest. 'But you have barely been wed five minutes! I thought I advised you to let her have her own way for the first few weeks, and only impose your will on her gradually, so she would not notice.'

'You did,' said Chaloner, recalling that he had thought it dubious counsel at the time; now he was sure of it. 'But she is safer away from me at the moment. Too many people mean me harm.'

'Because of your investigations?' asked the Earl uneasily. 'I hope no one sets murderous eyes on *me*, because I would not like that at all. Is that why you came? To warn me to be on my guard?'

'You should always be on your guard, sir, but I do not think the danger is any greater than usual. I actually came to report that I have had no success with your documents.' Chaloner was disinclined to admit that he had done very little to find them. 'However, if you tell me what they—'

'No!' snapped the Earl. 'All you need to know is that they are extremely sensitive. Why do you think I am so eager to have them back?'

Chaloner suppressed a sigh. 'If they contain details about

252

our navy, then perhaps someone in van Goch's delegation *did* lay hold of them. But if they relate to the new religious laws, then different people will be interested. As long as I know nothing about them, I have no idea where to look.'

'In other words, you have failed. I told you this was important, and you have let me down.'

'I am sorry, sir,' said Chaloner, equally cool. 'But in the absence of clues—'

'I do not know,' hissed the Earl angrily. He lowered his voice when Chaloner regarded him blankly. 'I do not *know* what is in these papers, so I could not tell you even if I wanted to.'

Chaloner frowned his bemusement. 'But you said you studied them all Friday afternoon – it was how you were able to say they were stolen between six and eight o'clock. How can you not—'

'I *intended* to read them, but I was tired after being with van Goch and Hanse all morning, and I fell asleep. They were stolen before I could open the packet. There! Are you satisfied now?'

Chaloner was still mystified. 'I do not—'

'I have no idea *what* secrets are now in the hands of the enemy,' snarled the Earl. 'Whoever that enemy transpires to be. And I *said* I read them because I did not want people to think me a fool.'

It explained his stubborn refusal to provide information that might help locate what had been taken, but went nowhere in terms of clues.

'Does Bulteel know what these papers were about?' Chaloner asked. 'He refuses to discuss them with me, because you ordered him not to. But if he has read them, *he* can tell me their contents.'

'I imagine he has,' said the Earl begrudgingly. 'He is

253

the most efficient secretary I have ever had. But I can hardly ask him, can I? It would tell him that I lied about reading them all afternoon.'

'He would not care, sir. His loyalty to you is absolute and unquestioning.'

Clarendon sniffed. 'I suppose so, although I have never been able to like the man. He is so . . . so *seedy*. But his cousin has taken him in hand, so perhaps he will turn respectable. And loyalty is not a virtue I should dismiss, especially given what is happening to others.'

'Sir?' Chaloner had no idea what he was talking about.

'Blackmail,' elaborated the Earl. 'Rich and powerful men are being held to ransom over intimate matters – at least ten have fallen victim to a villain who sends letters demanding payment in return for discretion. And *how* did this sly rogue learn these secrets? From loose-tongued servants!'

The hypothesis certainly made sense. 'Are you sure about this?'

'Well, no, but it stands to reason. A bishop, whom I had better not name because he is a friend, told me he has been targeted: the blackmailer knows about a lewd pamphlet he penned as a student. He will become a laughing stock if that is made public.'

'And you think one of the bishop's retinue gossiped about it?'

'I do,' nodded the Earl. 'The same is true for Lord Lauderdale, Lady Rochester, Buckingham, and even the reprehensible Downing. How else can a blackmailer have learned these things?'

'Well, you have no need to worry about Bulteel. He would sooner cut out his tongue than say anything to harm you.'

254

'True,' acknowledged Clarendon. 'Well, you may ask him about the contents of the papers. Say I give him permission to enlighten you, on the grounds that I am too busy to do it myself. But do not tell him the truth. I may not like him, but I do not want him thinking ill of me.'

Bulteel was relieved when Chaloner repeated the Earl's instructions. 'Thank God he has seen sense at last! They comprise minutes from seven Privy Council meetings – the unexpurgated ones, where secretaries have written down everything that is said. Later, they are edited, which is the version that will be stored for posterity.'

'And what was discussed at these gatherings?'

'Everything – the Dutch problem, religious laws, agricultural policy, taxation. They also touch on who is the most talented actress in *Worse and Worse*, which of the Queen's ladies-in-waiting has the largest bust, and whose horse will win the next race at Newmarket.'

'They debate all that?' asked Chaloner in awe. 'No wonder their meetings take so long!'

'The trivia occupies a lot more time than the serious subjects. And when I say the minutes need to be edited, I do not mean just deleting the irrelevancies. I mean they need to be rewritten in a way that ensures the participants do not look like complete ignoramuses on important affairs of state.'

'I see.' Chaloner frowned. 'Clarendon has been telling me about the White Hall blackmailer. Do you think he acquires his information through these unedited minutes?'

'No. As I understand it, the blackmailer has learned far more intimate secrets than anything aired in Privy Council meetings.'

'Well, this is all very fascinating,' said Chaloner with a sigh, 'but it does not help. The topics covered are so wide-ranging that half the country will find something of interest in them.'

Bulteel nodded his agreement. 'However, you can see why we must have them back as a matter of urgency. The opinions expressed, and the subjects aired, will expose the Council to ridicule, and make the general public even more certain than ever that our government is unfit to rule.'

A sudden blare of trumpets from outside drew them to the nearest window. Van Goch and his retinue had arrived at the Banqueting House, splendid in their ceremonial finery, so Chaloner and Bulteel joined the other courtiers and servants who left their duties to watch. They hurried across the Pebble Court, and took up station just inside the Banqueting House's main entrance.

The King, clad magnificently in red and gold silk, was sitting in a throne at the far end of the hall, surrounded by his favourites. The Queen was at his side, totally overshadowed by the glorious peacock behind him that was Lady Castlemaine. There was a short commotion when Clarendon waddled in at full speed, to take his place at the King's right shoulder – someone had neglected to send his invitation, and he had almost missed the occasion – and then all was ready. Chaloner looked around at the others who had gathered to take part.

Downing was nearby, standing rather closer than was nice to the buxom Lady Muskerry, while Kicke and Nisbett were with the Lady's retinue, looking smug, prosperous and confident. Kicke did not notice Chaloner, but Nisbett pointed a finger in a way that was meant to be intimidating. Chaloner stared back evenly, unmoved by the threat.

Then there was another fanfare, and all attention snapped towards the door, where the diplomatic parade was on the move. The standard bearers were first. They included Ruyven, whose eyes moved restlessly across the onlookers, as if hunting out potential assassins. His gaze lingered on Chaloner, but then he was past.

Van Goch was next in robes of blue and orange. The lesser members of his party followed. Kun first, his kindly face sober, then Zas, sharp-eyed and watchful. Jacoba was there, too, invited perhaps to take her mind off her grief. She smiled at Chaloner as she passed. De Buat the physician was at the very end, and when he saw Chaloner, he stepped out of line to speak to him.

'I have learned something more since we last met,' he whispered. 'It concerns Hanse's drinking. Do you recall me telling you that I thought he was imbibing more wine shortly before his death than when he first arrived?'

'Yes. You said it did not lead him to violent or unchar-acteristic behaviour.'

'And I still stand by that contention. However, I have been asking questions of his friends, and they tell me this increased consumption occurred within the last six weeks. I discussed it with Kun, who reluctantly admitted that he thought something had happened to drive him to it. He says he does not know what, though, and I believe him.'

'If Kun is ignorant, then what about Zas or Ruyven?' asked Chaloner, annoyed that this particular fact had not been aired in the Brown Room. 'What do they know about it?'

'They claim they have no idea what I am talking about.'

257

'Do *you* have any suspicions about what might have been worrying him?'

'None whatsoever. And there is another thing: the servants say Oetje owned no gun. Apparently, her brother was shot, and she owned a deep abhorrence of them. *Ergo*, the one I gave you must belong to her killer – he dropped it as they struggled.'

Chaloner's heart sank. As Williamson had commissioned the gun – and others like it – it seemed reasonable to assume that he was involved in her murder. Or was he? It was also possible that the killer had acquired the weapon from London's underworld, as Gunsmith Trulocke assumed Chaloner had done. In other words, de Buat's intelligence told him little that would help him unravel the mystery.

The physician moved away when another blast of trumpets announced the beginning of the speeches. Spitefully, Buckingham called on the Earl to begin, knowing perfectly well that the Lord Chancellor had had no time to prepare. But Clarendon was a statesman, and rose to the occasion with a prettily worded homily in Latin. Kun replied in kind, his strong, pleasant voice carrying to the farthest corners of the hall. When he had finished, others made contributions, and Chaloner eased towards the door, bored. It was far too hot to be in such a crowded building.

Chaloner was grateful to be outside, where the air was cooler, but had not gone far before someone stepped out of a doorway to intercept him. It was Williamson, with his assassin Swaddell at his side. The little dagger immediately dropped into the palm of Chaloner's hand.

'Small guns,' said the spy, going on the offensive

before they could regale him with questions about his foray to Newgate that morning. 'How many have you had made?'

'How small?' countered Williamson cagily.

Chaloner showed him the one de Buat had found. 'You pass these to your intelligencers. Of course, they are expensive, so I doubt you dispense many. Who owned this one?'

'I really could not say,' replied Williamson. He held out his hand. 'Although you are right in that they are expensive, and I am grateful to you for returning it to me.'

Chaloner had no intention of handing the Spymaster a loaded firearm; it might represent too great a temptation. 'I need to keep it a while. It may allow me to identify Hanse's killer.'

'I thought he drowned,' said Swaddell, puzzled. 'Are you saying he was shot?'

'Well, if he was, then *I* had nothing to do with it,' said Williamson, before Chaloner could reply. 'I can barely keep up with dispatching home-grown villains – assassinating foreigners would stretch my resources well past breaking point.'

There was an awkward silence. It was not an admission Williamson should have made.

'We have commissioned at least two dozen of those,' said Swaddell eventually, nodding at the weapon. 'And a number have been lost. *Ergo*, its presence in connection to Hanse's murder is not a reliable clue, because anyone might have come into possession of it. And that includes Dutchmen.'

'You think Hanse was killed by one of his own people?' asked Chaloner.

'It is possible,' replied Swaddell. 'They present a united

front to outsiders, but our spies tell us that divisions are rife. Hanse was frantic for peace, and was willing to offer generous terms to get it. But not every Hollander thought he was right to be so accommodating.'

Chaloner said nothing, but inwardly he groaned. It would not be easy to investigate the residents of the Savoy, and they would certainly resent any questions that looked as though he was going to lay the murder at their door.

'Better the culprit is a Dutchman than an Englishman,' said Williamson fervently. 'I have high hopes for the convention on Sunday, but the talks will fail if one of *us* killed Hanse.'

'What do you care about peace?' asked Chaloner, sufficiently disheartened by their revelations to let his bitterness show. 'The rest of the country does not.'

'The rest of the country does not have access to intelligence reports,' retorted Williamson. 'Ones that tell me to delay hostilities until we have at least a sporting chance of victory. At the moment, we have none. And if it is revealed that an Englishman killed Hanse, the Dutch will go home and we will be at war within weeks.'

'They will go home if they learn he was murdered by one of their own, too,' Swaddell pointed out. 'They will claim that our spies put the culprit up to it, regardless of whether or not it is true.'

'Well, one side or the other must have done it,' said Chaloner, exasperated. 'Unless you suspect a third party – the French, perhaps, to prevent two Protestant countries from forming an alliance.'

'Now there is an idea!' exclaimed Williamson, eyes gleaming. 'I may put that tale about, no matter who transpires to be the villain.'

'Keeper Sligo came to our offices earlier,' said Swaddell to Chaloner. 'He told us how Wiseman's assistant, Crane, made a horrible discovery in Calais.'

'Calais?' asked Chaloner innocently.

'It is where I deposit undesirables,' said Williamson smoothly. 'Men who are a nuisance.'

'Is that legal?' asked Chaloner, hoping the Spymaster would never learn about his mortal terror of prisons, because it would certainly be used against him.

'I am above the law,' said Williamson smugly. 'Spymasters are, where national security is concerned.'

'Crane uncovered an alarming fact,' Swaddell went on, while Chaloner regarded Williamson in distaste, thinking that Thurloe would never have made such an arrogant claim. 'Namely that two of the men incarcerated for plotting to steal the coronation regalia are dead, while the other escaped.'

'Dead of gaol-fever?' asked Chaloner. 'I heard it is rife in Newgate.'

'Murdered, according to Sligo. We have set guards on Falcon's Cheapside house and his known haunts, but there is no sign of him yet. He remains at large. And that is a problem.'

'Because he might make another attempt on the jewels?' asked Chaloner.

Swaddell shook his head. 'Because he is a very dangerous individual. We did not make the decision to put him in Calais lightly.'

'In what way is he dangerous?'

Swaddell grimaced. 'He seems to have a certain power about him. And he curses.'

'Lots of people curse,' said Chaloner. 'Especially when their plans are foiled.'

261

'Yes, but this is different,' said Swaddell. 'I am not a sensitive man. Indeed, I imagine I am less susceptible than most to this sort of thing – you cannot be too concerned about divine vengeance in my line of work, or you would never get anything done. But he unnerved me.'

Chaloner raised his hands in a shrug. 'I still do not understand.'

'There is a power about him,' snapped Williamson impatiently. 'It happens sometimes in those wholly dedi-cated to their cause. God knows, there were enough of them during the Commonwealth. You know what I mean – men who are so convinced of their rectitude that they are blind to all else.'

'A fanatic?' asked Chaloner.

'The term will serve,' said Williamson. 'He has curious eyes that . . . *burn*. Swan and Swallow were terrified of him. He unsettled Compton and his soldiers, too, and they are sensible sorts.'

'Three of those are dead,' said Chaloner. 'Two crushed by a speeding cart and one drowned.'

Williamson and Swaddell exchanged a glance that showed they were shocked by the news.

'Falcon represents a considerable risk to London and Londoners,' said Williamson. 'So if you hear rumours pertaining to his whereabouts, I would appreciate being told immediately.'

'Of course,' said Chaloner, although the Spymaster would only be told once Falcon had been thoroughly questioned about Hanse's murder, because Chaloner had no intention of visiting Calais a second time to secure an interview.

'Good,' said Williamson with his reptilian smile. 'And now let us return to Crane. We would like to speak to him, but the Company of Barber-Surgeons has no one registered under that name.'

'Crane,' mused Chaloner. 'A bird. Do you think he was another of Falcon's accomplices?'

'He had Swan and Swallow,' snapped Williamson. 'He did not have any one else.'

'But yet he must have done,' reasoned Swaddell. 'Because, according to Sligo, one came dressed up as a warden, and rescued him.'

Williamson did not deign to acknowledge the point. 'Wiseman is in trouble, though. It was his assistant who discovered what had transpired in Calais – a place this Crane should not have been.'

'Wiseman is lazy,' said Chaloner, alarmed that the surgeon might suffer on his account. 'He probably did not bother to check Crane's credentials, so he cannot be blamed for—'

'Crane was his responsibility,' said Williamson coldly. 'So we can blame him for whatever we choose. But we will find Crane, because Sligo is drawing a picture of him as we speak. And then we shall put *him* in Calais, since he was so eager to see it.'

The hot summer day suddenly seemed cold to Chaloner as he walked away, and he shivered.

Hannah was released from her duties early that evening, because the Queen expected to be at the Banqueting House until late and Judith Killigrew had offered to wait up for her.

'We shall go out together,' she announced, when Chaloner came to collect her. 'If we are to live separately for a while, then you can compensate by taking me somewhere pleasant now.'

Chaloner nodded absently, although his thoughts were still on Falcon, a man so clever and dangerous that his escape had disconcerted even the Spymaster. Had Falcon somehow learned about the message Hanse had left in his stockings, and the surveillance on Tothill Street was *his* doing? Given what had happened to Swallow and Swan, Chaloner knew he had to do everything in his power to keep Hannah as far away from the man as possible.

'Joseph Thompson has offered you a bed in his house.' He passed her the bag he had packed. 'You must stay there tonight, because Tothill Street is no longer safe.'

'But it is my home, Tom!' cried Hannah, distinctly unimpressed.

'I know. But it will not be for long. Please, Hannah. I would not ask if it were not important.'

Hannah stared at him. 'Will it always be like this? You will cross deadly villains, and I will be bundled off to some rectory until you have eliminated the threat they represent?'

'Not once I find different rooms,' said Chaloner, although he knew that even this would not entirely eliminate the problem. 'I should have done it sooner. This is my fault, and I am sorry. I think I have dragged Wiseman into hot water, too.'

'He will not be pleased,' predicted Hannah. 'And neither am I. You really should be more careful. But I have decided it will be the last one anyway.'

'The last what?' asked Chaloner warily.

'The last case like this. Sir William Compton has offered you a post – he told me. You will take it, and be done with that horrible old Earl.'

Chaloner smiled. 'I imagine the work Compton has

in mind will be just as risky. He is Master of Ordnance, and you do not encounter saints trying to steal weapons.'

Hannah put her face in her hands. 'I cannot bear this. I have seen one husband in his grave. Am I to be deprived of another? You have no idea what it is like to lose someone you love.' Then her head jerked up and she looked at him in dismay. 'But you do, of course. Your first wife . . .'

'Aletta,' said Chaloner, forcing the name out. As he did so, he realised how rarely he spoke it aloud. He hesitated, but then forged on. It was now or never. 'Her sister is in London with the Dutch delegation. It is . . . unsettling, because Jacoba reminds me . . . they look like . . .'

He was expecting anger for not confiding sooner, so was startled when Hannah took his hands in hers, and regarded him with compassion. 'Poor Tom! That cannot have been easy for you.'

'No,' he agreed fervently. He looked at his feet, not sure what more to say.

'I will go to Thompson,' said Hannah gently. 'But you must agree to two things in return: talk to Compton, and take me out somewhere now. It is a lovely evening, and we should spend it together.'

'Have you seen the crown jewels?' He had intended to visit them anyway, to assess for himself how secure they were, and there could be no harm in taking Hannah. Or could there?

'It is not quite as romantic as the cherry trees at Rotherhithe,' said Hannah, beaming. 'Which I was going to recommend. But it will certainly be more interesting.'

But Chaloner was having second thoughts. 'Or better yet, we could see whether Brodrick has any music planned. I have not played my viol in—'

265

'The jewels,' said Hannah firmly, leading the way towards the gate. 'Listening to you sawing and scraping is not my idea of doing something nice.'

As it was such a fine evening, they decided to walk to the Tower. They met Temperance and Maude on Fleet Street, out to take the air before things got going at the club. Fortunately for Chaloner, life at Court had made Hannah refreshingly liberal-minded, and she did not object to his friendship with the mistress of a bordello, as most respectable ladies would have done.

'Buckingham told me that Downing plans to visit us tonight,' said Temperance, after greetings had been exchanged. 'But I have ordered Preacher Hill to turn him away.'

'No,' said Chaloner worriedly. 'You do not want him angry with you, because he is vindictive. Let him in. He will not return once he learns how much everything costs.'

'Yes, I have heard he is miserly,' said Maude. 'Did you know he is being blackmailed?'

'No,' said Hannah, intrigued. 'What about?'

Maude grinned. 'Apparently, he has been tampering with his expense accounts – making claims for money that was never spent. I heard it from Mr Gardner, who works in the Accompting House, so it is certainly true.'

'If his secret is out, then there is no need for him to pay his blackmailer,' said Chaloner.

'There is evidence, apparently,' elaborated Maude. 'Documents. Until they are produced, the tale is just rumour, and the King is inclined to dismiss it. However, His Majesty will be forced to revise his opinion if he is shown papers *proving* what his Envoy Extraordinary has done.'

'The King is blind where Downing is concerned,' said

Temperance in disgust. 'The man is a rogue, and everyone can see it except His Majesty.'

'The blackmailer claims he has these documents,' said Maude. 'And Mr Gardner says Downing will do just about anything to get them back.'

Chapter 8

The Tower of London was a formidable place, a great, squat fortress surrounded by high walls and protective gates. There was also a moat, but much of the water had evaporated in the heat, leaving a stinking sludge that steamed in the evening sunlight. Hannah gagged as they crossed the drawbridge, overwhelmed by the reek of sewage, refuse and even dead animals that festered below.

'They should dredge it,' she gasped, bunching a scarf under her nose. 'It is horrible!'

Chaloner started to tell her about Amsterdam's moat-canals, which were kept far cleaner, when there was a strange, undulating cry. His hand dropped to the hilt of his sword.

'It is just an animal in the royal menagerie,' said Hannah, laughing at his momentary confusion. 'Did you not know that the King keeps lions, tigers and other exotic beasts here?'

Chaloner did know, because he had encountered one rather more closely than was pleasant the last time he had visited, but it had slipped his mind. He resumed walking, acutely aware that much of the complex was given over to housing prisoners, and it took considerable willpower to knock on the gate and ask to be admitted. Two gaols in one day was taxing the limits of his endurance, and he heartily wished they had gone to Rotherhithe instead. Hannah frowned as they waited for a yeoman to escort them to the Martin Tower, where the jewels were kept.

'Are you unwell? You are very pale.'

'I do not like places like this,' he replied, looking up at the sturdy grey walls and trying to suppress a shudder. Even after his wash and clean clothes, he fancied he could still smell Newgate.

'It was your idea to come,' she pointed out. 'But here comes the yeoman. Oh, look! Reverend White is with him. How nice! I am *very* fond of him.'

'Mr and Mrs Chaloner!' White smiled. 'I have had a long and difficult day, and the brightest part is seeing two people I recently married looking so happy in each other's company.'

Chaloner was not happy, but he smiled politely, while Hannah regarded the old man in concern.

'Are you still worried about your roof? I recall that you would not join us for our wedding feast, because you were so distressed by the damage that storm caused.'

'I *am* upset about the roof,' said White gloomily. 'But what *really* grieves me are these rumours about Cromwell. He did *not* excavate the royal tombs. The current Court is far more likely to indulge in that sort of thing than him, for a jape, or some bizarre quest for scientific knowledge.'

'Please do not say that to anyone else,' said Hannah soberly. 'It may be taken amiss.'

White rubbed a hand over his eyes. 'Lord! You are

269

right. I am not myself this evening – a combination of the heat and these dreadful lies.'

'Perhaps you should have stayed at home,' said Hannah unhelpfully. 'Or did you think that viewing the jewels or the royal menagerie would take your mind off your concerns?'

'I came to dine with my friend Talbot Edwards. But he had invited other guests, too, and they would not believe me when I said Cromwell was no grave-despoiler. And now I do not feel well.'

'May we take you home?' offered Chaloner, more than willing to postpone the jewels.

'Thank you, but that is not necessary,' replied White. 'I shall visit my sister in the country tomorrow. A spell in cooler air will put me right.'

'It would be no trouble,' said Chaloner, a little desperately.

White patted his hand. 'I would rather you spent the evening with each other. Have you come to see the jewels? Tell Edwards that you are friends of mine, and he will give you a special tour. He is terribly short-sighted, though, so watch he does not blunder into you and knock you from your feet.'

'And he is in charge of the coronation regalia?' asked Chaloner. 'A man who cannot see?'

'He can see well enough to polish them,' said White. 'But I had better go, because I am growing more weary by the moment. Good evening to you both.'

'Poor old fellow,' said the yeoman, leading Chaloner and Hannah through a series of locked and barred doors that made Chaloner feel queasy. 'He should just say Cromwell *did* do those terrible things, and let the rumours die a natural death. It is his fervent denials that keep them alive.'

Unfortunately for White, Chaloner suspected the yeoman was right.

Because the Assistant Keeper – the man charged with the daily care of His Majesty's jewels – did not earn a large salary, he had been given permission to exhibit them to the general public, and to charge a fee for the privilege. They were a popular attraction, and the yeoman who escorted Chaloner and Hannah to meet Talbot Edwards said they were shown off several times a week.

'Is he not afraid someone will steal them?' asked Chaloner.

Hannah jabbed him with her elbow, apparently thinking that this was an inappropriate question, and one that might see him arrested.

But the yeoman laughed. 'This is the Tower, sir! No one makes off with anything from here.'

Chaloner thought that he could: the Tower's locks were not state of the art, and he could pick them easily. Then it would be child's play to shove a sceptre under his coat and walk out the way he had come.

'Here you are, Mr Edwards,' said the yeoman genially, as the Assistant Keeper emerged from his domain with several courtiers at his heels. Chaloner assumed they were the folk who had so distressed White. 'Two more visitors for you. The gentleman seems to think our jewels are not very safe, so you had better watch him, or he might try to make off with them.'

Edwards, a portly fellow in his seventies, shared the yeoman's guffaw, laughing so hard that sweat beaded his forehead and ran down his face. He removed a cloth from the pocket of his overly tight coat, and dabbed at

271

it, while Chaloner wondered whether he would have been quite so amused had Falcon's plan succeeded.

'Come,' Edwards said, once the courtiers and the yeoman had gone, and he was alone with Chaloner and Hannah. 'You did not come to entertain me. You came to *be* entertained.'

'You will show us around by yourself?' asked Chaloner, startled. 'Are you not afraid someone will knock you over the head and steal your treasure?'

'And do what with it?' asked Edwards with a shrug. 'There is no great market for stolen crowns in London. And between you and me, the regalia is not even that valuable. Most of the so-called precious stones are nothing of the kind, because the best ones have been prised out and put in a safe place. The ones you will see are coloured glass.'

Chaloner regarded him askance, wondering whether that constituted fraud, given that people paid to see them. 'But, even so, they still must be worth something.'

'Oh, they are,' Edwards assured him. 'Just not as much as everyone thinks. Yet I *was* concerned about security at first, and consulted Sir William Compton on the matter. He is Master of Ordnance, and knows better than most how to keep things safe. He recommended that I hire a guard.'

'Then where is he?'

'Brown died of a fever last week, and I have yet to replace him. But enough chatter. Come.'

He began to walk away in entirely the wrong direction, and only after colliding with the Brick Tower did he realise he was well off course. With cool aplomb, he turned right, chatting gaily all the while about Cromwell's antics in Westminster Abbey. When he reached the

Martin Tower, he ran his fingers over the door until he located the keyhole. Keeping one finger on it so he would not lose it again, he fumbled for the key that hung on a chain around his waist, and unlocked it with a flourish. Chaloner watched with mounting horror. Surely, sharp eyes should be a requisite for such a post? Thieves were noted for their sleights of hand, after all.

Smiling genially, Edwards beckoned his guests into a low, dark chamber. There were no windows, and there was nothing in the room except a chest atop a table. He used a second key to unlock it, then stood back so his visitors could admire its contents. Half expecting it to be empty, Chaloner stepped forward.

The so-called Crown of England was the largest piece, a mass of sparkling colour in a frame of gold. Then there were the sceptre and orb, and various other head-pieces and accoutrements. Chaloner gave them no more than a cursory glance – he had never been very inter-ested in such items – but Hannah cooed appreciatively.

'May I hold the sceptre?' she asked, adding when Edwards looked wary, 'We are friends of Reverend White, and he—'

'Why did you not say?' cried Edwards, handing it to her. 'White and I have known each other for years. He is a lovely man, although I wish he were not so vocal about these rumours concerning Cromwell. It is not a good idea to say nice things about the Old Tyrant in this day and age. I know White was one of Cromwell's chap-lains, but even so . . .'

Hannah took the sceptre to the door, so she could admire it in the light, while Chaloner thought it would not need a cunning Falcon to make off with the King's treasure – anyone could do it.

'You chose a good time to visit,' Edwards said amiably, addressing the place where she had been standing. 'I am going to see kin in the country tomorrow, so had you left it a day later, you would have been disappointed.'

'No one shows the jewels off while you are away?' asked Chaloner.

'No. Visitor fees are my prerogative, and I do not see why I should share them with anyone else. But I shall not be gone long – a night or two, perhaps. The King sometimes likes to try his crown on, and it would not do to be away when he calls for it.'

'I understand there was a recent plot to make off with it,' said Chaloner, deciding to take the bull by the horns. 'A man called Falcon—'

'Falcon!' sneered Edwards, showing no surprise at the mention of the affair. 'He pretended to befriend me, but I saw through his antics in an instant. He stood no more chance of stealing the regalia than he has of flying to the moon. Spymaster Williamson arrested him in the end.'

'Did you know he has escaped?' asked Chaloner, watching Hannah return the sceptre to the box and turn her attention to the orb. 'And his accomplices have been murdered?'

Edwards's jaw dropped in disbelief. 'But that is impossible! No one ever leaves Calais.'

'Well, Falcon has. Do you think he might make another attempt on—'

'No!' declared Edwards vehemently. 'He will not chance his arm here again. He would not dare.'

'What does he look like?' asked Chaloner, before realising that he was asking the wrong man.

Edwards answered anyway. 'He always came dressed

as an affluent middle-aged cleric, which Compton said
he is. I did not see him after his arrest, but the yeomen
did, and they said he seemed younger, stronger, and
rather secular. They claim they have never known a fellow
able to change his appearance so completely, and declared
it uncanny and sinister.'

'Will you take additional precautions with the jewels,
now you know he is at large?'

Edwards nodded. 'And so will the yeomen, who are
as robust and reliable a corps as you could ever hope to
meet. But Falcon will not come here – he is not a fool.'

It was difficult to prise Hannah away, and when
Chaloner finally did manage, she enthused about the
jewels all the way to Thompson's house. Only when their
journey came to an end, and they were standing in the
rectory garden, Chaloner scanning their surroundings
for any evidence that they were being watched, did she
turn to face him.

'You have barely said a word all evening. Did you not
think the regalia fine?'

'Very fine,' replied Chaloner. 'And also very vulnerable. Stealing them would be easy.'

'You had better not say that to anyone else,' she said
with a grin, 'because if they do go missing, you will be
the prime suspect.'

Curious to know whether he had overreacted by taking
Hannah to a place of safety, Chaloner walked to Tothill
Street. It did not take him long to see that he had made
the right decision. The men watching his house were
smoking pipes or sipping ale outside the tavern opposite,
and might have gone unnoticed. But Chaloner knew what
to look for. There were six of them, stationed at the front

and the rear, and all were alert and vigilant. They became more so as dusk approached and the shadows lengthened and deepened.

He wondered what they wanted. Were they there to monitor his movements, or was their remit to lay hold of him? Regardless, he was not inclined to tackle so many in order to secure answers, so turned around and walked back the way he had come.

He took a carriage to Cheapside, where it was easy to identify Falcon's home – Swaddell and a companion were watching it, rather obviously, from the nearby Feathers tavern. Chaloner went to the side of the house, where he gained access via a badly secured window.

It was not very large, and had probably been neat and clean before Williamson had been through it. There was a huge stock of clothes and face-paints, suggesting the tales were true about the vicar's love of disguise. Chaloner stood in the house as darkness fell outside, and tried to gain a measure of the man. He found he could not do it. And even if he could, he doubted whether it would have helped: Falcon would already have assumed a new identity.

He sat on a chair and tried to think of ways to unmask him, because he was sure about one thing: Falcon was not the kind of person to accept defeat and slink away. He would be close at hand, plotting revenge on those who had foiled him. Or perhaps even working to resume the Sinon Plot, whatever that might entail.

Chaloner frowned. As a master of deception, it would be easy for Falcon to infiltrate White Hall, which was a transient place, always full of newcomers and visitors. And if he had, he might be anyone, even someone Chaloner had met. The spy rubbed his eyes wearily. The

276

task of exposing the fellow seemed impossible, but he knew he would have to try, especially if, as he was beginning to suspect, Falcon had killed Hanse.

There was no more to be gained from sitting in a deserted house, and Chaloner had the strong sense that the cleric had no intention of ever returning there, so he took his leave and went to the Golden Lion on Fetter Lane. The landlord was noted for his discretion: he did not ask why Chaloner wanted a room for the night, and Chaloner did not tell him.

Chaloner slept badly, waking each time there was a creak or a groan, and as the building was old, there were plenty of them. When he did doze, his dreams were plagued by muddled situations involving Newgate, Aletta and the Crown of England. He woke from one nightmare clutching a dagger, although he did not recall drawing it. Wryly, it occurred to him that Hannah was indeed safer with Rector Thompson, if her bed-mate was going to lay hold of sharp implements in his sleep.

When the stars began to fade and the first glimmer of dawn showed in the east, Chaloner rose and went to sit by the window. Opposite was a gap in the line of houses. He had lived there until recently, but the building had collapsed. Somewhere in the rubble that still littered the ground were his second-best viol, a cracked mirror that had been Aletta's, and a little jug his mother had given him. He wished he still had them, especially the mirror.

A sudden, vivid image of Aletta filled his mind, the clarity of which he had not experienced in years. He was honest enough with himself to know that theirs had not been a match made in heaven – all their friends had advised against it, on the grounds that the differences in

277

their characters would lead to quarrels and an eventual cooling of affection. But passion and youth had won out, and they had wed anyway. Plague had taken her before the predictions could come to pass, but he suspected that he and Aletta would not have been happy together in the long run.

Since then, he had stumbled through a series of hopeless relationships, mostly because he seemed incapable of choosing suitable partners. There had been a lady in Spain who might have been different, but circumstances had conspired against them enjoying a future together. And then there was Hannah. He believed he loved her, but the emotion was so different from what he had felt for Aletta that it was impossible to be sure. One thing was certain, though: the notion of her being in danger because of his work for the Earl filled him with a deep and all-consuming horror, and he knew he would do anything to protect her. Perhaps *that* was love.

To take his mind off matters that were so far beyond his understanding, he turned his thoughts to his investigations. He still had more questions than answers. How had Hanse learned about the Sinon Plot, and *was* Falcon responsible for his murder? Had Falcon killed Compton's soldiers? Why had Hanse met Surgeon Molins in the Sun tavern, and why had Hanse started drinking more heavily? Could Falcon be the mysterious vicar who met Molins and Hanse in the Sun? Who had stolen the Earl's papers? Who was holding half the Court to ransom with demands for money in return for keeping embarrassing secrets? And, right at the bottom of the list, was poor, forgotten Alden. His murderer had caught a lucky break, because Chaloner had not spared him a thought in days.

As soon as it was light, Chaloner walked to Lincoln's

Inn. It was already blisteringly hot, and the piles of rubbish that were usually washed along the drains at the sides of the road had grown so large that it would take a deluge of Biblical proportion to dislodge them. Most leaked a poisonous green-black slime that was treacherously slick, and undulated with maggots and flies.

He scaled a wall to enter Lincoln's Inn – he knew no one was following him, but was unwilling to take risks where his friends were concerned. As usual, Thurloe was in the garden, but Chaloner's heart sank when he saw he was not alone: a fellow bencher named William Prynne was with him.

Prynne was a pamphleteer, who liked to make scurrilous attacks on everything from religion and fashion, to playhouses and politics. He had been punished for his vitriol, though – no matter what the weather, he wore a woollen cap with long cheek-flaps, to conceal the fact that his ears had been lopped off and he had been branded. Unfortunately, not even that draconian measure had taught him to moderate his opinions, and he was a man most decent people tried to avoid.

'Tom!' exclaimed Thurloe, as the spy materialised next to him. He sounded relieved. 'You will want to tell me about your wife's health in private, so we shall retire to my rooms immediately.'

The removal of his ears had done nothing to impair Prynne's hearing, and he scowled his anger and disappointment at Thurloe's suggestion. 'But I was giving you my judgement on the Dutch delegation! You *must* be interested – you had dealings with them yourself during the Commonwealth.'

Thurloe looked pained. 'Your views are . . . enlightening, Prynne. Thank you. But Tom is—'

'*You* will be interested, too,' said Prynne, addressing Chaloner. 'You work at White Hall, so you will find this fascinating, although most courtiers are sinful heathens, who fornicate with Satan's—'

'Does your wife need one of my tonics, Tom?' asked Thurloe desperately. 'Shall I prepare it *now*?'

'As soon as possible,' agreed Chaloner.

'Secretary Kun is sly and deceitful,' Prynne went on, unfazed by Thurloe's transparent efforts to escape. 'A double-tongued viper, who pretends to be affable but who is actually full of wickedness. The lawyer named Zas looks like a fox, and owns that creature's cunning viciousness, so he cannot be trusted. And Ruyven, the soldier who protects them all, has a dark and deadly secret.'

'What secret?' Chaloner turned back suddenly, resisting Thurloe's attempts to pull him away.

'One of which he is deeply ashamed, but that he cannot help but pursue,' replied Prynne, pleased to have secured Chaloner's interest. 'I can smell it on him, and it is what makes him the man he is. I usually like Hollanders, but the ones in the Dutch delegation are agents of corruption and vice, and their women bear the badge of prostituted strumpets who ramble like harlots to—'

'No,' snapped Chaloner, knowing there was no point in arguing with a committed bigot like Prynne, but unable to overlook insults to Jacoba. 'Do not make such—'

Prynne overrode him. 'They revel in pernicious and intolerable corruptions—'

'Enough!' barked Thurloe, fixing Prynne with a furious glare. He rarely raised his voice, but when he did, wise men took heed, and Prynne, for all his faults, was not stupid. He bowed a hasty farewell and scurried away, muttering something about a pamphlet that needed his attention.

'I am sorry, Tom,' said Thurloe. 'He had no right to make those remarks. Come and sit in this arbour with me. We can talk in peace now he has gone.'

The arbour boasted a chamomile bench, and when they sat, it released a sweet, soothing odour.

'I had forgotten that you know some of Heer van Goch's delegation,' said Chaloner, breathing in deeply. 'You played host to them when you were Secretary of State.'

'I knew some rather well, and Kun has been to visit me here since he arrived this time. Prynne has a point, though: there *is* something hard and determined under that affable exterior.'

The same might be said of Thurloe himself, Chaloner thought. 'You do not like him?'

Thurloe shrugged. 'It is not a case of like or dislike. He just has hidden depths.'

'What about Zas? Did you meet him?'

'Yes. He *does* look like a fox, but I never found him vicious. Cromwell was fond of him.'

Chaloner was not sure the approbation of a military dictator said much that was positive. 'What did Prynne mean about Ruyven? What dark secret does he hold?'

'I have no idea, but I would not place too much faith in it. Prynne loves to cause trouble.'

Chaloner supposed he was right. 'Do you still have the receipts that prove I was in Middleburg when de Witt's bedchamber was burgled?' he asked, after a moment.

Thurloe's eyebrows went up. 'Why? Do not tell me you need them after all these years? I thought everyone

281

had agreed that that particular exploit would never be solved.'

'Downing has other ideas. He has mentioned it twice now, including once in the Savoy. I thought it was going to see me arrested. So did he, I imagine.'

'What is wrong with the man?' exclaimed Thurloe, shocked. 'Can he not see that the incident will reflect as poorly on him as on the spy who performed the deed? I know I told him I needed that information, but I never imagined he would order you into such a dangerous situation. It was bad enough telling you to steal the papers, but to then force you to put them back again . . .'

'They would have been no use to you if de Witt had known their contents were comprised. Downing was right about that.'

'Perhaps,' acknowledged Thurloe reluctantly. 'But the whole escapade was reckless and stupid, and would have caused untold damage had you been caught. You should have refused.'

'I did refuse, but he threatened to shoot Aletta's maid unless I did as I was told. He may have been bluffing, but I could not take the chance.'

'I will find those receipts today,' promised Thurloe. 'And if I have misplaced them, I shall arrange for more to be produced. Downing will *not* use this to hurt you.'

Chaloner left Lincoln's Inn glad he had a friend like Thurloe.

It was now a full week since the Earl's papers had been stolen, so Chaloner spent the first half of the morning in Worcester House, questioning the staff – again – about what they had seen or heard the evening the documents had gone missing. He did not expect anything new to come to light, and nor did it – the thief had slipped in and out without being seen by a single witness. Even Bulteel, who was more observant than most, had failed to notice anything amiss.

'Are you *sure* they are stolen?' Chaloner asked, exasperated. 'He has not mislaid them?'

'They have gone,' said Bulteel grimly. 'I checked very carefully, believe me. Is there *nothing* to help you trace them? This is important. I do not like the notion of them being in the wrong hands.'

But as far as Chaloner was concerned, the investigation had reached a dead end, and there was no more he could do unless someone gave him new information. Even learning the contents of the papers had not helped, because they were too wide-ranging to permit identification of relevant suspects. Virtually anyone might have taken them. Even, he thought caustically, the ladies of the Queen's bedchamber, eager to know what was being said about the size of their busts.

'I have every confidence that you will prevail,' said Bulteel, seeing his friend's disheartened expression. He looked around quickly, then lowered his voice. 'And if Clarendon threatens you with dismissal, I shall borrow a copy from someone else, and duplicate them for you to give him.'

Chaloner raised his eyebrows. 'That would be underhand.'

Bulteel blushed furiously. 'Yes it would, but I do not like the way he treats you. It is not right.'

'Perhaps I will have better luck with the other investigation – Hanse's murder. He may overlook his missing documents if I solve that.'

'Do you have any leads?' Bulteel tried to sound

283

interested, but it was clear he considered the papers more pressing. 'I have been listening for rumours, but have heard nothing yet.'

'I do have one clue: Hanse met a surgeon named Ned Molins in the Sun tavern. Wiseman is taking me to meet him this afternoon.'

'Then you may be in luck,' said Bulteel, smiling. 'Surgeon Molins is a disreputable, peculiar fellow who might well be involved in something untoward.'

'You think Hanse was untoward?'

'Well, I am convinced that he stole the Earl's documents. I know you disagree, but who else could it have been? No one else visited Worcester House that day except him and van Goch. And I doubt an ambassador would sully his hands with theft, so that only leaves one candidate.'

'But Clarendon says the documents went missing between six and eight o'clock on Friday night. Hanse has an alibi for then, because I was with him. He is not the thief.'

Bulteel sniffed and changed the subject, clearly unwilling to admit that his suspicions might be unfounded. 'I have never liked Molins. He is opinionated, loud and arrogant, and—'

They both turned as Griffith and his servant arrived. Bulteel's cousin was clad in a suit of pale pink, with enough ribbon to supply a maypole, while Lane was in his usual dowdy browns. Griffith minced towards them, and sank gracefully on to a chair, fanning himself with his lace.

'God's blood!' he exclaimed. 'Will this heat never end? I am all but overcome. Is there any wine? Fetch me some, will you, Lane? And quickly, because I think I am about to expire.'

Although Lane's expression remained faultlessly

neutral, he gave the distinct impression that he would not mind too much if that happened. Wordlessly, he bowed, and moved away.

'We were talking about Surgeon Molins,' said Bulteel. 'Do you know him, cousin?'

'I met him once,' replied Griffith, fanning vigorously and closing his eyes. 'I found him rather uncouth, and he smelled of pilchards. But he is an ardent Royalist, so he has his virtues.'

Lane returned with the wine, which Griffith swallowed as if it were medicine, wincing and cringing all the way to the bottom of the cup. Lane watched impassively, and it occurred to Chaloner that the fellow was actually rather sinister.

'Right,' said Griffith, when he had finished. 'Are you ready, John, dear? Where shall we do it?'

'Library,' muttered Bulteel, blushing red and not looking at Chaloner.

'Really?' asked Griffith, with an exaggerated moue of distaste. 'Can we not go to the Spares Gallery? I like that room, and it will be cool and empty at this hour of the day.'

'It will not,' countered Bulteel. 'Bates will be loitering there – he always is these days. Personally, I would rather do it in my Chelsey house, because that really is a long way from prying eyes, but I suppose no one will see us here.'

'No one will see them doing what?' asked Chaloner of Lane, after they had gone.

'Dancing lessons,' replied Lane, still with the same inscrutable expression. 'It is their third this week. The colonel maintains that light feet are the sign of a true gentleman.'

Chaloner passed the library on his way out, and, out of idle curiosity, peered through a crack in the door. Griffith was leading Bulteel around the room in a dance known as a courant, although Bulteel's stumbling and shuffling made it difficult to tell. The secretary's face was a mask of desperate concentration, but it was clear he was one of those men who would never be elegant, no matter how much time was invested in his training.

'This is hopeless!' he cried, pushing Griffith away from him in sudden despair. 'I move like a hippopotamus! No wonder Tom's wife did not want me at their wedding. They had a ball afterwards, and she was probably afraid I would take to the floor.'

'Nonsense,' countered Griffith good-naturedly. 'It just requires practise and patience.'

Bulteel took the proffered hands and they began to circle again. Chaloner left thinking the effete colonel was an incurable optimist, because Bulteel was right: there *was* something of the hippopotamus in his gyrations. Moreover, Hannah's dislike went a lot deeper than his abilities on the dance floor, and it would take more than mastering a courant to persuade her to like him.

Sorry that it was Hannah who was responsible for putting Bulteel through such torments, Chaloner went to White Hall, and divided his time between questioning Privy Council members about the Earl's missing papers and asking about Falcon. Neither enquiry yielded fruit: none of the Privy Council had sensible suggestions to offer regarding possible culprits for the theft, and were quite happy to believe the Dutch were responsible; and all he learned about Falcon was that those who had met him considered him enigmatic and frightening, and their

286

descriptions of him were contradictory. As Chaloner had feared, the man was going to be very difficult to track.

Later, simultaneously frustrated and despondent, he went to meet Wiseman.

'I am afraid my ruse to gain access to Newgate will bring you trouble,' he said apologetically. 'Williamson is suspicious of your so-called assistant.'

'I know,' said Wiseman grimly. 'I was subjected to an extremely unpleasant interview in his Westminster den yesterday. In order to extricate myself as quickly as possible, I told him the truth.'

'You did?' asked Chaloner uneasily.

Wiseman nodded. 'Yes. Which is that talented young surgeons queue up by the dozen, asking me to take them on, but that they rarely last more than a week. So I no longer bother to check their credentials. The Master of my Company tells me it is because I am abrasive, but he cannot be right.'

'Why not?'

'Because I am *not* abrasive. Temperance says so, and I trust her judgement.'

Chaloner fell into step at the surgeon's side as they walked along Fleet Street. People gave Wiseman a wide berth, and those who did not ran the risk of being shunted out of his way. There were a few resentful remarks, but nothing overt. It would be a brave and reckless fellow who picked a quarrel with the mighty Wiseman.

Ned Molins lived on Shoe Lane, an important thoroughfare that ran between Fleet Street and Holborn. It suffered from being near the Fleet River, and several unsavoury-looking lanes led off it, dark, uninviting slits that were used as dumps for all manner of refuse. The evil-smelling piles, combined with the eye-watering reek from the river, meant that not everyone who ventured down these alleys could expect to return.

'Ned lives here with his son Joseph,' said Wiseman as they approached a fine yellow-brick house. 'Joseph is a hopeless surgeon, but an excellent barber. His shaves are a true delight.'

'You say you chopped off Molins's leg,' said Chaloner, reaching out to stop Wiseman from knocking. 'Are you sure he will want to see you? Perhaps I should visit him on my own.'

Wiseman glared. 'Of course he will want to see me! The break was a dirty one, and it festered – I saved his life by whipping off his foot. Besides, although I was the one to perform the surgery, many of our colleagues were present, and they all agreed that amputation was the only recourse.'

The door was opened by a man with a Cavalier moustache, a black wig and simple but expensive clothes. When he saw Wiseman, he lurched forward with a shriek of anguish, hands scrabbling for the surgeon's throat. Chaloner braced himself to intervene, but Wiseman fended him off with ease, then grabbed the fellow by the collar, holding him at arm's length while the man howled unintelligible words and tried his damnedest to land a punch.

'Really, Joseph,' said Wiseman, when his captive's fury had subsided into shuddering sobs. 'Your behaviour is most unedifying, and people are looking at us. What in God's name is the matter?'

'How dare you come here,' wept Joseph, trying to slap him again. 'You have no right!'

'I have every right,' declared Wiseman indignantly. 'Your father is my patient.'

'My father is dead,' howled Joseph. 'And you killed him, you wretched butcher!'

Joseph's wails brought another man running. It was John Knight, a fierce bantam of a man with a bristling moustache, who was the current Master of the Company of Barber-Surgeons. Chaloner had met him on several occasions, and had found him pedantic, small-minded and unfriendly.

'Knight,' Wiseman nodded a wary greeting. 'What seems to be the problem?'

'The problem,' Knight replied coldly, 'is that Molins is dead.'

Wiseman shot him a withering glance. 'So Joseph has just declared, but I was hoping for more detailed information from you. Such as what killed him.'

'*You* did,' sobbed Joseph. 'Your surgery.'

'Rubbish!' declared Wiseman uncompromisingly. He turned to Knight. 'You observed the procedure, and you said it was the most elegant amputation you had ever witnessed.'

'Actually, *you* said that,' countered Knight. 'But I had reservations, and I was right. Poor Molins passed away an hour ago, from a poorly secured skin flap.'

'Nonsense!' declared Wiseman, although his face was pale. 'My flap was perfect.'

'It looked well immediately after the cutting,' acknowledged Knight. 'But it must have deteriorated. And you applied a plaister that you said should not be removed for a week, which meant that no one else was able to inspect it.'

'You killed him, Wiseman,' wept Joseph. 'Just as surely as if you plunged a dagger into his heart. The wound should have been inspected regularly, not left for days.'

'Poking about in new wounds encourages them to fester,' stated Wiseman angrily.

'You are wrong,' snapped Knight. 'And poor Molins has paid the price for your arrogance.'

'How dare you!' shouted Wiseman, affronted. '*I* am the King's personal surgeon!'

'Only because you marched to White Hall and informed him that you were taking the post,' Knight yelled back. 'But you are deeply unpopular there *and* in our Company. Everybody hates you, and your fall from grace will be spectacular and catastrophic.'

'What fall from grace?' demanded Wiseman dangerously.

Sensing he was skating on thin ice, Knight turned to Joseph, pointing at Chaloner as he did so. 'Here is one of Clarendon's gentlemen ushers. I imagine the Earl heard Molins was dead, and sent Chaloner to discover what villainy is at work.'

'How *dare* you imply—' spluttered Wiseman.

'Actually, I came to speak to Molins,' said Chaloner, interrupting before blood was spilled. He was cursing himself for agreeing to wait for Wiseman's introduction. If he had visited Molins the previous day, as his instincts had told him he should, he might have had some answers about Hanse.

'Where is the body?' demanded Wiseman, shaking with fury. 'I want to inspect it.'

'Upstairs,' sniffed Joseph. 'Follow me. You, too, Mr Chaloner. I want you to tell the Lord Chancellor exactly what this rogue has done to my beloved father.'

Chaloner started to decline, loath to become involved

290

in such a matter, but Wiseman gripped his arm and hauled him inside, muttering that he needed the support of a man he trusted. Chaloner tried to resist, but the surgeon was far too strong.

Molins had died in a first-floor chamber that overlooked the street. Wiseman whipped the covers from the corpse, revealing a neat bandage that swathed what was left of the patient's left leg. Chaloner stared at the body, recalling the description that Landlord Waters at the Sun had given: Molins was elderly, and did indeed have a birth-stain on his neck. He also saw that the dead man's clothes had been tossed to one side, as if death had come quickly – breeches, stockings, waistcoat, gloves and hat lay in an untidy pile on a chair.

'The cause of death is obvious,' said Knight quietly. 'The broken ankle released evil vapours into the vital organs, and bad surgery finished the business.'

Joseph gulped and darted from the room when Wiseman began to remove the dressing. The surgeon took a long time to examine the wound, while Chaloner and Knight watched in silence.

'The flap is inflamed,' Wiseman acknowledged eventually. His face was whiter than that of the corpse. 'Of course, redness and swelling are to be expected after surgery, so it is not *certain* that the procedure is to blame for his death, but . . .'

'Removing the foot should have saved his life,' said Knight harshly. 'It was as clear cut a case as I have ever seen. Young Molins is right: it *was* your plaister that killed his father.'

Uncharacteristically, Wiseman had nothing to say. He stared disconsolately at Molins, twisting his scarlet hat in his powerful hands. Knight watched him for a while, then announced that he was going to Chyrurgeons' Hall, to tell their colleagues what had happened – and no doubt use the opportunity to blacken Wiseman's name into the bargain.

'I honestly thought Molins would live,' said Wiseman in a low, strained voice, as he and Chaloner made their way down the stairs after him. 'In fact, I was certain of it. I have dealt with many such cases in the past, and I *know* I removed all the rot. I did *not* botch the operation.'

'Then perhaps there was an ingredient in the plaister that—'

'It came from a batch I used on three other people, all of whom are alive and well.'

Chaloner was thoughtful. Was it innocent chance that one of the men Hanse had met in the Sun was dead? Or had someone given Molins a push towards the grave? If the latter, then it meant Molins was the ninth person to die in connection with Hanse, Falcon and the Sinon Plot, and yet again, Chaloner was seized with the sense that something dark and deadly was unfolding.

'Could he have been poisoned?' he asked, whispering so Knight would not hear.

Wiseman stared at him. 'Why would anyone poison a man recovering from surgery?'

'Just answer the question.'

'There are no indications of it that I saw. And Knight may be a buffoon, but he would not have missed them, either. So I would say not.'

'I am going to talk to Joseph.'

Hope filled Wiseman's eyes. 'You are going to look into the matter? To prove me innocent?'

'Not exactly,' said Chaloner uncomfortably. 'But it is strange that Molins should die when—'

Wiseman clutched his hand in a grasp that threatened to break fingers, and Chaloner was horrified to see tears glittering. 'Thank God! You are a good friend, Chaloner. I will not forget this.'

Chaloner was alarmed, and wished he had held his tongue. 'Do not be too optimistic. It may be that there *is* no explanation, other than clumsy surgery.'

'You will not find that,' declared Wiseman with utter conviction. 'Because it would not be true. There *will* be answers to why this happened, and I feel a lot better now I know you are going to find them. God bless you, Chaloner. I shall always be in your debt.'

Raising his head and straightening his shoulders, Wiseman strode down the rest of the stairs and sailed into the street.

Joseph Molins was sitting in a parlour at the back of his house. For some reason, every scrap of wall had been covered with the mounted heads of dead animals, and the place reeked of whatever compounds had been used to preserve them, although some had evidently been unsuccessful because an aroma of decay lurked beneath the chemicals. A few beasts had been furnished with eyes fashioned from shells or beads, and the effect was a curiously disturbing sense of being watched by creatures who deeply resented what had been done of them.

'My father loved this room,' sniffed Joseph. 'He killed all these specimens himself. Take that enormous rat, for example. He caught that in the Anatomical Theatre in Chyrurgeons' Hall.'

'Did he?' Chaloner felt slightly ill when he reflected on the probable nature of the rodent's diet.

'He wanted me to inherit his hospital posts,' said Joseph, fresh tears falling. 'But I think I shall decline. It sounds girlish, but there is something about blood that makes me swoon.'

'I imagine that is true for most people,' said Chaloner consolingly.

'Yes, but most people have not been trained as surgeons,' Joseph pointed out. He wiped his eyes with the back of his hand. 'I am sorry for my display earlier. It was unseemly, but I could not help myself. I know people often die after amputations, but a dozen *medici* watched Wiseman, and one of them should have said something if they thought his technique was lacking.'

'It may not be his fault. Sometimes, men just die.'

'I know that,' said Joseph bitterly. 'Of course, none of it would have happened if some low villain had not attacked my father last Friday.'

'Friday?' asked Chaloner, more sharply than he had intended. Friday was the day Hanse had gone missing. Had there been two victims that night?

'It happened at the Devil tavern on Fleet Street,' Joseph went on. 'Although I cannot imagine what he was doing there. It is a rough place, and he had told me he was going out to see a patient.'

'Perhaps the patient was in the tavern,' suggested Chaloner.

'Not according to the owner – Barford said my father was there for a drink with four friends. My father later said the same, too, although he declined to tell me who had demanded his company at such an hour.'

'What hour was that?'

'It must have been well after ten o'clock. But he learned to his cost that the Devil was no place for him – some villain flailed at him with a sword as he left. He managed to duck, but he fell and landed awkwardly. According to Barford, my father's drinking companions saw the villain off. Then two of them left, but the other pair stayed with him until I arrived.'

'Did you know the names of these companions?'

'Sir William Compton was one of those who waited. Do you know him? He is the Master of Ordnance, and a very decent gentleman. The other was a Dutchman.'

'A Dutchman?' echoed Chaloner, thoughts whirling.

Joseph nodded again. 'A kindly-faced, amiable one, with a mass of yellow hair. He gave my father those nice white gloves that he liked to wear.'

Chaloner stared at him. The description fitted Hanse perfectly. Did this explain why he had refused the offer of an escort back to the Savoy? He had more socialising planned, and did not want anyone else to witness it? And what did it say about Ibbot, the hackneyman? That he had delivered Hanse to the Devil, rather than the Savoy, and had been murdered for it?

'Did you see his other two companions?' he asked hopefully.

'No,' replied Joseph. 'They had gone by the time I arrived. But the landlord said one was a vicar, while the other was fat and untidy.'

So, the five men who had met in the Devil on Friday night were the same as the ones who gathered in the Sun, thought Chaloner. But what did that tell him? He saw it raised more questions than answers, and supposed he would have to visit Compton and ask *him* why he had met Molins, Hanse, a vicar and a fat, untidy man late at night in London's taverns.

* * *

295

The afternoon heat hit Chaloner like a physical blow as he stepped outside. He turned into Fleet Street, which was full of dust kicked up by the traffic. Grit flew into his eye, momentarily blinding him, and causing him to trip over a sun-baked rut. A coach accompanied by horsemen rattled past, and one of the riders smirked as he witnessed the stumble. It was Ruyven.

'Been drinking?' he called. He spoke Dutch, and nearby pedestrians began to glare. Chaloner winced, thinking the captain was a fool for drawing attention to his nationality on such a busy highway.

'Stop the coach!' called Zas from inside the vehicle, hammering on the roof until it came to a standstill. Then he leaned out of the window. 'Climb in, Chaloner. We are going in the same direction, and it is too hot for walking. Especially for a man who has been at the claret.'

'No,' objected Ruyven, before Chaloner could inform Zas that he had been nowhere near wine of any description for days – he had not had time. 'It is not safe to offer rides to Englishmen.'

'He is not an Englishman,' countered Zas. 'He is Chaloner – Hanse's kinsman.'

They began to argue, and while Chaloner had no wish to accept Zas's invitation, a refusal was likely to prolong the incident and attract even more attention. Moving quickly, he opened the carriage door and clambered inside. Ruyven scowled, but Chaloner did not care what he thought.

It was cramped in the coach. Besides Zas, there was Secretary Kun, the burly sergeant called Taacken, and two more diplomats. All nodded politely, except Kun, whose greeting was cool. Chaloner could only suppose that he, like Ruyven, did not think that stopping to collect

296

passengers was a good idea. Everyone winced when there was a thump – a stone had been thrown. But then the driver flicked his reins and they were off, Ruyven and his men cantering along beside them.

'I am surprised you are out,' Chaloner remarked. 'Given what happened last time.'

'We have drivers we trust now,' explained Zas. 'There will not be a repeat of the incident at Charing Cross. But we are out because we were all tired of being cooped up inside the Savoy.'

'Where have you been?' Chaloner was aware of Kun staring morosely out of the window, which was unusual behaviour from the amiable secretary.

'St Paul's Cathedral,' replied Zas. 'It seemed a pity to leave London without seeing it. It truly is a wonder!'

'The wonder is that it is still standing,' muttered Kun uncharitably. 'It is virtually a ruin.'

Chaloner glanced at him, wondering what had brought about his sudden change of mood. Were Thurloe and Prynne right when they claimed he had another, darker side?

'It is precarious in places,' acknowledged Zas. He grinned at Chaloner, a brazenly vulpine expression that immediately put the spy on his guard. 'But we did not offer you a ride so we could talk about hackney drivers and architecture. We had a rather different discussion in mind.'

'One concerning Hanse, I suppose,' predicted Chaloner.

Zas nodded. 'Precisely. What more have you learned about his murder?'

'Progress is being made,' replied Chaloner shortly, resenting the fact that they felt free to demand answers when they had been far from open with him.

297

'What progress?' demanded Kun.

'We may be able to help,' coaxed Zas, when Chaloner declined to answer. 'After all, we want the same thing: Hanse's killer caught and the peace talks to succeed. We will achieve our objectives far sooner if we work together.'

'I thought we *were* working together,' said Taacken bitterly. 'Us and the English. But there are rumours – ones that claim we will not sign a trade treaty, when the truth is that we are ready to put pen to paper this very day. Someone is spreading lies about us, to damage our reputation.'

'The negotiations are *not* advancing as fast as they might,' agreed Kun, looking hard at Chaloner. 'Especially given the energy and goodwill that we have poured into them. So we have reached the conclusion that someone is trying to sabotage them. A traitor.'

'You mean a Dutchman?' asked Chaloner, recalling that the slow pace had been remarked upon by van Goch, Ruyven, Clarendon and even Thurloe. 'Someone in your delegation?'

'Of course not!' declared Zas, offended. 'All right – I accept that not everyone at the Savoy believes peace is our best option. But no one would actively work against it.'

'It is an outsider,' said Kun pointedly. 'Someone with an intimate knowledge of Dutch affairs.'

'Well, it is not me,' said Chaloner firmly. 'The talks have been in failure for months, but I have been in London for less than four weeks.'

'Of course it is not you,' said Zas impatiently. 'However, Hanse's murder is a major stumbling block to progress, and we desperately need a solution. So tell us what you have learned.'

'Very little,' said Chaloner, giving each of the Dutchmen a cool look. 'Which is not surprising, given that witnesses have not been honest with me. For example, it would have been helpful to know far sooner about Hanse's penchant for solitary walks *and* his sudden increase in drinking. But here we are at the junction with Wich Street, where our paths diverge, so let me out and—'

'No,' said Kun, reaching out to prevent him from knocking on the roof to tell the driver to stop. 'Tell us what you know, even if it is only a little.'

'I know I have wasted a lot of time learning facts that you could have confided days ago.'

'Because we did not want to mislead you,' said Taacken impatiently. 'His walks and drinking are irrelevant. Indeed, we are *all* imbibing more than is our wont, because we are worn out by these interminable delays. But neither it nor his nocturnal ambles pertain to his murder.'

Chaloner would make up his own mind about that. 'Perhaps. But withholding the information was not helpful, and your dissimulation is the reason why I have nothing more to tell you.'

With a sigh, Zas rapped on the ceiling, bringing the coach to a standstill. 'Then we are sorry. But please do your best to find answers. Peace between two nations may depend on what you learn.'

It was unreasonable pressure, and Chaloner grimaced as he turned to climb out of the carriage. Kun leaned forward as he passed.

'Be careful,' he whispered in a voice so low as to be virtually inaudible. 'Nothing is as it seems.'

Chaloner stared after the carriage as it rattled away.

299

Had he just been issued with a warning or a threat? And why had Kun been less friendly than usual? Had he tired of the negotiations, and decided there was no longer any need to present an amiable face to the opposition? Or was it the notion that Chaloner might be closing in on Hanse's killer that worried him?

Kun had looked different that day – smaller, older and thinner. How good a master of disguise was Falcon? Good enough to fool the friends of the man he was impersonating? With that unsettling thought, Chaloner turned and began to retrace his steps, hoping Compton would have answers to his questions, because if not, he was beginning to fear that he might never solve the mysteries that seemed to grow deeper and more entangled with every new piece of intelligence he acquired.

It was not far to Drury Lane, but it was now the hottest part of the day, and heat rose in wavy, shimmering sheets off the road. When Chaloner heard his name called, he was tempted to ignore it, wanting only to reach Compton's house, so he could step out of the sun. Moments later, a carriage rolled to a stop beside him. It was Murdoch, the hackneyman who had identified Ibbot.

'You are a difficult man to track down,' said the Scot, wiping his sweaty face with a rag. 'I would have given up, if the order to find you had come from anyone other than Mr Thurloe. But I would do anything for him, as you know. Even traipse around hot cities.'

During the Commonwealth, Thurloe had saved Murdoch's sister from wrongful execution, and had earned himself a devoted servant in the process.

'Why does he want me?' asked Chaloner worriedly. 'Has something happened to him?'

300

Murdoch shook his head. 'No, no. It is more a case of something happening to *me*. But, Lord, it is hot! The weather is an omen, you know.' He flicked his head to where the sun was a malevolent yellow eye in a cloudless sky. 'A terrible evil will befall us before the month is out.'

'People said that in February, when the old king's ghost took to wandering about and pieces started falling off St Paul's Cathedral. But we are still here.'

'Give it time,' said Murdoch darkly. 'My sister reckons it will be plague. After all, the disease is raging in Amsterdam, so the newsbooks say. But I had better tell you my story, because Mr Thurloe says it is important, and he charged me to relate it to you as soon as possible.'

'Yes?' asked Chaloner, when the Scot paused, apparently for dramatic effect.

Murdoch cleared his throat. 'I had a Dutchman in my carriage the other day. He spoke good English, but he scoffed cheese for the entire journey. That is how I guessed his nationality, see.'

'Right,' said Chaloner, wondering whether there was any point in informing him that the Dutch were no more enamoured of dairy produce than the average Briton.

'So, being a patriotic soul, I took him down a dark lane in the Fleet Rookery, and shoved a knife to his throat,' Murdoch continued, so blithely that Chaloner wondered how many other fares had suffered this fate. 'And I told him that if he did not confess to being a spy, I would kill him.'

'And did he?' asked Chaloner, sorry for the hapless foreigner.

'No.' Murdoch sounded disgusted. 'And then I was in a fix, because I did not really want to stab him. So I

301

ordered him never to spy on us again, on pain of death, and took him home to the Savoy.'

'The Savoy?' pounced Chaloner. 'He was one of Ambassador van Goch's people?'

'A diplomat,' agreed Murdoch. 'Maybe that was why he refused to admit being an intelligencer – he is skilled at reading minds, and could tell I was bluffing. Anyway, when we reached the Savoy, he flew out of my coach without bothering to pay, which was a damned cheek. But in his desperation to deprive me of my due, he left something behind.'

'What?' asked Chaloner, suspecting it had been fear that had led the man to bolt, not a ploy to gain a free ride – although most folk would baulk at paying for a journey that included unscheduled excursions to dark lanes and threats of murder.

'Something important,' said Murdoch smugly. 'Because the other hackneymen say he has been asking after it ever since – darting out to grill them as they drive past the Savoy. I rarely work that end of The Strand, so I have not seen him since. None of them told him anything, of course.'

'Of course,' said Chaloner. 'So I assume you took this item to Thurloe?'

'Today,' nodded Murdoch. 'When it occurred to me that I should probably hand it to someone in authority. And there *is* no greater authority than Mr Thurloe, as far as I am concerned, regardless of the fact that stupid Royalists have stolen away his power. Anyway, he took one look at it and told me to give it to you. So here it is.'

He reached behind him, and produced a package that was about the size of his head. Chaloner recognised the distinct colouring of one of the States-General's most famous cheeses, and supposed the diplomat *had* been gorging on it during his journey. He felt a surge of exasperation. What had the fellow been thinking? Had he *wanted* to perpetuate the stereotype?

'Look,' said Murdoch, removing the waxy paper in which the item was wrapped.

The middle of the cheese had been hollowed out and a sheaf of paper shoved inside. Clearly, the intention had been to conceal it by replacing the rind lid, but the diversion to the Fleet Rookery must have distracted its owner, and he had neglected to complete what he had started.

'Most are incomprehensible, because of word-shortening and code,' said Murdoch, watching Chaloner remove the documents and begin to sift through them. 'But there is an interesting bit about Lady Castlemaine's underwear.'

Chaloner took a page at random, and scanned it quickly. The 'code' was Latin, while the 'word-shortening' was the kind of shorthand all clerks employed. He had seen enough of such items to recognise notes taken at a meeting, and was also aware that 'Bu' probably meant Buckingham, while LC referred to the Lord Chancellor. They were minutes from a Privy Council gathering.

Were they the ones that had been stolen from Clarendon? Clearly, Thurloe thought so. Unfortunately, Bulteel said seven meetings' worth had gone, and there were not enough notes in the cheese to represent that many discussions. So where were the rest? And why had these been in the hands of a Dutchman? *Had* a diplomat taken them from Worcester House, and put them in the cheese to keep them safe, perhaps for transportation back to The Hague?

'When did all this happen?' he asked.

303

'Monday morning,' replied Murdoch, promptly and without hesitation.

Chaloner smiled. He had always known Hanse was not responsible, but it was still good to have it confirmed: Hanse was dead by the time the mysterious Dutchman had sat in Murdoch's carriage and fiddled with his cheese. 'Thank you. Is there anything else you can tell me?'

'Yes,' said Murdoch, pleased with himself. 'Something about Saul Ibbot. I know you are interested in him, because you asked after him earlier in the week. Well, there is a rumour that he was killed by Hectors, but I know for a fact that they stopped using him last year because of his wife's loose tongue. The rumour is false – he just had an accident.'

Chaloner mulled over the information. So there was nothing sinister about the hackney that had transported Hanse from the Sun. Hanse had probably asked Ibbot to take him to the Devil, rather than the Savoy, but it had been his decision, and had had nothing to do with criminal gangs. Ibbot's death *was* a coincidence, proving that they did occur from time to time.

Murdoch turned the discussion back to the papers. With a gleeful grin, he wrenched the minutes from Chaloner's hand and slapped a different page into it. This document was on thinner, cheaper paper, and was in different handwriting.

'The coded stuff is boring. *This* is the interesting bit, although Mr Thurloe did not agree.'

Chaloner saw the document did indeed contain details of Lady Castlemaine's nether garments. He gazed at it in confusion. Why should such a thing be among Privy Council papers? Or in the possession of a Dutch diplomat for that matter?

'When I dropped that butter-lover off at the Savoy, I heard his cronies call him Kern,' Murdoch was saying. 'At least, it *sounded* like Kern.'

'Kun?' asked Chaloner, his thoughts tumbling about like acrobats.

Murdoch snapped his fingers. 'You have it! The villain's name was Kun.'

Chapter 9

From being at a virtual standstill, Chaloner now had several leads to follow. He needed to see Kun, and demand to know why the secretary had been toting Privy Council papers around inside a cheese – and how he could have been so indescribably stupid as to leave them in a hackney carriage. Then there was the Devil tavern on Fleet Street, where he would ask what the landlord knew of the five men who had met there, and about the attack on Molins. And finally, there was Compton. As he was already at his house, he decided to interview the Master of Ordnance first.

He knocked on the door, and when it was opened, he was startled to find the house in an uproar, with servants standing in small, frightened knots.

'What is the matter?' he asked of the maid who had admitted him the last time he was there.

'The master is ill,' she replied with a sob. 'He was well this morning, but then he complained of pains in his stomach, and took to his bed. Surgeon Wiseman said he just needed to rest and drink lots of water. But he is getting worse!'

'Have you summoned Wiseman back again?'

The maid nodded fearfully. 'And a physician is already here.'

All heads turned as a man appeared at the top of the staircase. Chaloner could tell from his sombre clothes that he was a medical man.

'Are you a member of Compton's family?' the fellow demanded.

'He is the Lord Chancellor's envoy,' replied the maid before Chaloner could speak.

'He will do. Your master should have someone of quality with him, lest there is business he wants to complete before he sinks too far. And servants are hardly the thing.'

'Should we send for his brothers, then?' asked the maid, ignoring the slight.

'Yes,' said the physician urgently. 'And someone should hurry Wiseman along, too.'

'What is wrong with Compton?' asked Chaloner, shocked by the doom-laden words.

'It is too complex a matter to explain to laymen,' declared the physician haughtily, suggesting he probably did not know. 'Come with me. Quickly!'

Thoroughly alarmed, Chaloner followed him up the stairs and into a darkened chamber. Compton lay in a bed with a cloth on his head. Like Molins, his clothes had been tossed to one side – hat, gloves, stockings, breeches and coat.

'It is not the heat ailing me now,' he whispered, smiling wanly as he recognised his visitor. 'I am dying. I said I had a sense of impending doom, and I was right.'

'You cannot be dying!' declared Chaloner, although he was aware from the physician's grim expression that he might be right. 'I saw you yesterday, and you said you were fit and well.'

'But today, God has seen fit to call me to Him,' breathed Compton, his face serene. 'Will you stay until my brothers arrive? And if I am unable, tell them . . . tell them our problem is resolved. They will know what I mean.'

He lapsed into silence, and Chaloner wondered what to do. He was not so ruthless as to pump a dying man for information, but he was also aware that Compton would take his secrets to the grave unless questions were asked. Fortunately, he was spared from having to make a decision when the Master of Ordnance broached the subject himself.

'How goes your enquiry?' he whispered. 'Did you visit Newgate?'

'I did, but Falcon had escaped, and Swan and Swallow were murdered.'

Compton gaped at him. 'Falcon is on the loose? No! It is not possible!'

'He has probably been free for the last two weeks. When did the first of your men die, exactly?'

Compton swallowed hard. 'Twelve days ago. You *must* help me, Chaloner. Go to the Fleet Rookery and warn Fairfax. Four of us are gone; there cannot be a fifth.'

'You think your illness is Falcon's doing?'

'I am sure of it – his curses are very powerful. Will you do as I ask?'

'Of course. As soon as your brothers come.'

Compton closed his eyes in relief. 'My soldiers are important to me. All my people are.'

'Will you tell me something?' Chaloner began tenta-

308

tively. 'You met four men in two London taverns. One was Hanse, who is dead. Another was Ned Molins, and he is dead, too.'

Compton's expression was agonised. 'Molins? But Wiseman said he had saved him!'

'He thought he had.'

'Lord God!' Compton's face was a mask of despair. 'I lied to you, Chaloner, when you asked about the Sinon Plot. I did it to protect you *and* them, because . . . Visit the last two men . . . tell them they are in terrible peril. We should have known it was too hazardous a . . . You *must* help them!'

'Lied to me about what, exactly?'

'No! It is far too dangerous! Warn the other two. Please! Promise me you will do it.'

'It may be more dangerous *not* knowing what is going on,' said Chaloner, becoming frustrated.

Compton gripped Chaloner's hand with unexpected strength for a man on the verge of expiring. 'I misled you specifically to keep you out of Falcon's clutches. If *we* could not stop him, with all our combined resources, then how can one man expect to prevail? I will not see you dead, too. He is even beyond Williamson's skills . . .'

'I can look after myself. And to be blind to the risks is far more—'

The physician came to pull him away, seeing his presence was agitating the patient, but Compton tightened his hold on Chaloner's wrist, and it was the *medicus* who was obliged to retreat.

'I can tell you that the crown jewels were just a beginning,' Compton whispered, once the physician was out of earshot. 'They were needed to finance Falcon's *real* work – the Sinon Plot.'

'What *is* the real Sinon Plot?' pressed Chaloner urgently.

'Warn the last two members of our group,' ordered Compton. His voice was weakening, and perspiration stood out on his forehead 'One is Talbot Edwards . . . of the Tower. Go to him . . .'

The 'fat, sweaty, ordinary' man, thought Chaloner, recalling his own encounter with Edwards the previous evening: the rotund Assistant Keeper of the Jewels had perspired heavily under his unremarkable clothes. 'And the last one is a vicar,' he prompted.

'Yes. He is Edw . . .' The rest of the sentence was spoken too softly for Chaloner to hear.

'Enough,' said the physician sharply, stepping forward again when Compton's eyes closed and he slumped back, exhausted. 'Let him rest, or he will die before his family arrives.'

The agitation had gone from Compton's face, and Chaloner saw he thought his message had been delivered – that his companions were going to be safe. He started to shake him awake, to ask for the last name to be repeated, but the physician shoved him back.

'Do you *want* him dead?' he hissed. 'At least give his brothers a chance to say their farewells.'

But Chaloner thought the dying man would probably sooner save the life of a friend, and reached for Compton's shoulder again. Ignoring the physician's objections, he shook it, lightly at first and then harder, but the patient was past rousing.

It was not many moments before the door was flung open, and two men raced in. Chaloner recognised Compton's brothers from Court. The older one was the

Earl of Northampton, and the younger was Charles. Northampton immediately took command, firing questions at the physician and issuing orders to the servants. Both reeled with shock when informed that Compton was dying.

'He wanted me to tell you something,' Chaloner said, eager to deliver the message and be away to fulfil their sibling's last wishes. 'Your problem has been resolved.'

Northampton bowed his head in relief, still ashen from the physician's grim prognosis. 'Thank God! He doubtless explained it all to you? About Penelope, our sister?'

'No,' replied Chaloner. 'He just—'

'She fell in love,' Northampton interrupted wretchedly. 'And gave herself to a man. There was a child. We thought we had kept the matter quiet, that her reputation was intact, but . . .'

'But someone found out and is demanding money for his silence?' Chaloner was not surprised: the White Hall blackmailer seemed to know secrets about virtually every family at Court.

Northampton swallowed hard. 'Our honour is at stake, so we had no choice but to pay. My brother did it yesterday. As you no doubt know, that was the meaning of his message to us.'

In Chaloner's experience, once blackmailers had profited from their work, they tended to come back for more, and Compton's capitulation was likely to mark the beginning of the problem, not the end. But it was no time to say so. He became aware that Northampton was staring at him.

'Why did my brother confide in you? He has never mentioned you as a particular friend before.'

Chaloner did not want to distress him further by telling

him that Compton had confided nothing, and that it had been Northampton himself who had just let the family skeleton out of its closet. It was understandable enough: the poor man was in shock.

'He trusted me,' replied Chaloner simply, meeting his eyes. 'And so may you.'

'Thank you,' said Northampton gruffly, seeming to sense his sincerity.

'Your brother met four men in different London taverns,' said Chaloner, wondering whether Northampton could help him out with answers, given that Compton was no longer in a position to do it. 'They included Willem Hanse, Ned Molins and Talbot Edwards. Could he have been meeting them in connection with this black-mailer, do you think?'

Northampton looked bewildered. 'I doubt it. Edwards sometimes consulted my brother on security for the crown jewels, while Molins acted as surgeon to his troops. I had no idea he knew any Hollanders though. But you said four men. Who is the last?'

'Does he know any vicars?'

'Lots – he is a devout man. But I doubt *they* are the sort to gather in alehouses, and—'

He broke off when Wiseman exploded into the room. The surgeon dropped to his knees beside Compton, but it was clear the patient was past earthly help. He shook his head at the brothers' hopeful gazes. Northampton began to sob, so Chaloner left, to give them privacy. He was walking down the stairs, aiming to execute his promise to Compton straight away, when Wiseman came after him. The surgeon was pale.

'I thought it was the heat, so I recommended rest and plenty of water. How *can* he be dead?'

Chaloner had no answer, although it was the second time that Wiseman had misdiagnosed Compton. 'Could he have been poisoned? Falcon cursed him and his men for putting him in Newgate. Now four of the five are dead. That cannot be coincidence.'

Wiseman stared at him. 'I can take samples and test them on a few rats.'

'Do that,' said Chaloner. 'And let me know what you find.'

With the sense that time was of the essence, Chaloner left Drury Lane, and ran towards the Fleet Rookery, an area of tiny lanes, filthy runnels, creaking tenements and seedy yards. It was home to thousands of people, crammed twenty or thirty to a room, and the stench of sewage, poverty and filth that pervaded it that sultry June evening was enough to take his breath away.

It was no place for a man wearing Court clothes, and Chaloner, still clutching the cheese and its hidden papers, was obliged to fend off several attacks as he tried to learn where he might find Fairfax. He was beginning to think he might have to give up, when he remembered that Mother Greene lived nearby.

Mother Greene, a sprightly old lady with opinions, had helped him before. She owned a small but spotlessly clean house on Turnagain Lane, and claimed she had once been married to a wealthy actor. Her home was full of herbs and potions, and Chaloner was fairly sure she was a witch. She was pleased to see him, although her expression grew guarded when he explained what he wanted.

'I do not know Fairfax.' Fleet Rookery residents did not talk about their own.

'It is vital that I pass him a message. His life may be in danger, and he needs to know it.'

'Then tell me this message,' she ordered. 'And I will see what I can do.'

'Sir William Compton is dead, and so are three of the four soldiers who went with him to arrest a thief named Falcon. With his dying breath, Compton warned Fairfax to be on his guard.'

'Sir William is dead?' Mother Greene was dismayed. 'Then I am sorry. He was a good man – generous with alms for the poor, and kind to his servants. And young, too. How did he die?'

Chaloner wiped the sweat from his face with his sleeve. 'I am not sure.'

'That cheese smells nice,' she remarked, after a short silence during which they both reflected on the man who had been so widely admired for his integrity and courage. 'Did you bring it for me? It is a pity you have scoured out the middle, but I suppose beggars cannot be choosers.'

There was no reason not to let her have it – the Earl would not thank him for bringing something that reeked into his offices, not even to see how cleverly the documents had been concealed. He retrieved the papers, shoved them inside his shirt, and stood to leave.

'Wait,' said Mother Greene, climbing stiffly to her feet. 'I will go with you to the edge of the rookery. It will be dark soon, and you should not be unaccompanied at this time of night.'

'There is no need,' said Chaloner, reluctant to accept the services of an old lady as a bodyguard. 'And I am in a hurry.'

'In a hurry to die?' she asked archly. 'Let me walk with you. To repay you for the cheese.'

314

Biting back his impatience, he matched her stately pace as she led him towards Fleet Street. But then the hair on the back of his neck rose in the way it always did to warn him of danger, and he had the sense that he was being watched. He glanced around uneasily, and thought he saw shadows flitting in the doorways they had passed. Mother Greene was right: the Fleet Rookery was no place for an outsider after dark. Thus he was surprised to see a familiar figure materialise in the gloom ahead. It was Sir George Downing, a dozen thickset louts at his heels.

'Chaloner!' he exclaimed. 'I hoped I might run into you at some point. Of course, I did not expect it to be here – I thought you had more class than to frequent this sort of area. But then again, you always were an unsavoury villain.'

'What do you want?' asked Chaloner, forbearing to mention that it was no place for an Envoy Extraordinary, either, and the King would certainly disapprove.

'I was doing well in London,' said Downing sourly. 'But then *you* arrived. First, you expose two of my stewards as thieves, and it has been difficult to persuade people that I had nothing to do with their crimes. And then you steal something that belongs to me.'

Chaloner regarded him blankly, trying to imagine what it was that the envoy thought he had taken. He could feel the malice wafting from Downing in waves, and glanced uneasily at Mother Greene, wishing she was not there. It would be difficult to defend her if Downing's men attacked.

'What have I stolen?' he asked.

'Certain documents,' replied Downing coldly. 'Ones that show my expense accounts may not be entirely accurate. They are missing from my lodgings, and I know it was you who took them.'

'How can you think I would waste my time so?' asked Chaloner in disgust. 'I have better—'

'Of course it was you!' spat Downing. 'I have not forgotten your talents in that direction. So, you will give them back, or my friends here will find a way to persuade you.'

Chaloner did not grace the threat with a reply. He put his hand on Mother Greene's shoulder, and began to steer her through the watching ruffians, aiming to have her safely out of the way before the fighting – which he sensed was inevitable – began. Obediently, she began to walk, and he was surprised but relieved when the men shuffled aside to let them pass.

'What are you doing?' shouted Downing, gaping at his louts in disbelief. 'Stop him! Make him say what he has done with my property.'

Chaloner braced himself for an assault, but nothing happened, and Mother Greene continued to hobble forward, her eyes fixed straight ahead. Chaloner whipped around when Downing drew his sword, but Mother Greene grabbed his arm and pulled him on.

'You are not interested in them, sir,' he heard one of the hirelings say. 'Let them go.'

'I certainly shall not!' cried Downing, outraged. 'If those documents ever see the light of day, I will lose everything, and *you* will not get paid. So either stop him, or get out of the way so I can.'

There was no reply, and when Chaloner glanced around a second time, it was to see Downing deprived of his sword and fuming impotently behind a solid wall of men.

'You damned scoundrels!' he was howling. 'I will see you all hanged for this!'

'That fellow is not in his right wits,' murmured Mother Greene. 'It is hardly wise to make that sort of threat in the hearing of fathers, brothers, cousins and friends. He is asking to be dispatched.'

'I am not quite sure what just happened,' said Chaloner, when they reached Fleet Street. He had resigned himself to a trouncing – or worse – and was amazed to find himself in one piece.

'Downing hires local lads from time to time,' replied Mother Greene vaguely. 'For protection and for the occasional spot of rough work. Doubtless, he will be looking for replacements now these have defied him.' She chuckled to herself.

'But *why* did they defy him?' pressed Chaloner. 'Was it because of you?'

Mother Greene smiled enigmatically. 'Me? Why should I have such authority? Incidentally, next time you come, bring me a ham. I prefer meat to cheese.'

Chaloner flagged down a hackney, and climbed in wearily. Mother Greene might have saved him this time – probably because Downing's hirelings had not wanted to be turned into toads – but the envoy was likely to try again if he thought Chaloner was in possession of documents that showed him to be corrupt. He sighed. It was a distraction he could do without when he had so much to do – and so much to think about, too, after Compton's disclosures. And how was he to fulfil his promise to Compton when he had not caught the name of the last man he was to warn? All he could hope was that Edwards would tell him. Aware that time was of the essence, he

317

yelled for the driver to make for the Tower with all possible speed.

It was not long before they arrived. The Tower was foreboding and eerie in the half-darkness of the balmy summer night, all thick walls, jagged crenellations and lowered portcullises. Fighting down a wave of nausea at the sight, Chaloner forced himself to bang on a gate until a yeoman came.

'I need to speak to Mr Edwards,' he said urgently. 'It is very important.'

'Perhaps it is, but he is not here,' replied the yeoman. 'And I would not let you in anyway, not at this time of night. We have our security to think about, and I do not know you.'

Chaloner sagged when he recalled Edwards saying he was going to visit kin in the country. He cursed himself, knowing he should have remembered.

'Where has he gone?' he demanded, supposing he could ride through the night if necessary.

'He did not say,' replied the yeoman. 'But he has family in Chatham, Hampstead and Dorking, so I expect it will be one of those. Or perhaps Essex. He has an uncle there, I believe.'

It was hopeless – they were places in completely different directions. 'Is there anyone who might know?' Chaloner asked desperately. 'A friend here, or in the city?'

The yeoman shook his head. 'He might have told his guard, Brown, but Brown died of a fever recently, and Mr Edwards is a private kind of man. He always keeps his travels to himself.'

'Then will you give him a message when he returns?' asked Chaloner, defeated.

318

'Write it down, then. One of us will see he has it the moment he returns.'

'When might that be?'

'Tomorrow or the day after. He does not like to be gone for too long. Here is pen and paper.'

Chaloner took them, and wrote a note informing Edwards that Compton, Molins and Hanse were dead. He did not add that the Assistant Keeper should be on his guard, because it should be obvious, and he did not want to compromise the man, should the missive fall into the wrong hands. He gave the yeoman some coins for his trouble, and turned back towards the city, supposing he would have to revisit both Tower and Fleet Rookery the following day, to ensure his warnings had been received – and to ask Edwards for the name of the last member of his curious cabal. His own promise to Compton would not be discharged until he was sure the three men understood the danger they might be in.

The hackney carriage that had taken him to the Tower was still waiting, so he asked its driver to ferry him to the Devil tavern on Fleet Street, thinking to interview the landlord about the five men who had gathered there. But when he arrived, it was to find the place closed and shuttered for the night. He hammered on the door until an angry neighbour informed him that Barford was away, and was not expected back until the following evening.

Chaloner closed his eyes in despair. From having a number of leads, he was now reduced to one – and it was too late to interrogate Kun at the Savoy. Exhausted, he started to walk home, but then remembered that his house was being watched, and it would not be safe to sleep there. He would not endanger Thurloe or

319

Temperance by foisting himself on them, so he was effectively homeless.

With nothing else to do, he prowled, a silent shadow in the dark streets. The other London was awake now. Robbers and thieves roamed, ready to pounce, and prostitutes flounced in twos and threes, scantily clad in the sweltering heat. Court rakes travelled in carriages or on horseback, carousing in those taverns that catered to late-night patrons. Chaloner saw Kicke and Nisbett in a boisterous, belligerent throng. Whores followed them, hopeful for business.

He reached The Strand, and was padding past the maypole – demolished by Cromwell and replaced by the King – when he decided to visit the Savoy anyway. If the elderly secretary objected to being woken in the middle of the night, then he should not have dabbled in espionage.

Knocking on the front gate was out of the question – no guard would admit casual visitors after dark – so he went to Worcester House, and entered the Savoy's garden by scaling the wall that divided them. The night was clear but moonless, and he had no trouble evading the sentries.

As he drew near the State Room, he saw a soiree was in progress. Lights blazed, and its windows were thrown open in the hope of catching a breeze. The sound of civilised society drifted out: music, the clink of goblets against decanters, and the buzz of genteel conversation. The language was Dutch, and he surmised that a reception was being held for ex-patriot merchants. It was a relaxed affair, and people were enjoying themselves. Except three: van Goch, Zas and de Buat were standing by a window, speaking in low, strained voices. Chaloner edged closer.

'. . . no idea where he is,' the physician was saying. 'Ruyven has been searching all evening.'

Van Goch looked as though he might be sick, and Zas patted his arm. 'The Savoy is a big place, sir. Kun will have found himself a quiet corner somewhere, to sit and think quietly about how best to counter Downing's most recent effort to damage relations between our countries.'

'Then let us hope he is successful,' said van Goch worriedly. 'The convention is in two days, and we cannot afford yet another obstacle in the path of peace.'

'To which obstacle do you refer?' asked de Buat. 'The one that says the Duke of York has set to sea with thirty warships? Or the business with the vase?'

Van Goch sighed unhappily. 'Buckingham says the tale about the boats is a canard, and perhaps he is right. Such an action would be tantamount to declaring war, and I do not think the King would be so insensitive as to launch an armada while we are still in the country.'

'Clearly, this rumour is a ploy to create suspicion and mistrust,' said Zas. 'Like Downing's so-called discovery in the vase. We must ignore them – refuse to let them influence us.'

They moved away, leaving Chaloner wondering what Downing had found and whether he should search the precinct for Kun. He glanced around, then sagged in defeat: Zas was right when he said the place was huge, and he could not do it thoroughly, at night and on his own. It would be a waste of time.

Supposing his questions would have to wait until morning after all, he prowled until he reached Jacoba's lodgings. A lamp burned, showing she had declined to join the party in the State Room, but had not yet gone to sleep. He raised his hand to knock on her door, then let it drop when he heard the rumble of conversation through one of the open windows. Loath to disturb her when she had company, he started to leave, but then stopped when he recognised one voice as Ruyven's.

'. . . appreciate your position,' the captain was murmuring. 'But you *said* you loved me.'

'I do love you.' Jacoba's voice was unsteady. 'But Willem is dead, and I cannot escape the feeling that it is my fault – that I am being punished for betraying him. So, as I told you the last time we talked, I *cannot* see you again. Not ever. Now please leave, before someone sees you.'

'I will wait for you to change your mind,' declared Ruyven softly. 'Even if it takes years, you will be mine again.'

Chaloner hid in the shadows as the captain crept past, then leaned against the wall and stared up at the sky. So, he thought, poisonous old Prynne had been right: Ruyven *did* have a dark secret. Had Hanse known? Chaloner was inclined to suspect he had, and that it was the reason why he had turned to excessive drinking. But what did it say about Hanse's death? That *Ruyven* had poisoned him and pushed him half-dead into the river? Unpleasant though it would be, Chaloner knew he would have to find out.

The Golden Lion was too busy for Chaloner's liking, so, in the absence of anywhere else to go, he found a quiet spot under a tree in Lincoln's Inn's Fields. The night was warm, and it had not rained for so long that there was no dew to chill him. Moreover, the vegetation was dust dry, and anyone approaching could not do so without crunching, cracking or rustling, sounds that would rouse him. But no one came, and he woke just as the night sky was beginning to turn a lighter shade of blue.

He lay for a while, looking up at the fading stars, and inhaling deeply of air that was scented with seared earth and baked leaves. He thought about his investigations, wondering why Hanse had met Compton, Molins, Edwards and the still-unidentified vicar. Compton's reluctant admission – that the Sinon Plot was more than an attempt to steal the crown jewels – made him certain that the five men had met to discuss it. But *what* was it, and had they been aiming to stop it or further it?

Still, at least he could conclude that the mysterious vicar was not Falcon – Compton would have noticed if the man he had arrested was the same individual he had met in taverns. *Ergo*, it was another cleric who needed to be warned of the danger he was in.

Worriedly, Chaloner pondered the enigma that was Falcon. Compton believed Falcon was responsible for the deaths of his men, and Chaloner strongly suspected that he had had a hand in what had happened to Hanse and Molins, too. Williamson and Swaddell had remarked on how dangerous he was, and what a threat he represented to London and Londoners, so hunting him down was a matter of urgency. But *how* was it to be done when no one could say what he looked like?

Staring at the sky was bringing no answers, so Chaloner stood, brushed himself down, and began to make his way towards the road. Shadows moved in the trees ahead, so he slowed and inched forward carefully. In the predawn light, he could see a rough table on which weapons had been laid: a duel was about to take place. He started to move away, but stopped when he recognised one of the combatants. Charles Bates looked white and sick under his copper wig.

'I do not have a second,' he was saying unsteadily. 'I could not find . . . I did not want to tell . . .'

Kicke laughed. 'You kept my challenge secret, lest your friends see you as the cuckold you are.'

'I *will* kill you,' vowed Bates, swallowing hard. 'You insult Ann, as well as me.'

'She does not deserve you,' spat Kicke contemptuously. 'She deserves me, and I will have her when you are in your grave. So, shall we start, or do you need a moment to pray first?'

Bates tried to draw his sword, but his hand was shaking so badly that it stuck. Chaloner watched in horror. The contest was tantamount to murder, because there was no way Bates stood even the remotest chance of surviving the encounter. Hannah would be devastated – she was fond of the man who had been her father's closest friend. Moreover, what would she say if she ever learned that her husband had stood by and watched the slaughter from the safety of a bush?

Chaloner had seen Kicke fight: he was no Nisbett, and the spy knew he could probably defeat him. He closed his eyes for a moment, took a deep breath, then strode forward.

'Sorry I am late.' He smiled amiably when Kicke whipped around. 'I am Bates's second.'

'But he just said he does not have one,' objected Kicke uneasily. 'Go away. You—'

'No, let him stay,' said Nisbett, advancing from the gloom with his blade at the ready. 'And I move that the principals stand back and let the seconds settle this matter. Is everyone agreed?'

'Yes,' nodded Kicke quickly. 'Carry on.'

Wishing he had remained hidden, and sincerely

hoping Wiseman's report on Nisbett's weak knee was accurate, Chaloner drew his sword. Nisbett grinned his delight, and Chaloner knew he would have to act quickly, or it was going to be a very short – and fatal – encounter.

'No!' cried Bates, grabbing Chaloner's arm. 'Hannah will never forgive me.'

He jerked away when Nisbett launched a savage attack that had Chaloner retreating faster than was comfortable. Nisbett smirked his satisfaction when the spy stumbled.

'Remember what happened the last time you played with him,' warned Kicke. 'Finish him quickly, and then I shall dispatch the worm who married my Ann.'

Nisbett lunged again, forcing Chaloner to work hard to avoid being skewered, but the spy knew he was holding back – that despite Kicke's words, he intended to enjoy himself before delivering the final blow. The assault ended when the tip of his sword pierced Chaloner's coat, which would have hurt, had his shirt not been stuffed full of Privy Council minutes. Gloating, Nisbett strutted away, expressing his contempt by turning his back.

It was the opportunity Chaloner had been waiting for. He shot forward, and managed to score a gash in the man's thigh. It was a superficial injury, but it slowed Nisbett down. It also made him less agile, so he struggled to defend himself when attacked. And then he lost his balance. He landed on the ground with a screech of agony, clutching his leg and letting the weapon fly from his hand.

'I yield!' he howled. 'Fetch me a surgeon. Quickly! The pain . . .'

'What happens now?' asked Bates, regarding him dispassionately. 'Do I fight Kicke?'

'I will,' offered Chaloner. 'Or you can accept his apology. It is your choice.'

'I apologise,' said Kicke hastily, apparently unwilling to risk a bout with the man who had bested Nisbett. 'There. Now honour has been satisfied and I can tend my wounded friend.'

'I accept on one condition,' said Bates with sudden spirit. 'That you stay away from Ann. Decline, and Chaloner will dispatch you here and now.'

Kicke regarded him with blazing eyes. 'Very well,' he said, after a brief internal struggle, during which Nisbett howled, moaned and pleaded with him to hurry. 'You have my word.'

'The word of a scoundrel,' said Bates coldly. 'But it will have to do, I suppose. Good day.'

He strode away, head held high. Nisbett whimpered his relief, and there was a vengeful expression on Kicke's face. Neither would forgive what had happened that morning.

Chaloner accepted Bates's offer of a ride to Fleet Street, and they climbed into his carriage just as the twilight lifted and the first hint of gold in the east indicated that the sun was coming up.

'You risked your life, dashing in like that,' said Bates, when they were under way. 'Because they meant to murder me.'

'I imagine they still do, so be on your guard.'

'I will.' Bates looked out of the window. 'I had another demand for money this morning – the blackmailer is growing impatient. I am going to pay him, then take

326

Ann away. By this evening, we shall be gone from the city for ever.'

'Good. Hannah will be relieved to see you out of danger.'

Bates nodded. 'Yes, she will. But I am sorry I shall not be able to do as I offered – provide you with documents to bring Kicke down. However, Hannah told me you are also looking into the murder of that Dutch diplomat, so I wondered whether this might help you.'

He withdrew a sheet of paper from his pocket. It had been screwed into a ball at some point, because it was wrinkled. It was also partially burned at one end.

Chaloner took it cautiously. 'How did you come by it?'

'I found it in the Spares Gallery. Someone must have been working on it, then tossed it in the fire when he had finished. Unfortunately for him, the flames did not consume it all.'

Chaloner regarded him askance. 'Are you in the habit of picking through ashes, then?'

Bates shrugged. 'It caught my eye when I was re-arranging the fireplace. I like a tidy hearth.'

Chaloner turned his attention to the paper. 'A recipe for gingerbread?'

'Turn it over,' said Bates impatiently. 'Look at the *other* side.'

Chaloner did as he was told, and then it was difficult to prevent his shock from showing. There was a list of names, some with lines scored through them. It read:

~~Compton~~	~~Oates~~	~~Upton~~	Fairfax	~~Osborn~~
~~Molins~~	Joseph?	~~Hanse~~	~~Oetje~~	Chaloner?
Edwards	~~Brown~~	~~Pocks~~	Swan	Swallow

327

There may have been others, too, but the paper was too singed to tell. Chaloner gazed at it, thoughts churning. It comprised people he thought were associated with the Sinon Plot, with those who were dead crossed off. Compton said he had lost three of his four men – Upton, Osborn and Oates – with only Fairfax left alive, while Chaloner knew about Hanse, Molins, Oetje, Swallow and Swan. Moreover, Assistant Keeper Edwards had lost a guard named Brown to a recent illness. Did his name on the list suggest the 'fever' had been nothing of the kind? And did Edwards's own name mean he was marked for assassination, too?

Chaloner could only assume the list was Falcon's, and that he was eliminating anyone he considered a problem. After all, Swan and Swallow's names had been written, but Falcon's own had not. It was possible that it had been burned off the bottom, but somehow Chaloner did not think so, and the more he considered it, the more he became certain.

But who was Pocks? The last member of the group who had met in the taverns – the vicar, whose name Compton had spoken too softly to hear? If so, then the fact that it was scored through suggested that Chaloner was already too late to save him. And why were there question marks next to Chaloner's own name and that of Joseph? Did it refer to Joseph Molins?

Yet one thing was clear: Falcon had access to White Hall, and was sufficiently at ease there that he had lounged comfortably in the Spares Gallery and written a death list. Did that mean the Dutch delegation could be eliminated as suspects? Unfortunately, Chaloner suspected it did not – such an audacious master of deceit would probably feel at home anywhere he chose to be.

'Do you know a vicar called Pocks?' he asked Bates urgently. 'Perhaps Edward Pocks?'

Bates shook his head. 'I am sorry. And I would offer to help you find out, but I have booked seats for Ann and myself on the Oxford coach at nine o'clock.'

'Then be sure you do not miss it.'

Even though it was early, the Rainbow Coffee House was open for business. Chaloner knew it was risky to visit a familiar haunt when his home had been put under surveillance, but he wanted to see Rector Thompson and ask after Hannah. And meeting him in the coffee house was a lot safer than visiting his home or waylaying him in public.

Farr was roasting beans in a pan over a fire, and the air was thick with smoke. It billowed so densely that the skillet was invisible, and although Farr had once told Chaloner that he did not need to see the beans to know when they were ready – he could tell by the sound they made in the pot – Chaloner did not think he was very good at judging it. His brews always tasted burnt.

'Freshly ground this morning,' he announced, flapping his way out of the fug and coming to present his customers with a jug of steaming liquid. 'It does not come any better than this.'

Chaloner sipped it, and thought that if Farr's claim were true, then coffee would be a short-lived phenomenon. But he nodded polite appreciation, and Farr went to serve Stedman, who was holding forth about the religious significance of hailstones. Unwilling to listen to the ridiculous assertions being made, Chaloner withdrew to a corner while he waited for Thompson to appear, and

329

passed the time by studying the documents he had found in the cheese.

It did not take him long to realise that Bulteel had been right when he had said Privy Council secretaries wrote everything down: the documents contained a huge amount of irrelevant chatter. He learned that while Buckingham had no concept of the manoeuvrability of the navy's gunships, he owned a detailed grasp of the quality of the horses in the King's stables. He also discovered that the Duke of York liked women with short, fat legs in green stockings, and that Clarendon thought there should be a tax on traffic, as a measure to reduce London's congestion.

Reading on, he saw that military statistics given in one meeting were contradicted in the next, and that the 'expert opinions' of committee members changed constantly, depending on how they happened to feel at the time. As far as he was concerned, the minutes told the reader nothing more useful than that here was a group of men who did not know what they were talking about.

Would the papers be dangerous to national security if they fell into the wrong hands? They revealed the Privy Council to be a band of clueless idiots, but Chaloner suspected the Dutch already knew that. Moreover, the conflicting information did more to confuse than inform, and if van Goch believed any of it, then he was likely to do his own country a serious disservice.

The last document was the one that had intrigued Murdoch. It was written in bold roundhand, and said that Lady Castlemaine had stolen the veil the Queen wore to church, and had had it converted into some indecent underwear. It went on to describe the skimpy

330

garment. Chaloner knew the Queen would be horrified if she ever found out, and, because he would not want her quite so brazenly insulted, the King was unlikely to be amused. The letter went on to say that the Lady could have the item in question back, if she parted with fifty pounds.

Chaloner stared at it. Was the Lady guilty as charged? It was certainly the kind of prank that would appeal to her – and knowledge of it would appeal to the White Hall blackmailer. But how had Kun come to be in possession of such a note? With a sigh, Chaloner saw he would have to ask him as soon as he had delivered the papers to the Earl.

He was about to give up on Thompson and go about his duties, when the rector arrived.

'Your wife is charming company,' he enthused, all smiles. 'I may not let her go when you decide it is safe for her to return home, because she tells such entertaining tales of the Court . . .'

Chaloner was sure she did. 'Thank you for looking after her.'

'How are *you* faring?' asked Thompson in a lower voice. 'I have seen you looking better.'

Chaloner supposed his appearance did leave something to be desired. His night in the open had left him rumpled and unkempt, and he had not shaved in days. He decided he had better make a foray to Tothill Street before visiting the Earl.

'White Hall was in a frenzy just now,' Thompson went on, when Chaloner made no reply. 'Sir George Downing's house was burgled last night. Unfortunately for the would-be thief, Downing was up, frolicking with some hapless chambermaid, and there was a bit of a fight.'

331

'Is Downing harmed?' asked Chaloner hopefully.

'Unfortunately not,' replied Thompson with a rueful smile. 'Which goes to show the Devil always looks after his own. The felon was heavily disguised, but Downing is going around White Hall braying that the suspect is Lane – Colonel Griffith's manservant. Lane denies it, of course, and Griffith is defending him stoutly, although I can tell it pains him to do so.'

'Why?'

'Because he cannot abide the man, and longs to replace him. Unfortunately, anyone who applies for the post mysteriously withdraws his application within a few hours. The suspicion is that Lane warns them off. Poor Griffith! There is something about Lane that is very sinister.'

'Downing's accusations are a good opportunity for Griffith to be rid of the fellow. So why does he back him?'

Thompson shrugged. 'Principles, I suppose: Griffith feels obliged to stand by his own. He may be a cockerel, but he is loyal to his people. And that is not all that has set White Hall a-twitter today. Charles Bates announced just minutes ago that he is leaving on account of the plague.'

'He has it?' asked Chaloner uneasily.

Thompson shook his head. 'He says the heat will entice it to London. I heard him speak myself, and he was very convincing. There was none of the self-effacing fellow we have grown accustomed to, but a man who spoke firmly and with conviction. It was almost as if he was another person.'

Chaloner frowned. Had Bates's victory over Kicke changed him? Or had Falcon boldly assumed the identity of a shy, unassuming man whom no one had ever really noticed? Chaloner shook himself impatiently. Wild flights of fancy were not going to help him catch one of the most elusive criminals he had ever encountered.

Hannah's house was still under surveillance, but Chaloner had not put in an appearance for so long that the watchers had grown complacent. There were still too many to tackle for answers, but it was easy to evade the ones at the back and gain access to his home via a window.

Inside, the place was in a terrible state. Clothes had been hauled from chests and tossed on the floor, cushions had been slit and furniture upended. What did someone think he had? The Privy Council papers? Evidence about the Sinon Plot? The documents that proved Downing was a cheat? He looked around unhappily. It was not the first time it had happened to him, and would probably not be the last, but it would be the first time for Hannah, and he was sorry.

He shaved, found a smart blue waistcoat and black breeches, and left the way he had come. He had not gone far when he heard a shout, and a glance behind showed two men racing towards him. One carried a gun. Chaloner turned and fled, aware that others were joining the chase. But he had a good start, and was conveniently close to the maze of alleys around Westminster. He ducked into a doorway, and watched three men hurtle past. There was a fourth, but he lagged behind, fatter and less fit. Chaloner stuck out his foot and the fellow went sprawling.

'Answer some questions and you will live,' he whispered, hauling the fellow into his hiding place and pressing a knife to his throat. 'Refuse, and you will learn just how angry I am about the mess you made of my house.'

'Not me, sir,' bleated the man, frightened. 'I stood outside and kept guard, but I never went in. The one who hired us did, although I do not know his name and I did not see his face, so I cannot tell you who he is. He pays a dozen of us to watch your house full time, and says he will give us five shillings each if we lay hold of you and bring you to him.'

'Bring me where?'

'To the Heaven Inn, where we are to wait for someone to come and take you off our hands.'

The information did not help. The Heaven was a large, impersonal tavern, and Chaloner could ask questions there all day and not learn the identity of whoever wanted him.

'Then who are you?' he demanded.

'Just poor Richard Inch of Smithfield, sir. No one important.'

Clearly, Inch was a member of one of London's many criminal gangs, who hired their services to anyone who could pay. Such organisations were powerful and secretive, and Inch would be a lowly operative: Chaloner was unlikely to learn more by questioning him further. He put the knife in his pocket, aware that the interrogation had told him nothing he did not already know.

'Did your employer say why he wants me?' he asked, not really expecting a sensible answer.

'Not at first – he just said he needed to talk to you. But last night he told us that you are a spy, and a danger to our country.'

Again, the answer told Chaloner nothing, other than the fact that 'he' was aware the watchers had become complacent and hoped to give them added incentive for vigilance. Any one of his suspects – Falcon, Williamson,

Downing or Kicke and Nisbett – might have invented such a tale.

Chaloner heard the King's many clocks striking seven as he reached White Hall, and was surprised: he had been up for hours, and thought it was much later. He headed for the Earl's offices, relishing the cool emanating from the great marble staircase. He walked quickly, thinking of all he needed to do that day – confront Kun, visit the Devil tavern, ensure his messages to White and Fairfax had been delivered. And that was before he turned his attention to unmasking Falcon, and assessing whether Ruyven and Jacoba's affair had a bearing on Hanse's death.

'Wait!' hissed Bulteel, hurrying to intercept him as he passed. 'There is something you need to know before you speak to Clarendon. Come into my office.'

'What is the matter?' asked Chaloner, alarmed by the worry on the secretary's face.

'There is a rumour that says you are a spy for the States-General. Apparently, you were seen climbing into a carriage with some Dutchmen yesterday. Moreover, you make regular visits to the Savoy, and you met Hanse in suspicious circumstances.'

Chaloner sighed. 'Who started the gossip? Downing? Williamson?'

Bulteel pursed his lips. 'I would not know about Williamson. I did not like the atmosphere in his place of work when we visited it the other day, so I decided to cool our relationship. The Earl has never approved of it, and neither have you, so you should both be pleased. Moreover, he is unpopular at Court, and I will never be accepted in lofty circles as long as I fraternise with him.'

'The same might be said about your friendship with me,' said Chaloner, although he was relieved to hear Bulteel's curious association with the Spymaster was on the wane. He had never been comfortable with it.

'Downing would certainly agree,' said Bulteel. 'He claims you are related to Hanse through a secret former marriage, and he came here this morning with a band of louts to arrest you.'

'He cannot arrest me: he has no authority.'

'That is what Clarendon said, so he has stormed off to Williamson, to get some. You cannot stay in London, Tom. I know you are innocent and so does the Earl, but no one else will give you the benefit of the doubt. You are not safe here, and you should leave while you can.'

Chaloner understood exactly what the envoy was doing. 'Downing thinks I have papers that show him to be corrupt, and no doubt hopes that if I am in prison, they will be dismissed as forgeries. And he will escape prosecution.'

'I do not believe you have any such papers,' declared Bulteel stoutly. 'He is lying about them.'

'Oh, I imagine they exist. He would not be going to such efforts to defend himself otherwise. But they are not with me.'

Bulteel looked worried. 'Please say you will leave London. Downing is treacherous and selfish, and would think nothing of delivering you to a terrible fate in order to protect himself.'

'I cannot run away. People will assume I am guilty.'

'Better that than what Downing has in mind. Besides, Griffith told me last night that all manner of men are dying in curious circumstances – Hanse, Sir William

Compton, Ned Molins. I do not want your name added to this list.'

'Have you heard of a vicar named Edward Pocks?' asked Chaloner hopefully. 'He may have died recently, too.'

'*I* have not, but I will ask my cousin – he seems to be acquainted with half of London. Do you know anything else about this vicar? The name of his parish, perhaps?'

Chaloner shook his head. 'And I do not know how to begin finding out.'

'I do,' said Bulteel brightly. 'The Bishop of London is coming to visit Clarendon later. He has an excellent memory for names, so I shall ask him if he knows a clergyman called Pocks.'

'Thank you,' said Chaloner gratefully. 'Incidentally, I heard Lane is in trouble.'

Bulteel nodded. 'He is accused of burgling Downing, although I do not believe it, and neither does my cousin. Lane may be a sinister devil, but he is not a thief. I suspect Downing made the tale up to hurt poor Griffith.'

'What has Griffith done to annoy Downing?'

'He composed a scurrilous, but very funny poem about his greed and corruption.'

Chaloner grinned, and his opinion of Griffith rose. 'May I read it?'

Bulteel did not smile back. 'It is no laughing matter, Tom. First, it may damage my efforts to be accepted at Court – people know Griffith is my kinsman. And second, but rather more importantly, it may make Downing more dangerous than ever, which may harm *you*.'

'I can look after myself.'

'In a swordfight, perhaps, but Downing has other

337

contrivances at his disposal. Take this morning, for instance. He had a second reason for coming here – namely to return some of Clarendon's missing papers, which he says he found in the Savoy. They were in a vase, apparently.'

Chaloner regarded him askance, although he recalled what he had overheard van Goch, Zas and de Buat saying the previous night: Downing's 'so-called discovery'.

'Why would the Dutch treat potentially valuable documents in so bizarre a manner?' he asked dubiously. 'And why was Downing poking about inside their flower pots anyway?'

'Clarendon asked both those questions, but Downing declined to answer. He was unbearably smug when he handed the minutes over, though. He tried to make the Earl feel stupid for losing them in the first place, and kept saying that *you* did not retrieve them because your real loyalties lie with the States-General.'

Chaloner pulled the sheaf of papers from his waist-coat. 'But I *have* retrieved some.'

Bulteel snatched them, and began to thumb through them lovingly. 'I *knew* you would prevail! Where were they? Do you have the culprit under lock and key? Who is he?'

'Are they are all recovered now?' asked Chaloner, ignoring the flurry of questions.

'No – only about half.' Bulteel frowned when he found the letter pertaining to Lady Castlemaine. 'But this is not a document I recognise from—'

Chaloner took it from him. 'I think you might be safer not knowing the contents of that.'

Bulteel tried to grab it back. 'I am Clarendon's secretary. I know everything about his affairs.'

'It does not affect Clarendon,' said Chaloner firmly, declining to let him see it.

'As long as you are sure,' said Bulteel, unhappily. 'But I meant what I said about leaving London, Tom. I do not want to see your head on a spike outside Westminster Hall.'

With a strong sense that unless he found answers quickly, Bulteel's grim prediction might well come true, Chaloner stepped inside the Earl's office. That morning, even Clarendon had eschewed a fire, although his gouty foot was still swathed in blankets. He glared when Chaloner approached.

'Have you heard what Downing is saying? That your first marriage makes you a Dutch spy.'

'We have never seen eye to eye.'

The Earl grimaced. 'But he contradicts himself in his efforts to malign: he claims you gather intelligence for the States-General, but then brays a tale in which you invaded de Witt's bedroom and made off with his secrets. Obviously, you are unlikely to have done both. But the evidence against you is damning – your visits to the Savoy, your fluency in Hollandish . . .'

'I have been investigating Hanse's death and your missing papers,' Chaloner pointed out. 'Of course I have been to the Savoy. And it was necessary to speak Dutch, because some witnesses—'

The Earl cut across him. 'Moreover, you have just returned from the States-General. No one but I knows why you went there, and I am not about to announce that I ordered you to hunt for Lord Bristol. The King would not approve of that.'

'I suppose the situation does not look good for me,' conceded Chaloner.

'It does not. So you had better stay away from *me* until this business is over.'

Chaloner thought about Griffith's staunch defence of Lane. Clearly, the same courtesy was not going to be extended to him. Clarendon seemed to read his thoughts.

'I tried discrediting Downing's accusations, but my enemies immediately began to clamour that I am in the pay of the Dutch, too, which accounts for my determination to prevent a war. And as peace is more important than either of us, it is best if I just distance myself from you for a while.'

'Very well, sir,' said Chaloner flatly.

The Earl grimaced. 'None of this is my fault, Chaloner. *You* are the one who made an enemy of Downing, and now you must bear the consequences. However, you cannot leave London until the fuss dies down, because I need you here. You will just have to keep your head down.'

'I will try,' said Chaloner, not bothering to point out that it was difficult to conduct investigations without being visible to a certain extent.

'Good. But do not look so sullen! This unpleasantness will soon be over. The peace talks are failing, and van Goch is mumbling about going home. And when he goes, Downing will follow.'

Chaloner was horrified. 'You mean we are on the brink of war?'

'Yes, although I shall fight for conciliation for as long as I can. Who knows? Perhaps tomorrow's convention will see some progress – we can but hope. Incidentally, your failure to find my missing papers has caused me a great deal of embarrassment. I have had Downing gloating—'

Chaloner handed him the bundle. 'These were hidden

340

in a hollowed-out cheese in a hackney carriage,' he said, loath to reveal Kun's role in the affair until he understood what was happening.

'Lord!' breathed Clarendon, skimming through them quickly. 'A cheese in a hackney carriage is not a place *I* would have thought to look. And these are far more important than the ones Downing found, which transpired to be minutes of the discussion we had about the price of horses. He found them in a vase in the Savoy, so I was right all along: Hanse *did* steal them.'

'Or someone planted them there in an effort to undermine the peace talks,' suggested Chaloner.

'It is possible, I suppose,' acknowledged the Earl. 'But I do not like the notion of my papers in Dutch hands – not even ones about horses.'

'I doubt any harm has been done. The minutes expose the Privy Council as ill-informed and stupid, and will lull the Dutch into a false sense of security. That can only benefit England.'

The Earl gaped at him. 'Men have been hanged for making less acerbic remarks! Besides, *I* am on this committee, and *I* am not ill-informed *or* stupid.'

Chaloner was inclined to think he was, if the transcripts were anything to go by. He watched the Earl continue to leaf through them, and said no more.

'But what is this?' demanded his master, stopping suddenly. 'Not notes from the Council.'

Too late, Chaloner realised he probably should not have included the letter about the Lady, but it was too late to take it back, and he watched the Earl's eyes widen in horror as he read it.

'Is this your idea of a joke?' he demanded. 'To embarrass me with ribald missives?'

'I am sorry, sir. It was in the cheese with the other documents, and—'

Clarendon flung it back at him. 'I assure you, it has nothing to do with me. It is disgusting!'

'I will burn it, then,' said Chaloner, going towards the hearth and reaching for a tinderbox.

'Wait! If what it says is true, then it shows the Lady in a terrible light, does it not? To take a garment of deep devotional significance and turn it into lewd underwear?'

Chaloner turned towards him. 'It does not flatter her, certainly.'

The Earl held out his hand. 'Then we shall put it in a safe place. It might come in useful.'

'You would use it to . . .' Chaloner stopped himself from using the word blackmail, but only just.

'To encourage her to acknowledge certain points of view,' finished the Earl smugly.

'Well, do not leave it anywhere it might be stolen again,' advised Chaloner, thinking his master was making a big mistake. 'It might be more trouble than it is worth.'

'What do you mean by "again"?' demanded the Earl. 'This was *never* in my possession. The thief must have stolen the intimate papers of others, as well as my own.'

'Then it cannot have been Hanse. He did not have had access to Lady Castlemaine's quarters.'

Clarendon pursed his lips, not liking to be proven wrong. 'Have you found his killer yet? No? Then you had better go and do so. Perhaps it will help to persuade Downing of your innocence.'

Chapter 10

As Chaloner left White Hall, he found himself studying the people he passed, to assess whether one might be Falcon in disguise. He noticed that Sir Alan Brodrick moved more stiffly than was his wont, and that Kicke's luxurious mane was probably a wig. He began to feel overwhelmed. How was he supposed to stop whatever was being planned when he did not know what it entailed, or even what its perpetrator looked like?

He forced himself to concentrate on other lines of enquiry, in the hope that answers regarding Falcon might come if he was not straining so desperately for them. He decided to visit the Savoy, to see if he could prise some truth from Kun. He walked there too quickly, so when he arrived he was breathless, sweaty and tense. Before he could approach the gate, his shoulder was grabbed and he was swung around roughly. He found himself facing Killigrew.

'You have a damned nerve, coming here,' snapped the Master of the Savoy Hospital angrily. 'Downing says you are a spy, and I should have guessed it when you were so quick to defend Kun and Zas after they were attacked by that mob.'

'I said they had no choice but to accept the King's invitation to St James's Park,' objected Chaloner. 'That was not defending them – it was an explanation.'

'So you say,' sneered Killigrew. 'But you speak their language. It is damned sinister.'

'You speak French,' Chaloner pointed out. 'Does that make you a French spy?'

'Of course not!' snapped Killigrew testily. 'But I am above reproach, whereas you work for the Lord Chancellor – a man who itches for peace. And do not think you will be safe inside the Savoy, either, because I am going to tell Downing where you are.'

He strode away, all righteous indignation. Chaloner considered running after him, but doubted Killigrew would listen to reason. Aware that he had better hurry if he was to be gone before the envoy arrived, he stepped up to the gate and asked to see Kun. There were more soldiers on duty than usual.

'You cannot come in,' Ruyven said coldly. 'I have tightened security, because Downing claims to have found those stolen papers in one of our vases. But none of us put them there, so they must have been planted by someone who wants to damage the peace talks.'

'Who?'

'Someone who is underhand and disreputable. Someone like you, in fact.'

Nettled, Chaloner went on the offensive. 'How long have you and Jacoba been lovers?'

The blood drained from Ruyven's face. 'What? How do you . . . How *could* you . . .'

'I suspect Hanse knew, and that was why he turned to drink in the last few—'

Ruyven shoved him against a wall, glancing around uneasily to make sure they could not be overheard. 'This is none of your business. And if you breathe one word to anyone, I will kill you.'

'Is that what you did to Hanse? Killed him when he found out?'

'No! There was no need, because he did not care. All *he* cared about was peace.'

'Oh, I think he cared,' said Chaloner softly. 'Everyone here noticed his increased drinking.'

Ruyven could not meet his eyes, and released him abruptly. 'Well, perhaps he did turn to the barrel. But he never tried to stop us, and Jacoba needed more than the occasional kiss from a distracted husband. Besides, our affair is over now, and if you do not believe me, ask her.'

Chaloner stared at him. Ruyven had changed over the last twelve years. He was heavier, darker and his eyebrows were thicker. Moreover, the old Ruyven had been quick to lose his temper, and quicker still to draw his sword – Chaloner would have been battling for his life if he had made such remarks to the man he had known in Amsterdam. Was this the real Ruyven, or was it Falcon?

'I need to speak to Kun,' he said, not sure what to think.

'Well, you cannot. I am not having you regaling my colleagues with accusations about—'

'Accusations that happen to be true,' Chaloner flashed back. 'But your secret is safe with me; I have no wish to hurt Jacoba. However, I still want an audience with Kun.'

'I could not oblige, even if I wanted to,' snapped Ruyven. 'Because he is missing.'

Chaloner recalled the discussion he had overheard the previous night, when Zas had assured van Goch that Kun had found himself a secluded corner, in order to think. Was Kun still thinking? Or had he gone the same way as Hanse?

'Perhaps you will help us locate him,' came a voice from behind. Chaloner had heard Zas's soft-footed approach, but Ruyven whipped around in alarm, clearly wondering exactly how much of the discussion the lawyer had overheard. 'He went out after Downing found those stolen papers in the vase yesterday. He said he was going to prove our innocence.'

'Did he say how?' asked Chaloner, aware that if Kun was dead, the peace talks would founder for certain; van Goch could not be expected to overlook the murder of a second diplomat.

'No,' replied Zas. 'And we are all very worried. We are virtual prisoners in the Savoy now, and we need someone we can trust to search outside—'

'No,' interrupted Ruyven. '*I* do not trust Chaloner. I do not want him involved in our affairs.'

'Because you still smart over the woman he married?' demanded Zas coldly. 'She died years ago, man! Surely, it is time to forget this ancient rivalry? And Kun may be—'

Ruyven's face was white with fury. 'My past is none of your concern!'

'Perhaps not,' snapped Zas. 'But Kun is, and he is more important than your wounded pride.'

'My pride has nothing to do with it,' snarled Ruyven. 'Has it occurred to you that Downing is unlikely to have *guessed* where those papers had been shoved, so someone must have told him? Chaloner is the Lord Chancellor's man, and it was the Lord Chancellor's minutes that were stolen. In other words, *he* put them in the pot, then told Downing where to look. To cause trouble.'

'But you told Heer van Goch that you accompanied him every moment he was in the Savoy,' Zas shot back. 'If that is true, then how can he have slipped documents into vases?'

Ruyven regarded him with dislike. 'Spies have their ways. And someone has been working against the negotiations from the start – telling lies that make the two sides distrust each other, hiding documents that cause delays, killing our diplomats. I said it was a waste of time to come to London, and I was right.'

'I agree that there is a saboteur,' said Zas. 'But it is not Chaloner: he was not in London when the trouble started.'

'So he claims,' said Ruyven. 'But why should we believe him?'

The argument went on for some time, with Chaloner fretting at the wasted moments. He could scarcely credit that the Dutch *and* the English suspected him of espionage, especially as it was the one time in his life that he was innocent. How had it happened? Was it Falcon's doing, to slow him down and prevent him from discovering what was going on?

'Very well, then,' shouted Ruyven, throwing up his hands in a theatrical expression of disgusted capitulation. 'Let him in. But do not come crying to *me* when he betrays you.'

'Heer van Goch made a mistake when he appointed him to oversee our security,' said Zas with rank disapproval, watching Ruyven stalk away. 'He is loyal, but the task is beyond his meagre abilities. But never mind him. Come with me to the Brown Room.'

'Why?' asked Chaloner suspiciously.

'Because I am worried about Kun, and I am prepared to accept help from any quarter to find him. No matter what Downing and Ruyven say about you.'

It was hardly a resounding vote of confidence, and Chaloner followed him across the courtyard reluctantly. Several people scowled at him as he passed, indicating that the irascible captain was not the only one ready to believe the envoy's accusations.

'Unfortunately, Ruyven is right,' said Zas, as they went. 'Downing *did* go straight to those papers last night – I watched him. And the only way he could have known they were there was if someone had told him. In other words, we *do* have a spy in our midst.'

'But I am not in your midst,' Chaloner pointed out. 'I am an outsider.'

'Quite.' Zas smiled wryly. 'And it makes you a more attractive candidate – no one likes the thought of being betrayed by a friend. It is easier to blame the stranger.'

'Will Heer van Goch postpone tomorrow's convention?' asked Chaloner, thinking that an atmosphere of doubt and mistrust would do nothing to ensure a successful outcome.

Zas pursed his lips. 'He said that would be playing into the saboteur's hands, and is determined to go ahead, no matter what. He says it is our last chance.'

Chaloner saw preparations were already under way. Food and wine were being carried to the kitchens, an army of cleaners was at work, and van Goch's ceremonial robes had been sponged down and were drying outside his lodgings. The Savoy felt simultaneously industrious and uneasy.

They reached the Brown Room, where an immediate silence fell over the people who had gathered there. No one appeared to be working, and the faces of all were tense and unhappy.

'Chaloner has offered to help us find Kun,' Zas announced, although Chaloner had done nothing of the kind. However, with upwards of thirty men regarding him with open suspicion, he decided it was not the time to say so. 'So tell him what we know.'

'Kun is not in the Savoy,' said Taacken. The burly sergeant spoke haltingly, clearly torn between his disinclination to cooperate with a man who had been accused of espionage, and his desire to help the elderly secretary. 'We have looked everywhere. So he must still be out.'

'Precisely.' Zas looked around at his colleagues. 'And as we cannot go to look for him ourselves, we must rely on local help. Chaloner is Hanse's kinsman, so better him than anyone else.'

The Brown Room's occupants did not look particularly convinced, and Chaloner glanced at the door, wondering whether he could reach it if they attacked en masse.

'Kun said he was going to prove that we are innocent of stealing Clarendon's papers,' supplied Taacken, again speaking reluctantly. 'He did not tell me how, only that he had an idea.'

'He did not mention it to me,' said a clerk with a big nose, while others muttered that Kun had not spoken to them, either.

'If he has suffered Hanse's fate, then we should leave this benighted country,' said one of the lawyers. He glared at Chaloner. 'We should not stay here to be picked off by clever foreigners.'

'There is nothing to say Kun is—' began Zas.

'There is nothing to say he isn't, either,' countered the lawyer. 'We are risking our lives by staying, and I want no more to do with England or Englishmen. And I do not want their kind in the Savoy, either, no matter whose kin they claim to be.'

There was a general growl of agreement, and realising that prolonging the interview would serve no useful purpose, Zas declared an end to it. Chaloner was relieved: he could not recall ever feeling so vulnerable, not even when he really had been spying on the Dutch. They were almost at the gate when there was a shout, and Jacoba hurried towards them.

'Have you learned anything new about Willem?' she asked eagerly. 'Is that why you are here?'

Chaloner was tempted to make a remark about her relationship with Ruyven, but that would have been ungentlemanly in front of Zas, and he owed her some consideration. 'Not really.'

'He came to ask after Kun,' explained Zas. 'We are all anxious about him.'

'We should be,' replied Jacoba soberly. 'He was very upset about Downing finding those papers, and he told me he was going to Westminster to talk to Spymaster Williamson about them. I have heard rumours about that particular man, and apparently, he is not very nice.'

Before Chaloner tackled Williamson, he went to the Tower, to see whether Edwards had returned. The same yeoman was on duty, and informed him that the Assistant Keeper was still away, but that the message would be delivered the minute he returned. Frustrated, Chaloner hurried to the Fleet Rookery, where he sought out Mother Greene. Keen to stay on her good side, he took her a ham.

'Your warning has been delivered to Fairfax's favourite inn,' she said, accepting the gift with an appreciative nod. 'And promises were made to get it to him. It is the best I can do.'

'Then let us hope it reaches him,' said Chaloner worriedly, supposing he would have to return yet again, because his vow to Compton would not be fulfilled until he knew for certain that both men had received and understood the warnings.

When he arrived at Williamson's office, hot and agitated, he hesitated. It was the last place he should go, given that he was accused of espionage. But he desperately needed to interview Kun, and Williamson was the only person who might be able to say what had happened to him. He racked his brains for other ways forward, but nothing came to mind, and he was in the process of writing a note, asking Williamson to meet him in a nearby tavern, when the door opened and the Spymaster himself stepped out. He had three stout men at his heels, clearly bodyguards. Wondering what he intended to do that warranted such precautions, Chaloner began to follow.

They turned east, towards the river, and it did not take Chaloner long to guess their destination: the charnel house. When they reached it, Williamson strode inside while his guards took up station by the door, ready to repel other visitors. Chaloner climbed through a window at the back, and heard Kersey entertaining his guest in the handsome parlour at the front of the building.

He crept towards them, a route that took him through the mortuary hall, where the stench of death was over-powering and the buzz of flies was a constant hum. He soon saw why: every table held two occupants – victims of the unseasonable heat. Most were thin, pathetic bundles under their covers, but one stood out as bulky. Was it Kun? Chaloner took a deep breath to steel himself, and raised a corner of the sheet. But it was not the Dutchman who stared back at him, it was Nisbett, lank ginger hair framing his waxen face, and bulbous eyes beginning to glaze.

Chaloner lifted more of the blanket, and recoiled in distaste when he saw that the man's throat had been cut from ear to ear. Whoever had inflicted the wound had used a very sharp knife and a considerable degree of force. It was the work of someone who had wanted to ensure that his victim was dead. Chaloner replaced the sheet, and began to tiptoe towards Kersey's parlour again.

'. . . dispatched,' Williamson was saying. He was sitting in Kersey's best chair, and the charnel-house keeper was standing behind him, setting small honey-biscuits on a little silver platter. 'And this is an excellent vintage, by the way. French?'

'Italian, actually,' replied Kersey. 'I keep it for guests with discerning palates. Such as yourself.'

Chaloner winced. Kersey was not normally syco-phantic.

'In that case, I shall take a cask with me when I go,' said Williamson. 'My palette is more discerning than

352

anyone else you are likely to entertain here, and it would be a pity to waste it.'

'Are you *sure* Nisbett was the blackmailer?' asked Kersey, glaring at the Spymaster's back and clearly resenting the effrontery. 'The wretched fellow bled me all but dry with his demands, and I shall rest easier tonight if I can be certain my problems are over.'

'We are sure,' Williamson assured him. He took another sip of the wine. 'Well, we are sure he was *one* of the despicable criminal consortium who so suddenly decided to extort money from people. There are others – as yet unidentified – but I think Nisbett's fate should make them think twice about what they are doing.'

Chaloner recalled Daniel Cotton's predicament, and supposed he should have guessed that Nisbett was complicit in threatening to expose her. Nisbett had claimed to remember nothing about the frolic the following day, but he would have had to have been *very* drunk not to notice that the rough Yeoman Cartaker he had bedded was actually a woman.

'I am taking quite a risk, you know,' said Kersey uneasily. 'I am not in the habit of disposing of corpses surreptitiously. For a start, Surgeon Wiseman is often here, looking for specimens. Nisbett's is a nice cadaver, and if he sees it, he will want it for his researches.'

'Well, do not let him have it,' ordered Williamson, alarmed. 'We had an arrangement – I relieve you of your blackmailer, and you get rid of the evidence. Swaddell's work is well known, and people will guess he is the culprit if they see Nisbett's throat.'

'I will see to it. And Wiseman will probably stay away from work matters today, anyway, because he is out of sorts.'

'Upset, because he has been accused of incompetence,' scoffed Williamson. 'I would not mind Swaddell cutting *his* throat in a dark alley one day, and neither would anyone else at White Hall.'

'*I* would mind,' said Kersey, a little coldly. 'I happen to like Wiseman.'

'Let us drink a toast to our success,' said Williamson, after a brief and uncomfortable silence. 'You no longer need to fear exposure for dispatching your predecessor, and I have struck a major blow against these villains. It was courageous of you to insist on delivering the blackmail money in person, thus allowing Swaddell to do his business. We must work together again.'

'Actually, I would rather not,' said Kersey, making no effort to conceal his distaste. 'I did not like your men loitering in my domain day and night. They have no place in a decent establishment like this. I do not mean to offend, but I speak as I find.'

'Very well,' said Williamson stiffly. 'Now, you promised me a cask of claret. Will you fetch it yourself, or shall I ask one of my assistants to oblige? I have three of them outside.'

'I will go,' said Kersey, equally cool. 'You stay here.'

When Kersey had disappeared into his cellar, Chaloner emerged from his hiding place and went to stand behind Williamson. The Spymaster was lounging contentedly in his chair, pleased with what he considered to be a job well done, and when Chaloner spoke, he leapt so violently that the wine flew from his goblet.

'So you ordered Swaddell to murder Nisbett. I hope you had good evidence.'

'The best kind,' said Williamson, recovering quickly. 'He was caught in the act. And he admitted to his crime

354

once we had him. Poor Kersey's secret left him vulnerable to such vultures, you see.'

'Was the accusation true? Did Kersey really murder his predecessor?'

'He says it was self-defence. But the old man was a vile wretch, and no one mourned his passing. No one will mourn Nisbett's, either. He was a criminal, as you, of all people, should know.'

'Did Nisbett tell you about the White Hall thefts, too?' asked Chaloner. 'That he and Kicke had an accomplice – someone who immediately stepped in to rescue them when they were caught, and who had helped them to steal by staging distractions? One example was in St James's Park, when a diversion by the Canal allowed them to work without being noticed.'

'He did mention a certain arrangement with Lady Castlemaine,' acknowledged Williamson. 'She has debts and expensive tastes, so is always eager for money. Nisbett and Kicke were in Downing's service at the time, but that did not stop her from recruiting them. How long have you known?'

'Since about an hour after I began investigating. But I am not such a fool as to point fingers at the King's mistress. I hoped they would betray her themselves, in an effort to save their own necks, but she extricated them before awkward questions could be asked.'

'Bulteel told me you were remarkably sanguine about her interference with the course of justice,' mused Williamson. 'Now I understand why: you felt you had risked her wrath far enough.'

'She is a formidable adversary, and too strong for me. But she is not the blackmailer, lest you think to accuse her.'

Williamson steepled his fingers, and settled back in the chair. 'No? How do you know?'

'Because I discovered a document that was written to extort money from her – some of her underwear has fallen into the wrong hands. Obviously, she is not black-mailing herself.'

'You are right,' acknowledged Williamson. 'The Lady is innocent of that affair. But before he died, Nisbett told Swaddell that he and Kicke are now in the pay of *two* masters – Lady Castlemaine and one other. Can you guess the identity of the second?'

'Not really,' said Chaloner tiredly.

'Falcon,' announced Williamson with a flourish. 'Swaddell is looking for Kicke as we speak, to ask whether *he* knows the location of the villain's lair.'

Chaloner supposed it was possible: Kicke and Nisbett were greedy and unscrupulous, and exactly the kind of men Falcon might recruit. 'What was wrong with trying Nisbett in a court of law? Was it really necessary to dispatch him on the sly?'

'Yes, it was,' said Williamson firmly. 'Because none of his victims would make a formal complaint – not when they have spent a fortune to keep their peccadilloes quiet. A public trial would ruin them, and they are upright men of good standing.'

'Not all are decent. Take Downing, for example. He has been paying to ensure inconsistencies in his expense accounts do not come to light.'

'I knew he was a victim, but not the nature of his secret,' admitted Williamson. 'Although I cannot say I am surprised by it. But, of course, you *would* seek to malign him. He has accused you of being bought by the Dutch, and now there is a warrant for your arrest.'

'Have you stationed men outside my house, to execute it?'

'Of course not! I am not such a fool as to believe you can be cornered *there*. It would be a waste of my thinly stretched resources.'

'I see,' said Chaloner, not sure whether to believe him.

'But to return to our little problem in the mortuary, I did the right thing by letting Swaddell have Nisbett: he was an odious brute, who did not deserve to live. Not even in Calais. And speaking of Calais, it *was* you who sneaked in after I expressly declared the Sinon Plot off limits. Do not deny it: Keeper Sligo described you.'

'I did go to Newgate,' conceded Chaloner. 'But I did not speak to anyone connected with the Sinon Plot. How could I, when Falcon had escaped, and Swan and Swallow were murdered?'

Williamson winced at the reminder that his most formidable prison had been found lacking. 'Falcon is dangerous – perhaps the deadliest adversary I have ever faced. I am not ashamed to confess that he unsettles me with his diabolical powers and fearsomely devious mind.'

'Diabolical powers?' echoed Chaloner sceptically. It was unlike the Spymaster to make fanciful remarks.

Williamson regarded him oddly. 'If you do not believe me, then look at what happened to Compton and his soldiers. All were cursed, and now only one remains alive.'

'Is that why you sent them to arrest Falcon instead of going yourself? You were afraid of—'

'No!' snapped Williamson, although the guilty flicker in his eyes suggested that was exactly what had happened. 'Although Falcon hates me regardless.'

For the first time, Chaloner saw the Spymaster was afraid, which no doubt accounted for the bodyguards

357

outside. Yet he was still prepared to attack Falcon by depriving him of Nisbett. Grudgingly, Chaloner acknowledged his courage.

'It is imperative that he is caught as soon as possible,' Williamson went on. 'But he owns an unnatural talent for changing his appearance, which means I cannot circulate his description among my men. If I do, he will just turn himself into someone else.'

Clearly, Williamson had no more idea how to catch Falcon than Chaloner did, which was not a reassuring thing to hear a spymaster admit. 'I cannot help but wonder whether he is right under our noses,' he said worriedly. 'A servant, perhaps. Or a courtier.'

Williamson nodded wry agreement. 'I find myself looking hard at everyone these days. Indeed, I noticed only this morning that Griffith's manservant, Lane, seemed darker and smaller than I remembered, while Charles Bates has undergone quite a transformation.'

'What do you mean?'

'I spoke to him shortly before coming here, and he seemed younger and more confident. Or perhaps it was my imagination. I rarely give him more than a passing glance.'

'What time was this?' asked Chaloner, recalling that Bates's coach was to leave at nine.

'Ten o'clock, or a little after,' replied Williamson. 'He told me he was leaving London because he feared the plague, and he is taking his adulterous wife with him.'

Chaloner asked the question that had prompted him to follow the Spymaster in the first place. 'Why did Secretary Kun come to see you last night?'

Williamson's eyes widened. 'You *are* well informed! But the nature of our conversation was private, and if you use violence to make me tell, I shall holler and my men will save me.'

'You think they will be in time, do you?' asked Chaloner, amused. 'But the reason I ask is because Kun is missing, and he was last seen going to visit you.'

Williamson smiled unpleasantly. 'Is that so? Well, you will find that there is no one who can say whether he reached me or not.'

'You have just admitted to enjoying a tête-à-tête.'

'Admitted it to you. I shall deny it to anyone else.'

'Did you order Swaddell to cut *his* throat?'

'What a low opinion you have of me! No, I did not. We had our little chat, and he left in perfect health. I heard he did not return to the Savoy, but his disappearance has nothing to do with me.'

'There are rumours of a traitor in the Dutch delegation. It is unlikely to be Kun – he would not have told Jacoba he was going to see you, if it were. Did he confide his suspicions?'

'I told you: our discussion was confidential.' Williamson's eyes gleamed suddenly. 'But of course there *is* a traitor. There are several, in fact. It should not surprise you – it would be unthinkable for me *not* to recruit eyes and ears in a large foreign delegation like that.'

'But there is a big difference between spies who watch and listen, and those who intervene,' said Chaloner. 'Such as by leaving stolen papers in vases for Downing to find, and starting rumours that have the two sides at each other's throats.'

'Yes,' acknowledged Williamson. 'And I do not have any of those. Kun *did* express his concerns about that sort of conspirator last night, but I was unable to help him. Whoever this villain is, he has nothing to do with me. I *want* the talks to succeed, as I have told you before.'

'What time did Kun leave you?'

'Midnight, or thereabouts. I keep a discreet hack-neyman for after-hours work, and I told him to take Kun wherever he wanted to go. When I heard Kun was missing, I questioned the man. He said Kun had stopped him at Charing Cross, and said he wanted to walk the rest of the way – it was hot, and he needed air. My driver was telling the truth; Kun probably was not.'

'So you have no idea where he might have gone?'

'None at all.'

Chaloner left the charnel house when he heard Kersey returning, but had only taken a few steps before Williamson emerged to yell that there was a dangerous spy on the loose. The bodyguards gave chase, and he was obliged to race down a series of alleys before he was able to lose them. He was not very pleased: it was too hot for such antics. But he supposed he did not blame the Spymaster for trying: it would not look good if it later came to light that they had met, and Chaloner had been allowed to walk free.

He was tired, but there was no time to rest. He needed to go to the Feathers on Cheapside, to see whether its landlord could shed any light on Falcon. Then he had to visit the Devil tavern, to ask what had happened when Molins had been assaulted. *And* he was obliged to return to the Tower and the Fleet Rookery yet again, to ensure that his warnings had been delivered.

He went to the Feathers first, because it seemed the most urgent. The landlord, a Mr Benson, told him with an exaggerated shudder that he was glad Falcon no longer visited his establishment.

'Swan and Swallow are nice,' he said. 'But Falcon is horrible. I think he might be insane.'

'Why do you say that?'

'Because he *looks* insane – eyes that blaze, and a way of cursing. He cursed one of my pot-boys, and the next day, the lad broke his arm. Now, you may say it was co-incidence, but I am not so sure.'

'When was the last time you saw Falcon?'

'Not since Sir William Compton came and took him away. I can tell you one thing, though: Williamson reckons that Falcon is his real name, and that he is a canon in Canterbury Cathedral. But he is not.' Benson pursed his lips, waiting for Chaloner to ask him more.

Chaloner obliged. 'How do you know?'

'Because my brother is a verger at Canterbury, and he has been visiting me this week. *He* said there is no canon there called Falcon.'

'Where is your brother now?' asked Chaloner, intending to question the man himself.

'Gone home,' came the disappointing reply. 'But we discussed it at length, and he is quite certain: there is *no one* called Falcon at the cathedral.'

'What about a vicar named Pocks?' asked Chaloner, suspecting that Williamson would be galled when he learned that his efforts to ingratiate himself with the Church had been in vain. 'Have you met or heard of him?'

Benson smirked. 'Pocks? I must write that one down! My brother and I keep a list of amusing or embarrassing names, and have done for years. I have never heard of any vicar called Pocks, though – and he has not either, because, he would have mentioned it.'

Chaloner was beginning to be exasperated – not by Benson, whose testimony seemed sound, but by the lack of answers. 'Tell me about Falcon,' he said. 'Did you ever see him dressed as a vicar?'

Benson shook his head. 'He wore different clothes every time he came here, and sometimes I did not recognise him until Swallow and Swan arrived – they sat with him, which gave him away.'

'You are talking about Falcon,' said a man who had approached to have his ale jug refilled. He grinned, revealing himself to be sadly bereft of teeth. 'He was in Newgate.'

'I know,' said Chaloner, not without rancour.

'I saw him in a cell there about a year ago,' the man went on. 'And then he sails in here, giving himself airs, when he is actually nothing but a common felon. Mr Benson is right – he is no vicar. He did wear clerical garb on occasion, but he never swore any holy orders.'

'Are you certain?' asked Chaloner.

The man nodded. 'If I recall aright, he was in Newgate for stealing. He is just a thief, although not one *I* would want to cross. I am glad those soldiers came and took him away, and I hope I never set eyes on him again. Unless it is with a noose around his neck.'

'Hear, hear,' said Benson fervently.

Their declarations made Chaloner even more concerned for the men Compton had charged him to protect, so he went immediately to the Fleet Rookery. He sighed his relief when Mother Greene assured him that Fairfax had received and understood the message.

'Are you sure?' he pressed.

She nodded. 'Quite sure. I delivered it myself, and he told me to thank you. You can rest assured that Sir William Compton's last wishes have been fulfilled.'

He did not think she would lie to him, although he wished he could have spoken to the soldier in person. But there was no more he could do if Fairfax declined to meet him, so he returned to Fleet Street, where he flagged down a hackney carriage and told its driver to take him to the Tower. The same yeoman was on duty yet again.

'Mr Edwards is back, and I gave him your note. Stay here. I will fetch him for you.'

Chaloner took a deep breath, feeling some of his anxieties recede. Edwards would tell him what Compton had declined to share, *and* how to reach the last member of their cabal. Once Edwards and the vicar – if he was still alive – had been warned, Chaloner's obligations to Compton would be complete. He rested his forehead against the stone wall, seeking coolness, but it was as warm as blood in the heat of late afternoon.

Eventually, the door opened, and Edwards stepped out. He squinted around myopically until a cough from Chaloner made him turn in the right direction. His expression was one of bemusement.

'It was you who left me the note saying Compton, Molins and Hanse are dead?'

Chaloner nodded. 'Compton told me to warn you with his dying breath.'

Edwards continued to look bewildered. 'Warn me about what?'

Chaloner had not spelled out that Edwards needed to be on his guard, because he had assumed it was obvious. 'That your life is in danger, and you should take additional care until Falcon is caught,' he explained, a little impatiently.

'My life?' asked Edwards stupidly. 'But Falcon did not

kill the others! Molins and Compton died of fevers, and Hanse drowned. I am deeply sorry, because they were good men, and—'

'Hanse was murdered,' interrupted Chaloner curtly. 'The other deaths are suspicious, too, especially considering that Compton lost three soldiers to "accidents", and you lost one to sickness.'

Edwards blanched. 'I do not believe you.'

'You should – it might prevent you from joining them in their graves. Who was the last man in your group? The vicar? Is his name Edward Pocks?'

Edwards's face was ashen. 'I do not know anyone called Pocks. The last man is Edward *White*.'

Chaloner stared at him in surprise. 'He officiated at my wedding.'

Edwards blinked his bemusement. 'Did he?'

Chaloner's thoughts were a mass of confusion. So who was Pocks? And why was White's name missing from Falcon's list? Or had it been on the section that had been burned off? But Edwards was peering around uneasily, clearly unwilling to be out when killers might be at large, so Chaloner continued with his questions before the Assistant Keeper could scuttle back inside the Tower.

'What did you discuss when you met Compton and the others?'

'I cannot tell you. I swore an oath never to reveal anything about it. We all did.'

Chaloner sighed. 'People are dying, and more will follow unless this scheme – whatever it is – is thwarted. I know the Sinon Plot is nothing to do with stealing the crown jewels—'

'It *was*,' whispered Edwards. 'We believed Falcon wanted them to finance . . .'

364

'Finance what?' demanded Chaloner.

But Edwards shook his head stubbornly. 'No. There are some things more important than the lives of individuals. You can ask White, although I doubt if he will break his word, either. He lives on Fleet Street, near the Rainbow Coffee House.'

Chaloner leapt in a hackney carriage, and ordered the driver to take him to Fleet Street as quickly as possible. The city was full of people who had abandoned work early, because of the heat, and he chafed at the delay caused by a snarl of vehicles near Fish Street Hill, and then again by St Paul's. But there was nothing he could do, and he doubted he could make better time on foot.

To take his mind off the minutes that were ticking inexorably away, he thought about the last member of Hanse's group. It was a shock to learn that White was involved. But involved in what? He sincerely hoped White would not follow Edwards's example, and refuse to confide the real nature of the Sinon Plot. But White was an intelligent man – far more so than Edwards – and would see that silence might be dangerous. Or at least, Chaloner hoped so.

Unfortunately, when he reached White's home, there was no reply to his hammering. He clenched his fists in frustration when he recalled their last encounter: the vicar had been feeling out of sorts, and had declared an intention to visit his sister in the country. Was he still there? If so, how long would he be gone?

His mind teeming with questions, Chaloner hurried towards the Devil, but he had not gone far before a coach rattled to a halt next to him, and several rough men piled out. Another figure alighted after them.

365

'There is the spy!' shouted Downing, jabbing a finger. Excitement made his voice shrill. 'There is the man who has been selling English secrets to Hollanders. Stop him! Bring him to me!'

The envoy's face was vengeful, and Chaloner had the distinct sense that to be in his custody might prove fatal. He started to run, but the street was crowded, and Downing's accusing howls encouraged passers-by to snatch at him. He managed to slither away from three apprentices, but they slowed him down, allowing one of the envoy's louts to seize his coat. He used every trick he knew to escape, but the odds were against him, and it was not long before he was overpowered.

'Put him in my coach,' Downing ordered, grinning victoriously. He turned to the crowd that had gathered, and addressed the preening apprentices. 'Spymaster Williamson will be grateful to you for apprehending such a deadly villain. Here are a few coins for your trouble.'

'Sixpence?' asked one, regarding what had been dropped into his palm in disappointment. 'Between three of us? We should not have bothered!'

'Williamson will give *him* six pounds,' said Chaloner, as he was hauled to his feet.

'He is lying,' snapped Downing, shooting him an irritable look. 'Ignore him.'

'And a new horse,' Chaloner went on. 'And a set of silver spoons.'

'He is playing games,' declared Downing contemptuously. 'Do not listen to him.'

'*You* are the one playing games,' shouted a member of the crowd. 'These lads' help was worth more than sixpence. So come on, pay up!'

366

'I most certainly shall not!' cried Downing, miserly to the last. 'You can all go to hell!'

It was no way to appease an indignant horde, and the apprentices surged forward angrily. Downing shrieked as fists began to fly, and Chaloner used the opportunity to wrench away from his captors, and roll under the carriage. He was just emerging on the other side when a boot caught him on the side of the head. He stumbled, dazed, then hands fastened around him and he felt himself hoisted inside the coach. Downing leapt in on top of him and screeched for the driver to go. The coach lurched forward, followed by a barrage of missiles.

When Chaloner's senses cleared, his hands were tied, and he could feel blood oozing from a cut on his temple. Downing was glaring at him. The envoy had a swelling under one eye, and his fine clothes were torn. There was a hired man on either side of Chaloner, and another next to Downing. All had apparently been picked for size and strength, because they were enormous and looked fit. However, they were also incompetent, because although they had relieved Chaloner of his sword and the dagger in his sleeve, he still had a knife in his boot and the little gun in his belt.

'You will pay for that trick, Chaloner,' Downing snarled. 'Williamson has places for men like you – dark, deep dungeons, from which there is no escape. And do not expect Thurloe or Clarendon to save you, because they will never know where you have gone.'

Chaloner feigned indifference, but his stomach lurched. Behind his back, he began to assess the rope that bound him. The knots were tight, but manageable. The only question was whether he would be able to wriggle free of it quickly enough, because the coach was rattling along at a furious rate, and it would not be long before it reached Westminster. And then it would be too late.

'You are losing your touch,' Downing gloated. 'You would not have been caught so easily in The Hague. I was right to dismiss you in favour of better intelligencers.'

'Such as the one who told you to look in the Savoy's vases for Clarendon's missing papers?' asked Chaloner coolly.

'I have my sources,' said Downing smugly. 'Ones that will live to serve me again, thanks to your sacrifice. You see, I have fed Heer van Goch information that proves *you* are the spy, and your execution will stop him looking for the real culprit. And it will please me into the bargain.'

'I am sure it will,' muttered Chaloner, trying to intensify his struggles without the men on either side of him realising what he was doing.

'So will your wife's. Call it repayment for her rude remarks to me in St James's Park before that tedious music. No one calls me "loathsome" and goes unpunished.'

Chaloner regarded Downing in shock, escape forgotten. 'You would harm Hannah?'

Downing's eyes gleamed when he saw the effect his words had had. 'With the greatest of pleasure. And do not imagine she is safe, because *I* know where you have hidden her. You see, she regaled Rector Thompson with a lot of Court gossip, and he repeated it in his coffee house. My spies overheard, and we put two and two together. As soon as I have delivered you to Williamson, I shall collect her. She will hang by your side.'

'No!' exclaimed Chaloner, appalled. 'You *know* she is innocent. You cannot—'

'Oh, yes, I can,' countered Downing. 'I know what people said about us in The Hague – that my success derived from the intelligence *you* provided. Well, it is time to put the matter straight. I have outwitted you now, and it proves I was the better man all along.'

'You are certainly more devious,' acknowledged Chaloner, fingers now working frantically at the knots. 'But not quite devious enough. Have you forgotten the documents that show you have been cheating the government regarding your expenses? You accused me of having them.'

Downing narrowed his eyes. 'You told me you do not.'

'You believed that, did you?' taunted Chaloner. One hand came free.

'Stop the carriage,' ordered Downing, which was just the reaction Chaloner had anticipated.

The envoy managed to land two hard punches before Chaloner was able to wrench his other hand from the rope, but the moment he was free, Chaloner moved fast. He incapacitated the guard to his left with an elbow to the nose, and the one to his right with a backhanded blow to the jaw. The third, slow to react, was just drawing a dagger when Chaloner hauled the dag from his belt. Downing gaped in horror as Chaloner indicated that he was to alight from the coach.

'I really would not mind shooting you,' Chaloner said softly, when the envoy baulked. 'So you would be wise not to give me cause.'

Downing knew him well enough to appreciate he meant what he said, so he hastened to obey. Chaloner climbed out after him, and saw they were in a seedy part of Westminster, alarmingly close to Williamson's lair. It had almost been too late. He addressed the hirelings.

'Turn around and go back the way you came. If you return here within an hour, Downing dies.'

369

'Do it!' screamed Downing, when the men only exchanged uneasy glances. 'Now!'

'Well,' mused Chaloner, when the carriage had gone. He indicated Downing was to precede him down an alley that was no more than a dark slit between two buildings. 'What shall I do with you?'

'I was teasing.' Downing tried to turn, but Chaloner shoved him on. 'I was only taking you to Williamson so we can correct our little misunderstandings. I know you are not *really* Falcon.'

'You told him I was?'

'Yes, but I doubt he believed me. And I never intended to harm your wife, either. Please, Chaloner. Be reasonable!'

There was no reply. Downing walked a little farther, then stopped. It was shadowy in the alley, and he could not see very far ahead. Very slowly, heart thudding, he turned around.

Chaloner was nowhere to be seen.

Chaloner did not have much time. Downing would race out of the alley, demand men and a fast carriage from Williamson, and go directly to Thompson's house. And while Chaloner might not understand the complexity of his feelings for Hannah, he knew he would rather die than see her fall into Downing's hands. He flagged down a hackney and offered a princely reward for travelling to Fleet Street with all possible speed.

The driver did his best, but it still felt like an age before the coach rolled to a standstill outside the rectory. Chaloner shoved coins at him and raced towards it. He pounded on the door, then kicked it open when it was not answered immediately.

'Hannah is not back yet,' said Thompson, lowering his cudgel when he recognised the frantic invader. 'She said she might be late tonight, but you can wait in the—'

'Soldiers will come,' said Chaloner, feeling he owed Thompson some explanation for why his comfortable existence was about to be turned upside down. 'With Downing and Williamson. When they do, tell them I forced you to keep Hannah here. Do not say you offered willingly. I am sorry . . .'

He was hurrying back through the splintered door when a carriage drew up outside. He braced himself for trouble, but the vehicle bore Buckingham's coat of arms, and Hannah stepped out.

'Tom!' she exclaimed. 'Is that blood on your face? Has someone punched you? It is a—'

'Come with me,' he said urgently. 'Quickly.'

'Why?' demanded Hannah, and he cursed himself for marrying a woman of strong character with a mind of her own. Could she not see that there was no time for explanations?

'Do as he says,' ordered Thompson. 'There is trouble afoot, and he is trying to keep you safe. I shall help. I do not like Downing *or* Williamson, and if your bother is with them, then I am happy to—'

'No.' Chaloner did not want him involved any further. 'Stay here, and say you have no idea where we have gone.'

'They are no worse than my old adversary, the Devil,' declared Thompson with spirit. 'Follow me. I have a back entrance that no one knows about – one I use to avoid disagreeable parishioners.'

There was no time to argue, and Chaloner *was* grateful for his help. As they reached Fleet Street, he was aware of two coaches travelling fast from the direction of Westminster, but did not need to look around to know where they were stopping. He turned quickly into Chancery Lane, dragging Hannah behind him. There was only one man he trusted to keep her safe.

'How can I help, Tom?' Thurloe asked immediately, nodding a polite greeting to Hannah and Thompson. He was far too experienced an operative to waste time by demanding explanations.

'I need you to take Hannah somewhere safe. Do not tell me where.'

Thurloe nodded tersely, and left to make arrangements, while Thompson went to help the porter back a pony into the traces of a cart. The rector looked as if he was enjoying himself, and Chaloner hoped he would not regret his actions later – the Devil had nothing on Downing and Williamson.

'Tom,' said Hannah shakily, once they were alone. 'What is going on? Why did you tell Mr Thurloe not to say where he is taking me?'

Chaloner leaned against a wall. Now matters were being taken out of his hands, and he was no longer fuelled with anxiety, he found his legs were unsteady.

'You are in danger. Go with Thurloe, and do not come back or attempt to contact me until I tell you it is safe. Your life depends on it.'

'What about yours?' cried Hannah, alarmed. 'Come with us. You can protect me.'

'You do not want to spend the rest of your life as a fugitive, and neither do I. I need to resolve this case, and foil the people who are accusing me of . . .' He trailed off. The less said, the better.

'I am not leaving you,' said Hannah, tears sliding down her cheeks. 'We took vows to stay with each other through bad times, as well as good, and—'

Chaloner pulled himself upright. 'Here is Thurloe. Go with him.'

'We will remain hidden until you send word,' promised Thurloe. 'Contact me via Lincoln's Inn, and make sure you include the word rabbit, so I know the order is genuine, not coerced.'

'The horses are ready,' said Thompson, face alight with excitement. 'Where will you go?'

'Somewhere we will not be found,' replied Thurloe shortly. He gripped Chaloner's shoulder. 'Be careful, old friend.'

Chaloner hugged Hannah, then slipped out of Lincoln's Inn and loitered in the shadows opposite. After a moment, a carriage rolled out, and rattled towards Holborn. At the same time, two coaches tore around the corner, its passengers leaning out of the windows. They raced past Lincoln's Inn, and set off in pursuit. When they had gone, a cart trundled out and made its sedate way in the opposite direction. No one followed that, and Chaloner sighed his relief. Hannah was safe.

It might have been Chaloner's imagination, but there seemed to be more of Williamson's soldiers on the streets than usual, distinctive in their buff jerkins and striped sleeves. There were also an inordinately large number of men who looked as if they had no particular business; they slouched along in groups, scanning the faces of passers-by. A manhunt had been initiated, and someone – Williamson, perhaps, or Downing – had called up reinforcements from the criminal gangs. It was only a matter of time before he was challenged, so he decided to lie low until nightfall. But where? Not with Temperance or Bulteel, because he did not want to endanger friends.

He had just resigned himself to skulking in a thicket in Lincoln's Inn Fields, when he remembered Wiseman's house on Fleet Street. He knew the attic was empty, because it had been offered to him as lodgings. He would slip into it unseen, and the surgeon need never know that he had harboured a fugitive.

Wiseman's home was a four-storey affair with a cobbled yard at the back. Chaloner scaled the rear wall, and opened the door carefully. There was a servants' parlour to the left, where three men sat playing cards. He was disconcerted to note that two were missing limbs and one an eye. Had Wiseman been practising on them, or were they just old patients, hired because his ministrations had left them too incapacitated to work for anyone else?

He crept past them, and found himself in a laboratory, with shelves along the walls and a chemical odour in the air. The shelves held jars, but he did not inspect them too closely, lest one contained Wiseman's brother-in-law. He rubbed his head; the boot that had knocked him out of his wits earlier had given him a nasty cut, and it was beginning to throb now he had time to be aware of it. Pushing the discomfort to the back of his mind, he aimed for the stairs.

The middle two floors were occupied by Wiseman, while the attic contained nothing but empty boxes and dead flies. Chaloner went to the window and looked into the street below. Williamson's soldiers were questioning pedestrians, and the rough men from the gangs were everywhere. He could only suppose the Spymaster was hunting Falcon, although it would be like looking for a needle in a haystack given the man's talent for disguise.

There were at least two hours of daylight left, so Chaloner lay down and closed his eyes. The garret was too stuffy for comfort, and floors rarely made for easy sleeping. He did doze, but his dreams teemed with unpleasant images – Calais, Nisbett with his throat cut, and Downing stalking Hannah. He dreamt about Wiseman, too, and when he started awake for at least the tenth time, he was horrified to see the surgeon looming over him. He leapt to his feet, dagger in his hand.

'There is no need for that,' cried Wiseman, starting away in alarm. 'I was only trying to ascertain whether someone had left me a corpse to anatomise.'

'What are you doing here?'

'It is my house,' replied Wiseman indignantly. 'I live here. What excuse do *you* have?'

'None,' admitted Chaloner, sheepish and apologetic. 'What prompted you to come up here?'

'Blood,' replied Wiseman, eyes gleaming. 'There were splashes of it on the stairs. I knew *I* had not left them there, so I investigated.'

Chaloner supposed he must have reopened the cut on his head when he had rubbed it, and cursed himself for his carelessness. It was inexcusable in an intelligencer of his experience.

'A warrant has been issued for your arrest,' Wiseman went on. 'You are a Dutch spy, apparently, although Heer van Goch maintains you have been spying *on* him, not for him. So everyone thinks you are a traitor – Dutch *and* English. It is an impressive achievement.'

'Yes,' agreed Chaloner tiredly, thinking that Downing should congratulate himself. Or did he have Falcon to thank for the situation, with Downing as his unwitting – or willing – ally?

'Moreover, Clarendon is furious with you. There is a rumour that he had no idea what was in the papers that were stolen from him, and he has become a laughing stock. He told me you are the only person to know that particular secret, and thinks you started the tale to discredit him.'

Chaloner groaned. 'Why would I do that?'

'Well, if Downing is to be believed, because you are a Dutch spy who wants to bring ridicule and disgrace to our country's most respected ministers.'

'That makes no sense. If I were their spy, I would be denigrating the warmongers, not the doves.'

'That is what I said, but no one listened. Where are you going?'

'You will lose your Court appointment if I am found here. I should leave.'

'I might lose it anyway, because my enemies are making much of the fact that I killed Molins and Compton. My only hope is that you will prove my innocence.'

Chaloner had forgotten Wiseman's problems. 'Did the samples you took from Compton and Molins's homes reveal anything amiss?' he asked, loath to admit that he had done nothing about the matter lest Wiseman took umbrage. He did not have the energy for another confrontation.

'Not yet, although you must bear in mind that not all toxins work instantly, and it may take some time for symptoms to appear. But I shall not rest until I have exhausted all the possibilities.'

'Good. I shall leave you to your labours, then.'

Wiseman gestured towards the window. 'It will be dark

376

soon, and you look tired. Rest tonight, and start afresh tomorrow. Downing will not be back.'

'Be *back*? You mean he has been here already?'

Wiseman nodded. 'I tried to show him my anatomical collection, but he went quite pale, and I had to revive him with a sip a tonic. Then he claimed I was trying to poison him. If only I had!'

'He was looking for me?' Chaloner was appalled: it suggested Downing knew him better than he had thought, and that was dangerous.

'He asked if I had seen you, but I doubt he guessed that you are hiding here – he is just desperate. It is not because you are the one blackmailing him, is it?' Wiseman laughed, but not with his usual unrestrained vigour, and Chaloner saw the accusations against him were weighing heavily on his mind. Chaloner knew exactly how he felt.

'May I borrow some clothes?' he asked, indicating his own ripped, dirty and stained attire. 'Preferably ones that are not red.'

It took some searching, but the surgeon eventually produced some brown breeches, white hose and a black coat. He also owned plenty of pastes and powders that Chaloner could use to change his appearance. Then, as the daylight faded and night approached, Chaloner left the house and slipped out into the darkness.

The night was sweltering. It drove people from their homes in search of cooler air, and the streets were full as Chaloner made his way towards the Devil tavern. There were plenty of soldiers and watchful hired-hands about, too, and he discovered the reason when he overheard two of them questioning an onion-seller: there was a reward of five pounds for anyone who produced Falcon.

But there was a twist. Downing had offered a further *ten* pounds to the man who caught Chaloner, having declared publicly that he and Falcon were one and the same. It was not clear whether Williamson agreed, but it was irrelevant anyway – the point was that there were a lot of men determined to have the reward. Chaloner did not blame them. It was a fabulous sum, especially from a miserly man like the envoy, and underlined just how determined Downing was to see him in chains.

The Devil was not far. Chaloner pushed open the door and entered, fighting not to choke on the wall of smoke that greeted him: every patron puffed a pipe, and the lack of anything approaching a breeze rendered the air all but unbreathable. Landlord Barford was doing a roaring trade with cool ale from his cellar, and was in an affable mood. He watched his serving boys weave among the noisy throng, smiling his satisfaction. The hot weather was pleasing someone, at least.

'Yes, I remember Molins,' he said, when Chaloner broached the subject. 'Some villain lunged at him with a sword. I saw it happen, but it was dark, so I could not see the fellow's face. However, I did notice the unusually fine lace on his boot-hose, so we are not talking about a common felon here. Personally, I suspect someone from Court.'

'Why could it not be a merchant?' asked Chaloner. 'Or a wealthy visitor from the country?'

'Because White Hall is overrun by vicious rogues who are always duelling and fighting. But to get back to the tale, Mr Molins jerked away, and fell as he did so. I raised the alarm, and Sir William Compton came to his rescue. He and the Dutchman saw the villain off.'

'You mean they fought?'

'No, I mean the coward fled when he saw Compton and the Dutchman coming.'

'Did you see anyone watching Molins, or behaving suspiciously?' Chaloner was expecting at any moment for Barford to demand why he should want to know, but the landlord was apparently used to being pumped for gossip, and did not seem to find anything odd in the inquisition.

'It is strange you should ask, because someone *did* watch him and his friends like a hawk one night. Indeed, it was the day before poor Molins was attacked, now I think about it.'

'Can you describe him?'

At that moment, the door opened, and three ruffians entered. They sat not far away, alert and watchful, and Chaloner tensed. If they were halfway intelligent, they would notice a patron pressing a tavern-owner for information, and would be suspicious.

'Not really,' Barford was saying, 'because it is dark in here of an evening. He was well dressed, though. I remember that.'

'Could it have been the same man who attacked Molins?' Chaloner was aware of the three louts looking in his direction, and hoped his disguise would protect him.

'Yes, it could, now I think about it. The damned rogue! If he shows his face in *here* again he will be sorry!'

'Did you ever hear what Molins and his friends discussed?'

'Only once. He and the Dutchman liked a drink, so they were not always as quiet-voiced as the others. They were chatting in a foreign language, but I heard Molins mention an emissary.'

379

'Emissary?' Chaloner thought fast. 'Could it have been *emissarius*?'

Barford snapped his fingers. 'That was it! He must have been talking about sending someone on a mission, perhaps to get medicine or a surgical implement. It was all innocent enough.'

But Chaloner suspected otherwise. Molins, Compton, Hanse, White and Edwards were educated men. All five would have known Latin, and they had used it to converse, to reduce the danger of eavesdroppers. And an *emissarius* was a spy: they had been discussing espionage.

When Chaloner left the Devil, the three men followed him out. Unwilling to believe it was coincidence, he ducked down an alley, and only emerged when he was sure they had gone. Then he approached White's house again, but it was locked up very tightly, and no lights were lit. Breaking in would necessitate climbing to a second floor window, but he was too weary for such antics. It was too late to do anything else, so he returned to Wiseman's house.

This time, he was careful to leave no tell-tale drips of blood.

Chapter 11

Although Chaloner was used to sleeping in uncomfortable places, the night in Wiseman's attic was dismal by any standards, and he snapped awake at the slightest creak or groan. When dawn finally broke, it was accompanied by a light, clammy drizzle, not enough to shift the festering piles of rubbish, but more than enough to intensify their reek. Moreover, it served to render London's already polluted air heavy, stale and humid. All in all, it was not a change for the better.

He crept down to Wiseman's laboratory and used the surgeon's plentiful supplies of potions and greases to transform himself from a thirty-four year-old intelligencer into a sixty year-old merchant. Wiseman arrived just as he was finishing.

'I am not open for business until . . .' Wiseman began indignantly, then stopped when he recognised Chaloner's grey eyes. 'Breaking into my home is becoming something of a habit with you.'

'I will try not to do it again.'

'Clearing my name of these hideous accusations is taking you too long,' declared Wiseman, following him to the door. 'So I shall accompany you, to speed matters along before the damage to my reputation becomes permanent. Where shall we go first?'

'I work better alone, Wiseman. Besides, it is not a good idea to be seen with me at the moment.'

'I do not care about that, and I cannot go on with this Sword of Damocles hanging above me. I need you to prove that I did *not* kill Compton and Molins. This morning, if possible.'

Chaloner stifled a sigh; he did not have time for the surgeon's troubles. 'I doubt you are responsible – these deaths are connected to a case in which at least seven other people have been murdered. But you must be patient: finding the right answers takes time.'

Wiseman's expression was suddenly bitter. 'My critics might be right. If Molins and Compton *were* poisoned, then why did I not see it? Moreover, I misdiagnosed Compton twice – once when I thought a headache was a deadly fever of the brain, and once when I dismissed a serious sickness as the ill-effects of heat. Perhaps I *am* losing my touch.'

Chaloner was not sure what to say. 'The most productive thing you can do is stay here and keep working on the samples you took.'

'Very well,' said Wiseman reluctantly. 'But where are you going?'

'The Fleet Rookery,' lied Chaloner, unwilling for anyone to know his real plans.

Wiseman nodded in a way that said he knew he was not being told the truth, then handed the spy a tin. 'More grease for your disguise. You will need it, because not only is it hot today, but it is wet, too. Your pastes may wash off and give you away.'

382

Chaloner left through the back door, while Wiseman distracted the servants. Even with the disguise, he felt acutely vulnerable, and it was difficult not to break step and run when he saw a group of Williamson's guards marching towards him. One hand dropped to his sword, while the other gripped the little gun, but the soldiers passed by without giving him a second glance.

He grimaced. It was going to be a long day. As he walked, it occurred to him that it was Sunday, the day when the Dutch were due to host the conference that represented the last chance of peace. Would they succeed, or would two nations be plunged into bloody conflict? And would Chaloner himself be alive to see it?

There was still no reply at White's house, so Chaloner decided to go to White Hall, in the hope that Bulteel had asked the Bishop of London about Pocks. It was not a sensible place to visit, given the lies Downing had spread about him. Moreover, he was wary about revealing himself to anyone, even trusted friends, given that an incautious slip of the tongue on their part might see him arrested. But he was desperate for clues, and time was short, so he felt he had no choice.

Bulteel was in his office when he arrived, early even for him, because he had papers to assemble before the conference that evening. The secretary looked up irritably when he saw the old merchant hovering in the doorway.

'I am *not* wearing pink gloves to the Savoy,' he snapped. 'So if you have come to sell me some, you can just take them away again. I *know* my cousin claims they will conceal my ink-stained fingers, but I have not seen any other gentlemen wearing pink gloves, and I am beginning to wonder whether I should have asked someone else to oversee my training, because—'

'It is me,' said Chaloner, cutting into the tirade. 'Tom.'

'*You* should not be here!' hissed Bulteel in alarm, once recognition had dawned. 'Downing is telling everyone that you are Falcon. A spy.'

'I prefer the term intelligencer,' said Chaloner, sitting tiredly on the desk. 'It sounds less sordid.'

'Do not jest!' cried Bulteel, distressed. 'He has accused you of being a double agent, of passing secrets to England *and* the Dutch. You are in very real danger, because someone at White Hall *has* been feeding information to the enemy, and Downing makes a good case for you as the culprit.'

Chaloner was sure he had. 'Then I had better visit Williamson, and explain that—'

'No! I heard *him* tell the Earl that while he does not believe Downing's accusations, arresting you will relieve pressure on him to catch the real Falcon. And if he should let you fall into Downing's hands . . . well, suffice to say that your guilt or innocence will not matter, because you will die regardless.'

Chaloner did not doubt it. 'I do not suppose you have learned anything about Pocks?'

Bulteel shook his head. 'I could not corner the Bishop, because my cousin said—'

'I said we can no longer afford to help you.' Chaloner whipped around at the sound of Griffith's voice. He had not heard him approach, and realised weariness and strain were combining to make him careless. It was something he would have to rectify if he wanted to end the day a free man.

Bulteel dragged his cousin inside the office, pointedly

closing the door on Lane, whose face was its usual impassive mask. Chaloner had no idea whether the manservant had recognised him.

'How long have you been listening?' Bulteel demanded, his thin face full of anxiety.

'Long enough to know you have disregarded my advice,' said Griffith reproachfully. He turned to Chaloner, and the lace began to flap. 'It is nothing personal. Indeed, you are one of few men I have met in London who possesses an ounce of integrity. But espionage is a serious matter, and John and I cannot risk being seen as your confederates. I am sure you understand.'

Bulteel was dismayed. 'You defended Lane when Downing fabricated that tale about him being a burglar. So what is the difference between that and me defending Tom?'

'Lane is a servant, and masters have a duty to protect hirelings,' explained Griffith. He shot a pained glance towards the door, which said he had objected to the inconvenience. 'And he told me he is innocent, whereas Chaloner has made no effort to deny the charges brought against *him*.'

'He has no need to deny them, not to me,' Bulteel flashed back. 'His innocence is the one thing I *am* sure about in this treacherous city.'

Griffith softened, and the lace flapped a little less frantically. 'You are right, of course. Forgive me, Chaloner. John does not give his trust readily, and the fact that you have earned his should have told me all I needed to know. So we *will* help you. We shall give you all our money, and urge you to disappear before Downing catches you.' He produced his purse, a fancy thing in puce silk.

Bulteel nodded vigorously, and began to rummage in

385

his desk. 'It is a good idea. You must leave London, immediately, Tom. I will give you everything I have, plus a little of the Earl's—'

'No,' said Chaloner, backing away. 'It is better to stay, and prove Downing wrong.'

Bulteel regarded him in horror. 'But he will kill you before you succeed. See some sense!'

Griffith lowered his voice. 'Obviously, *we* will not betray you, but Lane has probably seen through your disguise, too. And I am beginning to wonder whether *he* is a spy. He disappears, and declines to say where he has been, he listens to everything, and then there is that horribly bland face. I do not trust him, and I wish I had never hired the fellow.'

'I do not trust him, either,' said Bulteel, also *sotto voce*. 'And if he comes after you, Tom, you must slit his throat before he slits yours.'

'Slit his throat?' squeaked Griffith, shocked. 'That is hardly a gentlemanly—'

'Please go, Tom,' begged Bulteel. 'And only come back when you are *sure* it is safe.'

Chaloner nodded agreement, although with no intention of complying, and took his leave, brushing aside the proffered money. He doubled back when he heard them begin to talk, slipping past their door unseen. He wanted to see the Earl before abandoning White Hall.

'Poor Tom!' Bulteel was saying tearfully. 'He is a good man, and my only real friend here.'

'I am leaving London today,' declared Griffith abruptly. 'Downing remains unreasonably vexed over that poem I wrote, and he is too vengeful an adversary for me. It is time to go home.'

*   *   *

386

A fire was lit in Clarendon's office, which was hot and airless. Chaloner padded across it and stood behind his master, coughing softly to announce his presence.

'Lord save us!' exclaimed the Earl, putting his hand over his chest after Chaloner had identified himself, and he saw he was not about to be assassinated. '*Must* you do that? What are you doing here, anyway? I told you to stay away until this business is over. Have you heard what Downing is saying about you now? That *you* stole my documents, and stuffed them in vases at the Savoy.'

'I doubt that tale will prove very popular. People are more interested in blaming Hanse.'

'Yes, but Downing is going around telling everyone that you know your way around Worcester House, including where I keep my papers. And he points out that your alibi is a dead Hollander.'

Chaloner stared at him. 'What do you believe, sir?'

'That Downing is an inveterate liar, who will destroy anyone for personal gain. But I cannot afford to protect you, Chaloner. I have already explained why. The peace talks . . .'

'It was not me who spread the rumour about you not knowing what was in your missing papers,' said Chaloner, unwilling to be blamed for that particular piece of nastiness.

The Earl pointed to the windows, now closed. 'Someone must have overheard us talking. When Wiseman reported the rumour to me, I admit my first thought was that you were the culprit. But then I reconsidered: you are no gossip. Quite the reverse, in fact – you never tell anyone anything. But why did you come? You do not need me to remind you that it is dangerous.'

'I came to tell you who has been blackmailing courtiers.'

'I do not care about them,' said Clarendon irritably. 'If they were decent, godly people, they would not have shady secrets. I am far more interested in getting the rest of my missing documents back. It was an audacious raid, stealing them from under my nose as I slept.'

'As you *slept*? You said they disappeared when you were dining with your wife.'

The Earl became flustered. 'Yes, well, they may have gone a little sooner than I led you to believe. The afternoon, for example.'

'The afternoon?' Chaloner was torn between anger and frustration. 'Are you sure? When did you last see them?'

The Earl looked sheepish. 'When Bulteel left them on the table after I had eaten breakfast. Do not look at me so accusingly! As I told you before, I *meant* to read them, but I dozed off. I am overworked, so is it surprising that I am always exhausted?'

'No,' said Chaloner, trying to hide his exasperation and failing. 'But the difference in time opens the theft up to a whole new range of suspects – the staff on duty during the day are not the same as the ones who work at night. I will have to start all over again.'

The Earl narrowed his eyes dangerously. 'How dare you berate me! And I—'

There was a clatter of footsteps on the stairs outside, and Downing's self-important voice echoed along the hallway. Chaloner glanced around quickly, assessing avenues of escape. They were limited, and he saw a confrontation was going to be inevitable. But the Earl had other ideas.

388

'Stand behind the curtain,' he ordered. 'I cannot afford to be caught consorting with you, especially today, with the conference looming. So stay hidden until I tell you to come out.'

'Downing is being blackmailed because he has submitted fraudulent expense claims to the government,' said Chaloner quickly. 'If you need to disconcert him, mention them.'

There was no time for further explanations, because Downing was outside, and Chaloner had only just stepped behind the draperies when the envoy marched in. He sported a spectacularly bruised eye from the scuffle in Fleet Street.

'What happened to you?' asked the Earl, eyeing him with dislike. 'Been brawling?'

'Chaloner attacked me,' claimed Downing, raising a tentative hand to touch it. 'He is a vicious brute, and I recommend extreme caution when dealing with him.'

'You no doubt deserved it,' said the Earl coldly. 'But what do you want? I am busy. Can you not do your business with my secretary?'

'I thought it best to see you in person,' said Downing, equally frosty. 'And do not look at *me* with distaste, My Lord. *I* am not the one who harbours criminals – betrayers of King and country.'

'I am not harbouring anyone,' asserted Clarendon, somewhat furtively. 'Search my rooms if—'

'I *have* searched them,' interrupted Downing curtly. 'Chaloner has been hiding somewhere these last few days, so I have been through your offices *and* your home.'

Clarendon was purple with rage and indignation. 'You impudent upstart! You have no right—'

'I have every right! I am looking for a dangerous

389

traitor,' snarled Downing. 'So do not presume to tell me my business, My Lord Chancellor.'

'Chaloner is not a traitor, and nor is he Falcon,' the Earl snapped back. 'You know it, and so does anyone with a modicum of intelligence. He was not even in the country when Falcon was arrested. Your campaign against him is petty and sly, and tells everyone that your success during the Commonwealth *was* due to his superior skills.'

Behind the curtain, Chaloner was astonished. He had never expected to hear such an endorsement of support from a man who had never made any attempt to conceal his dislike of him.

Downing did not grace the outburst with a reply. 'I did not come here to argue,' he said haughtily. 'I came to reason. Do you know where he is? Your enemies will have nothing with which to accuse you, if you are the one who gives him up.'

Chaloner held his breath: his master had a strong sense of self-preservation.

'Do not attempt to coerce me,' shouted the Earl, outraged. 'Catch him yourself. Or are you saying he is cleverer than you, Williamson and the entire intelligence service combined?'

'No!' barked Downing. 'But he will make a mistake soon, and then we shall have him. I thought he would have fled to Thurloe, but Thurloe is away and no one knows where. Meanwhile, I have questioned his other friends, including the brothel-keeper in Hercules' Pillars Alley and your secretary, but they know nothing. Damned simpletons!'

'What brothel-keeper?' asked the Earl, shocked.

Downing's smile was malicious. 'You do not know the kind of company he keeps?'

Fortunately for Chaloner, the Earl did not believe him. 'He has done nothing wrong. Unlike you, it seems. You may as well know now that I have decided to audit your expense accounts.'

Downing paled. 'Why?'

'Because I have reason to believe you are cheating the government.'

'No!' cried Downing. 'You have no proof. And if Chaloner has given you the papers he stole from my home, then they are forgeries. He wrote them himself!'

'Well, which is it?' demanded Clarendon archly. 'Did he steal them or fabricate them? He cannot have done both, and you contradict yourself in your oily efforts to extricate.'

Downing stared at him, then became greasier than ever. 'You understand how these things are, My Lord. Mistakes in accounting happen, and I cannot be responsible for the carelessness of my clerks. I can explain everything.'

'Oh, you will,' said Clarendon softly. 'To an investigating committee.'

Downing stared at him for a moment longer, then turned on his heel and stalked out, slamming the door behind him.

'That shut him up,' said the Earl gleefully. 'And he is clearly guilty. What has he done, exactly?'

Chaloner told him all he knew, hoping it would go some way to protecting his master against Downing, because he was beginning to fear that he would not be in a position to do it himself.

It was not easy leaving White Hall, because Williamson's soldiers were everywhere, scanning the faces of servants and courtiers alike as they passed through the gates. Chaloner managed eventually, but two followed him out. He itched to run, but sixty-year-old merchants did not sprint, and it would have shattered his disguise for certain. He thought he had lost the pair as he crossed the busy expanse of Charing Cross, but when he reached The Strand and glanced behind him, they were still there.

He escaped them in St Martin-in-the-Fields, which was busy because prayers were being said for cooler weather. Then he hurried to Fleet Street, and breathed a sigh of relief when White's door was answered by an elderly housekeeper. Filmy blue eyes indicated she was virtually blind, but she smiled when he asked to speak to the vicar.

'I recognise your voice! You married Mrs Cotton recently. I remember, because it was the day my master had that vile message that warned him against his good works.'

'Is he in?' Chaloner had no idea what she was talking about, but it was no time for idle stories.

'What really upset him was that a man was murdered to see it delivered,' she went on as if he had not spoken. 'Stabbed in the back, and the missive pinned to him. During a *wedding*!'

Chaloner stared at her: he had all but forgotten the hapless Philip Alden. 'The note advising someone not to interfere was aimed at White? What was he doing to warrant such a message?'

'Fighting evil,' replied the housekeeper promptly. 'And someone did not like it.'

Chaloner continued to stare. Was Alden's murder Falcon's work? Falcon had cursed Compton, but such tactics would not work on a devout cleric like White, so had he resorted to crude threats instead? But *what* was White not to interfere with? The Sinon Plot? Chaloner stepped inside the house, determined that the vicar would give him answers before anyone else lost their lives.

'Where is he?' he demanded.

'Dead, sir.' Tears slid down the old woman's leathery cheeks. 'He passed away on Friday night at his sister's home in Chelsey. We brought him home, and he is to be buried today. That is why it is raining – God is weeping for the death of a good man.'

Chaloner slumped against the wall, shocked and sorry. 'What killed him?'

'A fever. He was well one moment, and gone the next. Would you like to see him? He is on display, and several of his parishioners have already been to pay their respects.'

Chaloner closed his eyes as guilt flooded through him. He had let Compton down, failed to do the one thing he had asked. If only he had managed to catch White's name! Full of self-recrimination, he followed the house-keeper into a parlour, and looked inside the coffin.

White had been dressed in a smart long-coat, with a fresh falling band and white gloves to match. Chaloner frowned. The gloves were the same as the ones Compton had worn, *and* the same as the pair in Molins's pile of discarded clothes. He had been told that both were gifts from Hanse.

'Will you fetch Surgeon Wiseman?' he asked, as questions and answers began to rattle around in his mind in equal measure. 'He will want to pay his respects. Tell him Tom wants him to come.'

While he waited for the surgeon to arrive, he tried to inspect the body, but did not know how to find what

393

he was looking for, and chafed impatiently until Wiseman marched into the room a short while later. The surgeon dropped to his knees and began to pray. Touched by his piety, the housekeeper withdrew. Wiseman leapt to his feet the moment the door was closed, eyebrows raised.

'Examine his hands,' ordered Chaloner urgently.

Wiseman blinked. 'Why?'

'Because Hanse gave gloves to Molins and Compton, and now we discover that White had some, too. I suspect they have been treated with poison. I wonder whether Talbot Edwards was sent any.'

'Talbot Edwards is not dead. I saw him this morning.'

'He is a sweaty man, and it is hot for gloves – perhaps he has not worn them yet. But Compton and Molins have. And van Goch's physician told me that the substance that killed Hanse and Oetje was not administered in anything swallowed. He thought it might have been introduced by means of a sharp object, but some toxins can be absorbed through the skin . . .'

Wiseman began a detailed and, to Chaloner's agitated mind, aggravatingly time-consuming examination. It involved inspecting White's throat, removing clothes to look for marks, and examining hands and gloves with a magnifying glass. It felt like an age before he had finished.

'You are right,' he said eventually. 'White *has* been poisoned, and the gloves are responsible. Can you see this stain by the seam? It is where powder or liquid has been pressed into the material. It has a rank stench, and is almost certainly deadly.'

'Deadly enough to kill?'

'Perhaps, although do not forget that the victims would

394

have removed the gloves to eat or drink, leaving residues on their fingers. The poison could have gone into their bodies that way, also.'

'How long would it take to have an effect?'

'I will have to perform experiments to tell you that. However, there are potions that can lay a man low, then let him rally before killing him. That must have been what happened to Compton – he was ill, felt better, and finally succumbed. No wonder I misdiagnosed!'

'But the process was inevitable, once started?'

'Yes, if the source of the trouble was not removed. Of course, one symptom may have been cold hands, leading the victim to reach for his gloves, thus perpetuating the cycle.'

'We need to recover the ones from Molins and Compton,' said Chaloner. He was aware of the despair in his voice – he could not track down dead men's clothes, elude the grasp of everyone who thought he was a spy *and* thwart Falcon. 'No one else must put them on.'

'I will do it,' offered Wiseman. 'They are proof of my innocence, so you can trust me to succeed. Does it mean Hanse is the killer? The wretched things were gifts from him, after all.'

'Hanse cannot be the culprit for three reasons. First, he was poisoned, too – and perhaps he was stripped of his clothes to allow the real killer to reclaim the garments that brought about his death. Second, he would not have sent gloves to his friends—'

'You sound very sure.'

'I am sure. He *was* in the habit of giving gifts, but only stockings – someone else sent the gloves in his name. And third, he had received a pair himself. He wore them the night we met in the Sun. How could I have sat with him all that time, oblivious to the fact that he was being murdered?'

'Because you had no reason to suspect it. Had he complained of—'

'He mentioned pains in his stomach,' said Chaloner bitterly. 'And now I know why.'

'I was going to say that had he complained of irritated skin or swollen fingers, then it might have been different. But I saw no damage to his hands. Or to White's, Molins's or Compton's, for that matter. You could not have known.'

Chaloner was not so sure, and knew his lack of care would plague him for a long time to come.

'Swan and Swallow were probably poisoned, too,' Wiseman went on, placing White's gloves in a bag for safekeeping. 'It would explain why they were compliant when they were doused in oil and set alight – they were incapable of doing anything but scream.'

Chaloner thought about it. 'In other words, they were burned to eliminate evidence that they had swallowed a toxin. But why bother? Any fool could see they had been murdered.'

'The answer is obvious,' said Wiseman disdainfully. 'We have been looking for a man who kills by setting his victims alight, and it has not occurred to us that we may be hunting a poisoner. It was a ruse, to throw investigators off the real trail.'

'The real trail,' muttered Chaloner. 'God only knows what that is. But we know that Falcon killed Swan and Swallow, so perhaps the gloves are proof that he dispatched Hanse, Molins, Compton and White, too. The connecting factor is poison.'

Wiseman grimaced his disgust. 'It is a ruthless way to kill, regardless. The man is deranged!'

Chaloner agreed. 'The Privy Council – and possibly Williamson, too – believe his sole intention was to steal the crown jewels. But Compton and Edwards thought he wanted the treasure to finance something more significant. Meanwhile, the landlord of the Devil heard them mention a spy—'

Wiseman looked bemused. 'Falcon is an intelligencer? Whose? Ours or the Dutch?'

'Both and neither. No one understands why the negotiations are not working. We should have had a treaty long before now, but there is suspicion and mistrust on both sides—'

'And the moment progress is made, a rumour starts to circulate, which sets it back again,' nodded Wiseman. 'It is Falcon, keeping us and the Dutch in a state of unease. But why?'

Chaloner shrugged. 'Perhaps because he can. You look disbelieving, but he has held two nations at each other's throats for months. Such power must be intoxicating. And addictive.'

Wiseman shook his head in incomprehension. 'What will you do now?'

'Find Talbot Edwards and *force* him to tell me what he knows about the Sinon Plot.'

Leaving Wiseman to explain to the housekeeper why they had tampered with her master's body, Chaloner left White's house. The ruffians from the gangs were everywhere as he flagged down a hackney carriage and ordered the driver to take him to the Tower, although whether Williamson's or Downing's was impossible to tell. Two watched him as he climbed into the coach, but neither followed, and he was soon rattling down Ludgate Hill to cross the Fleet River.

Once across the fetid, evil-smelling stream, there was a problem, because the cobbles on the other side of the valley had been rendered slick by drizzle, and several vehicles had slithered out of control to cause a blockage. Chaloner itched to burst out of the coach and run, but it would demolish his disguise for certain, so he forced himself to stay. Chafing impotently, he willed the traffic to ease, but it took an age, and the clocks were striking ten by the time he reached his destination.

Then there was another delay, because the yeomen were at their Sunday devotions, and the one who eventually answered his insistent hammering was not pleased to have been dragged away. He conducted Chaloner to Edward's lodgings with ill grace, although his jaw dropped in horror when they arrived: the Assistant Keeper was lying on his bed clutching his stomach, his face as white as snow. A hat and a pair of gloves had been tossed on to a nearby chair.

'Fetch Surgeon Wiseman,' Chaloner ordered the yeoman. 'He will know what to do.'

'What is wrong with me?' gasped Edwards when the soldier had gone. His weak eyes were watering, so his cheeks were wet with tears. 'I was well this morning, but now I feel dreadful.'

'White was murdered on Friday night.' Chaloner was sorry to be brutal to an ailing man, but there was no time for niceties. 'Like Hanse, Compton, Molins and now you, he was poisoned by a pair of gloves – which were *not* from Hanse, but from Falcon. It is time to tell me what is going on.'

'No!' whispered Edwards, glancing towards the offending items in horror. 'I cannot . . .'

'Then you will die, too,' said Chaloner harshly. 'If not today, then later, when Falcon will avenge himself on you for what you have done to thwart him already.'

'I will stop him,' declared Edwards unconvincingly. 'It is why we came together in the first place. Compton overheard him plotting, and he told three men he trusted – Molins, White and me. And we included Hanse, because of what Falcon did.'

'He circulated rumours to impede the peace talks,' said Chaloner, watching surprise light Edwards's face that he should know. 'You needed Hanse to repair the damage from the Dutch side.'

'Our strategy was working! Then Compton had a brilliant idea: to tell Williamson that Falcon planned to steal the crown jewels. Falcon could not play his evil games in prison. But he escaped . . .'

'Are you saying Falcon is innocent of plotting to steal the regalia?'

'Oh, no! He intended to have it sure enough. He was outraged when Williamson ordered his capture, and he cursed Compton . . . but you know all this.'

Chaloner was struggling to understand. 'Did you tell Williamson that Falcon was doing a lot more than plotting to make off with a few baubles?'

Edwards was ill enough to overlook the slight to the treasure in his care. 'We did not dare! It would have unleashed even more suspicion and mistrust than ever.'

'He is the Spymaster,' said Chaloner, disgusted. 'He is paid to handle this kind of business.'

'But his intelligencers are next to worthless,' whispered Edwards in despair. 'They are corrupt, too – anyone can

399

buy them for a few pounds. And this is too sensitive a matter to be left to chance. We decided it was better to tackle it ourselves.'

'Your arrogance has allowed Falcon to inflict all manner of damage on the negotiations.'

'I suppose he *has* proved too wily for us,' admitted Edwards tearfully. 'When he was arrested, he accused Swan and Swallow of giving him up, although they did nothing of the kind . . .'

'Wait a moment,' said Chaloner uneasily. 'You let Williamson incarcerate Swan and Swallow in the same cell as a man who thought they had betrayed him?'

Edwards closed his eyes. 'I know we bear some responsibility for their fate, but it was necessary – as long as he blamed Swan and Swallow, he would not think others were working to foil him. The means really did justify the end, and Swan and Swallow were hardly angels.'

Chaloner was appalled. 'But Newgate only held him for a day, and he learned the truth as soon as he escaped. Hanse, Molins, Compton and White have paid the price for trying to thwart him.'

Edwards opened his eyes, and spark of defiance flashed in them. 'But I still live, and the real Sinon Plot has not come to fruition yet. I can still stop him.'

'How?' demanded Chaloner. 'And what *is* the real Sinon Plot?'

Edwards swallowed hard and muttered a prayer. For a moment, Chaloner thought he was going to refuse to break the oath he had sworn, but he began to speak after a moment.

'The peacemakers have one thread of hope left: the convention at the Savoy this evening. If that fails, Heer van Goch will go home.'

'Falcon intends to sabotage it?'

Edwards nodded. 'But we have not been able to discover how. He might have hired assassins, planted a bomb or even prepared documents . . .'

'What kind of documents?'

'Neither government has been entirely scrupulous in its dealings with the other, and it is possible that Falcon has obtained written evidence of it. If he has, making it public will destroy friendly relations between our two countries for ever.'

Chaloner was exasperated. 'I do not see why you and your friends went to such pains to keep this a secret. Williamson is perfectly capable of—'

'Because of Falcon himself,' whispered Edwards. 'He is *not* just the impostor-vicar from Cheapside. He is also someone powerful and wealthy – a high-ranking diplomat or politician, probably one who thinks anarchy will make him rich. Williamson is *not* capable of handling a traitor of such magnitude.'

Chaloner still did not understand, but there was no time for more explanations. 'Who is he?'

'We never managed to find out, although we have our suspects: Ruyven, Zas, the conveniently missing Secretary Kun—'

'I had better visit the Savoy, then,' said Chaloner, turning towards the door.

'Wait! They are not the only ones. Why does Charles Bates spend so much time in the Spares Gallery, and can we be *sure* he left London yesterday? Then there is Kicke, who stole from White Hall using some very good disguises. And finally, Griffith's manservant is sinister, and I distrust him intensely, although Compton never shared my suspicions.'

401

'You said you were going to stop Falcon today,' said Chaloner, supposing it was down to him to put the plan into action. 'How?'

Edwards swallowed hard. 'I shall go to the conference and look for him.'

Chaloner was bemused. 'But you have just listed six suspects, most of whom will have a legitimate reason for being there. How will you know which one to challenge? Moreover, Falcon is a master of disguise, and might decide to be someone else today. You may not recognise him.' Especially, he thought, as Edwards was as blind as a bat.

'Well, what *would* you have me do?' cried Edwards, distraught. 'I dare not go to Williamson or the Privy Council, lest one of *them* transpires to be the villain.'

'Can you walk?' asked Chaloner. The plan was feeble, but he could not think of a better one.

Unfortunately, Edwards fell back on the bed when he tried to stand, moaning and clutching his middle. Chaloner was on his own.

'Rest now,' he said, wishing five amateurs had not meddled in matters best left to professionals. 'And when Wiseman arrives, tell him everything. Perhaps he can devise a plan to—'

'No,' sobbed Edwards. 'I will not bring Wiseman into Falcon's sights. You are already doomed, but I will not damn anyone else.'

Once outside the Tower, Chaloner hesitated, not sure what to do first, but acutely aware that time was passing. He pretended to be inspecting fruit on a barrow when two rough villains strode past, and fumed at the wasted moments. How could he concentrate on foiling Falcon

402

when he could not move about the city without fear of being apprehended? Or should he give himself up, and use his capture as an opportunity to tell Williamson all he had learned?

But then he thought about Edwards's contention that Falcon was a high-ranking politician or diplomat. *Williamson* might be Falcon, and marching into his lair might see him executed on the spot. And then no one would be left to stop him. So whom could he trust?

The only person who came to mind was van Goch, who had worked so hard for peace. Chaloner brightened as he thought it through. But how was he to reach him? He could hardly walk into the Savoy and demand an interview when the entire delegation thought he was a spy. Mulling the problem over, he hailed a hackney and ordered it to The Strand as quickly as possible.

Once there, he hid in the alley opposite, reflecting on how best to get in. Ruyven had not been exaggerating when he said he had improved security – especially on the day when the place would be flooded by high-ranking men from both nations – and the grounds and the front of the hospital complex were thick with soldiers. He could not sneak past them in broad daylight, so he needed to gain access another way.

He hurried to Covent Garden, where it did not take him long to find what he was looking for – a cart piled high with vegetables from the country. He experienced a pang of guilt when he punched the owner and shoved him into a convenient coal shed, but his conscience did not prick him for long. Within minutes, he was driving down Bow Street, all his attention on the task in hand. He crossed The Strand and steered the pony towards the Savoy.

'What is this?' demanded Ruyven, on duty at the gate. 'We did not order these.'

He spoke Dutch, so Chaloner pretended not to understand, keeping his head down and hoping Ruyven would not see through his disguise. Fortunately, a much larger wagon laden with firewood arrived at the same time, and Ruyven decided that represented more of a threat. Chaloner's little vehicle was waved through impatiently. He abandoned it near the kitchens, and made his way towards Jacoba's quarters. She would help him reach van Goch.

The Savoy was busier than he had ever seen it. Its courtyard had been swept and carpets set down, so visiting dignitaries would not soil their shoes in the mud produced by drizzle and dust. Retainers were everywhere, pinning up banners, carrying platters of food and jugs of wine, and giving windows and doors a last-minute polish. Zas and Taacken stood near the State Room, heads together as they discussed some urgent point of business. Taacken looked tense and unhappy, although Zas was full of fierce good humour, his foxy eyes everywhere.

Chaloner listened outside Jacoba's door for a moment, to ensure she was alone, then entered. She was sitting in the window, reading. She turned sharply, and opened her mouth to scream.

'It is me,' he said urgently, raising his hands to show he meant her no harm. 'Tom.'

She peered at him fearfully. 'Things are being said about you, and now you arrive in disguise!'

He closed the distance between them quickly, and knelt at her side. 'I am not a spy, but there *is* one at large – a very dangerous one. His name is Falcon.'

Jacoba swallowed hard. 'Falcon? There is no one here called Falcon.'

'It is an alias,' explained Chaloner tiredly. 'He might be anyone – Kun, Zas . . .' He did not mention Ruyven, but she read it in his mind anyway.

'It will not be Ruyven,' she said, shaking her head firmly. 'He is . . . not that kind of man.'

'You think you know him because he was your lover,' said Chaloner bluntly. There was no time to mince words. 'Hanse found out about your relationship, which led me to wonder whether Ruyven had killed him. But it was Falcon.'

'We never meant to hurt Willem,' said Jacoba in a small voice. 'But he walked in on us one evening. When you offered to find out who had murdered him, I repeated what he had said about Ruyven being a bad enemy in the hope that it would keep you and Ruyven apart.'

'To protect me?' asked Chaloner, a little coolly. 'Or him?'

'Both. *And* my reputation. Ruyven is not clever, and I knew you could trick him into a confession. But how *did* you find out? We were very careful, and no one else knows.'

It was a sordid business, and Chaloner was sorry that Hanse had spent the last few weeks of his life distressed by it. But Jacoba's infidelity was not relevant to his duties that day.

'Has Kun been found yet?' he asked.

'No.' Jacoba gazed at him with huge eyes. 'But I fear he may be dead – poisoned and drowned, like Willem. And it is horrible here without them to calm ragged tempers. Downing's accusations have the whole place in an uproar, especially the ones about you.'

Chaloner was beginning to feel overwhelmed. 'Downing is playing right into Falcon's hands,' he said

405

bitterly. 'As long as attention is focused on me, Falcon is free to do as he pleases.'

'How do you know *Downing* is not Falcon?' asked Jacoba. 'You mention Kun and Zas as suspects, but there is nothing to say this evil is the work of a Dutchman.'

'No, there is not. But regardless of who he is, we *must* stop him before he damages both our countries. Will you take me to Heer van Goch?'

'No!' Jacoba was appalled. 'You will be arrested and shot before you can explain yourself.'

'Please, Jacoba. I would not ask if it were not important.'

She put her head in her hands. 'I do not know what to think! You are no spy – Aletta would not have married one of those – but Ruyven says you are dangerous, and so does Downing.'

'Then I will find my own way to the ambassador. All I ask is that you do not raise the alarm until I have had a chance to talk to him.'

Jacoba shot him an anguished look, but rummaged in a chest to emerge with a voluminous gown and a feminine wig. She helped him don them, and told him to wash the first disguise from his face. Then she led him along a series of corridors. She was obviously frightened, and her behaviour when she met friends was suspicious, to say the least. Chaloner braced himself for capture, but although there were raised eyebrows at her uncharacteristically curt salutations, no one challenged them.

'We made it,' she murmured eventually, heaving an unsteady sigh as she stopped outside a heavy door. 'But I still think you are insane. Leave, before you are caught.'

'Go back to your rooms,' instructed Chaloner. 'If I

am . . . if matters do not go according to plan, I will not tell anyone you helped me, so do not admit it.'

When he was sure she had gone, he opened the door and stepped inside. He found himself in an antechamber, where visitors waited for private audiences with the ambassador. It was empty, so he aimed for the door at its far end. This opened into a handsome parlour, and a third door led to a bedchamber. It was closed, suggesting van Goch was resting within, rallying his energies for the looming convention. The middle room contained only one occupant.

'Kun!' exclaimed Chaloner. 'Where have you been?'

Kun's jaw dropped when Chaloner flung off the wig and gown. The secretary was pale, unshaven, and his eyes were hollow. He shot an agonised glance towards the bedchamber, then beckoned Chaloner out of van Goch's quarters, to an adjoining set of rooms. From the teetering piles of legal papers that filled them, Chaloner assumed they were Kun's own.

'You are accused of espionage!' the secretary hissed, checking the corridor carefully before closing the door. 'Are you insane, to come here so brazenly?'

'You are hardly the man to talk,' retorted Chaloner. 'You, who totes stolen Privy Council papers around London in cheeses, and leaves them behind in hackney carriages.'

Kun put his head in his hands with a groan. 'They have been found?'

'When did you take them?' demanded Chaloner. 'I know Hanse did not do it.'

'Actually, he did – when he and van Goch were visiting Worcester House that Friday morning. He saw them on

407

a table and slipped them in his bag. It was a blunder of monumental proportion.'

Chaloner recalled the Earl's confession: that the papers had gone missing earlier than he had led everyone to think. But even so, Chaloner still did not believe that his kinsman was a thief. He started to shake his head, but Kun overrode him.

'He came straight to me, and told me what he had done. I was horrified, and ordered him to return them the very next day, before Clarendon missed them. But he went out that night and never returned, so the problem devolved to me. I cannot tell you what a strain it has been.'

'So what did you do?'

Kun looked as if he might be sick. 'I decided to send them back to Clarendon in a cheese, in the hope that the matter would be quietly forgotten. But . . .'

'But a rogue hackneyman whisked you down an alley and threatened you. He brought you home, but you were so frightened, you ran, leaving them behind in your panic. Or some of them, at least.'

Kun slumped on to a chair. 'Putting them in the cheese was harder than I anticipated, so half were still in my pocket. I hid some in a vase, for want of somewhere safer. And look at the trouble that caused! The rest I managed to burn. But I wish to God I had set fire to them all, instead of trying to be clever, and attempting to mitigate the damage.'

'But why did Hanse steal them in the first place?' Chaloner was appalled. 'He wanted peace, and removing papers from a house in which he was a guest was hardly the way to achieve it.'

'He hoped they would reveal the identity of a traitor

408

– a man whose machinations are damaging the negotiations. It was a desperate measure taken by a desperate man. And to rub salt into the wound, the papers were a lot of nonsense anyway – contradictory, irrelevant and misleading.'

'It is a sorry mess,' said Chaloner, disgusted. 'Surely, you have professionals to manage this sort of thing? You and Hanse did not have to dabble yourselves.'

'But we do not know who to trust!' cried Kun. 'Because of the man called Falcon.'

'You know about Falcon? How?'

'Hanse told me. He described how he met four honourable Englishmen who are committed to thwarting him. *Falcon* is the one who has been sabotaging the negotiations, you see.'

'What did Hanse tell you about the Sinon Plot? And do not deny knowing about it this time.'

Kun hung his head. 'The Sinon Plot is Falcon's final *coup de grâce*, a scheme that will destroy the friendship between our two nations for ever. Hanse also said he suspected Falcon was not in Newgate, and was going to visit the place to find out. But he was murdered before he could go there.'

So he had left messages telling Chaloner to do it instead. Unfortunately, missives without explanations were useless, and Chaloner had unravelled the mystery far too late.

'I went to your Spymaster on Friday night,' said Kun brokenly. 'I told him Falcon was trying not only to sabotage the peace talks, but to damage our governments, too. He listened politely, but I could tell he did not believe me. So I have been trying to find this villain myself.'

'Is that why you have been missing? Your friends have been worried about you.'

'I dared not tell anyone what I was doing, lest I inadvertently confided in Falcon or his agents. The only person I trust is Heer van Goch. He knows I am back, but no one else does.'

'Falcon's agents?' asked Chaloner uneasily.

'Of course. He cannot have achieved all this on his own. Besides, the intelligence he has used to create confusion and distrust comes from leaks at the very highest level. We are not talking about State-Room gossip here, but highly classified information.'

'You do not think I am Falcon, then?'

'You cannot be – you have not been in London long enough. He is either a Dutchman who travelled with us, or an Englishman who was already here.'

'He plans to make his move today,' said Chaloner. 'At the convention. You must tell van Goch, so he can be on his guard. Meanwhile, I will try to—'

'You two will not be doing anything,' came a quiet voice from behind them.

Chaloner spun around. It was Ruyven.

Chaloner knew, from the expression of gloating malice on Ruyven's face, that he was in serious trouble. The Dutchman held a gun, and it was primed and ready to fire. Behind him were Zas and Taacken. Zas's expression was troubled, while Taacken's was unreadable.

'How much did you hear?' demanded Kun uneasily.

'Most of it.' Ruyven shot Chaloner a disdainful smile. 'This may come as a surprise, but Jacoba cares more for me than she does for you. She told me what you forced her to do.'

Roughly, Taacken relieved Chaloner of sword, daggers and even the little gun. He tossed the latter to Ruyven, who regarded it admiringly before slipping it into his own pocket.

'You have been a fool, and so was Hanse,' said Zas to Kun in disgust. 'Playing such games when so much was at stake! How could you have been so stupid?'

'I did what I thought was right,' said Kun with quiet dignity. 'For peace.'

Zas rubbed his chin as he looked at Ruyven. 'The best way forward is to execute Chaloner. The atmosphere in the Savoy will lighten when people know he is dead, and it may buy us the time we need to catch the real traitor. Falcon, as Kun just called him.'

'I shall oblige you with pleasure,' replied Ruyven with a grin.

'No!' cried Kun, appalled. 'You cannot murder an innocent man!'

'Consider yourself lucky that we do not shoot you, too,' said Zas coldly. 'Your actions have harmed our country, and that makes you guilty of treason, as far as I am concerned.'

'Kun, warn van Goch,' called Chaloner urgently, as Ruyven started to manhandle him towards the door. 'About Falcon's plans to—'

'Stay here and make sure he does not escape,' Zas ordered Taacken, treating the secretary to a look of utter disdain. 'And if he gives you trouble, kill him, too.'

'How dare you—' Kun's outraged objections stopped abruptly when Taacken, unwilling to take chances, bundled him unceremoniously into a closet and locked him in.

'Please,' Chaloner begged, appalled that van Goch

would go to the convention blithely unaware of Falcon's intentions. 'If you overheard us talking, then you will know that Falcon plans to—'

Ruyven struck him with the butt of his gun, driving him to his knees, stunned.

'Make sure Jacoba stays in her room,' said Ruyven to Zas, grabbing Chaloner's arm and hauling him upright again. 'She will not want this villain shot, regardless of what he has or has not done, and she will make a scene. That will be unpleasant for everyone.'

'It will,' agreed Zas. 'However, while I have no stomach for executions, I had better see this one through. It would not be the first time a spy has survived this sort of situation.'

Ruyven laughed mirthlessly. 'He will not escape from me. When you hear the gunshot, you will know it is done. Jacoba may guess what has happened, so stop her from rushing to investigate. Her distress will distract Heer van Goch, and we need him at his best this evening.'

Chaloner felt his last hope evaporate when Zas went to do as he was told. Ruyven had been waiting a long time to avenge himself on his hated rival, and the chances of reasoning with him were non-existent. He reeled dizzily when he saw his battle against Falcon was over, but made no attempt to right himself. Ruyven grunted with the effort of supporting him.

'For God's sake, Chaloner,' he muttered. 'Do you have to make this quite so difficult?'

Chaloner did not reply, and it was not long before they reached the wall that separated the Savoy's grounds from Worcester House. It was shielded from the hospital buildings by trees, and was the perfect place for an execution. Ruyven shoved him against it, then stood back.

'Can you climb over this wall unaided? Or must I help you?'

Chaloner regarded him suspiciously. 'Why? So you can shoot me trying to escape? What purpose would that serve, other than to salve your conscience?'

'I do not have a conscience,' replied Ruyven shortly. 'I seduce the wife of my oldest friend, and I betray my country. For money. Does that sound like a man with a conscience to you?'

Chaloner struggled to understand what he was being told. '*You* are a spy? Do not tell me you are Falcon, because I will not believe it. You are not nearly intelligent enough.'

Ruyven regarded him wryly. 'You might at least *try* to phrase your remarks in a conciliatory manner, given that I am the one holding a gun. But no, I am not Falcon. I *am* a spy, though. I am surprised you did not guess. You saw me with my paymaster once.'

'With Downing! In the Savoy's yard. I assumed you were pumping each other for information.'

'He was pumping me. It was I who told him that Clarendon's papers were in the vase. Does it surprise you to learn we are on the same side?'

Chaloner was more than surprised, he was dumbfounded. Ruyven was the last man alive he would have imagined corruptible. 'And you did it for money?'

Ruyven laid his gun in the grass. 'For a pension, actually. I have never been paid enough to invest in one, despite risking life and limb for the States-General since I was twenty.'

'A *pension?*' echoed Chaloner in disbelief. He had met many traitors in his life, but none who had been motivated by the chance to save for the future.

413

Ruyven grimaced. 'I asked Heer van Goch to raise my salary dozens of times, but he always palmed me off with excuses. Well, there is only so far I am willing to be abused – passed over, while less worthy recipients are rewarded.'

'Christ!' muttered Chaloner. He knew he should take advantage of the opportunity Ruyven had presented by setting down his weapon, but he was too dazed by the captain's startling revelations.

'There are intelligencers galore in the delegation,' Ruyven went on. 'For example, Zas spies *for* Heer van Goch. Why do you think he wants you dead? Because he hopes you will be blamed for some of the things *he* has done. He does not know I am Downing's man, of course.'

'Of course,' said Chaloner weakly. 'But if we really are on the same side, then warn van Goch to be ready for whatever Falcon is planning. It is—'

'He will not listen to me,' interrupted Ruyven bitterly. 'I am far too lowly.'

'Then take me to someone who isn't,' said Chaloner desperately. 'Or Falcon will succeed.'

'Perhaps he will,' agreed Ruyven with a sigh. 'But I am unequal to stopping him, and so are you. Downing lied when he concocted that tale about you and de Witt's bedchamber. You do not have the mettle for espionage, and I am beginning to realise that I do not, either. But hop over the wall, or Zas will catch us, and then I *will* have to shoot you.'

'I have no idea what is happening,' said Chaloner tiredly. 'Why are you letting me go? Especially now I know you are a spy.'

'Because of Downing.' Ruyven's voice was resentful.

414

'He has not paid me what he pledged, and I suspect he never will. In other words, I have squandered my principles for nothing. Killing you will please him, and I am not inclined to do anything that will make him happy.'

'He does have a reputation for reneging on promises.'

Ruyven smirked suddenly. 'The only good thing to come out of this was hitting you just now – consider it revenge for winning Aletta all those years ago. She is the only woman I have ever really loved. Jacoba is all right, but she does not have Aletta's courage or her intelligence. Besides, Hanse's death has filled her with guilt, and she has ended our association.'

Impatiently indicating that they had talked enough, he made a stirrup of his hands. Chaloner stepped into it, and pulled himself to the top of the wall. Ruyven tossed him the little gun, then pointed his own dag at a nearby tree and squeezed the trigger. The resulting crack set a number of gulls to screaming their alarm.

'Goodbye, Chaloner,' he said softly. 'We shall not meet again.'

Chapter 12

Chaloner stumbled through the grounds of Worcester House in a daze, staggered by Ruyven's revelations. Unfortunately, they told him nothing that would help him trap Falcon, and the clocks were striking four. Surely, he would not be reduced to following Edwards's plan – of loitering at the convention in the hope of spotting something amiss? He had to find *something* to give him an edge.

'Look!' came a howl of disbelief as he stepped into The Strand. It was Killigrew, and he was jabbing a forefinger that shook with righteous indignation. 'There is the traitor!'

Chaloner cursed himself for forgetting that he no longer wore a disguise. He saw two ruffians immediately break into a run, so he jigged to his left and, when they changed course to intercept him, shot off to his right, tearing eastwards.

It was not an easy journey. There was a lot of traffic, and drivers cursed him as he cut in front of their carts. A glance behind told him that his pursuers were experiencing similar problems, but were gaining anyway. He tried to run harder, but the street was too crowded. He reached Temple Bar, and shoved his way to the front of the queue that had formed to file through it, earning himself kicked shins and a punch. But then he was past it, and into Fleet Street.

Unfortunately, his pursuers' brutish appearance meant people jumped aside for *them*, and they burst through, hot on his heels. Aware that he needed to aim for quieter pastures if he wanted to escape, he ducked down a lane that led towards the river. When they followed, he jigged left, along an alley that had the wall of the Inner Temple's garden to the south and its stately buildings to the north. There was a gate in the wall, and by miraculous chance, it was open. He shot through it, and secured the other side with a bar. Moments later, it shuddered under the impact of a kick. There was a brief silence, then a scraping sound told him that the wall was being scaled.

He looked around quickly. He was in a large arbour, as fine as the one in Lincoln's Inn. Mature trees graced it, and it was neatly dissected by paths and flower beds. It was brown from lack of rain, but well tended and clearly loved. Cut off from the noise and bustle of the city, it was an unexpected pocket of stillness and tranquility.

His lame leg burning from overexertion, Chaloner hobbled to a compost heap and crouched behind it. The two men were soon over the wall, and began hunting for him. He fingered the gun in his pocket, and supposed he could shoot one, but the discharge in this quiet place would attract attention and make it difficult for him to escape afterwards.

Almost as if he could scent his prey, the larger of the two suddenly gazed directly at Chaloner's hiding place.

He muttered something to his companion, and they started to walk towards it. Chaloner looked around desperately. There was nowhere else to go, and he knew he could not scramble over the wall before they caught him. He waited until they were almost on him, then leapt to his feet, gun in his hand. Both stopped dead in their tracks.

'There is no need for that,' the larger one said, raising his hands. 'We just want a word.'

'A word about what?' asked Chaloner.

'About Falcon. Stop your questions and your meddling, and stay away from him.'

'Who is Falcon?'

The big man smiled without humour. 'He ordered us to issue you with a kindly warning. Heed it; there will not be another. He also told us to tell you that if you disobey, Hannah will die.'

'Hannah is safe,' said Chaloner, although he did not like the notion that these two brutes should know about her. 'Even I do not know where she is.'

'No, but Falcon does,' said the smaller man with a sly grin. 'You should choose your friends more carefully, because Rector Thompson is not very brave with a knife to his throat. He told us to leave a message mentioning rabbits with one John Thurloe at Lincoln's Inn.'

Chaloner's stomach lurched. 'No! You cannot—'

'We already have.'

Chaloner stared at them, and suddenly, his wits were sharp and clear. Who had the contacts and resources to hire men such as these – strong louts, but ones with a modicum of intelligence – and order them to deliver ultimatums? There was Downing, but he wanted Chaloner dead or caught, not warned off. Nisbett was murdered;

Kicke, Lane and Bates were not sufficiently wealthy; and the Dutch would not know how to recruit gang members. And then there was Williamson. Chaloner's anger was a cold, hard knot. The Spymaster had crossed the line, and he would pay for it.

'Where is Falcon now?' he demanded, pointing the gun at the larger man's head.

The fellow cringed, seeing he was in earnest. 'We do not know! He issues us with orders through a captain – Abraham Kicke, who works at White Hall. We have never met him in person.'

'He is telling the truth,' said the smaller man, smug grin gone. 'And Falcon *does* have your wife. He sent someone to collect her the moment Thurloe dropped her off in Tothill Street.'

'Thurloe thought all was well,' added his friend. 'But it is not, and Falcon will kill her if you interfere with his plans.'

There was a sudden shout, and Chaloner saw a gardener striding towards them, clearly angry that trespassers should dare to set foot in his domain. His indignant yell alerted his fellows, who began to converge, all clutching a variety of tools that could double as weapons. Chaloner swore under his breath. They were an inconvenience, but he did not want them hurt.

'What now?' asked the big man, confidence returning when he saw what was happening. 'Will you kill us in front of witnesses? Let us go, then make your own escape. It is your only option.'

Reluctantly, Chaloner conceded he was right. He lowered the weapon, and the two moved away quickly. He followed, aware of the gardeners breaking into a run. The big man ripped the bar from the gate, and then he and his companion were gone. Chaloner was not far behind them.

He knew they had been bluffing about 'Falcon' having Hannah, because Thurloe would not have taken her to Tothill Street – he would have gone to Lincoln's Inn, and not let her leave until Chaloner himself had arrived to collect her. But if Williamson had sent a letter using Thurloe's codeword, then he and Hannah would certainly be on their way home. Williamson might not have Hannah yet, but it was only a matter of time before he did. And while Chaloner's feelings towards his wife might be confusingly ambivalent, he knew one thing for certain: that he did not want her in the Spymaster's ruthless hands.

Chaloner's breath came in agonised gasps as he sprinted towards Lincoln's Inn, and he vowed that if Williamson had laid so much as a finger on Hannah, the Spymaster would die.

Williamson's men were out in force, not the soldiers in their buff uniforms, but the rough villains who shouldered their way along, peering into the faces of passersby. Chaloner kept his head down as he ran, bracing himself for trouble when one fellow gave him a long, hard look. But the man was distracted by a prancing horse, and Chaloner was able to slip past unimpeded.

He cursed himself for not appreciating sooner that Falcon was someone with the resources to play deadly games – to dabble in high-level espionage, spread misleading rumours, and kill those who tried to stop him. And how many had that been? Hanse, Compton and his soldiers, White and his guard, Molins, Oetje, Swan, Swallow, Pocks. And who knew how many more names had been written on the part of the death list that had been burned away?

But what was Williamson thinking? He claimed to want peace, so why was he trying to provoke a war – and damage two governments into the bargain? For money? Chaloner supposed he should not be surprised. He had met many spies – Ruyven being the most recent – who were not ashamed to admit they were driven by a desire for wealth.

He was breathless, limping and hot when he arrived at Lincoln's Inn. But there was bad news. Thurloe had arrived with a woman beside him, and a messenger had been waiting.

'He told Mr Thurloe that he and the lady were to get into his carriage, and go with him to see Tom's rabbits,' said the porter, shaking his head, perplexed. 'Why would they want to—'

'What did this man look like?' Chaloner demanded, stomach churning.

'I could not see. It was drizzling, and his hat was over his eyes.'

'Then in which direction did they go?'

'I did not look.' The porter's expression turned from bemused to anxious. 'Is Mr Thurloe in danger?'

Chaloner was in an agony of despair, thickly overlain with guilt. It was bad enough that Hannah had been dragged into his murky affairs, but to endanger Thurloe, too . . . He knew he would never forgive himself if anything happened to either.

But self-recrimination could come later: now he needed to force his fears to the back of his mind and think rationally. Where had they been taken? To Newgate, where they could be incarcerated until they were quietly

421

dispatched? He did not think Williamson would be rash enough to take his prisoners to his Westminster lair – someone would see them, and awkward questions would be asked. But the Spymaster was likely to be there himself. Chaloner set off at a run again, ignoring the porter's wails for answers.

Fortunately, Murdoch had parked outside Lincoln's Inn, lounging with his feet up while he ate a pie. He hurled it away and snatched up his reins when Chaloner yelled at him that Thurloe was in trouble, and they rattled at a furious pace towards Westminster. It was quicker than running, and also served to keep Chaloner off the streets and away from anyone who might recognise him.

'Mr Thurloe is in there?' asked Murdoch in horror, when they reached New Palace Yard and Chaloner alighted. Like all Londoners, he knew what went on in Williamson's domain.

'Wait here,' ordered Chaloner. There was no time for explanations. 'I may need you to take me somewhere else when I have finished.'

His inclination was to storm the building with his sword flailing, but common sense told him that was unlikely to help Thurloe and Hannah, so he forced himself to hide in the shadows of a nearby doorway while he studied the place, chafing at the passing moments.

The front was protected by two guards – not the ones in uniform, but the ruffians. It did not look good to station members of criminal gangs at the entrance, and Chaloner wondered whether the Spymaster had lost his mind. However, the building gave the impression of being other-wise empty – Williamson's clerks did not work on Sundays.

Unwilling to tackle the sentries in the street, lest cronies came to their assistance, Chaloner made his way to the back door, which was locked but unguarded. He picked his way inside, and immediately tripped over a body. It was a man in a buff uniform, and he had been stabbed. Confused and uncertain, Chaloner armed himself with the fellow's sword and selection of daggers, and made sure the dag was in a place where it could easily be reached.

The main chamber, where the clerks worked, was deserted with the exception of two secretaries. Both were dead. Chaloner stared at them: something was badly wrong. He crept on, aiming for the Spymaster's office on the upper floor.

Swaddell lay near the door. His eyes were closed, and there was blood on his face. Chaloner paused to put his hand on the assassin's neck. Swaddell was alive, and stirred when he was touched. There was a nasty gash on his head, and it was apparent that he had been struck from behind. Had Williamson tired of his faithful henchman and ordered him dispatched? With infinite care, Chaloner eased open the door to the Spymaster's office, just enough to let him see inside.

Williamson was sitting at his desk, hands clasped in front of him. Kicke was in the centre of the room, pacing back and forth. Two more men stood to one side, and the stains on their clothes indicated they had been responsible for at least some of the killing.

Chaloner reviewed his options. The gun would eliminate Kicke, while a lobbed dagger would dispatch one lout and the other could be finished with a sword. And Williamson represented no threat – while no coward, the Spymaster preferred to let others do his fighting, and was not an accomplished warrior. The only question was whether there were more men who were out of sight.

He pushed the door open further, trying to see, but

Williamson chose that moment to look in his direction. Their eyes locked, and the Spymaster's jaw dropped in astonishment. Desperately, Chaloner began to haul the dag from his belt, knowing he *had* to win the confrontation, because it was not just his life in the balance, but Thurloe's and Hannah's, too.

'How much longer will you and these four villains keep me prisoner in my own office, Kicke?' Williamson demanded quickly. 'I have no idea what you think you are doing, but holding me here against my will and slaughtering my people is extremely unwise.'

Chaloner stared at him in confusion. What was going on? Kicke could not have worked out that Williamson was Falcon, because he did not have the wits. Had Lady Castlemaine? That did not sound very likely, either. But, more to the point, how was Chaloner going to demand Hannah's whereabouts when Williamson was being guarded? The answer was obvious: Chaloner was going to have to rescue him. Clearly, Williamson was expecting him to try, because he had passed him a message: that Kicke had two more men who were not visible from the door.

Kicke strode towards the Spymaster and leaned menacingly across the desk. His expression was malevolent, and Chaloner could see it was all Williamson could do not to flinch.

'I will keep you prisoner until my master tells me otherwise,' he snarled. 'And do not expect to be saved by your minions: you were very convincing when I forced you to tell them that Chaloner is Falcon, and not to show their faces until he is caught. They will be ages looking for him, because if he has any sense, he will have fled London and will never be found.'

424

'You are making a serious mistake, allying yourself with Falcon,' said Williamson quietly. 'He has over-extended himself with his villainy, and will soon fall. And you will fall with him.'

Chaloner closed his eyes in despair. If Williamson was not Falcon, then who had Hannah and Thurloe? And how much time did he have before Falcon decided they represented a risk he did not need to take, and they suffered the same fate as his other victims?

In the office, Kicke released an unpleasant laugh. 'Falcon is your superior in every way. He hoodwinked you into thinking the Sinon Plot was just an effort to steal the crown jewels, when the reality was something far more significant. And you still have no idea who he is.'

'But you do?' asked Williamson. 'Tell me. Surely, you must see that I have a right to know the name of the man who has . . . bested me.'

His pained expression showed how much it galled him to admit his failure. Chaloner held his breath, willing Kicke to answer.

'I am not inclined to gossip,' came the disappointing reply. 'He would not like it.'

'Then tell me about his achievements,' urged Williamson. 'Surely, he cannot object to that?'

'Who knows what he might object to?' muttered Kicke, and Chaloner saw he was frightened of the man he had chosen to serve. 'I am not so stupid as to risk his ire.'

'Then let me tell you what I have learned,' said Williamson. 'He is the White Hall blackmailer, which means he must be a courtier himself, or he could not have learned such devastating secrets. He preyed on Buckingham, Lady Muskerry, Daniel Cotton, Charles

Bates, Penelope Compton, and a host of others. He even tackled Downing.'

So Downing and Bates were not Falcon, either, thought Chaloner, in growing dismay – they would not have black-mailed themselves. So who was left? He had discounted the Dutchmen and Lane, on the grounds that foreigners would not know London well enough to recruit gang members, and Lane would not have the resources. Or was he underestimating them? Ruyven had already proved himself to be more than he seemed, while Lane spoke so rarely that Chaloner had no idea what he was capable of.

'He has amassed himself a fortune,' agreed Kicke. 'All his victims paid, rather than have their nasty secrets made public. I helped, and so did Nisbett. You should not have let your henchman murder Nisbett, by the way. I would not have killed Swaddell if you had not killed Nisbett.'

Pain flashed across Williamson's face; he was fond of Swaddell. 'Five brave but rash men tried to stop Falcon,' he went on, his voice unsteady. 'Compton, Molins, White, Edwards and Hanse.'

'Falcon sent them poisoned gloves,' said Kicke, gloating now. 'But they took too long to work, so he told me to expedite matters. I followed Hanse one night, and pushed him in the river.'

'I heard all his clothes were missing,' said Williamson, shooting a desperate glance towards the door to commu-nicate that he was running out of things to say.

'Falcon did that. He was looking for something, although he did not find it. The gloves killed White, Molins and Compton, and they will soon make an end of Edwards. And no one will guess.'

'But Molins was attacked as he left the Devil tavern—'

426

'I am no good with swords. Not like Nisbett. But the injury Molins sustained when he fell weakened him, and *then* the poison did its work.'

Chaloner glanced at Kicke's boot-hose and saw the elaborate lace. The landlord of the Devil had been right to suspect that the culprit was a courtier.

But every minute spent listening to Williamson coax scraps of information from Kicke was another minute in which Falcon could decide to kill Hannah and Thurloe. Williamson was not in a position to demand Falcon's identity more forcefully, so Chaloner saw he would have to do it himself.

He looked around desperately, trying to devise a way that would eliminate the four guards but leave Kicke alive. He jumped when he saw Swaddell's black eyes open and staring at him.

Slowly, the assassin climbed to his feet. 'I did not think *we* would ever work together,' he whispered with the ghost of a smile. 'But here we are. Do you have a plan?'

'I do now there are two of us.'

It took no more than seconds for Chaloner to outline his idea to Swaddell. The assassin lay on the floor again, and began to groan. When a guard emerged to make an end of him, Chaloner felled him with a blow to the head. The sound promoted a second man to investigate, so Chaloner hit him, too.

'Now it is just two more and Kicke,' Swaddell murmured, scrambling to his feet. 'You take the one on the left, and I shall deal with the one on the right.'

Chaloner hurled open the door, his knife flying through the air at the same time. It embedded itself in the guard's arm, and the man dropped to his knees, screaming, although he stopped when he saw Swaddell's blade flash across his companion's neck. Kicke's jaw dropped in horror when he recognised Chaloner.

'You—' he began.

But he got no further. Williamson had reached into his desk the moment Chaloner and Swaddell had burst in, and now he held a gun. Kicke froze.

'No!' shouted Chaloner, as Swaddell advanced on the wounded guard. 'He may answer—'

'He knows nothing Kicke will not tell us.' Swaddell cut the man's throat.

Chaloner turned towards Kicke. 'What is Falcon's real name?'

'That *is* his real name,' bleated Kicke, backing towards the window. It was the one Bulteel had stood at, to look down into New Palace Yard, and it was open. 'Mr Falcon. I cannot say more.'

'Do not play games,' snapped Williamson. 'Tell us his identity, or I will let Swaddell have you.'

Kicke's face was agony of indecision: neither option appealed. Williamson nodded to Swaddell, who began to advance. Kicke turned and leapt at the window. Chaloner dived towards him, straining to lay hold of him before he could go out, but his fingers closed on air.

Kicke would probably have survived had he judged the jump properly, but his foot caught on the sill, and he went out head first. Chaloner leaned through the window and looked down at him. Kicke's back was broken, and although he was trying to speak, no sound emerged. Chaloner knew Kicke would be dead before he could run all the way down the stairs to put his questions, so he climbed on to the sill and prepared to drop next to him.

'No!' Williamson yanked him back. 'Are you insane?'

Chaloner struggled free of him, but when he reached the sill again, a crowd had clustered around the fallen man. Among them was de Buat. The Dutch physician sensed movement above him, and squinted upwards, shaking his head to tell them Kicke was dead. Chaloner sagged in defeat.

'Clarendon is always telling me you are dedicated,' Williamson was saying as the spy staggered away from the window, 'but hurling yourself out of windows to inter-view suspects defies reason. It is hardly—'

'Falcon has Hannah and Thurloe,' whispered Chaloner wretchedly, feeling hope disintegrate within him. 'Kicke was my best chance of saving them.'

'Lord!' Williamson stared at him. 'Does this mean we are going to have to work together? You to save your wife and friend, and me to lay hold of a dangerous villain who wants to plunge us into a bloody war for reasons I cannot fathom?'

Chaloner barely heard him as he tried to devise another way forward. Unfortunately, he was too agitated for rational thought, and all he could think was that Williamson and Swaddell had deprived him of his best opportunity – Swaddell with his over-eager blade, and Williamson by preventing him from reaching Kicke. He itched to slam their heads together as hard as he could, and scream at them for their stupidity.

'I see now that Kun spoke the truth when he came to see me the other night,' Williamson was saying to Swaddell. 'He warned me that Falcon's eyes were fixed on more than the crown jewels, but I thought he was just distressed because the peace talks are floundering. I should have listened.'

'I thought you were Falcon,' said Chaloner dully. He sank on to a bench and put his head in his hands, taking a deep breath in an effort to control his rising panic.

'Me?' demanded Williamson, shocked and offended. 'You think I am the kind of man who plays one nation against another?'

'Why not? You think I am.'

'That is different. *I* have not spent years in the States-General, insinuating myself into their society. However, Thurloe wrote me a letter yesterday, pointing out that he would not have maintained an association with you, had you been a traitor. And now you have risked your life to save mine. So I am willing to acknowledge your innocence. Of this, at least.'

'I told you he was not a defector,' said Swaddell, before Chaloner could remark that he had *not* saved Williamson's life – his sole intention had been to interrogate Kicke. 'He is not sufficiently interested in power or wealth to sell himself to another country.'

'You must have some suspicions about who Falcon might be,' said Chaloner desperately, not really caring whether they thought him innocent or not. 'Or who he is not.'

Williamson winced. 'It pains me to admit it, but Kicke was right: Falcon *has* been too clever for me. I know he is someone in a position to do a lot of damage, so he will not be some inconsequential minion. But he might be anyone – courtier, cleric, envoy, even Dutchman.'

'He plans to disrupt the conference at the Savoy,' said Chaloner tiredly. 'I am not sure how – perhaps with a bomb or an assassination, or even with documents. I tried to warn van Goch—'

430

'Why him?' demanded Williamson. 'Why not Clarendon or the Privy Council? Or me?'

'Why do you think I came here?' lied Chaloner.

Williamson snatched up his gun from the desk. 'This villain will *not* succeed. I swear it. He—'

He stopped speaking when there was a clatter of footsteps in the hallway outside. It was de Buat. The physician regarded Chaloner uneasily.

'It is all right,' said Williamson, beckoning him in. 'Chaloner will not betray you. We have just established that he is not a Dutch spy.'

Chaloner's mind reeled as the implications of that remark sunk in. 'De Buat is *your* man?'

'Yes, and has been for years,' replied Williamson. 'Ever since he was rash enough to fight for Cromwell during the civil wars. More recently, he has been my eyes and ears in the Savoy.'

'But it is a pity he cannot tell us the identity of Falcon,' muttered Swaddell.

'Who was the man you tossed out of the window?' asked de Buat, as he stepped into Williamson's office. His jaw dropped in horror when he saw Swaddell's handiwork – the assassin had added the two guards Chaloner had stunned to his tally, and was casually cleaning his knife on a piece of linen.

'We did not throw him. He fell.' Williamson saw the Dutchman's sceptical look and grimaced. 'I know we have made that claim before, but it is true this time. Why?'

'He could not speak,' said de Buat. 'But he could move his mouth, although no sound came out.'

'And you read lips,' said Chaloner, hope stirring. 'What did he say?'

De Buat shook his head. 'It made no sense. He said that Falcon is the mincing man.'

Chaloner gazed at him. Surely, he could not mean Griffith? He groaned as several facts came together in his mind. The effete colonel had made many friends at Court since arriving in February, and might well have learned how to blackmail them. And he had hired Lane, a man who was sinister by anyone's standards. Moreover, he had expressed his intention to leave London that day, perhaps because his sly work was almost done.

Meanwhile, Swaddell shot Williamson a triumphant look. 'I *told* you there was something odd about Colonel Griffith.'

'He claimed he came from Great Hampden,' said Chaloner, speaking more to himself than the others. 'But I was born near there, and would have heard of his family. *Ergo*, he either lied about his name, or about the place of his birth.'

'That was careless of him,' said Swaddell. 'He should have asked Bulteel where you—'

'He might have done, but Bulteel did not know,' interrupted Chaloner, his mind running ahead, focusing on how he was going to corner Griffith. 'I never mentioned it to him.'

'Then why did *you* not challenge Griffith?' demanded Swaddell. 'If you knew he was lying?'

'Why would I? Lots of people lie about their origins in these uncertain times.'

'So his real name probably *is* Falcon,' said Swaddell. 'And he was never a Royalist colonel during the wars. Clarendon was deceived by him, though, because they spent hours reminiscing.'

'He did remark that Griffith had changed,' said

432

Chaloner, desperately racking his brain for places Griffith might take Hannah and Thurloe. 'But with wigs and face paints . . .'

'No,' said Williamson quietly. 'Griffith cannot be Falcon, because—'

'He deceived us all,' interrupted de Buat. 'Dutch *and* English. But his guilt is obvious now I think about it. He haunts White Hall, for a start, and where better a place to learn secrets for blackmail and spying?'

'Moreover, he arrived when Chaloner was away,' added Swaddell. 'He would not have been able to insinuate himself here had there been a vigilant spy to hand. And by the time Chaloner returned, Griffith was too well established.'

'No,' said Williamson, more loudly. 'You are wrong. The man is Bulteel's cousin, for God's sake, and you all know *he* is above reproach.'

'Griffith deceived Clarendon,' said de Buat. 'Why not Bulteel, too?'

Poor Bulteel, thought Chaloner with a pang. He would be devastated.

'Griffith is *not* Falcon,' snapped Williamson, temper fraying. 'And if you must know why I am so sure, it is because he works for me. Like you, de Buat, he reports on the Dutch.'

'Christ!' muttered Chaloner. 'Am I the only man in London who is not currently hired to spy on someone else's government?'

Williamson ignored him. 'However, while de Buat supplies me with gossip and inconsequentialities, Griffith provides proper information.'

'Well, there you are then!' said Chaloner, disgusted that the Spymaster should not have seen it sooner. 'Falcon!

Providing high-level intelligence. But not just to you – to both sides.'

'I suppose he might . . .' acknowledged Williamson reluctantly.

'We have a name at last,' said Swaddell, suddenly all business. 'So let us act on it, and save Chaloner's wife and our reputations before it is too late.'

Out in New Palace Yard, Williamson, Swaddell and Chaloner piled into Murdoch's hackney, while de Buat was instructed to round up any of the Spymaster's troops who had escaped being killed by Kicke and his minions, and escort them to the Savoy with all possible haste. Once they were on their way, Chaloner's thoughts returned to Griffith.

'Bates gave me Falcon's death list,' he said, furious with his failure to put facts together sooner. 'He found it tossed on the fire in the Spares Gallery, a place where Griffith likes to lurk.'

'Listening for gossip to tell the Dutch,' nodded Swaddell, clinging on for dear life as Williamson yelled for Murdoch to go faster. It was not far to Bulteel's house, and they would soon be there. 'But how do you know the list was Griffith's? Lots of courtiers haunt the Spares Gallery.'

'But lots of people do not have recipes for ginger-bread,' explained Chaloner. 'It was written on the back. Bulteel likes to cook, and Griffith must have used some scrap paper from his kitchen.'

'Damn!' muttered Williamson. 'The clues were there, but we were all too blind to see them.'

Chaloner regarded the Spymaster in alarm when Murdoch turned north. 'Where are we going? Bulteel's house is in the opposite—'

'We are not going to Bulteel's house,' said Williamson impatiently. 'We are going to the Savoy.'

'But Griffith is going to leave London today,' shouted Chaloner. Hannah and Thurloe were not going to be in the Savoy, and he was a lot more interested in rescuing them than in salvaging a truce that was in tatters anyway. 'He will be packing his—'

'He will be in the Savoy,' snapped Williamson. 'I am the Spymaster here, Chaloner. I do know something about my trade, and—'

'But the meeting is not due to start for an hour!' yelled Chaloner, desperately aware that every second was taking him farther from the people he cared about. 'He will not waste that time. He will be gathering his belongings, so he can make a quick getaway.'

'Enough!' snarled Williamson. 'I am in charge here, and . . . What are you doing?'

Chaloner threw open the door and jumped out. The coach was travelling fast, and he bounced and rolled painfully as he landed. Williamson leaned out and made a gesture of anger, but Murdoch did not see and whipped his horses on. Yet Chaloner *knew* Williamson was wrong about the Savoy.

He scrambled to his feet and started to run, and had almost reached Old Palace Yard, when he saw Griffith. The man was ahead of him, striding along confidently with two burly gang members at his heels. There was no sign of the mincing courtier now, and even his effeminate clothes could not disguise the lean, efficient strength of his body. He turned down an alley, little more than a dark slit even on the brightest of days, which was a short-cut to Bulteel's home.

Chaloner drew his gun and set off after him, trailing

him and his companions until they were well out of sight of the main road, lest some passer-by thought to interfere. Then he made his move.

'Put your hands in the air,' he ordered softly. 'Or I will shoot.'

Griffith whirled around, and his eyes widened in shock when he saw the dag. 'Chaloner! What do you think you are doing? You should have left London hours ago. What is wrong with you? Do you *want* to be hanged as a spy?'

One of the ruffians started to edge away, so Chaloner threw one of the knives he had taken from Williamson's dead guard. It entered the man's thigh, causing him to curse vilely as he slid to the ground, both hands clutching the wound.

'Stay where you are,' he told the other villain. The man saw he meant it, and quickly raised his hands. Chaloner turned back to Griffith. 'I want my wife back.'

'Your wife?' echoed Griffith. The mince was back in his movements, but Chaloner was not deceived. 'What makes you think I—'

Chaloner darted forward and pressed the gun against Griffith's temple. 'I am not interested in a debate. Tell me where she is.'

'Wait!' cried Griffith in alarm. 'If you kill me, you will never find her.'

Chaloner took the gun from Griffith's head and aimed it at his middle instead. 'Tell me.'

Griffith paled. As a soldier, he knew what it meant to be gut-shot. 'Is this about my little lie? That I am not Griffith, and do not hale from Buckinghamshire? I can explain!'

'I am not interested. Where are Hannah and Thurloe?'

'The real Griffith died in my arms years ago, after

436

regaling me with tales of his escapades in the wars. I admit to that deception. And I will even admit to organising the watch on your home – my "cousin" brays about your skills constantly, so keeping you under observation seemed a wise precaution. I searched it to look for any reports you might have written for the Earl—'

Chaloner's finger tightened on the trigger. 'Hannah and Thurloe.'

'It was me who slipped into Newgate, too,' Griffith went on, a little desperately. 'I am good at disguises. I pretended to be a warden, and getting into Calais was easy.'

'I am sure it was, but did you have to murder Swan and Swallow so horribly?'

Griffith looked away, and Chaloner was surprised to see the incident haunted him. 'It was not my idea, it was Falcon's. He said we needed to make people see he is not someone to be crossed.'

Chaloner narrowed his eyes. 'Do not lie. *You* are Falcon.'

'Me?' Griffith started to laugh. 'I am merely his servant. I was—'

'I do not believe you,' snapped Chaloner. 'So, for the last time, where are they?'

'Stop!' shouted Griffith, when Chaloner began to squeeze the trigger. 'I am Williamson's spy, working for England against the Dutch. Kill me, and you damage your country. My lies have been for England, and are a necessary part of my disguise.'

Chaloner was not sure what happened next, only that the man he had injured had hauled the dagger from his leg and lobbed it. He ducked instinctively and it missed, but Griffith's reactions were frighteningly fast. He

437

whipped his sword from its scabbard, and while Chaloner's attention was on him, the second ruffian knocked the gun from his hand.

Chaloner managed to evade Griffith's first swipe, but the wounded man grabbed his foot, causing him to fall. Then the second ruffian produced a cudgel, and struck him an agonising blow on the leg. Griffith moved in for the kill. Chaloner tried to struggle away, but it was hopeless.

Suddenly, there was a deafening report. The lout with the club dropped to the ground and lay still. Griffith dropped to a fighting stance, gazing around wildly.

'Step away from him, Griffith,' ordered Lane. There was anger in his usually impassive features. 'You and your kind are not killing anyone else.'

'What are you doing here?' demanded Griffith furiously. 'I told you to pack my—'

He did not finish, because Lane charged at him. Both crashed to the ground. Chaloner hobbled towards them, but it was too late. Blood seeped through Lane's clothes, although he still clawed furiously at his opponent. Griffith punched him away, scrambled to his feet and fled. Chaloner tried to follow, but Griffith was fast, and Chaloner's injured leg meant there was no chance of catching him. He limped back to Lane.

'Do not waste time with me,' Lane gasped. 'Find Griffith and stop him before he does any more harm. My master would wish it.'

'Your master?' Chaloner's mind reeled. 'But Griffith is—'

'Do you think I would demean myself by working for that villain? My master was a great man, and I am proud to have served him.'

'Compton?' suggested Chaloner tentatively, his thoughts in chaos. 'Did *he* ask you to monitor Griffith? Because he suspected something amiss?'

Lane nodded, his face white with pain. 'He ordered me to stop when his other men died, because he said it was too dangerous. But when he became a victim, I decided to disobey him for the first time in my life, and bring his killer to justice. I am usually good at keeping Griffith in my sights, but I lost him today in the traffic around Charing Cross. And it almost cost you your life!'

'You are Fairfax!' exclaimed Chaloner in understanding. 'You did not let me give you Compton's message in person, because I would have recognised you.'

'Lane' gave a wan smile. 'I appreciated your efforts to protect me. But do not linger here. Go!'

Chaloner thought about his promise to Compton. 'I cannot leave you—'

'I have friends here, and my injury is not fatal. Stop this evil, or it will all have been for nothing.'

Chaloner stumbled down the lane, aiming for Bulteel's house. It felt like an age before he arrived, gasping for breath, with sweat stinging his eyes and his leg aching viciously. The building sat small and pretty, with roses growing around the door – a small haven of peace and colour in the dirty metropolis. It was difficult to believe that a monster lodged there.

Common sense prevented Chaloner from staging a frontal assault, and forced him to go around the back. The gate was barred, so he scrambled over a wall and dropped silently down the other side. The garden was full of the herbs that Bulteel liked to use in his cooking, and bees buzzed among them. Chaloner reached the kitchen door and listened hard. He could hear someone inside. It was Bulteel, standing at his table as he rolled pastry. He was humming, happy and content.

Chaloner felt sick. Bulteel was cooking, something he had been unable to do while Griffith was staying with him. Did it mean Griffith had already gone? He opened the door and stepped inside, raising his finger to his lips when Bulteel looked up in surprise.

'Where is Griffith?' he whispered.

'He arrived in a terrible fluster a few moments ago, and is upstairs, packing. I am fond of him, but it will be good to have the house to myself again. I am baking him a pie for the journey to—'

'Did he mention Hannah and Thurloe?' asked Chaloner desperately. 'Falcon has them.'

'Falcon?' echoed Bulteel, confusion suffusing his face. Chaloner felt like grabbing him by the throat. Could he not see that it was an emergency? He took a deep breath, to calm himself.

'Yes,' he managed to reply. 'Have you seen them?'

'No,' said Bulteel. 'But I can ask my cousin. Wait here while I fetch him. You—'

'No! Do you have a cellar?'

Bulteel gaped at him. 'A cellar? Why do you—'

'John, please!' begged Chaloner. 'Where is it?'

'This way,' said Bulteel, regarding him in concern. 'And then you had better sit down, because you look terrible.'

Chaloner followed him along the corridor, to where a low door led to a place where coal and firewood could be stored. A stout bar was placed across it.

'Here,' said Bulteel. 'I keep it locked because I had rats last year. Do you want to see inside?'

Chaloner did not answer. He removed the bar and

peered into the blackness within. The familiar fear of cell-like places gripped him as he took one step down the stairs, and then another. It was dank, cold and smelled of decay, like a prison. The notion distracted him, and by the time he realised something was amiss, it was too late. He heard Bulteel's shriek of alarm before the door was slammed closed, plunging him into pitch darkness.

Chaloner was not alone. He could hear snuffling farther inside the chamber, and he stumbled down the uneven steps towards it. His groping fingers encountered hair and a face, wet with tears. He tugged off the gag.

'Tom!' sobbed Hannah. 'Oh, thank God! We received a message from you that it was safe to come home, but it was a trick, and we have been locked in this miserable place for days.'

'Hours,' corrected Thurloe, when Chaloner removed the gag from him, too, and set about sawing through the ropes that bound their hands and feet. 'But we must escape. Now. I overheard talk of plans to disrupt the conference – plans that will end any hope of peace for a very long time.'

'What plans?' demanded Chaloner.

'I am not sure,' confessed Thurloe. 'But I do know they will be devastating, and we *must* stop them, no matter what the cost to ourselves.'

'He has been trying to spoil the negotiations for months,' added Hannah. Her voice shook, although she tried to keep it steady. 'Ever since the Dutch arrived.'

'Who has?' asked Chaloner. 'Griffith, who is not Griffith at all, but Falcon?'

'Griffith is not Falcon,' said Thurloe grimly. 'He has been receiving orders, not giving them. Falcon is someone

441

else – someone who holds a respected post at Court, and has access to powerful men. I have two suspects. Killigrew of the Savoy occupies a unique position to cause trouble . . .'

'And his other suspect is Charles Bates, although he is loath to say so in front of me,' said Hannah in a choked voice. 'Because of Charles's sudden departure from London, which means no one expects him to be here, so he is free to move about unfettered. But whoever it is means to cause untold damage. It is his revenge.'

'His revenge for what?' asked Chaloner.

'On the many good, brave men who have tried to stop him,' explained Thurloe. 'They are mostly dead, so it is up to us now.'

Chaloner groped his way up the cellar steps and began inspecting the door. He pushed on it, but it was immovable. Fear washed through him. Griffith would kill Bulteel and abandon them there. It would be every bit as bad as Calais. Worse, because Hannah and Thurloe would be beside him. He saw a shadow flit across the bottom of the door.

'John?' he called softly. 'John, are you there?'

'Tom!' Bulteel sounded terrified. 'What is happening? My house is full of ruffians.'

'Can you let us out?' asked Chaloner.

The door began to rattle. 'No! He must have jammed it. I do not understand—'

'Fetch Williamson,' ordered Chaloner. 'He is at the Savoy.'

'I cannot! My cousin has just produced several barrels of something that looks like gunpowder, and I think he means to use them. I must try to reason with him, before it sees him in trouble.'

442

Griffith would kill him, thought Chaloner. 'He is not your cousin.'

There was a startled silence. 'Of course he is!'

'He has already confessed to deceiving you. Please! There is no time for explanations. Go to the Savoy. It is our only hope.' Chaloner's voice broke as he added, 'Hannah and Thurloe are in here.'

Bulteel gulped, and Chaloner heard him scurry away. The spy leaned against the door and closed his eyes, his head pounding with tension and worry. But it was not many moments before Bulteel was back.

'I cannot get out,' he squeaked, his voice shaking almost uncontrollably. 'All the doors and windows are locked. I do not understand what is happening!'

'Griffith is in the pay of a deadly agent known as Falcon,' supplied Thurloe. 'A man who has blackmailed his friends, and damaged his country.'

Chaloner had a small packet of gunpowder in his belt, for priming the gun, and an idea began to unfold in his mind. While Thurloe regaled Bulteel with an account of Falcon's misdeeds, he emptied it into the tin of greasy paste that Wiseman had given him for his disguise. Then he smeared the mixture on the door's leather hinges.

Enough light was filtering under the door for Thurloe to see what he was doing. Wordlessly, he handed Chaloner the tinderbox he used for lighting his pipe. Chaloner struck a flame and touched it to the hinge. For a moment, he thought the leather was too damp to ignite, but it flared suddenly, and began to burn. Chaloner blew on it, to coax it along.

'You should have stayed away,' Bulteel was saying. 'You should not have interfered.'

Chaloner stopped blowing as the final piece of the

mystery snapped into place. He had encountered those words before – on a message attached to a corpse at his wedding.

'It is you,' he said in a low, shocked voice. '*You* are Falcon.'

There was a silence from the other side of the door, then a bemused laugh. 'What?'

'Griffith would not have left you running free inside the house if you were not involved,' Chaloner went on, stomach lurching at the implications of the realisation. 'He would have killed you. So you pretend to be a victim, but your aim is to learn how much we have guessed about you.'

'Tom!' cried Bulteel, hurt in his voice, while Thurloe and Hannah regarded Chaloner in astonishment. 'What are you saying?'

'It was your choice of words: *do not interfere*. The same as those pinned on Alden in St Margaret's Church. White thought they were aimed at him. Perhaps he was right.'

'You mean at your marriage?' Bulteel sounded puzzled. 'Hannah did not invite me, so how—'

'You came to the church,' countered Chaloner. 'I saw you standing at the back.'

'What is that burning smell?' asked Bulteel, suddenly suspicious. 'What have you done?'

'And there is more,' said Chaloner. 'Hanse's body was stripped, because his killer was looking for something – Clarendon's lost papers. The Earl misled me by saying they were stolen on Friday night, when Hanse had an alibi. But the killer knew the truth, which is that they went missing much earlier, when Hanse was in Worcester House.'

444

'Hanse probably did steal them, as I have said all along. But I do not see how that proves I—'

'You know everything about Clarendon's affairs, so you would have known exactly when the papers went missing. Moreover, you were eager to have them back, not to protect your master, but because some of the documents you used to blackmail people were among them. The Lady's—'

'Tom!' cried Bulteel, distressed. 'This is logic gone wild. But what is that smell—'

'*Bulteel* is the blackmailer, too?' asked Hannah, shocked.

'Yes, ably assisted by Griffith, Kicke and Nisbett,' replied Chaloner, blowing on the fire again. He sincerely hoped his plan would work and the hinges would soon disintegrate, or he, Hannah and Thurloe were going to be trapped inside a burning cellar.

'I do not fraternise with thieves,' said Bulteel coldly. 'And what are you doing in there? I can definitely smell smoke. You had better not be—'

'I do not care about the Court rakes – they make their own choices,' Chaloner went on, to distract him. 'But how could you pick on Compton? He was a good man.'

'It was his wanton sister who transgressed,' muttered Bulteel. 'Not him.'

'And there is an admission of guilt!' pounced Chaloner. 'The family told no one about Penelope's indiscretion. Only they and the blackmailers knew.'

'And you, apparently,' Bulteel flashed back. 'There is smoke oozing under the door. Do you want to choke to death? Stop whatever it is you are doing, or—'

'A rumour started that Clarendon did not know what was in his missing papers,' Chaloner forged on. 'He blamed me for spreading it, because he said I was the only one he had told. But *you* knew, because you eavesdropped on us. In fact, you eavesdrop on a lot of people.'

'You are despicable,' shouted Hannah suddenly. 'A monster, who preys on the vulnerable. I have never liked you, you treacherous little snake, and I am glad I told Tom to reject your overtures of friendship. I cannot imagine why he wasted his time in the first place.'

'Because *you* cannot cook,' Bulteel yelled, abruptly abandoning any pretence at innocence. 'And he does not love you, anyway. How could he, when you are both so different? You will hate each other within a year, and then he will be glad of loyal friends.'

'He will never hate me,' began Hannah, shocked by the outburst. 'He—'

'I despise you and everyone like you,' Bulteel raged on. 'People who think themselves superior to me. I am sorry Tom must be sacrificed, but I am glad *you* will be blown to pieces.'

'John,' called Chaloner reasonably. 'It is not too late to end this. We can—'

'No!' cried Bulteel. 'I know you. You will hunt me down, and I will never rest easy again. Why could you not have left London when I suggested it? Why could Clarendon not have dismissed you in revenge for the rumour I started about his lost papers? Then you would have been safely away.'

'You warned me against antagonising Kicke and Nisbett—'

'They are malicious and unforgiving, but good at their work, which is why I hired them. But I did not want them to hurt you – the one man in White Hall who has been kind to me.'

'Then help me now,' urged Chaloner. 'Open the door and—'

'I cannot! It is too late.'

'Despite my reservations, Tom *is* fond of you,' shouted Hannah. 'And he always defends you against those who say nasty things. But how do you repay him? By locking him in a cellar and threatening to blow him up! You are incapable of friendship, you loathsome little worm.'

'I have friends,' objected Bulteel, although there was pain in his voice.

'Who?' demanded Hannah ruthlessly. 'And do not say Williamson, because he cultivated you for information, not affection.'

The hinges were burning merrily now. Unfortunately, the flames had not confined themselves to the leather, and were greedily consuming the door, too. Chaloner coughed as smoke billowed over him. He indicated that Thurloe and Hannah were to lie on the floor, where the air would be fresher.

'Williamson has been cold and distant of late,' said Bulteel. 'I let him use Griffith as a spy, so perhaps bad things were reported about me. Regardless, we are no longer close.'

'Griffith plans to betray you,' lied Chaloner, willing to say anything to open cracks in Bulteel's defences. 'To steal all the money you have acquired, and leave you to answer charges of—'

'I thought he might,' interrupted Bulteel. 'Men like him do not know the meaning of loyalty, and I am still angry about the poem he wrote regarding Downing's corruption. All my courtly training will have been for nothing if that scurrilous nonsense sees him ostracised,

447

because *I* will be ostracised with him, as his so-called kinsman. I was livid when I read it.'

'What did you do?' asked Chaloner uneasily.

'I slipped him some poison,' replied Bulteel coldly. 'He is upstairs, and when my house is destroyed, people will assume Falcon died setting the explosion. And I shall be left in peace.'

'Never!' shouted Hannah furiously. 'Too many people know *you* are the culprit.'

'On the contrary,' said Bulteel. 'No one else has guessed, and you will not be here to put the matter straight. I shall visit the Savoy shortly, and then my revenge will be complete. Everyone who has shunned and mocked me will be repaid in full. And it serves them right!'

'John, please,' said Chaloner, shocked by the venom in his voice. 'Do not do this.'

'It is already done.'

Hannah was choking, and Thurloe struggling to breathe. Chaloner closed his eyes in despair. *He* had brought them to this terrible end. In a sudden fury at the futility of it all, he kicked the door as hard as he could. But the flames had done nothing to weaken the hinges, and the door was sturdy. It did no more than shudder. Bulteel sniggered on the other side.

'You will never escape. There is no lock for you to pick, and you cannot break the wood.'

Chaloner slumped to his knees. 'You will not get away with this,' he rasped. 'When you are suddenly rich from your crimes, people will notice and ask why.'

'This is not about money. It is about punishing the people who have been unkind to me. The English Court, the aloof Dutch diplomats, Clarendon . . . I shall have the last laugh over them all.'

'The cost of your vengeance will be war,' gasped Chaloner, becoming dizzier by the moment. 'Hundreds of lives lost, and untold misery for many more. How could you—'

'I do not care!' shouted Bulteel. 'Everyone sees me as a quiet mouse with no spine, but I am more powerful and determined than any of them. I have recruited Hectors and dangerous men like Nisbett and Griffith, and I have kept them all under my control. *Everyone* has underestimated me.'

The door was now a sheet of flames. Coughing almost uncontrollably, Chaloner forced himself to his feet and kicked it again. Nothing happened.

'Save your strength,' jeered Bulteel. 'I told you: you cannot escape.'

Chaloner kicked the door a third time, and something cracked. His eyes were streaming so badly that he could not see, and every breath was like inhaling boiling acid. Then there was another crack, and he was aware of Thurloe next to him, pitting his own strength against the burning wood.

There was silence from the corridor, and Chaloner knew Bulteel had gone to set his fuses. Thurloe kicked with all his might, but although the wood splintered, it was nowhere near enough, and Chaloner saw they were going to be too late. Then he saw Hannah, frightened but calm, and he felt his resolve strengthen. She was *not* going to die because he had made a bad choice of friends.

Fighting the giddiness that threatened to overwhelm him, he took several steps back, then hurled himself at the door with every last ounce of his strength. It collapsed outwards in a spray of sparks and splinters, and he went sprawling among them. Smoke billowed everywhere.

'Run!' he gasped, staggering to his feet. 'Back door.'

'It is locked,' cried Hannah, reaching it and giving it a vigorous shake.

Still struggling to breathe, Chaloner dropped to his knees and inserted one of the tools he used for burgling houses, hoping it was not a new lock that would take him longer to defeat, because he could hear a furious hissing that told him the fuses were lit. Meanwhile, Thurloe picked up a chair, and in a display of power that belied his claims of delicate health, he swung it at the front window. Glass flew, and the wooden frame cracked. Hannah went to help him.

The first explosion occurred upstairs. It rocked the house and sent a good part of the ground-floor ceiling crashing down. Chaloner stared in horror at the mountain of rubble that lay where Thurloe and Hannah had been. But then he heard Hannah screaming his name and Thurloe urging her to climb through the window. They were alive! At that moment, the lock sprang open, and he staggered through the door and into the garden, racing for cover behind a shed.

It was not a moment too soon. The second explosion blew out all the windows, and Chaloner put his hands over his head as fractured glass rained down around him. The third blast was more of a pop, but flames started to lick through a hole in the roof.

'You should have stayed where you were,' said Bulteel softly. Chaloner raised his head, and saw the secretary armed with a gun.

'Why?' asked Chaloner, staring up at him. He no longer had the energy to bandy words.

'Because it would have been a quicker death – I am not sure how cleanly these little things kill. It was a gift from Williamson. One of a pair.'

'You lost the other when you murdered Oetje. She was the spy you hired to watch Hanse.'

Bulteel grimaced. 'Yes. And when I saw it tucked in your belt, I knew it was only a matter of time before you or Williamson worked out who had owned it. But you were both slow-witted, and now it does not matter. You will die and I shall tell people that Griffith did it, using a gun he stole from me. All my loose ends will be neatly tied.'

'What will you do at the Savoy?' asked Chaloner. 'Kill someone else? Blow the place up?'

'Nothing so dramatic.' Bulteel indicated the parcel he carried under his arm. 'I shall just circulate a few letters that discredit Clarendon. There will be no peace without its main supporter, and I shall have my revenge on the man I truly hate – the one whose treatment of me has been so cruel and disdainful.'

He took aim, and Chaloner forced himself to meet his eyes. There was something unrecognisable in the once-familiar face, and had Chaloner been an impressionable man, he might have said it was evil.

A report cracked out, loud and sharp, but from another direction. Bulteel stood for a moment, the dag still pointed at Chaloner. But then his knees buckled and he crumpled to the ground. Chaloner scrambled to his feet as Williamson walked towards him. Swaddell was at his side, blowing on the smoking barrel of a gun.

'I apologise, Chaloner,' said Williamson quietly. 'I was

451

wrong about Falcon running to the Savoy. Indeed, it seems I was wrong about a number of things, including the quality of my friends.'

Chaloner stared at Bulteel's body. 'I think that is true for both of us.'

Epilogue

London's weather soon reverted to normal: cool, wet and windy. Its residents complained, of course, claiming summers had been better when they were children – skies had been blue, the sun kindly and it only ever rained at night. But Chaloner was relieved by the change.

'Excessive heat makes Englishmen irrational,' he told Thurloe, as they strolled around the gravelled paths of Lincoln's Inn's gardens one evening. 'Perfectly normal men become violent, or engage in strangely uncharacteristic behaviour.'

'You cannot blame Bulteel's misdeeds on the weather, Tom. He managed those all by himself, with no help from the elements. I know you liked him, but there is no excuse for what he did.'

'Yes, I *did* like him,' said Chaloner sadly. 'He was not a bad man, and deserved better than he was given.'

'Not a bad man?' echoed Thurloe. 'Do you want me to list all the people he killed? Oetje, Hanse, Molins, White and Compton. And he would have had Edwards, too, if Wiseman had not saved him. Then there was Edwards's guard and Compton's soldiers, including Lane . . . I mean Fairfax—'

'Fairfax is mending. Mother Greene told me.' Chaloner tried to change the subject. 'Did I tell you that he confided that it *was* him who burgled Downing? He was looking for evidence to tie Downing to Falcon, although he was wrong on that score. Downing was innocent.'

Thurloe continued as though he had not spoken. 'Swan and Swallow, murdered solely to put the fear of God into anyone thinking of challenging him, while Kicke and Nisbett—'

'Swaddell killed Nisbett,' objected Chaloner. 'And Kicke jumped out of the window.'

'No,' said Thurloe firmly. 'They died because of what Bulteel did. And let us not forget those whose names we never learned – the clerks and soldiers who were slaughtered when Kicke was ordered to invade Williamson's offices.'

Chaloner supposed he had a point. 'He tried to remove me from danger, though. He offered me money to leave, and started a rumour that he thought would see me dismissed and sent away.'

'And then he tried to kill you. I admire your compassion for a lonely, unhappy man, but the truth is that he was no friend to you. Your name was on the death list Bates found in the Spares Gallery.'

'With a question mark,' argued Chaloner. 'Like Joseph Molins's. He did not *want* to hurt me.'

'So you say. But bear in mind that both Downing *and* Williamson have since told me that he fed them information to make them think you were a spy, purely to direct attention away from himself. Not to mention the fact that he tried to blow you up and shoot you.'

'That was not the worst of it. You and Hannah . . .'

'Quite. He struck at two people dear to you. He even killed his kinsman, Griffith.'

'Griffith was not his cousin. The real Griffith died years ago. The impostor arrived in February, and set about convincing Bulteel that he was long-lost kin. But Bulteel saw through him . . .'

'And promptly decided that Griffith was exactly what he needed to help him create Falcon and set the Sinon Plot in motion,' finished Thurloe when Chaloner could not bring himself to go on. 'However, I am deeply unimpressed with Clarendon, who spent hours "reminiscing" with the man. How *could* he have been so easily tricked?'

'Because he had not seen Griffith in twenty years, and the impostor was good at impersonating people – as his foray inside Newgate showed. Moreover, the real Griffith shared a lot of personal information with the false one on his deathbed. Except the place where he was born, apparently. Records indicate that Griffith hailed from Bedfordshire, not Buckinghamshire.'

They walked in silence for a while, savouring the damp freshness of the air.

'I still cannot believe how close Bulteel came to succeeding,' said Chaloner eventually, still unsettled by the whole affair. 'I would never have guessed he was Falcon if it had not been for a phrase he happened to use – the same words as in the note pinned on Philip Alden.'

'The corpse at your wedding,' mused Thurloe. 'And the warning was intended for White.'

'White was horrified. At the time, I thought it was just

shock at a murder in his church, but with hindsight, I see it was more than that. I imagine Compton and the others were similarly threatened, but they kept meeting anyway, doggedly determined to foil the danger Falcon represented.'

'So Bulteel sent them poisoned gloves, although I am not surprised he became impatient when they failed to work and sent Kicke to speed matters along. People do not wear gloves in heatwaves.'

'And the recipients should have been suspicious of them, anyway,' added Chaloner. 'Hanse's passion was stockings, not gloves. And there is the fact that the gloves were sent while Hanse was still alive. Had one of the others thought to thank him for them, the ruse would have been exposed.'

They lapsed into silence a second time, and Chaloner thought about the interview he had had with Williamson the day after Bulteel's death. It had been decided that the Dutch delegation did not need to know what had really happened, lest it destroyed what feeble hope remained for peace. So a drunken thief had 'confessed' to killing Hanse and Oetje, and official apologies had been issued and accepted. Chaloner had agreed to the deception readily enough – to do otherwise might mean war, and it would be unfortunate if Bulteel's plot should succeed after all.

'Of course, Williamson should bear some of the blame in this unsavoury affair,' said Thurloe, after a while. 'He naively let himself be convinced that the Sinon Plot referred to a scheme to steal the crown jewels, when it was actually far more. Spymasters should be less credulous.'

'But Falcon *did* intend to have the crown jewels.'

'I know, but Williamson should have probed deeper.'

456

'That was partly Compton's fault. *He* knew what the Sinon Plot entailed, but did not tell Williamson, because he did not trust him to thwart it. Unfortunately, he, Hanse, Molins, White and Edwards were amateurs, and their bumbling efforts almost ended in disaster.'

'Well-meaning amateurs,' said Thurloe. 'They thought they were doing the right thing – that by foiling the plot quietly, they were giving peace the best possible chance. But to return to my original point, if Williamson had possessed an ounce of competence, none of this would have happened.'

Chaloner smiled. 'You would have seen through it, but he is not you, and never will be. Do you think the King will dismiss him?'

'No. The man is a survivor. Besides, he did save your life. He told me afterwards that it was one of the most difficult things he had ever done.'

'What was? Saving me?'

'Ordering Swaddell to shoot Bulteel, especially as he had not been party to the confession that had gone before. He saw only Bulteel pointing a gun at you, and had to make a quick decision. Thank God he made the right one. He is not all bad, Tom. Perhaps this business will see an easing of relations between you.'

'It might,' acknowledged Chaloner. 'Although I doubt it will last. Clarendon is sending me to Tangier tomorrow, to investigate a major mismanagement of public funds, and I have a bad feeling some of Williamson's spies are involved. We shall soon be back to our usual state of animosity.'

'You seem to attract the dislike of unpleasant men. Downing, for example.'

Chaloner grinned. 'He is in a lot of trouble at the

457

moment. He recruited two spies in the Dutch delegation. One was Ruyven, who was next to useless, but who is demanding a lot of money that our government will have to pay in order to avoid embarrassment. And the other was Zas.'

Thurloe frowned. 'Zas? But I thought he was spying *on* us. *For* the Dutch.'

'He was, and Downing lost far more secrets than he gained – Zas was too clever for him, and led him a merry dance.'

'So, to summarise,' said Thurloe, 'Ruyven, de Buat and "Griffith" were spying for England, Zas pretended to be Downing's man but was actually Heer van Goch's, and Bulteel was in the middle, confusing everyone.'

Chaloner grinned. 'Yes. It makes me quite nostalgic for my days as an intelligencer.'

'Espionage can be a very dirty business,' said Thurloe, not smiling back. 'Especially when men like Downing are involved.'

'He slithered back to The Hague before Clarendon could examine his expense accounts.'

'Good! Peace stands a better chance with him gone. He is hardly what I would call a dove.'

'Which is precisely why His Majesty wanted him here, of course. The King stands to make a lot of money if we acquire the States-General's trading routes – he *wants* war.'

'Everything seems to boil down to money in the end,' said Thurloe in distaste. 'Although it was not Bulteel's motive. I heard him say so myself.'

'He was lying. He owned a house in Chelsey, which I visited with Williamson two days ago. He said he had inherited it from an uncle, but the truth is that he bought

458

it with the money he made from blackmailing people – which he must have been doing for months, because I have never seen so much treasure in one place. He was fabulously wealthy.'

'What will happen to it all?'

'Williamson will return it to Bulteel's victims. He offered me a finder's fee, but the whole affair was sordid, and I wanted nothing to do with it.'

'I heard you discovered else that was unpleasant, too.'

Chaloner nodded. 'The body of the original "Falcon", who plotted in the Feathers tavern with Swan and Swallow. Griffith rescued him from Newgate, but then Bulteel ordered him killed.'

'Why? I thought he was one of Bulteel's minions – the one who would actually steal the jewels.'

'He was, but Bulteel must have decided he was too great a liability with his curses and his sinister stares. His real name was Edward Pocks.'

'The name on the death list!' exclaimed Thurloe. 'But I do not blame him for preferring to be called Falcon. I might change *my* name, too, had I been burdened with Pocks.'

'The "Falcon" we hunted was an amalgam of characters, which was why he was so difficult to find. He was an unsettling felon, a master of disguise and a cunning intelligencer. In other words, he was a combination of Pocks, Griffith and Bulteel. Falcon did not exist in one sense, although the damage he did was real enough.'

'White's name was not on this death list,' said Thurloe. 'Why was he omitted?'

'It must have been written on the burned part. God alone knows how many more were there – victims claimed and others pending. But I am sorry about White. I might have been able to save him had I known his identity sooner . . .'

'Do not blame yourself,' said Thurloe. 'He knew the risks when he elected to tackle Falcon. But let us turn to happier matters. I enjoyed hearing you play your viol at the Savoy last night, and so did Heer van Goch. He asked me to tell you.'

'I performed abominably,' said Chaloner gloomily. 'Because I can never practise. Since we married, Hannah has confessed to a deep dislike of the solo viol.'

'All marriages have their problems,' said Thurloe sagely.

'Not ones of this magnitude,' muttered Chaloner.

A short distance away, a man lay in bed, swathed in bandages. He was miserable and in pain, although his physician had assured him that he would make a complete recovery.

'How much did you salvage from this debacle?' he asked of the visitor who sat at his side.

'Almost all of it,' replied Williamson. 'Your victims must show me the original blackmail notes if they want to reclaim what they paid. And as they paid because they want their dirty secrets buried, few have come forward. Chaloner is an odd devil, though – he refused to accept any of it as a reward.'

'Decent to the end,' said Bulteel savagely. 'Honest, incorruptible Tom.'

'You should have come to me with your plans,' said Williamson reproachfully. 'We have always worked better together than alone. And you almost brought me down.'

Bulteel winced. 'Well, you *did* bring me down. You ordered me shot.'

'I did nothing of the kind! Swaddell acted before I understood what was happening. Assassins have a habit of squeezing a trigger first and asking questions later, and he always was jealous of our association. But you will recover, and then we shall turn our attention to the future. Together.'

'I am not sure I trust you any more,' said Bulteel resentfully. 'I almost died.'

'But you survived,' Williamson pointed out tartly. 'And you tried to kill me, anyway – sending Kicke and his villains my way.'

'No! I told them to keep you in your office until I had delivered my carefully forged papers to the delegates at the Savoy. I expressly ordered them *not* to harm you in any way.'

'Well, that makes two of us, then,' said Williamson. 'We are even.'

Bulteel regarded him suspiciously. 'I still do not understand why I am not in prison. I blackmailed half the Court, and went a long way to sabotaging the negotiations with the Dutch. The former showed you in a bad light because you could not solve the case, and you will disapprove of the latter because you want peace.'

'Peace is certainly the more sensible option, but it was never really on the table. The talks were doomed long before you became involved.'

'What about the blackmail?' asked Bulteel. 'How can you forgive me for that?'

'The generous donation from Chelsey went some way to salving my wounded pride.'

'Then why did I detect a cooling of our friendship these last few weeks?'

'Because Griffith was always in your company, and

461

one needs to be careful around professional spies. Of course I maintained my distance – as I would have explained, had you asked.'

Bulteel continued to scowl. 'What happens if Tom learns I am alive? He will not overlook what I did to Thurloe and Hannah. He does not understand that he would have been better off without them – a relic from a lost regime and a woman who will make him miserable.'

'Do not worry about him. He is going to Tangier soon, and by the time he returns, he will have forgotten all about you.' Williamson hesitated. 'But I have one question. It concerns the death list he passed me. He thinks the "Joseph" refers to Molins's son, but I would like to hear from your own lips that he is right – that you were not thinking of Joseph Williamson when you penned it.'

'Of course not,' said Bulteel flatly. 'I have already said that I went to some trouble to keep you safe.'

Williamson smiled, although there was no warmth in the expression. 'Good. Now drink the wine I bought you. It is Kersey's best, and will soon have you strong again.'

Bulteel did as he was told, then lay back on the pillows. After a while, his breathing became laboured. His eyes snapped open in alarm, and his frightened gaze settled on Williamson.

'There, there,' said the Spymaster gently. 'It will soon be over, and this is a lot more pleasant than what Swaddell had in mind for you.'

'Why?' Bulteel managed to gasp. 'I thought we . . . allies again . . .'

'That was before you lied to me,' said Williamson softly. 'You *did* plan to kill me, just as you planned to kill Chaloner.

462

I could see it in your eyes. He mourns the loss of a friend, but I shall not. You were never a friend to me.'

Bulteel released a strangled gurgle, although whether it was a denial or a death rattle, Williamson did not know. He sat quietly for a moment, lost in his thoughts, then stood to close the dead man's eyes.

Historical Note

The peace talks between England and the Republic of the Seven United Provinces – also called the Dutch Republic or the States-General – in the summer of 1664 did not go well. A large delegation, headed by Ambassador Michiel van Goch (or Gogh), had arrived in London, but relations between the two countries had been deteriorating for some time. The Dutch government was eager for a treaty, probably because of the cost involved in staging a war and the disruption to trade.

Unfortunately, van Goch's efforts were in vain. The moderate voices of men like the Earl of Clarendon, then Lord Chancellor, were drowned out by the warmongers – the dukes of Buckingham and York. As conflict was not really in Britain's interests, either, historians have debated long and hard about why two Protestant countries, surrounded by enemy Catholic states, should want to damage each other. The most likely explanation is that there was not enough room for two powerful maritime nations, and England intended to rule the waves. It sounds petty, but one of the sticking points in the negotiations involved the dipping of flags – a previous treaty stipulated that the Dutch should salute the British first; this they did, but the Dutch captains were understandably offended when their salutes were not acknowledged or returned.

It was not the first time trouble had erupted between the two nations. The First Dutch War (1652–1654) had been won handily by Cromwell, but his ships had been well maintained and had full complements of sailors. The same could not be said for Charles II's navy, and a second victory was by no means certain. Contemporary broadsheets and newsbooks bray about the fleet's state of readiness, but Samuel Pepys, navy clerk and diarist, did not agree, and was deeply concerned. Heer van Goch failed to reach any agreement, and the delegation left London in September.

The Envoy Extraordinary to The Hague at the time was Sir George Downing. He had held the post under Cromwell, and had been so determined not to lose everything he had gained just because of a change of regimes that he promptly abandoned his old master (John Thurloe, Spymaster General and Cromwell's Secretary of State) and swore undying loyalty to the Crown. Amazingly, Charles II not only accepted his pledge, but knighted him into the bargain. To demonstrate his new allegiance, Downing engaged in a nasty piece of skulduggery that involved luring three regicides into a trap, and smuggling them back to England to face the horrors of a traitor's execution.

It is difficult to find a contemporary with anything good to say about Downing. The most common words used to describe him include unscrupulous, petty, mean, greedy, duplicitous and unsavoury. He was doubtless no worse than any other ambitious man in those turbulent times, but probably attracted dislike because he was good at earning himself riches and power. He travelled from The Hague to London in the summer of 1664 to advise the government, although he misread the situation badly, and many said he did more to aid the cause of war than of peace.

He recruited a number of spies, including the ex-patriot merchant Abraham Kicke, and the Royalist officer (once a spy for Clarendon) Colonel John Griffith, both of whom helped him catch the regicides. He was not a good master. He neglected to pay his intelligencers, blithely sent them into dangerous situations, and treated them with open disdain.

Nevertheless, he was proud of their achievements, and in one letter, he boasted how his spies were so skilled that one broke into Grand Pensionary Jan de Witt's house while he was in bed, stole his keys and used them to enter the closet where he kept his confidential papers. These were delivered into Downing's hands for an hour, then returned to the closet and the key slipped back inside de Witt's pocket, with the hapless Dutch head of state none the wiser.

Naturally, the Dutch had their agents, too. Zacharius Taacken was arrested in Ipswich in 1667 and was eventually brought to appear before the Privy Council, while van Goch's secretary, the aged Latin scholar, Peter van der Kun (his pen name was Petrus Cunaeus) was arrested on charges of watching the English fleet. Gerbrand Zas was also a Dutch spy; he was arrested and taken to the Tower in the 1660s.

Joseph Williamson, who eventually stepped into Thurloe's shoes as Spymaster General, also recruited intelligencers. The native Dutchman Dirk van Ruyven was banished from Holland for *his* association with Williamson; Henry de Buat, an Orangist Franco-Dutch officer, was executed; and John Nisbett had a narrow escape. Philip Alden was an Irish spy who was rewarded with a pension of £100 a year.

During the summer of 1664, London was full of rumours about the war and England's chances of winning one. Some were reported in *The Intelligencer* and *The Newes*, and others were just gossiped about in the coffee houses. These included the tale about the Duke of York setting to sea with thirty warships, and the story that the Dutch had launched forty ships of their own. Both were later found to be untrue.

Many of the other characters in *A Body in the Thames* were real people. Richard Wiseman was appointed Surgeon to the Person in June 1660, and John Bulteel was Clarendon's private secretary. Thomas Chaloner was a regicide who died in Holland in 1662; he had several siblings, one of whom may well have had a son named Thomas.

Daniel, Josias, Nathan and William Cotton were all Court officials during the early years of the Restoration. Nathan died in 1661, but Daniel kept his post as Yeoman Cartaker until his resignation in 1682. Charles Bates was a minor courtier who had a wife named Ann. Henry Killigrew was Master of the Savoy in 1664; his wife was Judith.

Sir William Compton was a son of the second Earl of Northampton. He fought for the Royalists during the civil wars, and co-founded the secret organisation known as the Sealed Knot. At the Restoration, he was made Master of Ordnance, and became MP for Cambridge. He was highly thought of, even by Parliamentarians, for his honesty and integrity, and died suddenly and unexpectedly in October 1663. He was 38 years old.

Edward Molins the surgeon lived on Shoe Lane. He also died in 1663, following a botched operation to remove his leg – he had broken his ankle, and the wound had become gangrenous.

There was a rumour circulating in 1664 that Cromwell had opened the royal tombs in Westminster Abbey, and swapped the bones about. One of Cromwell's chaplains, Edward White, denied the tale vigorously.

Finally, Talbot Edwards was Assistant Keeper of the Crown Jewels in 1664, and did indeed show them to paying guests. A few years later, he almost lost them when the infamous Colonel Blood staged an audacious raid on the Tower, and started to make off with them. But that is another story . . .